D0206282

GREENWAR

Steven Gould and
Laura J. Mixon

TOR ®

A TOM DOHERTY ASSOCIATES BOOK
NEW YORK

This is a work of fiction. All the characters and events portrayed in this book are either products of the authors' imagination or are used fictitiously.

GREENWAR

A Tor Book
Published by Tom Doherty Associates, Inc.
175 Fifth Avenue
New York, NY 10010

Tor Books on the World Wide Web:
http://www.tor.com

Tor® is a registered trademark of Tom Doherty Associates, Inc.

Visit the authors' website at http://www.thuhtek.net/~scg

ISBN: 0-812-57116-9
Library of Congress Card Catalog Number: 97-1618

First edition: June 1997
First mass market edition: November 1998

Printed in the United States of America

0 9 8 7 6 5 4 3 2 1

This one's for my mother,
Elizabeth Mixon. Love you,
Mother.
                    —LJM

What a coincidence!
For my mom —Carita Gould.
                    —SG

NOTES AND ACKNOWLEDGMENTS

This was a true collaboration. There was no senior or junior writer. The novel was plotted together, with Laura writing substantial portions of the first draft and Steve writing most scenes involving diving, certain aspects of the facility description, and some of the Keith Hellman viewpoint. (Oh—and explosions. Steve likes explosions.) Each author then made multiple passes through the manuscript.

Thanks are due to several people who helped us make this book more and better than it would have been.

Regina and Earle Tarr, in particular, deserve our gratitude; they went far beyond the line of duty in providing us truckloads of useful info about Melbourne, including photos and legwork, and subsequently vetted the manuscript for geographic accuracy.

Dr. Rodney Fujita of the Environmental Defense Fund was also a wonderful resource—he provided lots of useful information on marine ecology, sustainable mariculture, and ocean thermal energy technology.

Joe Haldeman and William S. Gross gave us good boom—details about plastic explosives.

Sue Bottom, vice president of Environmental, Health, and Safety for Basis Petroleum, gave us some useful tips on our hydrogen plant design.

Jake Varn, an environmental attorney in Florida, helped us with some environmental compliance issues.

Dan Hatch shared his sordid past in the Coast Guard.

Tim O'Donnell, vice president of Corporate Insurance for Salomon Brothers, told us things about corporate insurance.

Venkat Venkatraman, a vice president in Salomon Brothers' Mortgage Lending group, told us some things about merchant banking and deal funding, and he let us use his name.

Sage Walker, an M.D. with lots of experience as an emergency room physician, gave good gore—she helped us get the medical trauma right.

Martha Wells and Tom Knowles, fellow writers, read the tome on a short turnaround and gave us excellent plot critiques.

Valerie Davis of Holmes Regional Medical helped us improve the hospital settings.

Any errors that remain are, of course, our own.

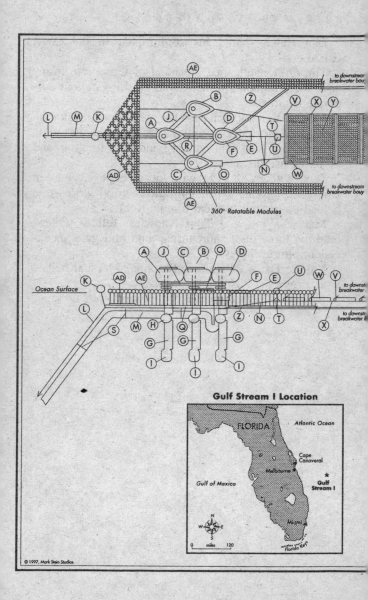

to downstream
breakwater bou

to downstream
breakwater bouy

360° Ratatable Modules

Ocean Surface

to downst
breakwater

to downst
breakwater

Gulf Stream I Location

FLORIDA

Atlantic Ocean

Cape
Canaveral

Melbourne

Gulf of Mexico

★
Gulf
Stream I

N
W   E
S

0   miles   120

Miami

Florida Keys

© 1997, Mark Stein Studios

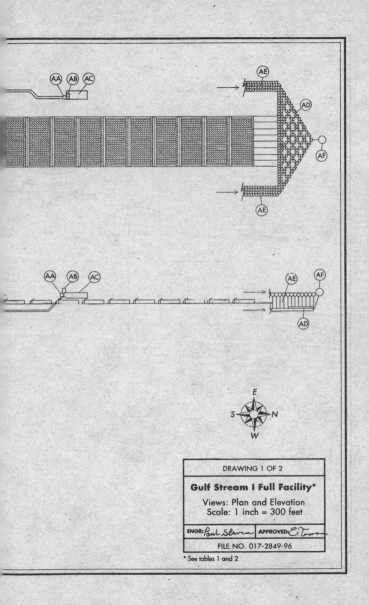

AA AB AC   AE
                                                   AD

                                                      AF

AA AB AC   AE   AF

                                                 AD

E
S   N
W

DRAWING 1 OF 2

Gulf Stream I Full Facility*

Views: Plan and Elevation
Scale: 1 inch = 300 feet

ENGR: Paul Slavin   APPROVED: E. Turner

FILE NO. 017-2849-96

* See tables 1 and 2

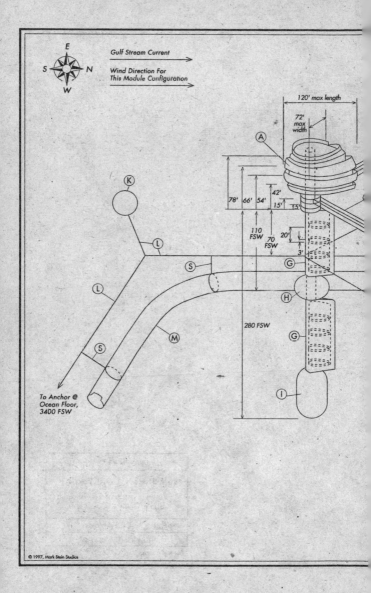

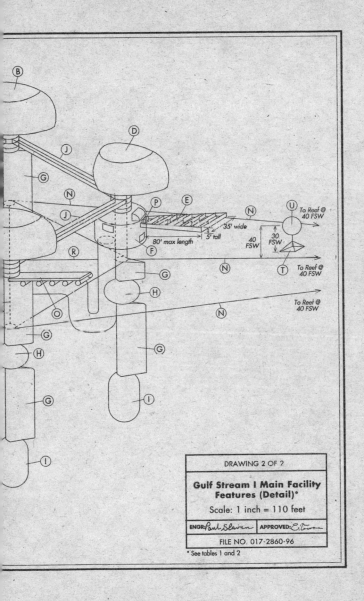

DRAWING 2 OF 2

**Gulf Stream 1 Main Facility
Features (Detail)***

Scale: 1 inch = 110 feet

ENGR: *Paul Slavin*   APPROVED: *E. Turner*

FILE NO. 017-2860-96

* See tables 1 and 2

Table 1. Gulf Stream 1 Facility Drawings—Legend

Item	Shown on Drawing #	Description
A	1, 2	Residential module. (Major features not shown: outer staircase on west side of module; roof gardens; life rafts.)
B	1, 2	Science module. (Not shown: outer staircase; analytical and communications equipment on roof; outer walkways; life rafts. Outer walkway detail is same as for A.)
C	1, 2	Mariculture module. (Not shown: outer staircase; helicopter landing pad; outer walkways; life rafts. Outer walkway detail is same as for A.)
D	1, 2	Engineering module. (Not shown: hydrogen, ammonia, and nitrogen storage on roof; hydrogen flare; outer walkways; outer staircase; lift rafts. Outer walkway detail is same as for A.)
E	1, 2	Plant effluent seawater spillways.
F	1, 2	Submersible Ocean Thermal Energy Conversion (OTEC) plant for conversion of thermal gradient between surface seawater and seawater at 3,400 feet below sea level to electricity.
G	1, 2	Beanpole with interior buoyancy chambers for adjusting facility lift. (Detail for B, C, and D beanpoles' buoyancy chambers is same as for A.)
H	1, 2	Primary buoyancy tank for module.
I	1, 2	Ballast bulb for stabilizing module.
J	1, 2	Catwalk. (Not shown: piping and conduits beneath catwalk for transmitting electricity, fresh water, seawater, wastewater, air, nitrogen, etc. between modules.)
K	1, 2	Main facility buoy.

L	I, 2	Underwater cable connecting facility to the main buoy at 70-foot depth, and connecting main buoy to anchor at 3,400-foot depth.
M	I, 2	Cold water intake pipe.
N	I, 2	Underwater lines connecting facility to artificial reef at 20- to 80-foot (typically 40-foot) depth.
O	I, 2	Facility boat dock.
P	I, 2	Mixed warm and cold water effluent to spillways.
Q	2	Rigid, hinged structure connecting all four beanpoles at 70-foot depth, for stabilizing relative positions of modules.
R	I, 2	Cross-linked cables connecting beanpoles at 70-foot depth for stabilizing relative positions of beanpoles.
S	I, 2	Support for cold water intake pipe.
T	I, 2	Diver's platform at 30-foot depth, at reef marker buoy.
U	I, 2	Reef marker buoy.
V	I	Leading baffle at leading edge of each artificial reef segment.
W	I	Buoyancy tank for reef segment.
X	I	Interstitial line.
Y	I	Main reef support platform. (Not shown: individual reef segment fittings and features, such as seaweed forests, carbonate structures, etc.)
Z	I	Underwater pressurized hydrogen line.
AA	I	Hydrogen barge buoy.
AB	I	Hydrogen manifold.
AC	I	Hydrogen barge.
AD	I	Breakwater system—rigid section. 3-foot buoys tethered to triangular grid, placed every 4 feet.
AE	I	Breakwater system—main section. 3-foot buoys tethered to 4-foot-square, interlocked plates.
AF	I	Facility downstream buoy.

Table 2. Gulf Stream I—Main Function Spaces:

Module A: Residential

Suites and dormitories
Cafeteria
  Eating area
  Kitchen
  Pantry
  Walk-in refrigerator
  Walk-in freezer
Lounge
  Large-screen TV
  Game room
  Library
Medical center
Module water reservoirs—fresh
  and seawater
Roof gardens
Satellite dish for TV
Crane bay
Warehouse
  Bulk food storage
  Equipment and cleaning
    supplies
  Waste storage

Module B: Science

Offices
Cubicles
Technical library
Laboratories
  Analytical
  Ocean Chemistry
  Bioassay (aquarium work)
  Mariculture support
Conference room
  3 TVs (1 lg-scrn, 2 std size)
    with teleconferencing
Module water reservoirs

Crane bay
Warehouse
  Cold rooms
  Chemical storage
  Equipment storage
  Waste storage

Module C: Mariculture and Fisheries

Offices
Cubicles
Coldwater lobster, shrimp, and
  abalone projects
Biomass processing
Edible algae processing
Dive center
  Divemaster/Open Water
    Safety Office
  Dive equipment
  Maintenance and storage
  Outboard motor storage
  Scuba tank compressors
  Zodiac (inflatable boat)
    storage
  Freshwater rinse station
  Gasoline and oil storage
Crane bay
Water reservoirs
Warehouse
  Cold rooms—food storage
  Biomass storage
  Waste storage

Module D: Engineering

Control room
  Weather

Communications
  Phone lines (5) via
    microwave relay
  Data links (2) via
    microwave relay
  VHF (with roof mast)
  Shortwave (with roof
    mast
Buoyancy
  Beanpoles
  OTEC plant
  Spillways
  Reef
Radar (2 with different
  ranges and resolution)

Power production
Hydrogen production
OTEC power plant
Hydrogen production plant
Water desalination plant
Engineering pilot projects
Machine shop
Buoyancy compressors and
  accumulators
Water reservoirs
Crane bay
Warehouse
  Miscellaneous chemical and
    solvent storage
  Waste storage
Roof storage—hydrogen,
  nitrogen, and ammonia

Prologue

In the few moments it took Gabriel to scale the last
twelve feet of cliff above Cañon Abajo and heave himself over the lip onto the mesa, a hazy, roseate band
had formed in the sky, splitting the heavens in two.
He shrugged his backpack off and lowered it to the
invisible ground with a grunt, and turned off his night-
lensed flashlight; the red glow winked out. Then he
dropped onto a boulder to catch his breath and await
the others, leaning back on his arms to look at the sky:
a large slice of dusky blue covered a third of the heavens, cut out of a wan and colorless expanse.

The line was the Earth's shadow, rolling slowly
across the sky like a lifting blanket as Earth's face
turned to the sun. But sunrise was still a good half
hour away, and west of the shadow's terminus, a few
stars were still visible.

The others were nearing the cliff edge now; he
heard their grunts and gasps. Gabriel stood and helped
Jax, then Mark, over the lip of the cliff. Then he
straightened with a groan, hands at the small of his
back.

A chill autumn gust smelling of sage, dead leaves,
and New Mexico dust cooled the sweat from his
cheeks and neck. He licked his chapped lips and tasted
salt and iron. His shoulders ached, and his feet; every
muscle in his body hurt. The mud of Rio Abajo—
tainted with the gluey stink of wood-treating toxins—

lingered in his nostrils and clung to his gloves and hiking boots.

Gabriel pulled off his black silk mask, used it to wipe the grime and sweat from his face and neck, and took another look at the fiberboard manufacturing plant in the canyon below.

Ugly was too kind a word for it. An obscene geometry of mercury lights glared onto two aluminum prefab buildings with cheap, green fiberglass windows and turned the surrounding scrub and pine trees and cacti to monochrome plastic. The stacks of lumber piled high behind the buildings bled sap onto the ground near a jumble of drums and carboys. The dirt parking lot on the other side was empty. A twelve-foot-high chain-link fence with barbed wire coils atop it surrounded the plant, and Gabriel could see the gaping hole they'd made in the fence from where he stood.

On this side of the river, mostly hidden by cottonwoods, junipers, piñons, and ash trees, a gravel logging road wound off up the canyon. A short stretch of river was exposed alongside the plant. Pipes appeared from beneath the asphalt at the plant's fence, ran down the river's bank, and disappeared into the rocks and weeds at the river's edge.

Factories were generally disgusting, but Woodland Products was bad even for a factory. Looking down at it, Gabriel felt almost physically ill.

It was bad enough that Woodland Products razed old forests in the Jemez Mountains to the east. Say "habitat preservation" to company officials and they'd call you a nut case or a communist. Gabriel knew that from personal experience. But there was more. With the waste waters from its fiberboard manufacturing process, Woodland Products Inc. was creating a plume of blight and destruction. Regardless of the evidence brought against them, they'd refused to

stop discharging their poisons, their creosotes and phe-
nols and aldehydes, into Rio Abajo. And they'd
bought off enough public officials that no one could
touch them.

Ecological criminals. Neither legal means nor
peaceful civil disobedience had done any good. Gabriel had, finally, had enough of playing by the rules.
Woodland Products had it coming.

He turned. Jax and Mark were lifting up a large, flat
boulder nearby, revealing the hole they'd dug earlier.
They dropped their ski masks into it and Jax dropped
in the wire cutters he'd used on the fence. When they
left this spot, they wanted to look like hikers—back-
packers out for three days of camping. Which was also
why they had left the car a county away, in the Jemez
wilderness.

Gabriel removed the radio transmitter from his pack
and began inserting batteries. Meanwhile Mark and
Jax took their turn at the cliff edge.

"So," Mark said, "who do you want to play you?"

Jax thought it over. "Keanu Reeves."

"No, *I'm* Keanu Reeves. You have to pick someone
else."

"All right, all right. Alec Baldwin, then. Or maybe
Pierce Brosnan. *Anybody* but Bruce Willis. I hear he's
an asshole."

Mark shrugged. "Hey, if the shoe fits . . ."

Jax glared. "Well, only if Gabriel is played by Ri-
cardo Montalban." He lowered his voice. "This company is polluting the environment with the richest
Corinthian leather."

"Nah," Mark said. "Antonio Banderas is the only
one to play Gabriel. He'll probably get the big sex
scene."

They both laughed.

Gabriel smiled, too, but didn't laugh. All the months
of careful planning, the fear, excitement, doubts—all

were gone now. He had moved, finally, to some serene, purposeful place in his mind.

"Detonator's ready," he said.

The dry air had a bite to it and the silk gloves Gabriel wore provided little insulation. He pulled the collar of his denim jacket up and came over, bringing the detonator, to crouch with Mark and Jax at the cliff edge.

Jax pointed his flashlight at the detonator in Gabriel's hands: a small box with vertical and horizontal joysticks and an on/off switch. It was a cheap radio control set, designed for flying model aircraft. Gabriel had had Jax buy it with cash the week before in Lubbock, well away from the target. Mark had converted the small receiver so that, instead of twisting ailerons and rudder, it fed a minute amount of current to a blasting cap.

"Ready?" he asked. Mårk and Jax looked at each other and, somber now, nodded.

He took a breath. "Then let's do it." He held up the detonator. "Who wants to do the honors?"

Mark and Jax exchanged glances.

"Be my guest," Mark said. Jax held out his hand, and Gabriel gave him the detonator.

"Hold on till I give the signal," he said, and pulled the cellular phone, taken from its charger in the office of the plant manager below, out of the waistband of his jeans. He covered the mouthpiece with his bandanna and switched the phone to active. It took a second to get a dial tone. He looked up.

Dawn was near. Overhead, a wedge of sandhill cranes flew southward—and among their chorus of deep-throated warbles was the trumpet call of a whooping crane. That brought a startled smile to Gabriel's lips. There were only a handful left; he couldn't ask for a better omen. He dialed 911.

"Nine-One-One Emergency."

"Listen—record this if you can; I won't repeat any of it."

"What is the nature of your emergency? Are you in need of police, fire, or ambulance services?"

"Yes. You'll find out if you let me talk."

"What is the address of your location?"

Gabriel closed his eyes, started the speech he'd prepared. "This is Wild Justice. We have judged Woodland Products Inc. and found them guilty of grievous crimes against the ecosystem. With the collusion of the state and federal governments, they have destroyed old-growth forests and desert habitats. They have poisoned the waters of the wilderness and have killed aquatic and desert species. They have flagrantly ignored warnings, demonstrations, and lawsuits and have continued to pollute. They are guilty of the crimes of murder and rape. Rape of the Earth."

There was a heartbeat's pause. "Who? You judged who?"

"Woodland! Woodland Products Inc.! Clean out your ears." Gabriel forced himself to lower his voice and calm down. "For these crimes they have been sentenced to the fate they have already inflicted on many other species. Annihilation."

Gabriel turned and looked down Abajo Canyon, to the street-lit glow of San Carlo two miles away. "Look out your west window, operator. The one that faces Calle del Monte." He paused. "Are you looking?"

A longer pause, a reluctant, "Yes."

"The sentence is now to be carried out. Woodland's fiberboard manufacturing plant in Cañon Abajo, and its rape of Mother Earth, are now a thing of the past."

He nodded to Jax. The younger man put his hand on the right-hand joystick and shoved the switch.

The concussion knocked them all to the ground.

The explosion was far bigger than he had expected.

They'd packed half their dynamite around flammable tanks of formaldehyde, cresylic acid, and diesel oil, but the other half was under the plant's huge propane tanks. Gabriel scrambled to his knees in time to see a fireball climb several hundred feet above the rim of the canyon. Twisted corrugated roofing and siding tumbled in lazy circles in the sky. Billows of black smoke rose from the torn roof and tongues of flame licked the twisted edges of gaping holes.

Someone, Jax or Mark, whispered, *"Jesus."*

Gabriel shook his head, swallowed hard. Exultation rose in him. No more wheedling, picketing, pleading for mercy on behalf of the planet—

He turned his back on the burning plant and made a fist. *Yes*.

The phone. He'd dropped it. He snatched it up and put it back to his ear. He barely heard the operator's voice over the ringing in his ears, but the voice stopped when he said, "We are Wild Justice. This is the first. There will be others."

Gabriel turned the phone off and threw it in the hole, followed by the gloves. Jax added the transmitter and his gloves; then they all shoveled loose dirt in, stamped it down, and pushed the boulder over, to cover everything.

Whiffs of black smoke scudded by. Its chemical stench made Gabriel gag. He sprinkled pine needles around the boulder and then eyed the sky. The sun was rising in a crevice in the Jemez Mountains, flinging sharp shadows far across the desert hills and erosion-carved mesas. Above the sun hung a faint, argent sliver of moon and the morning star. Angel-hair clouds of spun copper and gold drifted high above.

As they shouldered their packs and headed eastward up the ridge the thin wail of sirens rose from behind them, in San Carlo.

PART ONE

WIND

Chapter 1

The day started out bad and got worse.

Eighteen minutes before the press conference, in the suite where Emma sat drinking coffee and chatting with Dennis MacNichols, the firm's chief financial officer, her chief landside engineer in Melbourne called on her cell phone.

She glanced at her watch, surprised. Angelo never called before nine-thirty, and it was only eight-thirty, Florida time.

"What gives?"

He said, "We had a break-in last night."

She winced. "What did they take?"

"Computer equipment, mostly. The AutoCAD station, the plotter, a couple of fax machines. They only hit the engineering area. Nothing else seems to be missing."

She covered the mouthpiece and repeated the news to Dennis, who scowled. "I've been telling Pendleton we need better security."

"Guess he'll believe you now." She said to Angelo, "Did we lose anything irreplaceable?"

"Nah. I had everything backed up and they didn't touch my optical disks at all." He paused. "Sorry for the bad news."

She sighed. "Oh well. I've been wanting to upgrade, anyhow."

"Right. Uh, how's the conference going?"

"It hasn't really gotten started yet. Listen," she said as the door opened, "I've got to go; Pendleton's here. Go ahead and get started ordering replacements. Don't look so sour," she told Dennis, hanging up and tucking the phone into her satchel as Brad Pendleton, billionaire, Gulf Stream's CEO and majority partner, entered the suite. "We're insured."

"You're starting to sound like me," Dennis said.

"Emma, Dennis." Pendleton measured at least six feet five or six from stem to stern. This Emma knew from experience, because he loomed over her and she was six feet even, barefoot. His frame was so lanky that his three-piece, pin-striped suit seemed to hang off him despite all the strategically placed darts, nips, and tucks. He wore a Gulf Stream I logo lapel pin of diamond, emerald, and gold, with matching cuff links. His hair was the color of Florida sand, dusted with silver, and his face was deeply creased.

Ordinarily he moved with the happy and enthusiastic energy of a boy, but Emma noted that at the moment Pendleton's expression had a fixed quality to it, and his manner was subdued. Phillip Evans III, general counsel, right behind him, looked downright grim.

Pendleton closed the door and looked around. "Where's Thomas?"

"He had a commitment at Rice he couldn't put off," Dennis said. "A meeting with their board of directors about some possible funding."

Pendleton nodded, seeming distracted. Emma said, "You should be aware there's been a break-in at Gulf Stream Melbourne."

That got his attention. "Oh?"

"It doesn't look too bad. Easily pawnable electronics, mostly. A computer, a printer, and some fax machines."

Pendleton exchanged a look with Phil. "The day keeps getting better and better."

Phil looked pained.

Emma asked, "What is it?"

Pendleton sighed and sat down at the table, folding himself into a chair. He spread his big hands across the polished, gnarled wood. "General Motors has backed out."

Emma gaped. Dennis crushed his cigarette, rising to his feet abruptly. His grey business suit shifted uneasily on his overweight frame.

"The hell you say!"

The timing was exquisitely bad. The press conference coming up in, now, fourteen minutes, was intended to announce the details of their recently formed joint venture with General Motors and Pacific Gas & Electric to produce a line of hydrogen-powered cars and buses for the California market, and the infrastructure to fuel them.

Pendleton spread his arms in a shrug, wordless.

Dennis sat down again, his face red as rhubarb. "Those bastards. They can't. We'll sue."

Phil sat, too, and shook his head. "As I've told Brad already, we can try. But the contract gives them an out if the price of crude drops below twenty-five dollars per barrel. And it did, last week. Not for long, but long enough."

Pendleton rubbed at his forehead. "They were only looking for an out. They've clearly decided fuel cell technology in passenger vehicles just isn't worth pursuing."

"But why?" Emma asked.

"They say that public perception problems with hydrogen have caused them to reconsider. A contact of mine gave me a copy of a public opinion analysis being circulated to top management over there. The scuttlebutt is they're investing in a new flywheel pilot project instead." He shrugged. "The truth is, though, Jim Morris left GM three months ago, and this project

was his baby. I think his successor decided to dump
this one and put *his* pet project on the front burner."

"Christ." Dennis slumped.

Emma eyed Pendleton, a sour ache gnawing her
stomach. "I should have seen this coming."

Dennis glowered. "Nonsense. How could you have
predicted this?"

"Do we have any recourse?" Emma asked Phil.

He tapped his pen on the table and gave her an arch
look. "GM is one hell of a lot bigger than we are. A
long, drawn-out court battle is going to hurt us a lot
more than it is them."

Pendleton said, "It might be worth the fight, anyway. The price of oil barely dipped below our cutoff,
only for a day or two, and it's above that now. They're
not going to want to appear to be acting in bad faith."

Phil looked thoughtful. "True. Depends a lot on
current case law. I'll get my staff on that right away."

"Do that," Pendleton said.

"What's this bullshit about flywheel technology?"
Dennis demanded. "Battery-powered cars can't com-
pete with fuel cell cars. We've been over that before.
Emma, you reviewed their earlier work."

Emma met Dennis's gaze, troubled. "Something
might have changed in the interim. I'd like to see this
new analysis, if that's possible," she told Pendleton.

"Check with Kyle in Melbourne. He can fax it to
you this afternoon."

"Sure." Emma made a note in her electronic calendar. "I'll have something for you by tomorrow
morning." To Dennis she said, "I'm guessing, but
they may be talking about an epoxy resin flywheel that
was developed by the military some time ago. They're
much more efficient than the old metal ones, and safer
than metal flywheels because when they fail structur-
ally, they just turn into a bunch of fuzz instead of
shrapnel. I read a few articles about the technology

last spring. The technology has been around for a while, but no one has been pursuing it.''

"It looks like GM was persuaded to give it a closer look,'' Phil said.

Emma added, "It's a fascinating technology. It has certain advantages over fuel cells.''

Dennis scowled at her. "Don't tell me that.''

Emma shrugged. "The jury's still out on alternate technologies. I believe fuel cell cars are the best bet. But they have their disadvantages over a lightweight flywheel technology. They're heavier—so it takes more power to move the car. And hydrogen is no more dangerous than gasoline, but epoxy resin flywheels are safer than either.''

Dennis ran his fingers across his balding scalp with a sigh. "Christ. We're already topped out in the NASA shuttle hydrogen market, and our hydrogen inventories are growing. I'll have to look at our balance sheet, but this is going to have a serious impact on our finances." He sighed again, and looked at Pendleton. "What are we going to tell the press? Should you cancel?''

Pendleton shook his head. "We can't risk it. GM is going to issue a press release today announcing cancellation of the deal. The rumors will start flying if we don't implement some swift damage control. I'm going to go out there with Phil, read a brief prepared statement, and eliminate the question-and-answer session—with the promise of a follow-up later, once we have a chance to restrategize.''

"What does Rambort have to say about all this?'' Dennis asked. Rambort was PG&E's chief executive officer.

"I haven't spoken to him yet. I just found out myself." Pendleton shrugged. "I imagine he's baffled, or furious. Or both. I know *I* am. I'll be speaking to him later on today.''

Dennis said, "We have the hydrogen; PG and E can create the fuel distribution infrastructure in California . . . why not go it without GM?"

Pendleton shook his head. "We lack the capital. PG and E won't pony up GM's share and *we* certainly can't."

"And we lack the know-how," Emma added. "Face it. Without an auto manufacturer to build the fleet, the deal is deader than a three-day-old corpse. And GM was the only one of the Big Three that had a serious interest in the technology."

They were all silent for a moment.

"Do you expect hostility from the press?" Emma asked finally. Pendleton gave her a long, thoughtful look, chin in his hand.

"I expect there'll be an I-told-you-so reaction from certain members of the energy sector press—they've always been cynical about our chances for success. We've also invited members of the Big Ten environmental nonprofits. I'm hoping they will be more sympathetic. The Environmental Defense Fund, Natural Resources Defense Council, and National Wildlife Federation have already issued statements in support of Gulf Stream."

"That's no big surprise," Dennis said. "Thomas tells me NRDC, the Center for Marine Research, and the National Coral Reef Alliance have all approached him about a joint research effort using Gulf Stream's scientific facility for a series of longitudinal studies. And I know the NCRA has ties with the Environmental Defense Fund."

Emma made a sour face at the mention of Thomas's name.

"But Greenpeace and the Sea Shepherds will be there," Pendleton continued, "and they've made some cynical remarks recently about big technology and my other business connections." He sighed. "We'll have to see."

Emma frowned. "How can they bitch about Gulf Stream?" The OTEC plant was benign use of the sea to generate energy and they'd gone out of their way to design it in an environmentally friendly fashion. The facility supported all kinds of marine and climate change research and they'd signed voluntary compliance agreements with Florida, to operate under U.S. environmental laws even though the plant was in international waters.

"Some people think *any* technology is wrong," Phil said.

"It's just so infuriating. You can't win at this game. No matter what you do, they're convinced you're bad because business is bad."

"Anything else," Pendleton asked, "before I go out there?"

They shook their heads. He gestured at Emma.

"What's the word on that tropical storm?"

"It's been upgraded to a hurricane," Emma said. "But it's heading more northwestward now—away from us and toward the Gulf. We're watching it but not overly concerned."

"Good." Pendleton glanced at his watch. "It's press time."

"Do you still want us there?" Emma asked.

He shook his head. "Don't waste your time. Get started on your analysis. Dennis, you brief Thomas on what's happened as soon as he gets back and then get started on the financials. I have a conference call with the other two partners tomorrow at nine-thirty A.M. I'll want reports tomorrow morning by eight, from you three and Thomas. Include recommendations for ways we can change our business strategy. They are going to have a lot of questions."

He stood, and took hold of the back of the chair.

"This isn't good news, folks, but we're not dead in the water yet. I want your ideas, alternatives—other hydrogen markets, plant modifications to produce other materials, ways to restructure the company to trim expenses, legal strategies. We'll talk tomorrow."

Emma was seven feet underwater when the next bad news came.

Emma's main motivation for attending the conference in the first place was that it let her finally arrange a large enough block of time away from work to get her dive certification. She'd felt guilty taking time away from the analysis she was preparing for Pendleton, but decided, screw it; she'd been trying to get her c-card for too long.

The assistant instructor, wearing only mask, snorkle, and fins, kicked down to where Emma and her dive partner were experimenting with buoyancy control a foot off the bottom of the deep end. He signaled *surface* with his thumb and, surprised, Emma and her partner complied.

When her head broke water, she saw Gulf Stream's computer systems manager and her sometime administrative assistant, the normally unflappable Gloria Tergain, kneeling at the edge of the pool.

Right now, Gloria had none of her usual serenity. She was out of breath and had a rather wild expression.

"What? What's wrong?"

Gloria laid a hand on her chest and caught her breath. "You wanted to be updated," she panted, "on Sophronia."

"Where is it?"

"It's turned again, and sped up. The eye is passing over southeast Cuba now." Another breath. "It looks like it's going to rip right up the Bahama Banks now.

Landfall on Nassau or Andros expected in twenty-four to twenty-eight hours."

"Shit. And then right over the top of Gulf Stream I." Emma stripped off her diving equipment with a swift efficiency that would have amazed her if she'd thought about it. Gloria grabbed the equipment as she handed it up—another Gulf Stream–acquired ability, assisting divers. She heaped the rental equipment on the pool edge as Emma rocketed out of the water.

"Have the Streamers been put on alert? Does Pendleton know? And Dennis?"

"Yes, they're on alert; I don't know if Pendleton knows but Dennis does—he sent me after you—"

"Where are you going, Tooke?" her instructor bellowed from the pool. "We ain't done yet! Get back in the water!"

Emma threw an apology over her shoulder in his general direction and grabbed Gloria's arm, dripping all over the beautiful outfit that she'd bought specially for the convention. With a guilty grimace Emma let go, but Gloria was too distracted to notice.

As they hurried toward the locker room a dour little voice inside Emma's head whispered, You're *never* going to get that damned certification, are you?

As she drove back to the hotel she reached Pendleton by phone. "Yes, Dennis already gave me the news." He sounded concerned. "Give me regular updates. Interrupt me, if necessary."

Dennis was wrestling with a huge, rolled-up map of some sort when Emma and Gloria entered his suite. The map appeared to be winning. Dennis was wearing white linen slacks and a Hawaiian shirt with big, raucous parrots on it, turquoise, red, and yellow. It was overlarge and hid the folds of fat around his middle. The sparse tufts of black hair on his head were stand-

ing out as if he'd just received an electric shock. He
was cursing.

A look of relief passed over his face when he spotted Emma and Gloria. "Emma, thank God! Where've
you been?"

Thomas Reynolds was there, too, slouched in the
easy chair by the glass doors with his characteristic
languor. Thomas was a Ph.D. chemical oceanographer
with several impressive fellowships on his curriculum
vitae. He was almost embarrassingly handsome: hair
of gold monofilament; lips curved as sensuously as a
longbow; heavy-lidded, deep amber eyes; a tall, slim
bone structure clothed in a distance swimmer's lithe
musculature.

Emma dumped her soggy tote bag on the couch and
pulled out a satin wrap against the a/c's chill.

"What's the latest word?" she asked Dennis.
"Have you sent for a copy of the Storm Response
Plan? Who's the on-scene coordinator?"

Dennis looked alarmed. "Has anyone taken care of
that yet? Whose responsibility is it?"

"It's all right; I've sent for the plan," Thomas said.
Gloria looked surprised and opened her mouth, then
gave a little shake of her head at Emma's curious
glance.

Dennis swiped at his hair, blew out a breath. "Good
thinking."

"They're faxing the relevant pages from the Melbourne office," Thomas went on. "Melbourne reports
that Gulf Stream has already started implementing the
protocols. Flo is coordinating."

"Flo." The first good news she'd heard so far.
Emma pulled the wrap on and tied the belt. Some of
the tension in her belly eased. "I'll want a copy of the
fax as soon as you get it."

Thomas gave her a smile and a nod. "But of course.

Gloria, take care of it, won't you? If that's all right with you, Emma."

Emma raised her eyebrows with a glance at Gloria, who shrugged slightly. Emma had the feeling she knew exactly what was going on.

"But of course," she replied, with a wolfish smile. *You son of a bitch.*

"Give me a hand with this damned thing, won't you, Emma?" Dennis said. "Why they make maps that won't stay open is completely beyond me."

Emma held out her hand; the map flipped shut when he passed it to her, with a snap like a window shade closing. Gloria cleared the coffee table. Emma pried the map open and pinned the curling corners down using a glass ashtray brimming with cigarette butts, the room service menu, a copy of the *Houston Post,* and a horror novel.

The map was a National Weather Service hurricane tracking map for the Bahamas and the east coast of Florida. Emma tossed Gloria her room key and sent her for Emma's notebook computer, with its hurricane tracking software. Meanwhile, Emma borrowed a mechanical pencil from Dennis. She ripped a page from his *Newsweek* to use as a straightedge. As she was about to fold the page she took a closer look, and her jaw dropped. There, glaring up at her, was an out-of-focus picture of Gabriel Cervantes being taken into custody. "Well-known radical environmentalist questioned in connection with bombing," the caption declared.

Shit. No way. It just wasn't his style.

There you go, Gabe, she thought with a sigh. Being harassed by the authorities, no doubt, just for being the world's biggest, most opinionated asshole.

The others were looking at her.

"What is it?" Gloria asked.

"Nothing." Emma ran the fold through Gabriel's

face and pinched the crease decisively closed with her fingernail. She used her fifteen-mile pinkie knuckle to estimate the Gulf Stream facility's position off the east coast of Florida.

"What are Sophronia's latest coordinates?"

Dennis grabbed a piece of hotel stationery by the phone on the end table, and glanced at his watch. "About ten minutes ago, the eye was at twenty degrees, fifteen minutes, and thirty-two seconds north; seventy-five degrees and twenty seconds west, moving at ten point two knots at a heading of, let's see—is that a three or a five?" Dennis squinted and held the paper at arm's length. Emma glared; he gave her a sheepish smile. "I'm sure it's a three. A heading of three hundred thirty-nine degrees. That's according to the National Hurricane Center in Coral Gables."

She marked the hurricane's location, did some quick calculations on the hotel stationery pad, and then traced Sophronia's projected path onto the map. She stood back, sucking on the metal stub of the mechanical pencil. Thomas stood up so he could see the map past Dennis.

Gulf Stream I was a circled X the diameter of a pencil eraser, and the path of Sophronia's eye came within a hair's width of the circle. Emma had marked Sophronia's projected path with time increments in four-hour segments.

"Wow, that doesn't look so good," Thomas said. He peered at the map. "It might really hit the facility."

Emma blinked at him, gave a snort, and opened her mouth. Then she caught Dennis's warning glance and cleared her throat instead, avoiding sarcasm by milliseconds.

"It's a crude estimate—but it does look like we're almost dead in the path of the eye. Unless Sophronia's path or speed changes in the next twenty hours."

Thomas gave Emma a wordless look. Then he shook his head with a frown. "It's changed twice already. It's bound to change again."

"Maybe." Emma pushed her hair back and released a breath. She sat on the edge of the table and rechecked her calculations, then her tracings. Nothing changed. "We'll retrace the path more accurately when Gloria gets back."

She gave Dennis what she hoped was an encouraging smile. "Besides, well, I built Gulf Stream to withstand a hurricane. I just wasn't expecting it to be tested so soon."

She grabbed the notepad, dropped onto the couch, tucked a leg under herself, and started making a checklist of things to do. Then she tugged her lip. "I should head out tonight."

Dennis looked at her. She could tell that he didn't want her to go at all, and they both knew there was no way he was going to stop her. "Pendleton needs that report for his conference call tomorrow."

"So I'll finish it tonight and have it delivered to his suite."

"Why not book a flight out tomorrow morning? That will leave you available for any last-minute questions Pendleton might have, and you'll still be able to reach Gulf Stream before nightfall."

Emma eyed Dennis. He was right; she'd be working on her report for most of the night. She would likely have finished in time to catch a late evening flight if she hadn't tried to take that damned diving class. She slumped in her seat.

"Why can't we ever have just one crisis at a time?"

When she returned to her hotel room later, a message in her voice mail from Dennis asked her to drop by after dinner for a little chat.

His door had a *Do Not Disturb* sign hanging from

the handle, but the door was also slightly ajar. She knocked and someone inside, someone with a deep voice, made a noise. She decided to assume it was Dennis telling her to enter, and pushed the door the rest of the way open.

The room was dark, sodden, and warm, filled with the sour-sharp smell of ozone, with breezes and traffic noises. Headlights from the street flickered across the walls and bedspread. Tires on wet pavement made sounds like ripping cloth. The sheer curtains that covered the wall with the sliding glass door billowed above the air-conditioning unit. Then she saw the glow of his cigarette: he was out on the balcony, seated in one of the white, wrought-iron chairs.

Emma stuck her head around the glass door. Enough reflected light came from the streets and the mall across the interstate for her to make out his form, but not to read his features. He gestured at a chair next to his.

"Sit down."

With sunset the clouds had opened up and dumped rain on the city; the chair was still wet. Emma sat anyway, lifting her hair from her neck, and strips of cold spread across the seat and back of her cotton summer dress. It felt good. The western sky still held a trace of color; piles of thunderheads spat faint lightning and streaked rain across the distant strip of dull yellow along the horizon.

"Thanks for coming," he said.

A draft carried cigarette smoke to her; she pinched her nose and waved a hand. "Dad's told you a hundred times, you're begging for lung cancer with that habit. Or a heart attack."

"I pay Mike to lecture me about my health. You, I don't."

She made a face at him that he probably couldn't

see. "Your message was cryptic. I take it you want an update on the hurricane?"

"Oh. Yes. Have you talked to Flo? How are the preparations coming?"

"I called her about a half hour ago. Sophronia's still headed right for them. ETA between ten A.M. and noon on Friday."

"What's the status of the preparations?"

"We've had one stroke of major good luck—the trawler just went into dry dock in Port Canaveral yesterday for repairs, so it and the crew are out of harm's way. We're having a tug pick up the hydrogen storage barges this morning. The onboard staff are finishing Phase I of the Storm Response Plan right now with evacuation of nonessential personnel. Flo and the rest are in the process of shutting down operations and battening everything down." Emma paused. "I plan to fly out tomorrow at eight A.M. I've arranged for a charter plane from Tampa to Melbourne, and helicopter transport from there, which will put me on Gulf Stream by three-thirty tomorrow afternoon."

Dennis's eyes glinted at her; he took a drag from his cigarette and blew smoke upward. "It's not necessary for you to put yourself at risk."

Emma shook her head. "There's no real risk unless Gulf Stream sinks, and that won't happen. The beanpoles are tightly moored and most of their mass is well below any significant wave action." She slouched down in the chair. "Frankly, I'm more concerned about flooding and wind or wave damage."

"What do you mean?"

"The storm will threaten the reef and the mariculture farms. And the chemical storage tanks and hydrogen flare have been designed for up to one-hundred-eighty-mile-an-hour winds, but it's still a little nervous-making." She paused. "We could also get some damage to the modules, depending on how well my bulkheads and storm windows hold up.'' The ends of her hair snagged on the chair; she flipped it all over the back again.

''I don't see why whatever you need to contribute can't be done via telephone,'' Dennis said. She couldn't see his expression, but she could hear the frown in his voice.

''Look. With this GM fiasco, now is the worst possible time for us to get hit with costly repairs to Gulf Stream. I know the physical structure, and the facility design, better than anyone. I should be there. It could make a difference. I appreciate the concern, Dennis, but you really have nothing to worry about.''

He fidgeted; his chair skittered on the concrete. ''What am I going to tell Mike if something happens to you?''

''That's irrelevant.'' Which it wasn't, perhaps, on one level, because Dennis was a longtime friend of the family. But Emma was not about to grant the point. ''I mean it. Pendleton gave me operational control of Gulf Stream; it's my decision.''

''Yeah. Okay.'' After a pause, Dennis sighed. ''That's not what I wanted to talk to you about, anyhow.''

''What, then?''

''I want you to stay out of Thomas's face when he issues his report to Pendleton tomorrow.''

She stiffened. ''What are you talking about?''

Dennis didn't answer.

''Come on. Give.''

Dennis seemed to be looking at her, though she couldn't be sure. The silence stretched. He lit a cigarette, cupping the flame in his hand, and the light revealed deep lines in his face. After a moment he said, ''Emma, you're not going to like what I'm about to say.''

"Well, stop upsetting me with all these dark hints and just say it."

"You know our biggest income stream right now is the scientific grants we get."

She snapped her head around. "You're not suggesting that we modify our entire five-year plan to accommodate *his* grandiose schemes—"

"Hear me out."

Emma slapped the arm of her chair. "I've already heard it. And I'll tell you right now, it's a stupid plan. I killed it six months ago and I'll kill it again. I'm not going to have the hydrogen plant and all my engineering research projects gutted to turn the Engineering module into a haven for his petty projects. Damn it, we *can* make money with our hydrogen! If we have to, we'll convert over to fertilizer manufacture."

With a grunt he stood, went to the rail, and leaned his elbows against it, silhouetted against the Houston skyline. "Not profitable enough to justify the expense."

She eyed his silhouette. "The plant generates twenty-six hundred megawatt-hours per day of electricity; we'd be wasting power in fistfuls by converting the Engineering module to scientific research instead of hydrogen production and engineering research."

The tip of his cigarette flared. "And do what with your precious hydrogen? If there's no one to buy it at a price we can afford to sell it, we're out of business. Is that your aim?"

"Don't be ridiculous! There'll be markets for our hydrogen. We just have to look a little harder." She pinched her lip. "Besides, we have other important income streams that'll hold us for a while. The existing mariculture projects are already profitable. The seafood, the pearls, the guar all sell like crazy. And Flo has developed some great new markets for the guar and for biomass methane.

''And my engineers have several bench-scale pilot projects going: wave energy conversion pumps; calcium carbonate piping molded with seawater, chicken wire, and a little electric juice; I just okayed a proposal to extract precious metals from seawater—''

''All of those are maybes. Uncertain markets, deals not yet made.'' His sigh made her neck hairs stand up. ''We can't handle maybes, Emma; we need funds now. Not tomorrow. Not next year. Reynolds has the contacts and professional credibility to get those funds quickly. To put those funds to use he needs more space. And space is at a premium at Gulf Stream. Research labs are worth a lot more right now, per square foot, than your hydrogen production plant.''

''Bullshit.''

''What have you got against research?''

''I don't have anything against research. Ninety percent of the projects I just listed are ongoing partnerships with university researchers. Look at Tetsuo's marine biology research and Flo's Mariculture division—they're inextricably linked.

''The trouble is that Reynolds doesn't look for ways to benefit Gulf Stream as a whole. He looks for ways to increase his own turf at everybody's expense. Not to mention being an incompetent, arrogant asshole and a liar—''

''Emma.'' Here it came, as predictable as heartburn after Tex-Mex. ''Lay off him.''

She slouched in her chair, grinding her teeth. ''Yeah, yeah.''

''I mean it. He has powerful connections with several national and private funding institutions and we can't afford to alienate him. Lighten up.''

''I'm serious about him being a liar,'' she said. ''You should know that it was Gloria who initiated the on-land response procedures today, not Reynolds. He was lying to you. And that's just one example of the way he climbs over the backs of others and tries to make himself look good at others' expense."

"It doesn't matter who initiated the procedures." Dennis sounded weary. "They were initiated. Reynolds is a jerk, fine. But he's a valuable jerk. He brings in more external funding than you do."

"Damn it, Dennis, that's not fair. Finding funding is in his job description—not mine—and I *still* get external funds."

"We need him, Emma." Dennis stabbed out his cigarette. "Lay off. I mean it."

She pressed fingers against her lips. Getting sidetracked on Reynolds's incompetence had been a mistake.

"Here's the bottom line. The whole purpose behind Gulf Stream is sustainable energy. That OTEC plant is Gulf Stream's heart. Generating energy from the sea. Turning it into useful power." She lifted her hands. "It was our vision. You were there; you were part of it, too. Energy from the sea, benign technology, supporting a seagoing community set up to study and protect marine life. *Diversity* of projects, of income streams, to protect us from failure."

"But if a part of our vision has failed, if it's not profitable, we need to change that vision." He sat down next to her again, laid a hand over hers. "Even if the OTEC plant fails, commercially, it doesn't reflect on you, you know. The markets just aren't ready yet. It's not an economically feasible technology. Not quite."

Emma slid her hand out from under his.

"If Gulf Stream doesn't start earning its way," Dennis said, fanning the air with his cigarette, making tight, glowing circles with it, "we'll go down in history as the world's biggest high-tech boondoggle this side of Biosphere II."

Emma shook her head. "You're missing the point."

"I don't think so. I'm asking you to search your heart and look past the personal. We're facing some tough choices, Emma." He took a deep drag from his cigarette; the ember flared and lit up his face again, briefly. "You're in charge of Gulf Stream, you know, even more than Thomas and Flo. Everyone looks to you for answers. We need your leadership now."

"I won't support it."

But her heart wasn't in the protest.

He crushed the glowing ember of his cigarette into the ashtray balanced on the arm of his chair. "At least think it over."

She was silent. She felt him looking at her.

Why did he wield such influence on her? They were supposed to be peers. But he had a good deal more business experience than she; if he was right, how could she put her own agenda above the continuance of Gulf Stream as a commercial venture?

"Please?" he said.

Emma rubbed her arms, sighed, nodded numbly. "Okay."

He nodded slowly, and tapped another cigarette out of the pack. "Thank you. Oh, before I forget— Pendleton wants us to stick around for a ten-thirty meeting after his conference call."

"He does? Even with the storm?" That surprised her, briefly, out of the depression that had settled over her. It would upset her travel plans. She'd have to change them tonight, but she could catch a noontime plane and still be at Gulf Stream before dusk. "What's it about?"

"I don't know. He said he had some announcement to make. He specifically asked for you to be there and it was after he knew about the storm."

She looked at him, sitting there in his porch chair with his eyes glinting at her.

"Yeah, okay."

"See you in the morning," he said.

Emma didn't reply. She hung her thumbs in the pockets of her dress and left the room, feeling as battered and hagridden as if she'd been through a hurricane already.

At Emma's knock, Gloria came to the door. She wore a flannel nightgown and her hair was down, tumbling in a cascade of red streaked with white, around her face and down her back. Her mouth foamed with Uncle Malcolm's All-Natural Baking Soda Toothpaste and her hand clutched a toothbrush. She had the lights off and at least thirty votive candles burning in little glass cups on the dinner table, the dresser, and the bedside table. The scent of sandalwood drifted out around her.

"Can I come in for a minute?" Emma asked.

Gloria made a mushy, indistinct sound and motioned her inside, then closed the door and went into the bathroom to spit out the toothpaste. Emma sat down in a chair at the table. Set in front of the dozen or so candles was a geode with indigo crystals inside. She picked it up and turned it over.

"Praying Sophronia off in another direction?" she asked Gloria, who came out drying her face with a hand towel.

"Whatever aid the Goddess is willing to give, my dear. I don't presume to dictate to her, only petition."

Emma tossed the geode from hand to hand. "It's not working so far. At least, not since seven-thirty."

Gloria tossed her head back and laughed. "Give me time. It's a big storm and I've just gotten started." She tossed the towel on her bed and sat in the chair across from Emma. "You upset about Sophronia? Or something else?"

Emma growled. "I want to throttle that bastard."

"Dr. Reynolds?"

"Dennis."

Gloria's eyebrows went up. "That's a switch."

"He's putting pressure on me over Reynolds's proposal to gut the Engineering module and replace everything with more of his projects."

"Anything I can do?"

Emma shook her head with a sigh. "Afraid not."

"Maybe Flo can help."

"Yeah, maybe. But this is no time to distract her with office politics."

"Oh!" Gloria jumped up and picked up some faxed sheets and some small objects from the dresser. She handed her the fax. "These are for you." They were the Storm Response Protocols: several pages of names, phone numbers, and instructions.

"Thanks."

"And so are these." Gloria dropped two sea shells into Emma's palm. "For your collection. I found them on the beach in Galveston this morning."

Emma held one of them close to the candles, studying it. It was a shell as large as her palm in the shape of a child's top. Beads the color of butter and a thin ribbon of maroon encircled it.

"What kind is it?"

"A top shell of some kind. I'll have to look it up when I get home." She gave Gloria a smile. "It's pretty."

"And that one is really weird," Gloria said as Emma held up the second shell. "It must be a genetic fluke."

It looked like a shell that had come off its spool. A rusty brown, it was a coarse, heavily weathered tube a good five inches long. Emma smiled. "Not a fluke, though I'm surprised you found it here. It's a worm shell. A West Indian worm shell, if I'm not mistaken. Thanks."

She slipped the shells into her pocket. At the door,

she turned. "Just for the record, you *were* the one who
initiated the landside storm response, weren't you?"

Gloria gave her a wry smile and a shrug. "It doesn't
matter."

"Yes it does. Good work. Good night. And don't
stay up all night meditating. You need your rest."

Gloria blew her a kiss and sat down on her bed. She
was tucking her legs into a lotus position as Emma
pulled the door closed.

Chapter 2

GABRIEL: **Wednesday, 30 September, 8:03 A.M. MDT**
City-County Jail, Albuquerque, New Mexico

"Come on, Cervantes, you're only hurting yourself,"
Officer Tompkins said. "You have a rap sheet this
long on the Woodland Products plant alone! Now that
we've got evidence linking you to the explosion, all
we want are the details. Who was in it with you?"

Gabriel merely looked past the cop's shoulder at the
one-way mirror there and, pointedly, stifled a yawn.
He'd been arrested before and he knew better than to
let them get his ire up.

"You eco-freaks are all alike," Officer Fell said.
"You think you're so goddamn smart, and you're so
self-righteous, aren't you? One big family." He got
right in Gabriel's face. "So how come one of your
family squealed on you?"

That got Gabriel's heart going. He stared at Fell.
They'd been at him part of yesterday afternoon and
for almost an hour this morning. Up till now he'd just
let all their insults, questions, and demands wash past

him. But the idea that someone had turned him in—
that cut deep.

It couldn't be Mark or Jackson. He was sure of that.
They were like brothers to him. He could trust them.
But they *were* young and a bit rash; either might have
blabbed to someone, who'd blabbed to someone
else . . .

"Who did?" he said. "Who accused me?"

The two cops exchanged a meaningful smile.

"Maybe it was one of your accomplices, asshole.
Come on. Talk to us and maybe we can cut a deal.
Who was your demolitions man?"

Gabriel opened his mouth, but there was a knock
on the door, and a man in a three-thousand-dollar Ar-
mani suit entered.

"George R. Branscombe," he said, presenting his
business card to the cops. "I'm here to represent Mr.
Cervantes."

Gabriel stared. He had a large circle of friends and
admirers, but few of them had two ten-dollar bills to
rub together at a time, much less enough to hire an
expensive lawyer. Maybe they'd taken up a collection.
Ha.

"Now," the lawyer said, "I'd like a word with my
client. In private."

Gabriel eyed Branscombe while Tompkins exchanged a frowning look with his partner.

"Whoa, just a minute, here," Fell said. "You're *his*
lawyer?" He jerked his thumb at Gabriel, in his plaid
Wal-Mart–special shirt with its rolled-up sleeves, his
faded and worn jeans and dirty tennis shoes.

"That's correct. Excuse us, please." Branscombe
turned his back to the cops.

Tompkins took Fell's arm. "Come on, Alan."

"And keep away from the one-way mirror," Branscombe added, gesturing at the mirror, "or I'll have
your badges."

"Who sent you?" Gabriel asked as the door closed. The lawyer waved the question away.

"Let's get you out of here first, and deal with your questions afterward." Branscombe pulled up a chair across from Gabriel and leaned on the table. "I've seen the DA's—"

Gabriel put up his hands. "Stop right there. In the first place, I don't trust lawyers. And I'm not willing to take help from some unknown benefactor."

Branscombe leaned back and studied Gabriel. "As to your second point," he said, "this is a public service—a donation—from someone with money who believes in your cause. You're under no obligation to pay the money back or perform any action as a result of this. And as to your first point . . ." He spread his hands. "You don't seem to me to be a stupid man. Not getting a lawyer when you're under suspicion for destroying an eighteen-million-dollar facility—"

Gabriel's mouth quirked. "An eighteen-million-dollar polluting pus pocket of a facility."

"—is stupid," Branscombe finished. Gabriel leaned forward on the table, his eyes narrowing.

"All right, then. Let's cut the crap. I've known a few good lawyers, but that monkey suit tells me you're no public defender or altruist." He waved a hand at Branscombe's suit. "I'll give odds your typical client is a wealthy corporado who's ripped off the company and wants to get off lightly. Or maybe your usual business is even defending polluting companies. And that kind of help, my friend, I don't need."

Branscombe studied him thoughtfully. He gestured at his business suit. "This intimidates the opposition. A simple power move. And, while I *have* handled a number of white-collar-crime cases, I've never defended a company in an environmental violation." At Gabriel's incredulous look, he held up one hand and put the other one over his heart, striving for, and achieving, a sincere expression. "It's not my field. I specialize in criminal law."

Gabriel held out a hand for his business card, and Branscombe provided it. "Hinkle, Phelps, Wiggman?"

"That's correct."

"Out of Santa Fe."

Branscombe nodded. "I'm a partner there." Then he leaned forward and spoke more softly. "Now, this is not a condition of my employment, but an addendum, perhaps. Your benefactor *has* agreed to a meeting afterward. If, and only if, you desire one."

Gabriel frowned. It made no sense. "That's the only catch? Someone wants to meet me?"

"Only if you wish to. If not . . ." Branscombe shrugged. "You'll go your own way and that'll be the end of it."

Gabriel frowned, eyeing the other man. Finally, he nodded, with a sigh. "Go on, then. You were talking about the DA."

"I've seen the DA's case. The police received an anonymous phone call the other day, identifying you as responsible, but they have no witnesses, no physical evidence from the scene or your home. And most important, there was a second bombing last night, while you were in custody. Same MO as the bombing last week—done at night; no one was injured, detonated by radio. And, as before, Wild Justice claimed responsibility."

Gabriel stared. "*What?* Where?"

"Another Woodland Products plant in southern Colorado."

Gabriel knew of the plant. It was as much a pig of a polluter as its sister plants in San Carlo and Ruidoso. He rubbed at his mustache. Worry gnawed his gut. A copycat bombing. Mark and Jax wouldn't have acted without his knowledge and couldn't have gotten it together so quickly, in any event. So, who?

· "Now, according to the booking log, they brought you in at ten-oh-five yesterday. That means they can only hold you another"—he glanced at his gold Rolex watch—"hour and fifty-eight minutes without charging you. And they don't have a case. In less than two hours, maximum, if you do what I tell you to, you'll walk right out of here."

"So what do you want me to do?"

"What have you told them so far?"

Gabriel shook his head. "Nothing. They claimed someone fingered me so I asked who."

"From here on out, don't say a word. Not a word. Don't give them *anything* they might be able to twist around and use on you."

"Fair enough. What next?"

Branscombe bared teeth. "We'll see if we can save you a couple of hours of your time."

He stepped out into the hall and signaled to someone. Fell and Tompkins came back in, looking decidedly grim.

Branscombe brought his hands together with a smack. "Here's what's going on. My client has nothing more to say to you. If you have any questions, you may talk to me, and I will speak for Mr. Cervantes. Now, you arrested my client exactly twenty-two hours and three minutes ago." He took off his watch and set it on the table. "You know and I know that you don't have a case."

"Says who?" Tompkins demanded.

Branscombe spread his hands, smiling mildly. "I've seen the files, Officer. If you've got enough evidence to charge him, I think you'd better do so, right now. You're running out of time." He pulled a chair out next to Gabriel, and sat down. "If not, and if you have nothing better to do with your time, well, I suppose we can all just sit here for the next hour and fifty-seven—no, make that fifty-six—minutes, during which time you won't say a word to Mr. Cervantes, since he doesn't want to talk to you. And then he and I will leave.''

The two cops looked at each other. A long pause ensued. Then Fell sighed and shrugged at Tompkins, who went over and opened the door.

"Walk," Tompkins said, looking like he'd sucked a lemon.

Outside the courthouse was a mob scene: trucks with antennae and cameras on top, microphones on poles, people with headsets and earphones. Gabriel stared. He glanced at Branscombe.

"Is all this for *me*?" he asked.

Branscombe gave him a wry nod. "Let me do the talking," he said, pushing the door open for Gabriel.

As they exited, at least a dozen people came running up, shouting questions. Branscombe held on to Gabriel's arm and shouted, "No comment, no comment," barging through the reporters, and then they were through, and made a dash to Branscombe's car, which sat in a lot across the street.

As they sped away up Fifth Street, Gabriel said, grudgingly, "Thanks."

"Not a problem," Branscombe said.

Gabriel pocketed his billfold and relaced his shoes. "Any sign of a tail?"

Branscombe squinted at the rearview mirror. "Can't tell. Let me make a few diversionary turns . . .''

A few minutes later, Branscombe gave a little nod. "I think we're okay. Where would you like me to drop you?"

They were now on Coal, just past Broadway. Gabriel gestured at the curbside beyond the light. "Anywhere along here is fine."

"Are you sure? I don't mind giving you a lift."

"Thanks, but I've been cooped up too long. I'd rather walk." Branscombe pulled over, and Gabriel opened the door. The air was cool and fresh; he drew a deep breath. Yes, walk, definitely. Tompkins had recommended it, after all.

"Well, best of luck." Branscombe shook Gabriel's hand and then handed him a slip of paper. "Goodbye."

After Branscombe had pulled away, Gabriel looked around. He didn't appear to be being followed, but it never hurt to be a little paranoid. He headed over to the nearby strip mall, went inside the grocery store, and stepped into a public rest room. In a stall, he read the note. It was handwritten.

BEST PRICE BOOKS AND COFFEE, CENTRAL AND UNIVERSITY, 11:30 A.M., BACK ROOM.

He knew the place. That was about three hours from now—time enough to get home and take a shower—and close to where he lived, in the student ghetto south of the UNM campus.

An unknown, wealthy benefactor, and a mysterious meeting. Phooey. Manipulation. With a disgusted noise, he crumpled up the note and flushed it down the toilet.

On the way home he picked up a paper, and read about the Durango plant bombing as he walked. The destruction was not complete, but it was enough to shut the plant down for a good long while.

Another Woodland Products factory out of commission was all to the good, but he didn't like this copycat business. First off, he knew—or had thought he'd known—the terrain of the underground radical environmentalist movement quite well. No one else active right now had the skills—or the will—to act with explosives, or on such a large scale at all.

That meant there was someone new on the land-
scape. Someone who was hiding behind him and his
group. Or worse, trying to get to him, somehow. To
goad him.

After a shower and a shave, Gabriel checked his
voice mail—several reporters had left messages asking
for interviews—and then made some calls. He chatted
with a friend or two—carefully, in case he'd been
tapped. They expressed relief that he'd been released
and promised to pass the word. No one had heard any
scuttlebutt about the Durango bombing; one or two
obviously thought Gabriel had somehow engineered it.

He finally hung up, still disturbed. He didn't contact
Mark and Jax; they were lying low in a friend's cabin
out east of Madrid. With their Navy SEAL demolitions
training, any association with Gabriel right now would
spell trouble for all three of them.

He looked out the window. A woman walking her
dog; a man sitting in his parked car, eating a sandwich;
some young men Rollerblading in a nearby parking lot
. . . any of them could be feds, or reporters.

You wanted to go major league, Cervantes, he
thought; get used to it.

Deliberately ignoring the time, he went carefully
and thoroughly through his snail mail—mostly bills
and junk—and his E-mail—mostly responses to his
on-line radical environmental newsletter, *Untamed*.
Then he wrote a scathing editorial for the next issue,
implying that Woodland Products's management had
probably blown up the plants themselves for the insurance money. Tongue-in-cheek, between the lines,
he laid hints of the truth, of course; that was part of
the fun of monkey-wrenching: mind-fucking the opposition.

When he resurfaced from his creative fugue, the
clock on his computer read 11:28 A.M. He frowned. If

only the editorial had taken a little longer to write. He couldn't make it in time, but if he hurried he wouldn't be too terribly late. He hadn't wanted a choice.

Aw, hell. He'd dodged as best he could, but curiosity had him by the short hairs.

For the moment, at least, no one seemed to be watching his house. Gabriel dashed out the door, unlocked his bike, zipped down Silver to University, and pulled into the tiny parking lot of the book- and coffeeshop at 11:41. Panting, sweating, he locked up his bike and stepped inside.

The door was propped open. Shelves of old books filled the place, amid antique wood-and-wrought-iron tables and ornate figurines on stands. There was a long counter with pastries under glass, and a drink fountain and cash register, racks of postcards, and to one side, big bins with coffee beans. Fans on stands rotated slowly back and forth, moving air around. Windows showed traffic moving down Central and students sitting in the grass at the university campus across the street. A handful of people, mostly college-aged, sat at the tables, reading or sipping coffee and chatting.

The back room was beyond the coffee bins. It, too, was filled with shelves of used books, many of them ancient hardcovers—up to a hundred years old or older—along with more recent paperbacks. There was an unconvincing pretense of organizing the books by category. Tables were scattered through the room amid the shelves. A fan blew in here, too. The heady smell of old books blended with the aroma of brewing coffee.

Despite the fan this room was rather warm and close, and only one person sat there, a woman in perhaps her early to mid-thirties, with white-blond hair and small, rose-tinted, black-rimmed reading glasses. She was sipping an iced coffee and browsing through an old encyclopedia—"Brachiopod to Continental

Shelf.'' She didn't look wealthy. She had a neon pink bandanna rolled up and tied in her shoulder-length hair, and wore no makeup or jewelry—only a tie-dyed pale pink T-shirt, cut-offs, and Birkenstock sandals.

He glanced at his watch. It was 11:42. Either his benefactor had gotten tired of waiting and left, or this woman was it.

He cleared his throat. She looked up at him, seeming startled. Through the tinted glass, her eyes looked darker than any *gringa*'s he'd ever seen. He wondered if she bleached her hair. No dark roots showed, though, and except for some color in her cheeks that might have been a fading wind- or sunburn, her complexion was pale as eggshells. The muscles in her arms and legs stood out starkly, like iron cabling just beneath the skin. This was a woman who used her body *hard*. She didn't shave, though with hair as light as hers it hardly mattered. Her breasts were small, her shoulders broad, and her hips rather boyish; she wasn't an especially attractive woman, but there was *something* about her . . . something intriguing.

''It says here,'' she said, putting her finger on the page, ''that the king cobra can reach up to eighteen feet in length. Don't you think that's cool?''

''Umm, yeah.'' He paused. ''Excuse the intrusion, but . . . are you waiting for someone?''

''Not anymore.'' She flashed him a smile. ''Gabriel Cervantes?''

''Yes.''

She held out her hand and he shook it, waiting for her to provide her name. Instead she said, ''Why don't you go get yourself something? If you're into caffeine, try their iced chocolate **zip**. It's so caffeinated you'll break out in a sweat.''

After consideration he went for an iced herbal tea instead, and a bagel with cream cheese.

This was a woman; he felt obliged to apologize for

being late, as he sat. She waved the apology away with a smile that softened her sharp features, and removed her sunglasses. Her eyes were an odd color: a grey as dark as charred wood.

"I'm Boadica," she said.

"Is that your first or last name?"

"Neither." She snapped the encyclopedia shut and slid it back onto a shelf, then crossed her legs and leaned forward. "Forgive the melodrama at the courthouse, but I don't really want to come to the attention of the police. I'm, well, not to embarrass you, but I'm a fan of yours."

"Oh?" A mixture of pleased embarrassment and skepticism filled him. Skepticism won out. This wouldn't be the first time a woman had come on to him—in certain circles he was seen as the environmental movement's answer to Robin Hood, and groupies and hangers-on of one kind or another went with the territory. But while he'd never done anything like blowing up a plant before, he *had* broken plenty of laws, and he hadn't gotten this far by trusting strangers.

She went on, "I suppose you have a lot of questions—like why I hired a high-powered lawyer to get you out of jail and who I am. What's in it for me."

"As a matter of fact, that's exactly what I want to know," Gabriel said.

She pursed her lips and was silent for a moment, stirring her drink. "Have you heard about the Durango plant bombing?"

"Yes."

She didn't say anything else, merely smiled at him and waited. He cocked his head. "Are you implying that *you* were responsible?"

"I didn't plant the charges, myself—that's not my specialty—but yes, I made it happen."

His disbelief must have shown on his face. She merely shrugged.

"Why?" he asked.

"First of all, to get your attention. And second, because Woodland Products is a scum-sucking polluter of a company and they had it coming."

Gabriel's lips twisted in a wry smile. Then he frowned. "You blew up a plant just to get my attention?" She nodded. "You have an odd way of introducing yourself."

"I like making a dramatic entrance."

"So, if you *are* the instigator, why are you telling me? You don't know me from Adam. I could turn you in for both bombings—"

"And get yourself off the hook. Not really. I have an alibi for the first bombing and I was careful about evidence during the second. It's a calculated risk." She lifted her straw out with a finger over the top and sucked smoky liquid from the bottom. Her gaze was penetrating. "But in fact, I do know you, Gabriel. We've been following your career for some time."

This was getting too *Twilight Zone* for his tastes. "'We'?"

"Let's just leave it at that, for now." She stuck the straw back into her drink and put her elbows on the table. "I'll cut to the chase. I want you, Gabriel. I want your leadership, your intelligence, your dedication. I want you to help me wage war. It's time for us to plant a seed of fear in the hearts of corporate heads across the U.S. I want each and every CEO to believe that, unless he cleans up his act, his company might be next."

"Talk is cheap," Gabriel said.

"I've got more than talk. I have *resources*."

He remembered the expensive lawyer.

"Go on," he said.

Her voice was low and intent. "I want you to head

up a small team. Highly secret. We're going to hit a
big target. I mean *big*. A target that makes the Woodland Products bombings look like child's play.''

Gabriel raised his eyebrows. "What target?"

"I'll tell you tomorrow." She stood. "For now . . .
well, just make sure you have an ironclad alibi tonight
around . . . oh . . . you pick the time."

"Beg pardon?"

"Pick a time. Anytime between eight-thirty tonight
and six A.M. tomorrow."

He sighed, intrigued; exasperated. "Oh, okay, how
about nine-thirty?"

"Nine-thirty it is. Make sure you're covered from
nine to ten."

It was possible she was blowing smoke. Possible?
No—likely. She'd probably read about the Durango
explosion and was trying to use it to get to him for . . .
something. She was playing with his head. Tomorrow
she'd come up with some phony reason why nothing
had happened at 9:30 P.M., or something. He knew a
setup when he smelled one.

But just to be on the safe side, he returned a local
newspaper reporter, Cara Halloway's, call and agreed
to an interview at nine that evening. Besides the alibi
angle, publicity was all to the good, and in the past he'd
found Halloway's articles reasonably sympathetic . . .
though hideously naïve about the extent to which corporations would go to avoid environmental accounta-
bility.

Cara Halloway turned out to be half Indian—
probably Navajo, though perhaps Hopi or Pueblo—
and half white. She was in her forties, wore light
makeup, and was decked out in Santa Fe chic: a billowing, raw silk kimono over a silk tank top and blue
jeans, with a squash-blossom necklace in turquoise
and silver, a turquoise, coral, and silver bracelet-

watch, and heeled white sandals. She was friendly and professional, and quickly put him at his ease.

They met at Los Cuates, a New Mexican food restaurant, and over fiery-hot chimichangas and green chile enchiladas she asked him lots of questions about his background, his views on assorted local and regional environmental issues. Late in the meal, as they studied their menus and tried to decide whether to order flan or ice cream with their coffee, she came to the point.

"Everybody says you are one of the best-connected activists outside the East Coast power block of big environmental groups. Who is Wild Justice? What is their mission?"

He shrugged. "Nobody knows anything about them yet. They didn't exist until the Thursday before last, so far as anyone knows."

"Oh, come on." She leaned forward and lowered her voice. "Off the record—did you do it? Or do you know who did? I promise to keep your confidence."

Gabriel raised his coffee cup to his lips, and smiled at her. He let the pause lengthen. "Surely you don't expect me to answer that. But Woodland Products was due a comeuppance, and I'm glad they got it. Maybe corporations will start to take their responsibilities more seriously, if they realize that the public won't take any more of their excuses and lies. They may be able to buy off government officials, but the average citizen is tired—tired of stewing in pollution, tired of breathing air that makes our children ill, drinking water that is slowly poisoning us, watching as our national parks and natural wonders are destroyed and defaced by corporate America's irresponsible acts."

"But don't you think that the destruction of property is going too far?"

"I think destruction of property is what corporate America is all about." He paused, considered his words. "All right, that's a tad facetious. I think violence should be used only as a last resort, when all efforts to force a company to clean up its act have failed."

"Hmmm. What sort of violence? Do you draw the line at property damage, or do you advocate acts of terrorism against people as well?"

He was shocked. "In the first place, I don't advocate terrorism of any kind. Punishing a polluter when the government refuses to is vigilantism, not terrorism. And second, I would *never* advocate harming people!"

"You sound as if you feel strongly about that."

"Of course I do. Life is sacred."

She smiled at him, her eyes crinkling. "That sounds a lot like a pro-life stance . . . an odd position for a radical environmentalist to take."

He pursed his lips, and then smiled back. "Well, it's not my usual soap box. I will admit to internal conflict over the idea. I was brought up a strict Catholic, and while I no longer am, and while intellectually I see the need for stringent population controls, some of those old values linger." He lifted his eyebrows, and dropped them. He started to add that he'd had a relationship go to pieces over that very issue, but thought better of it.

"Ah," she said.

"But even leaving aside my personal beliefs, there's an important practical reason why it's critically important not to harm other people. The damage done to your cause in the public's eyes, if someone is hurt even accidentally due to your act of protest, is huge. It's just not worth it."

She jotted something in her steno pad, then looked up at him consideringly. "So you advocate violence against property, as a last resort."

"That's correct."

"Over the past two years you've been arrested three times, and convicted two of those times, for increasingly provocative, albeit nonviolent, protests linked to Woodlands Products Inc. Do you consider the bombing of their San Carlo plant an action of last resort?"

He laughed. "Well, *somebody* certainly did."

"You're toying with me."

"Only in good fun."

"Good fun. Hmmph." A frown had gathered on her brow. "You must know that the people in San Carlo are pretty stirred up about the bombing. Almost two hundred jobs were lost when that plant went up in smoke. People with families. Mostly Chicanos and Indians, you know? *Our* people. And it's a small town, with no other real job opportunities. The loss of the fiberboard plant will probably mean the end of San Carlo. That's harming people, isn't it?"

He nodded. "In a manner of speaking, it is. That's why violence against property should only be used as a *last* resort. Companies should be given plenty of opportunity to mend their ways. If not, though, like any criminal, they must pay." He made a sweeping gesture. "Let me give you an analogy. Suppose there is a man with a large family. He has a wife, he has several children. He provides for them well. How? By stealing from his neighbors. He must be stopped from stealing—he must be punished. It's very unfortunate that his family suffers, too, but you wouldn't allow him to go on stealing, would you?"

She shook her head, still frowning.

"A company that doesn't control its use of resources and stop its polluting," he went on, "is stealing. Stealing from our children and their children after them. If we don't tread lightly on this world there will be nothing left for our descendants. And countless other species will have been destroyed—irretrievably lost!—in the meantime. Either poisoned directly, or left with no place to go when their habitats and breeding grounds are destroyed. If the government won't take seriously its responsibility to make polluters pay for their criminal acts, then it's up to the citizenry to make them pay."

She looked at him, sipping her coffee.

"Vigilantism."

"Only if the government persists in not doing its job."

"And to what do you attribute the government's recent shift away from environmental regulation?"

He stroked his mustache. "I think there are a number of factors. The general populace has gotten complacent. Washington is in the pocket of big business, which has a clear economic incentive to avoid environmental regulation, and the media has gotten tired of covering environmental issues. Not enough drama in it, I suppose. The very real abuses—abuses that are worsening daily—aren't getting press anymore." He shook his head with a sigh. "Someday people are going to wake up, look out their window, and find out the world has been completely trashed while they weren't looking. That the Apocalypse is upon us—worldwide famine, drought, flooding—and it's too late to do anything about it."

She shifted, with a tight little smile, then glanced at her watch. "Oh, I do need to go."

Cara tucked her steno pad into her purse. Slinging the strap over her shoulder, she stood.

"This has certainly been educational for me." She shook hands with him. "Thank you for your time."

He glanced at his watch. It was 9:52. He tapped it, then shook it. "Speaking of time, my watch has stopped. Can you tell me what time it is?"

"Certainly." She looked at her own watch. "It's about five till ten."

Hope that'll do, he thought, and realized with a start that he did believe the other woman, Boadica. Something, somewhere, was going to blow. Or already had.

Chapter 3

EMMA: **Thursday, 1 October, 10:30 A.M. CDT
The Ritz-Carlton Hotel, Houston, Texas**

Emma entered the hotel function room to find Pendleton and Phil helping themselves to coffee from a big, sterling pot at one of the side tables. Morning sunlight streamed in the picture windows behind them, across a groomed lawn with fir trees. Beyond, traffic crawled along the street, amid orange barrels. Dennis entered behind Emma and closed the door.

She spotted Reynolds at the rosewood conference table. Across from him sat a man Emma didn't know. The man had wide-set, dark brown eyes, a pointed chin, and auburn hair worn short. His skin was pale with dark brown freckles scattered across the cheekbones. He wore a black suit and slacks, a stark white shirt with no vest, and a silver bear-claw bolo. Beneath the table she caught a glimpse of black dress cowboy boots. His build was rather shorter and broader, more powerful, than that of either Thomas Reynolds or Brad Pendleton. He had a piquant look, as if a wellspring of mirth were waiting to erupt from beneath his sober veneer.

A bit of an eccentric, she guessed. A wealthy Texan, perhaps: a potential investor.

Reynolds leaned toward the man, gesturing, going on in a low voice. Sucking up to him. Thomas must have reached a conclusion similar to hers. The man sat back in his chair with his boots crossed at the ankles and his hands linked behind his head, listening to Reynolds with a polite expression on his face that seemed, somehow, to communicate intense boredom.

He stood suddenly with a smile, interrupting Reynolds in midsentence. "I'd love to hear more about it sometime."

He then strolled over to join Pendleton at the coffeepot, leaving Reynolds looking rather deflated.

A smile slipped onto Emma's face.

Pendleton turned when Dennis shut the door. He appeared pleased to see them, and motioned them forward with broad sweeps of his arm. "Dennis, Emma. Come in! Have some breakfast! Come sit down."

Emma guessed his conference call—and/or the press conference—had gone better than he'd expected. Either that, or it was sheer relief at being past the ordeal. Phil looked troubled, though. Emma raised her eyebrows at him, but he only shook his head.

Once Emma and Dennis had helped themselves to coffee and pastries and seated themselves, Pendleton spoke.

"I got your reports." He looked at each of the four of them in turn. "They were quite helpful. I'd like to schedule a planning session in the Melbourne corporate offices on October fifth. That's next Monday. Two P.M." They all got their calendars out and made notes. "But that's not why I asked you here today." He gestured at the stranger. "Folks, may I present to you Keith Hellman, a top-notch environmental scientist, trained in marine biology and environmental law. Keith is lately of Groman Environmental Services here in Houston.

"Keith, this is Dennis MacNichols, our CFO.

Emma Tooke, the engineer who designed and built Gulf Stream I, and our chief operations officer. Thomas Reynolds, head of scientific research. Phil Evans, our general counsel, you've already met."

They shook hands all around with "hi's" and "how do you do's." When Emma's turn came, she found his grasp firm and his hand pleasantly fleshy and warm. He gave her a speculative look, which she returned.

"Keith is here at my invitation. He's—" Unaccountably, Pendleton broke off and exchanged glances with Phil, appearing uncomfortable. Hellman seemed unruffled, though wary. Pendleton cleared his throat and started over. "I have brought Keith on board to be our new environmental manager, in charge of regulatory compliance at Gulf Stream. He'll report to you, Emma."

Emma blinked. She threw a confused look across the table to Dennis, who shrugged.

"This is a surprise," Reynolds remarked around a bite of cheese Danish.

Emma framed her words carefully. "While I appreciate your suggestion, we've already got the selection process underway to replace Franz Uhlmann. I have several interviews scheduled for next week. No offense to Mr. Hellman."

"None taken."

Like hell. She returned the man's cool stare.

Pendleton seemed to have overcome his initial nervousness. He placed his palms flat on the table, stood, and leveled a gaze at Emma. "Mr. Hellman has been carefully screened for this position. He has handled all aspects of compliance for marine facilities for years, has extensive experience in spill response, and is ideally qualified."

Emma glanced at her watch. It was 10:45 and she

needed a full hour to get to the airport or she'd miss her flight. She didn't have time for this.

Again, she chose her words carefully. "It would have been better for me to have been involved in the selection process, given that he's to report to me."

Pendleton had the decency to blush, but his gaze didn't so much as flicker. "I realize I should have given you some advance notice. My apologies for that. However, I am decided on this issue. Mr. Hellman has my full support, and I expect him to be treated with the utmost respect and cooperation."

"Delighted," Reynolds said, smiling. He threw Emma a glance. "Welcome aboard, Hellman."

Phil reached across the table and shook Hellman's hand. Emma had a gut sense he wasn't all that thrilled about Hellman's presence, either.

Dennis mumbled a welcome and shook Hellman's hand.

Emma picked up her coffee cup, took a big gulp of cold coffee without really tasting it. Pendleton was looking at her now, with his eyebrows raised, awaiting her response.

What else could she do? She bolted her objections whole and said only, "Very well."

"Dennis tells me you're heading out to the facility," Pendleton said to her.

"I am." She stood. "In fact, I need to leave immediately to catch my flight—"

He waved her back down. "There's no need. I've arranged for you to take the corporate jet. The jet will get you there much sooner than the commercial airlines. It's waiting at Houston Hobby and the pilot has instructions to fly you directly to Melbourne." He glanced at his watch. "My car will pick you up at eleven-thirty. Meet the driver in the lobby at that time."

The last thing she wanted right now was to be beholden to him.

"Thank you," she managed. "Gloria is booked for the same flight. May she accompany me?"

"Of course." He gave her his winning smile, and then turned it on Hellman. "This is clearly a perfect opportunity for you to bring your expertise in spill prevention to bear, Keith. I'd like for you to accompany Emma to Gulf Stream and provide her with guidance on storm-proofing the chemical storage areas."

"I'd be glad to," Hellman said.

Slam. Bang. This morning was turning into the emotional equivalent of Space Mountain.

"Give me updates, as conditions warrant," Pendleton said.

Avoiding a direct gaze at anyone for fear of meltdown, Emma made her hurried good-byes and went upstairs to pound the bed and scream a little before she broke the news to Gloria.

Chapter 4

KEITH: Thursday, 1 October, 10:40 A.M. CDT
The Ritz-Carlton Hotel, Houston, Texas

Keith Hellman sat at the conference table while the rest of the Gulf Stream I staff left. He wasn't at all happy, but then, he hadn't expected to be.

What's-his-name, the head of scientific research, was bending Pendleton's ear, talking about the research projects under his supervision. Pendleton listened for about five minutes, but when the man showed no sign of stopping, he raised his hand. "I'm glad things are going so well, Thomas, but I'll have to hear the rest later. Mr. Hellman and I have some things to discuss before he has to leave. And don't you have to pack?"

"Why, no. My people have things well in hand so there's no point in me going along. I'll take in the rest of the conference. Somebody should."

"Fine, fine." Pendleton walked Thomas to the door. "You can fill me in on the research later. Perhaps in *writing*." He shut the door behind Thomas and shook his head.

Evans, the lawyer, had remained seated. He was scrutinizing Keith with a neutral expression.

Keith stood and walked quickly to the other end of the room, where a door led to adjoining function space. He pulled it open and two men and a woman came in.

"They seemed to take it well," said Barnes, one of the two FBI agents. He was a man in his forties with a high, lined forehead that seemed even higher because of a receding hairline. He wore a grey suit that seemed too large and a red tie pulled scrupulously tight. In the two days that Keith had known him, he'd never seen that tie loosened.

The other FBI agent, Gorey, rolled his eyes but didn't say anything. He wore a dark blue suit with a yellow paisley tie. He was at least ten years younger than Barnes and Keith *had* seen his tie loose. It was loose now.

"Bullshit," said the woman. She was short and solid-looking, and carried herself with a self-assurance that was almost regal.

Keith laughed quietly. Unlike the FBI agents, he'd known Jennifer Murdley for a long time. For the last six years she'd been his boss in the Enforcement Division of the Environmental Protection Agency. She wasn't about to gloss anything over.

Jennifer continued. "They're taking it, but they don't like it a bit and if Keith makes himself a pain in the ass at Gulf Stream, you'll have serious personnel problems. I know *I'd* be royally pissed if my boss shoved employees down my throat."

Pendleton gave her a sour look. "Yes, well, you people convinced me it was necessary. I still don't believe any of my people are involved."

Barnes spread his hands. "The same rumor that targets Gulf Stream talked about an inside contact. We can't take the chance. It's critical that you not reveal Mr. Hellman's real purpose to any of the Gulf Stream staff. For any reason."

"And if nothing happens?" Pendleton asked.

"Then we'll celebrate. But if we did nothing and a radical environmental group *did* strike at Gulf Stream, I wouldn't be doing my job. Those fiberboard plants Wild Justice blew up in New Mexico were worth almost fifty million dollars, not to mention the jobs lost. What would you be out if Gulf Stream was destroyed? Fifty million? A hundred?"

"A hell of a lot more than that," said Pendleton. "Enough, already. I agreed."

Keith smiled again. Apparently the FBI had wanted to put one of their own men in and had come to Jennifer for help navigating the maze of EPA regulations. It had fit in so perfectly with an undercover investigation the Environmental Protection Agency was pursuing against certain Florida Department of Environmental Protection personnel that she'd used some of her political muscle to get Keith in instead.

They had sold it to Pendleton as better cover; if he was going to force an environmental compliance manager on his people, he couldn't afford anything less than extreme competence without raising suspicions among his staff. Jen had told Keith privately, right before the meeting, that Evans had raised a big stink during their first discussions. But Pendleton had over-ruled him and agreed to let Keith come aboard.

Keith's smile soured. Ah, well, that was where the humor ended.

"Is there anything further we have to discuss?" Keith asked. "I've got to move my luggage down to the lobby and check out in the next twenty minutes."

Agent Barnes cleared his throat. "We'd planned on briefing you on communications procedures and what to look for. This hurricane is complicating things."

Jennifer shook her head. "This is too good an opportunity. With this emergency, he'll be on site before anybody has a chance to hide things or cover them up. Give Keith a little credit. He's been investigating polluters' criminal negligence for six years. You haven't *seen* cover-ups and stonewalling until you get into environmental compliance issues. Keith has a very good nose for this sort of thing. He can tell when people are hiding things."

Keith looked at his watch, embarrassed. "Time is running short."

"Okay," said Barnes. "We'll try and squeeze something in later, on a weekend perhaps." He handed Keith a card. It was blank except for a phone number—no name, no FBI logo. "This is our office in Orlando. When you call, ask for me or Gorey. If you have to leave a message, identify yourself as Mr. Peters and *don't* leave a number. We'll get back to you."

Keith frowned. "Don't you trust your own people?"

"It's just good security."

Brad Pendleton held out his hand. "Good luck, Mr. Hellman. I hope you find there's nothing to worry about, but if not, I hope you can stop it before anybody gets hurt."

Keith shook Pendleton's hand. "I'll do my best." He was impressed that Pendleton mentioned people's lives instead of the many millions of dollars' worth of capital investment. Even if it was probably on his mind.

Jennifer walked with Keith as they left, though they separated in the public areas and Keith checked that the hallway was clear before letting her follow him into the room. His luggage was packed: two soft-sided suitcases, a briefcase, two cardboard boxes, and a large, soft-sided equipment bag almost four feet long.

He phoned for a bellman with a cart and checked his watch. "Not much time. Any last words?"

"You know what to look for. Look hard at all their permits. Find out who their contact was at the Florida Department of Environmental Protection. And I want to know how well Gulf Stream's consent agreement conditions map to the DEP's track record on other offshore permits. You know what a good-old-boy network the DEP is, and Pendleton's people are plugged right into it."

"But you do have someone specific in mind."

Her lips thinned. "Yeah, I've got someone in mind. Chuck Pinkle. Look for his name."

"Chuck Pinkle."

She nodded. "In Permitting. I know he's taking bribes, and I intend to catch him. It's only a matter of time. What's so funny?"

Keith shook his head. "It's the irony. The FBI wants to catch terrorists. You said yes to them because it will let you catch the Florida DEP making shady deals with polluters. And the only reason I said yes to you—the *only* reason I'd be willing to sneak around like this—is because it's Gulf Stream and because I want to get some diving in. All of us have different reasons for this farce."

Jennifer scowled. "Farce? You don't believe the DEP's in up to their necks with local industry?"

He held up his hands. "Whoa. They probably are, and if the Gulf Stream consent orders were acquired improperly, we'll screw them to the wall. But the FBI? Jeeze, Jen, we're talking about the same organization that incited Earth Firsters to violence so they could bust them. Do you really think this eco-terrorist thing is for real?"

Jennifer shrugged. "I don't know. It's possible, though, and you shouldn't blow it off because of your opinion of the FBI."

There was a knock on the door. And Keith frowned. "Okay. I'll treat it and the environmental issues seriously. But, damn it, I'm going to get in some diving that isn't in half industrial sludge and the other half silt!"

Jennifer opened the door for the bellman while saying, "Nobody ever said you had to do all your own silt and water sampling."

"I'm not complaining about collecting my own samples. I'd just like to be able to see more than three inches in front of my face underwater, for a change. It's been a while, okay?"

She smiled. "Okay."

The bellman heaved on the equipment bag's handle and grunted when it didn't move. Keith said, "Here, let me help you with that. It's a little heavy." They piled it and the rest of the luggage onto the cart and Keith asked the bellman to meet him downstairs. The young man took off down the hall.

"Keep me informed, okay?" said Jennifer, her voice quieter. She reached out and touched his arm.

Keith nodded. "You're my boss. Not the FBI. Not Pendleton. Not Tooke. I'll be in touch."

Impulsively, she hugged him, surprising them both. "Be careful, Keith."

"I will."

Chapter 5

The night before, Gabriel had gotten home in time to catch the last few minutes of the ten o'clock news, and there had been no talk of a bombing . . . though he might have missed it. Then his sleepless night in jail caught up with him; he'd gone straight to bed and slept later than usual in the morning.

As soon as he woke up, with a mixture of nervousness and rising excitement, he ran out to get the morning paper. It lay on the grass in a plastic sleeve; he pulled it out and read the front page as he walked back to the house. There it was.

"Three strikes and they're out!" the headline said in inch-high letters. "Woodland Products Inc.'s Ruidoso plant bombed."

A tingle coursed up his spine. Despite additional security put in place after the San Carlo bombing, the blast had taken place at exactly 9:30 the night before. A phone call from "Wild Justice" five minutes before the blast had given the on-site security force time to evacuate. The damage hadn't been extensive, but it was almost certainly enough to put the company out of business. Good, thought Gabriel, folding the paper back up with a satisfied smile.

As he touched the doorknob, a car pulled into his dirt driveway, crunching gravel. He turned to see Detectives Tompkins and Fell get out. He waved as they approached.

"Hey, dudes," he said, smiling. "Long time no see." He held up the paper with the headline facing them. "Let me guess . . ."

Tompkins rolled his eyes up. "You want to answer a few questions, Cervantes, or do we have to take you downtown and call that fancy lawyer of yours?"

Cervantes grinned. "If the question is 'where were you last night?' I'll be glad to answer it. I'll even lend you my phone to check it out."

Cara Halloway wasted no time in providing him an alibi . . . and from the sound of things, must have reamed Fell a new one while she was at it. Gabriel didn't know exactly what she said, but the detective hung up the phone a shade or two paler than he'd been going on. Ah, the power of the press. Bless you, Cara, he thought, with only a twinge of guilt.

"It could've been a timer. Your alibi is irrelevant, really," said Fell, hanging up the phone.

"Right. Between spending twenty-two hours in jail and going to dinner last night, I had *lots* of free time to build a bomb, drive three and a half hours down to Ruidoso, plant the bomb in a heavily guarded facility, and drive three and a half hours back. Or maybe I flew, but frankly, my red cape is at the cleaners."

With a deadpan expression, Tompkins said, "Thank you for your time, Mr. Cervantes. We'll be in touch."

Forty-five minutes after they left, the phone rang.

It was a female voice. "How'd you like to go hiking?" Boadica.

He blinked—so soon? Well, why not? "I'll bring lunch."

"Great. Meet you the same place?"

The bookstore. "When?"

"Well, I'm hungry now."

She hung up without saying good-bye.

He dressed in his hiking clothes and packed a few

supplies—a canteen of water, trail snacks, turkey sandwiches, peaches, and his first-aid kit—then left the house at a brisk walk. There were a few people out. To be on the safe side, he dodged down an alley, sprinted down a side street, and ducked behind a vehicle. A moment later an out-of-shape man in a jogging outfit ran past, swearing and breathing heavily. Gabriel got a glimpse of him as he headed up Lead, and recognized him as one of the mob of reporters who had been shouting questions at him the day before. Sheesh. What a way to earn a living.

Gabriel doubled back and crossed to Central. Boadica pulled up beside him in a beat-up tan Jeep.

He appreciated the subtlety.

"I thought we'd head out east of the Manzanos," she said.

"Sure."

She took a roundabout way to I-40, threading through some of the residential streets around the university and then up Carlisle. On the freeway the wind blasted them, making conversation difficult, so neither spoke as she drove up through Tijeras Pass, then took the turnoff south onto State Road 14. She kept a close eye on the rearview mirror.

"Still looking for a tail?" he asked.

Her only answer was a quirked eyebrow and a smile.

After a while she turned onto a dirt road that headed up toward the peaks of the Manzano Mountains, and the going got bumpy. They wound around into and through a forest, along hillsides and cliffs, and finally came to a stop at a dirt parking lot on a hillside. No other cars were there.

Gabriel stepped out onto the dirt and breathed in the smell of evergreen needles and fallen leaves. The sky was clear and the air dry, just the right temperature; mountain ash and birch—whose leaves were turning firecracker yellow and orange—firs and juniper whispered secrets to the wind; bees buzzed past as they lifted their knapsacks from the back of the Jeep. Birds and squirrels teased them from high up among the branches.

Boadica spotted something and stooped, picked it up, and slipped it into the zippered pocket of her knapsack. Gabriel recognized it belatedly as a candy wrapper of some sort. The matter-of-fact way she did it, without making a fuss or prompting him to compliment her for doing so, impressed him.

"I've never been up this way," he said.

"Me neither, but my informant says it's one of the area's best-kept secrets." She set off, and he followed, up a trail that wound up into the forest.

It was a great hike. She spotted the fossilized imprint of a three-toed sloth in a tilted slab of sedimentary rock. Then they made their way up a dry, rocky wash. The climb was quite steep in a couple of places. He followed some bird tracks and found a quail's nest: four eggs buried in tall grass beside a shrub. He showed it to her, and then they covered it back up and moved away, grinning, as the mother bird hurled herself into the air, flapping her wings in their faces.

By about 1:00 P.M. they reached a rocky promontory overlooking the eastern foothills, and beyond, the high plains. The sky was dark, dark blue; the sun beat down, desert-strong, countering the air's coolness, making the hair on top of Gabriel's head hot. Thunderheads whose underbellies were smeared with verga clung to the horizon in the south and east. The breeze was strong enough to whip Boadica's white hair wildly around the edges of her cap. She brushed it away and smiled sidelong at him.

"It's something, isn't it?"

"Sure is." He took a slug of water and handed her the canteen; she drank deeply. Gabriel handed her a sandwich and a peach. "I forgot to ask, are you a vegetarian?"

"No, definitely a carnivore." She tore into her sandwich, and Gabriel bit hungrily into his. They ate in companionable silence.

After they'd finished and packed their food and wrappings away, Gabriel said, "You certainly put on a convincing show last night."

"If you'll join forces with me, it's only the beginning."

"What did you have in mind?"

She leaned forward onto her knees. "To have a real impact, we need to hit a high-visibility target. These small-time operations are just not newsworthy enough."

"We got a lot of press," Gabriel said. "We made *Newsweek* last week."

"Right, and I'm sure that corporations all over the country have upped their security precautions as a result. Look, no offense, but as manufacturers go, WPI is penny-ante stuff. The bombings will make a few bigwigs squirm in their leather chairs for a minute or two, but nobody is going to seriously worry about being a target unless the biggies—the billion-dollar-asset companies, the Fortune Five Hundred—feel it in their balls." She made a fist. "We have to threaten their bottom line. We need a big, expensive target."

Gabriel shook his head. "There are a lot of problems with that."

"Such as?"

"Well, for one thing, the bigger plants are a *lot* harder to hit. They have better security. And their sheer acreage makes it hard to total them. It would take a huge amount of explosives—which costs lots of money, and which our purchase or theft of would attract attention. We'd have so much heat on us so fast we'd be squashed like bugs."

"Not if we're smart," she said. "And as I said before, money's not a problem."

"But that's not the only issue. Bombing a big plant would cause a huge mess. It'd get cleaned up, eventually, probably . . . but creating a major environmental disaster defeats the purpose, doesn't it?"

"True." She was still smiling, though. His frown deepened.

"And those big plants are twenty-four-hour operations. No matter what kind of precautions we took, people would get hurt."

Her eyes gleamed. "I'm surprised to find you so squeamish."

"I'm disturbed that *you* aren't," he countered.

"How many died in Bhopal? How many in Chernobyl? How many species were decimated by the Prince William Sound spill, and during the Gulf War?" She lifted a hand in a shrug. "I agree with you we should try to avoid hurting innocent bystanders, and yes, let's take precautions against it, but let's also be realistic. It's a war we're waging. No matter how careful we are, people will get hurt."

"I've managed to avoid hurting people."

"With one bombing under your belt?" She gave him a wry glance. "Give it time. But we can minimize the likelihood of casualties, if we pick the right target."

"Such as . . . ?"

"Gulf Stream I."

He eyed her, shocked. "You're joking, right?"

"I'm deadly serious."

He thought about his old flame, Emma Tooke, who had—or so he'd heard from a mutual friend—gotten the career opportunity of her lifetime, a few years back, to design the facility. "Why pick on them? There are more companies out there than we can possibly put out of business, pillaging and despoiling for all they're worth. It'd be nuts to hit an environmentally friendly technology.''

'' 'Environmentally friendly'?'' She scoffed. ''My friend, you've been reading too many of their press releases.'' She ticked facts off on her fingers. ''They use their electrical power to generate hydrogen—a highly explosive element, that they sell to the government for military purposes. Their chairman and CEO has other businesses a good deal dirtier than Gulf Stream—all he's interested in is a high-visibility, tax-deductible red herring to take attention off his other, polluting enterprises.

''And furthermore,'' she said, ''my sources have uncovered more dirt on them. Gulf Stream built their rig in international waters, to avoid having to comply with U.S. laws. Their 'voluntary consent orders' that they brag so much about are much more lax than they would have been if the facility had been built in U.S. waters. They don't even have an environmental compliance person on staff right now, much less someone who has any real influence on company policy She shook her head. ''Gulf Stream is the worst kind of business. It's using the environmental movement to its own ends, pretending to be Earth-friendly technology when it's anything but. They offend me, Gabriel, in a deep and personal way.''

Gabriel massaged his scalp with his fingers and shook his head, but didn't say anything, just looked at her. After a moment she said, ''But in answer to your other points, there are some practical reasons why they're a good target. They're an expensive, high-profile facility. Hitting them really *will* strike fear into the hearts of corporate America's power brokers. And the facility is compact enough that—especially if we use their own hydrogen stores against them—we won't need an inordinate amount of explosives. If we plan carefully and hit them right, the plant will sink to the bottom of the ocean with barely a trace of pollution being released, without a single injury. And . . . um, what was your last point?''

"Security."

"Oh, yeah. According to my sources, they rely heavily on their isolation at sea for security. So we don't have to overcome a lot of electronic security measures, or anything like that.''

"I have another objection, then," Gabriel said. "I prefer to start out with less drastic methods—to give companies an opportunity to mend their ways, before putting them out of business.''

She looked skeptical. "That attitude is exactly what got you into such deep shit with Woodland Products, Gabriel. Your gradual approach makes you a prime suspect, when the inevitable happens. How many more targets do you think you'll be able to hit, if you keep up the way you've been?" He didn't answer. "And frankly,'' she went on, "what good did that approach get you with Woodland Products? Companies that are already flouting federal environmental laws are not going to give a tinker's damn about some wild-eyed radical chaining himself to their fences.''

He winced. He hated to admit it, but she had a point.

She leaned toward him, eyes gleaming. "We can do it, Gabriel. Together, with a single strike, we can affect business environmental practices nationwide, for decades to come. A single act that will completely transform the face of the corporate world. What do you say?''

He opened his mouth, closed it, then stood.

"I need to think," he said. "I'm going for a walk."

She nodded, serious. "I understand. Take as much time as you need.''

From a short distance away, amid some trees, he looked back at her through the screen of pine. She hadn't moved; she sat there on the rock, looking out over the plains.

He'd very nearly said yes, back there—thrown his lot in with her on sheer faith, alone. That terrified him.

I've only known her one day, he thought. *And she's holding a whole lot back from me. I don't dare. It's potential suicide.*

He found a stream and squatted, splashing his face with the cool, clear water. He wet his bandanna and tied it on top of his head in a makeshift cap, to cool the burning.

No way she could be a fed. No government agent, no matter how deep her cover, would blow up not one, but two manufacturing plants, just to convince him she was for real.

But I need answers, he thought. *I need to know who she really is.*

He headed back.

Boadica was doing stretches on the rock. She straightened when he came into view.

"I think you have some interesting ideas," Gabriel said, "but that's not enough. You know an awful lot about me, and I know nothing about you."

She nodded, slowly, and started back down the trail. He followed.

"What do you want to know?"

"You've said 'we' a couple of times, and you obviously have access to extensive intelligence. What group are you connected to? Who are you? Where do you get all your money? Radical environmental groups are not usually so well bankrolled."

Her mouth twisted. "True." She looked at him consideringly for a long moment, and then nodded. "All right. You have a right to know. You must swear never to tell *anyone* what I'm about to tell you. If you do, I swear to God I'll find you and you will pay."

Her tone was dead serious, and so was her gaze. He believed her. "Fair enough."

She looked out at the distant hills. "Ten years ago, shortly before she died, a wealthy, eccentric woman with strong environmental sympathies set up a trust fund. The fund had two missions—one public, after a fashion, and one completely secret. First, a low-profile, information-gathering and -interpreting network was to be created. Like a think tank. It was to access existing, publicly released information, but also to create a web of 'sources' throughout the country, focusing particularly on key industries and positions inside the government. The network would feed information to various grassroots environmentalist groups to help them in their fights against polluters. These activities would all be legal, for the most part. But the network would also funnel information to a secret activist team that would be created."

"And that's you?"

She nodded.

"How come I've never heard of this information-gathering network?"

"They keep a *very* low profile. When they release information, it's via individuals—members of other environmental groups, to whom they pass along critical information, 'rumors,' or whatever."

Gabriel absorbed this. "And why are you coming to me?"

She pursed her lips. "The think tank has been around a long time, but the activist team is only now being formed. It's hard to find people who are willing to do what our mission requires."

"Hmmph." He knew that problem. Most people were all talk.

"When you hit the San Carlo plant, we knew you were the right man for us."

"And what makes you think I was responsible for that?"

She gave him a sidelong look. "You should have a talk with Mark Flyer." Gabriel started. "When he drinks he talks too much."

So Mark was the source of the leak. "You do have good intelligence," he remarked.

"Yes, we do. You, Mark Flyer, and Jackson Amis make a good team—we'd like them in, too. *If* you can keep them under control."

Gabriel sighed. "They're *good*. Totally dedicated, tough, loyal. Just a little young, is all. I'll talk to Mark."

"Well?" she asked again, after a moment.

"How do I know you're telling me the truth?"

She shrugged. "I don't know. There's nothing I can show you, really. I could produce a couple members of the sister organization, the think tank, but they couldn't really prove we are what we say we are, either. It's our actions that define us, ultimately, isn't it? That's all you've got. I was hoping the other two bombings would convince you. If not, well . . . we'll just go our separate ways, and good luck to you."

He looked at her. Why do I hesitate? he thought, and realized that that whiff of deep fanaticism he'd detected in her, of her potential for violence, scared him.

I'm being overcautious, he thought. She had a steel core, yes—a willingness to do whatever it took to accomplish her goals. But it was no different from his own, was it? That very willingness to approach the edge, that fanaticism, was what it took. This—a big mission and the resources to accomplish it, a chance to make a huge impact, and working with someone who shared his own vision—was the chance of a lifetime. He wasn't about to pass it up.

Sometimes, he thought, you just have to act on faith. He drew a deep breath. "I'm in."

Chapter 6

It seemed as though nothing Keith did would please Emma.

The conference's morning sessions had let out by the time he reached the elevators, and they were so slow, and packed so full, that he sent the luggage on ahead. After waiting in vain for another five minutes he jogged down twenty flights of stairs to get to the lobby.

So he was eight minutes late.

Bad enough, but when Emma saw the bellman pushing Keith's mountain of luggage toward the car, her already tight lips compressed until the color left her mouth.

"Sorry. Had to take the stairs—the elevators weren't stopping at my floor." He decided not to fall all over himself with further apologies. If she was pissed, so be it.

"I hardly see how we can take all of your luggage. This is an emergency flight, not a moving van! What on earth is all of this?"

"My things," Keith said mildly. "I told Mr. Pendleton how much luggage I had. He said there'd be no problem with the jet. If it's a matter of space in the car, I can take a cab."

Gloria, a pained expression on her face, intervened. "Lord, no. Pendleton sent a limo. We might be a little crowded, but we can manage. By the way, I'm Gloria Tergain.''

Keith offered his hand. ''Keith Hellman. Glad to meet you, Gloria.''

By putting the equipment bag on the spacious floor of the limo's passenger compartment, the cardboard boxes in the front seat, and the suitcases in the trunk, they managed to fit everything in.

Gloria sat between Keith and Emma, in the backseat. ''Is it okay to put my feet on this bag?''

''No problem. It's padded pretty well.''

''What's in it?''

''Diving equipment.''

Emma stopped looking out the window. The expression on her face, disdain struggling with interest, made Keith want to smile. She said, ''Have you been diving long, Mr. Hellman?''

''It's Keith. Yes, twenty years. Since I was fourteen.''

For some reason this seemed to annoy her. ''Does everyone on the planet have their certification but me?''

Keith blinked.

''Emma was taking a scuba course while she was here in Houston,'' said Gloria. ''She had to abandon it when Sophronia changed course.''

''Ah. That's too bad. What flavor?''

''Pardon?''

''Professional Association of Diving Instructors? National Association of Underwater Instructors?''

''Oh, PADI. What certification do you have?''

Keith shrugged. ''I have a NAUI advanced diver's, but I got my teacher's certification through PADI.''

Emma thawed perceptibly. ''Really?''

''Honest. Boy Scout's honor. I was even a Boy Scout.''

Emma actually smiled at this and Keith revised his opinion of her.

At the private aviation terminal on the southwest side of Hobby airport, the driver spoke to a guard and then drove the car all the way to the aircraft, a small, twin-engined jet. The copilot helped Keith stow his luggage, then saw them safely aboard and the door shut.

The plane had two seats directly behind the cockpit, then a work area, two seats facing inboard with a folding table, and six more pairs of forward-facing seats behind. They three were the only passengers. Gloria and Emma sat in the third row, and Keith took one of the sideways-facing seats.

The ceiling wasn't high enough to stand upright. The copilot crouched down after closing the door and said, "I see everybody knows what a seat belt is. How about a life jacket? Oxygen mask?" Everybody nodded. "Emergency exits are this door and that one. There are procedures cards in the pockets. Don't use your cell phones during the flight, and don't use *any* electronic devices during takeoff and landing.

"Okay. Our preflight is done and they've got us scheduled for takeoff in five minutes. Any questions?"

"What's our ETA for Melbourne?" asked Emma.

"Flight time is two hours, twenty-five minutes. If we get off on time we'll get there at three-fifty-five eastern daylight."

"Okay. Can you radio ahead to York Aviation and tell them to be ready for the Gulf Stream I charter?"

The copilot blinked. "We can do that when we're in range, if you want, but you can reach them by phone sooner." He pointed at a phone set mounted above the folding work table.

Emma blushed. "Oh. I should've known. Thanks."

The copilot joined his colleague in the cockpit. They were airborne in ten minutes.

Keith pulled the technical specs out of his briefcase and began studying them. Emma used the phone. After five minutes she hung up. "Freddy will be standing by when we get in. They also gave me the storm's latest coordinates."

She opened her laptop and booted it up. Keith moved his briefcase. Emma punched some numbers in and said, "Hmm. Sophronia's speeding up. Average speed over the last four positions is seventeen knots. If she keeps that speed up—oh crap." She picked the phone back up. After a minute's worth of talk, she hung it back up and exhaled sharply. "Flo went to Phase II thirty minutes ago—thank goodness."

"Phase II?" Keith asked.

Emma said, "Evacuation of all research personnel. It's supposed to be completed twenty-four hours before storm contact. The hydrogen storage barge is towed to shore in this phase. With the new heading *and* the increase in speed, it's more like twelve hours before contact."

"What about the rest of the staff?"

Gloria said, "They're evacuated during Phase I— yesterday. All nonessential personnel. We've got some kids who live aboard and some interns. We were supposed to evacuate them with our trawler, to get her to safety, too, but she's in dry dock right now getting new engines. So we sent them in on one of the work boats, which is fast enough to get back for Phase II. Here." Gloria handed Keith a set of Xeroxed sheets. "An extra copy of the Severe Storm Response Plan. It wouldn't hurt you to be familiar with it."

The copilot came back into the cabin to show them how to use the bar, and to point out the coffee thermos and the small icebox filled with plastic-wrapped sandwiches and fruit.

Keith studied the Storm Response Plan while he ate, referring back to the facility specs in his briefcase for detail. He would have liked to ask Emma more questions, but she got back on the phone and stayed there for most of the flight. And he couldn't ask Gloria because she drank a beer with lunch and promptly fell asleep.

They were five minutes early into Melbourne and the jet taxied directly to a small white building set away from the regular terminal. A large helicopter put down as they approached and its rotors coasted to a stop. Ten men in grease-stained coveralls climbed out, carrying overnight bags with them. Signs on the helicopter and the building said YORK AVIATION.

The jet stopped and they deplaned. It was humid and warm, in the high eighties, perhaps, and clouds were scattered across the sky. The winds were mild and the sun beat down. Still, two men were fastening sheets of plywood over the glass windows of the building's office. Nearby, men were rigging tie-downs on several small planes.

Emma and Gloria disappeared into the office and Keith, grateful for the chance to stretch his muscles, helped the copilot unload their luggage. Since the jet promptly taxied away for refueling and the return to Houston, he moved the luggage over by the building, out of the way.

Emma and Gloria came back out of the building, followed by a man wearing aviator's sunglasses and carrying a clipboard.

Emma pointed at the pile of luggage. "Can we put some of this in your building, Freddy? Until later?"

"Well, I'd rather not. Last time we had a sizable storm we had three feet of water here. Is this stuff going out to the rig eventually?"

"How many times do I have to tell you, Freddy? It's not a rig."

"Same ol', same ol'," Freddy said. "Is it going out?"

"Sure, eventually."

"Well, why not take it now? You three aren't exactly pushing the limits of my machine, you know. Flo said I'll be bringing back eight people and light luggage." He pointed at an approaching fuel truck. "I can't take off until we refuel, anyhow, so there's plenty of time." He paused for a moment and then said, "Of course if you're afraid Gulf Stream won't survive the storm, I can understand . . ."

Emma hit Freddy lightly on the shoulder. "Gulf Stream will be fine! You, on the other hand . . ."

She turned abruptly, gave Keith a dark look, then grabbed her own suitcase from the pile and carried it toward the helicopter.

They loaded all the baggage and had time to use the rest rooms before the helicopter was refueled. Emma and Gloria climbed into the back. Freddy offered Keith the empty copilot's seat. They crossed over a big river, a thin strip of land, and then out over the Atlantic at twelve hundred feet, doing one hundred and twenty knots. Freddy pointed out Cape Canaveral and the Kennedy Space Center, thirty miles north.

He'd been in offshore helicopters before, investigating air emission and wastewater discharge violations on offshore oil production platforms, so the straps and the headset were familiar to him. Freddy pointed out more landmarks visible from the coast, before the sea below abruptly changed color to a deep, cobalt blue.

"There's the Stream," said Freddy.

Keith saw several fishing trawlers and shrimpers. All of them were headed east, to get to shelter before Sophronia rolled up the coast.

Thirty minutes later Freddy pointed straight ahead and his voice sounded in Keith's earphones. "There she is."

It took Keith a moment to spot the structure, but he

finally located four small white dots on the horizon. "How far out are we?"

"About forty-five miles. Call it twenty more minutes."

In ten minutes the four dots grew to rounded, streamlined structures, perched well above the water on shafts sticking out of the water.

He'd seen pictures in the press. There'd been several articles on it, and *Scientific American* had done a good overview, but the pictures hadn't done it justice.

From this angle they looked like sails. Like square-rigged sails atop thick, concrete masts, frozen in the act of billowing toward him. He smiled at the image and looked closer, noting first the navigation lights blinking atop each module, then the walkways that ringed each of the modules' four levels.

The shafts supporting the modules were spaced in a diamond shape, maybe a hundred, hundred and fifty feet on a side. Long catwalks connected them, joined to the shafts below the modules, perhaps twenty feet above the waves.

Three of the shafts passed into the water without further ado, but the northernmost shaft passed into the OTEC power plant at the waterline: a squat cylinder perhaps eighty feet in diameter, awash with water except for a raised deck with a hatch. Blazoned across the long side of the module towering above the power plant were the words GULF STREAM I and the Gulf Stream logo, in blazing green on white.

Also awash, stretching north from the plant, was a long, green apron. Beyond the apron, the water changed color to light blue, an area several hundred yards long and several dozen yards wide. A grid of bright orange buoys dotted the water over it. Keith sat forward, trying to get a better glimpse. It had to be Gulf Stream's artificial reef.

Surrounding everything—the reef, the apron, and

the four modules—was an enormous, wobbly-shaped rectangle of more orange buoys. He pointed at it and started to ask, but realized that it must be the floating breakwater that protected the reef and the power plant from ocean swells.

From overhead, as they neared, he saw that the modules were teardrop-shaped, like cross sections of a wing. The modules were tapered vertically as well, such that each of the four decks was a different size. The largest deck was the third from the top, with the others tapering inward above and below. Attached to each module, at the lowest level, were a set of orange lumps that must be lifeboats. He could imagine the modules to be oddly shaped, tethered blimps, only resting on the shafts that supported them, and he half expected them to float into the sky if he looked away for too long.

Freddy switched radio frequencies. "Gulf Stream, this is York One. Come in."

A voice came back, "York One, this is Gulf Stream. You got Emma with you, Freddy?"

"Ten-four. Did you take down that volleyball net?"

"Give us a break, Freddy. Wind is one-two-three degrees at seventeen knots. You copy?"

Freddy laughed. "Copy."

He swung around to approach the structure from the northwest.

The modules' roofs differed. Communication aerials, two rotating radar antennae, a satellite dish, and a microwave dish pointed back toward Cocoa Beach topped one. Another sprouted greenery, parklike. White pressure tanks and pipes crowded atop the module with the power plant, along with a tall, unlit flare. The fourth was flat, with a low railing, a helicopter landing pad at the wide end, and an elevated wind sock at the other.

"They play volleyball on the helicopter deck,"

Freddy explained. "I came out for an appendicitis case once and it was still up. Had to wait while they took it down. It was while they were still under construction, but I've never let them forget it."

He touched down on the pad with only the slightest of jolts. A line of men and women came up a stairway at the edge of the roof, all of them carrying overnight bags except for a small woman in front with a clipboard.

"Watch your head getting out. Be sure to get all of your luggage."

Keith pushed the door open and climbed down. The wind battered him. The woman with the clipboard hugged Emma and then Gloria as each got out. Among them, they got the luggage pulled out and dumped on the deck in less than a minute, and then the outgoing passengers loaded quickly. Keith started to move the luggage toward the stairway, but Emma pulled him toward the other end of the deck.

"After he takes off," she shouted in his ear.

They went partway down the stairs that ran along the outside of the module while Freddy lifted off. He banked away to the west, climbing and gaining speed as he went. Almost immediately, the noise lessened. The difference made Keith realize how oppressive it had been, how exhausting, to have that noise constantly hammering at him.

They moved back up the stairway. Emma gestured at Keith and said to the woman who had met them, "Keith Hellman, this is Floreen Jonas, head of Mariculture and Fisheries." She paused for a moment to look back at Flo. "Keith is our new environmental compliance manager."

Flo looked at Keith, curiously. "I heard. Nice to meet you. Call me Flo."

Flo was a small black woman with very dark skin and close-cropped hair, almost a head shorter than

Emma. She was wearing white shorts, a short-sleeved, red pullover sports shirt, and deck shoes.

Back on the roof they grabbed luggage. "We'll drop it in my conference room," Flo said. "We can sort it out later."

To get all the luggage took them two trips. The conference room where they deposited it turned out to be back down the stairs and around the curve of an outer walkway lined with window portals.

As they went back and forth ferrying luggage, Keith decided that Gulf Stream I looked more like a ship than an offshore rig—the outer walkways were railed, the decks covered in dark green, nonskid strips. He glanced inside the windows as they passed. Several of the rooms were large, crammed with big PVC tanks and piping, or big glass tanks with fish or shellfish inside. One appeared to be a lab. Some were small, clearly offices, with desks and phones. Inside one room, two people were beheading and packing what seemed to be lobster at first, but on closer look he saw that they were extremely large prawns.

One of them looked up, spied Flo, and shouted, "Hey, Flo, do you know where they moved the filters?"

Flo stepped back and stuck her head in the door. "Which ones, the glass fiber or the cartridge?"

"The glass fiber—they're overdue and I don't think they'll get changed during the hurricane."

"They stacked those in the main deck janitorial closet—outside of Junior Lobster."

"Junior Lobster?" Keith repeated.

Gloria laughed.

Flo looked over her shoulder. "It's the first part of the lobster line: brooding females, larvae, settled juveniles. They're moved over to Senior Lobster when they're big enough."

All the doorsills were raised, to prevent water from

running under doors, and the doors themselves closed on gaskets. If it weren't for the module's height above the waves and the empty flower boxes mounted on the outside of most of the railings—and the smell of fish that permeated the module—Keith could imagine himself on a large cruise ship.

After depositing the last of the luggage in the conference room, instead of using the stairways outside the module, Emma and Flo, talking quietly to each other, led the way down a corridor to the center of the module. This hallway intersected another corridor that circled the beanpole, the fifteen-foot-diameter shaft that supported the structure. Potted plants, apparently from the empty flower boxes outside, were set in neat rows on the floor, against the walls. They walked around the shaft until they came to a doorway set into the beanpole.

"Watch your step—there's a gap," Gloria said.

Keith knew that the module pivoted on the beanpole; he just hadn't expected it to be so obvious. A three-inch crack gaped between the floor and the beanpole's concrete surface. Small rubber wheels met the concrete below. When he looked up, he saw the same arrangement.

Emma said, "Elevator's leaving!"

He stepped quickly through the doorway. Inside was an antechamber whose walls were the curving interior of a cylinder, lined with conduit and piping. A narrow metal stairway climbed along the wall from an opening in the floor to another in the ceiling. The room smelled of fish, oils, and solvent. He joined the others in the wire cage elevator at the back of the chamber and pulled the door shut behind him. It lurched downward when Emma hit the second button from the bottom on the control panel.

"Where are we going?"

Flo answered. "Over to Control." At Keith's blank

look she said, "It's in the Engineering module. We're in Mariculture right now, my bailiwick."

The elevator stopped four levels down, at an ante-chamber virtually identical to the first, and Emma led the way outside; Keith emerged onto a metal walkway that circled the beanpole and went to the railing. Below their feet, visible through the metal mesh, was another circular walkway to which a long dock was attached. A good dozen Zodiacs were docked there, bobbing furiously. Overhead loomed the module itself, shaped like a teardrop, lined by more walkways.

The catwalk they crossed seemed impossibly long and narrow to Keith, especially when compared to the bulk of the module that loomed overhead. But as they crossed he saw that the railing was shoulder-high, with mesh beneath it—and four people could easily walk abreast on it. It wasn't bad at all to walk across in this light wind, but he wondered how it was in a storm, or, come to think of it, a hurricane.

At the base of the next beanpole, the circular mass of the OTEC plant was awash. On the elevated deck on one side, a man stood smoking a cigarette. Emma waved at him and he straightened. Emma called down, "How's she running, Mac?"

"Perfectly. Oleg rebuilt Number Seven again and the bearing is holding this time."

"Great."

They passed on into the antechamber inside the beanpole and rode its elevator up. This time Keith got a look at the controls. From bottom to top they read: *Dock, Catwalk, Utility, Main, Mid*, and *Top*.

They left the elevator on the top deck and wound around the module's center to a door labeled *Control*. Beneath the sign someone had taped a picture of Don Adams as Maxwell Smart talking into the sole of his shoe.

Inside, Keith came to a halt and stared. He felt as

though he'd stepped onto the bridge of a submarine
or mission control for somebody's space program.
Gloria saw his expression. "More gizmos than you
can shake a stick at, huh?"

He nodded, mute.

It was a big room, curved, following the leading
edge of this module. The windows pointed southeast,
into the wind, and Keith could see two of the other
three modules from where he stood.

Inside the room, facing the windows, was a bank of
computer consoles with eight graphical displays, keyboards, and mice. There were also two radar sets, two
radios, and a loran set. As Keith watched, a laser
printer produced a high-resolution weather map.
Above the printer was a poster-sized photograph of an
octopus squirting an ink cloud; the photo was labeled
Louie-Louie.

Two men sat before the control panel. The man
leaning forward to watch a screen seemed older, with
dark hair turning grey and deep lines in his forehead,
like a bloodhound's. The other man, his chair pushed
away from the console and his legs stretched out, was
blond, young. Both of them looked around when the
small group entered.

"Hi, guys," said Gloria.

" 'Bout time," said the blond, a smile on his face.

Off to one side stood a chart table, rolled blueprints
and maps tucked into cubbies beneath. Emma walked
to the table and leaned against it, facing away from
everyone. Keith saw her shoulders rise as she took a
deep breath, then fall as she exhaled sharply. When
she turned around she was all business.

"Flo, I'm coordinating now."

Flo's shoulders came up, as if a weight had been
lifted. "You bet," she said, and handed her clipboard
to Emma.

Emma turned to the older man at the console. "Lee,

when are they predicting forty-knot winds for us?''

Lee reached across and took the weather map out of the laser printer. His voice was morose, as though he were depressed or worried about something. ''I don't give a lot for the accuracy of this, but it looks like about ten-thirty, eleven.''

''Okay, get on the phone to York Aviation and schedule the last evacuation run for nine P.M. Warn them that we'll be hollering for it earlier if the winds pick up prematurely.'' She flipped through the pages of the clipboard, then ran her finger down the list. ''Hmm, looks like we'll only need one run.'' She looked up, then, and spotted Keith. ''Oh, yeah. We need to get you on the roster. Even with you, though, one chopper.''

Keith had no intention of being on that chopper, but he wasn't going to fight that battle now.

Emma belatedly introduced him. ''This is Keith Hellman, our new environmental compliance person. Lee Attewell is our chief of staff for Facilities and Control. The infant is Rob Kling, the engineer on duty.''

Keith nodded from his spot by the door, amiable outside, tense within. He was waiting for an opening, waiting for the right time. Emma gave it to him.

''Now,'' she said, ''I suppose we should get you someone to give you the grand tour, to get you oriented and assign you living quarters.''

He pushed off the wall. ''Save it. You don't have the time and I sure don't. I want to see the storage areas for hydrogen, ammonia, diesel, gasoline, and your, er, *our* hazardous waste storage areas. I want to see the chemical storage room in Science, lubricant storage in the maintenance shop, the OTEC, hydrogen, and wastewater treatment plants and the intermediate sewage storage tanks in each module, and most of all, *our* spill response equipment and procedures manual for same.'' He paused, noting that Emma's eyes were wide, her mouth tight; then he smiled. ''If that wouldn't be too much trouble.''

Chapter 7

EMMA: **Thursday, 1 October, 6:03 P.M. EDT**
Gulf Stream I, approximately ninety nautical miles
east-southeast of Melbourne, Florida

Emma frowned at Keith. Behind her, Rob coughed. Gloria and Flo exchanged a glance.

''Fair enough,'' she said finally, and turned. ''Rob, give him a radio and tell one of the Engineering team to meet him in Mariculture at the catwalk deck. Gloria, show him which catwalk to take, then''—she flipped through the pages of the checklist with the pencil eraser, scanning—''then go help out in Residential. They're behind.''

Gloria said, ''Check.''

Emma stuck the pencil behind her ear and glanced back at Keith. ''I'd like you to report on each module as you complete it.''

''You got it.''

Meanwhile, Rob sprang up, went into the small, windowed supervisor's office next to the switch room, and dug around in a locker. He came out and handed Keith a belt and holster with a two-way radio. As Keith removed his suit jacket and buckled the radio on, Emma went on, ''You've got four modules to inspect, as well as the power plant, and less than three hours before the last dust-off. Keep your eye on the clock.''

"Right.''

When Gloria pulled the door to the outer walkway open, wind gusted across the maps and papers. A sheet of paper tumbled into the air. Keith snatched the paper from midair as he crossed the room and handed it to Emma. Then, from a good five feet away, he tossed his jacket onto a hook among the rain ponchos and followed Gloria out the door.

Flo whistled. "Quite a hotshot.''

"Yeah. We'll see.''

At that moment one of the television monitors mounted above the screens caught Emma's eye. Dan Rather moved his lips while in an image projected behind him, fifty-foot palms whipped wildly against a black sky, bent nearly double. A Volkswagen overturned and skidded down the curb, shoved aside by brown gushing water. Wind snatched the thatched roof off a small home, which flew away amid a blur of flying debris. A wall of rain fell *sideways*. Overlaid on the broadcast was *Recording—Freeport, Bahamas— Hurricane Sophronia*.

"Holy smokes,'' she muttered. But the others were looking at her, so she smiled around. "Believe me, she's built to take a bigger pounding than Sophronia can dish out.''

Everyone looked at her. She couldn't tell if they believed her. Emma leaned on the console between Lee and Rob and tapped a pop-up menu on the middle touch screen to call up some meteorological displays. Rob had slipped on his headset and was talking into his mike.

Lee said, "Here, I've got a quick-screen set up,'' and pressed a finger to the menu bar at the base of the screen.

The power plant schematic blinked out and four

graphs appeared, accompanied by bell-like tones: swell height, wind speed, wind direction, and barometric pressure, plotted against time in bright colors: red, yellow, blue, and purple. Digital readouts tracked up and down as the graph lines wormed toward the vertical black line that cut all the way up the screen at 0230 hrs/06 Oct. The line was labeled *Sophronia*. There was also a digital readout of temperature.

On the top radar screen in front of Rob, small blobs of light appeared and faded as the scan needle circled counterclockwise. Rob called up on his touch screen a maritime map with Gulf Stream I at its center. A hurricane icon appeared south of the facility, a little yellow pinwheel. Three successively more shadowed icons trailed it at four-hour intervals: the hurricane was now dragging its way across the islands of the Little Bahama Bank.

Emma looked back at Lee's weather plots. The storm's direction had remained essentially constant over the past twenty-two hours. Sensors reported that swells were now almost eight feet high, up from three this morning, and in the past few hours wind speed had risen sharply from thirteen, stable for the moment at twenty-five knots. Temperature hovered around eighty-two degrees Fahrenheit. Barometric pressure was dropping steadily, now at about 29.1 inches of mercury.

"Lee, give us an alarm when the wind reaches thirty knots."

His fingers played across icons at the base of the screen and then across the keys set into the console. A horizontal red line appeared on the wind speed graph at the thirty-knot mark. At the same instant a bell icon labeled WINDSPD appeared on the alarm master screen on the far left, amid a field of labeled alarm bells. Emma straightened with her arms akimbo and took a breath.

"Well, folks, I guess it's about time to get started with the dunks."

Lee planted his heels, scooted his wheeled chair across the floor to call up buoyancy and pressure schematics for the power plant. Flo touched Emma's arm, and Emma had known her long enough to read the worry behind her impassive gaze.

"Let's take care of the farms and reef first. The plant is safe for now, and the experimental habitats are already taking punishment."

Emma nodded. "Good point."

"Don't worry, Flo," Rob said. "We'll take good care of Louie for you." Louie was a big, purplish octopus who was one of the reef's oldest residents. The streamers had appointed him official mascot, and he seemed to like the attention the divers gave him—or perhaps it was the fish they brought him.

"And how about we get Mac to toss Bowser in the water, while we're at it?" Lee asked. "Wouldn't hurt to monitor the dunk visually, too."

"Okay. But keep an eye on the swells. This late in the day, with all the turbulence, visibility's bound to be poor and we'll have to take him in close. If the surge gets too bad down there he could foul on the reef."

Flo, who had frowned at the mention of the remotely operated underwater camera, Bowser, was now nodding.

Emma cocked a finger at Rob. "Your turn to walk the dog."

He gave her a big grin. "Right, Chief."

Lee canceled the power plant graphics and called up the reef schematics while Rob got on the radio to Mac, down below.

Flo handed her a radio. She brought the receiver to her lips and depressed the talk button. "Residential, come in."

"Residential team here." It was Angus, the facility maintenance and services manager. Emma checked the lists.

"What are you doing in Residential? I have you on the Mariculture team. Oh—never mind; I see Flo's note."

But Angus was already talking over her. "—tootin' I'm in Residential. The last dust-off happened five hours too quick. It messed them up over here. And they were already way behind—the reefer and pantries are a disaster. Charles Lawson is a disorganized boob. He shouldn't be put in charge of his own checkbook, much less facility stores."

Emma lifted her eyebrows at the radio. "Save it for the post-storm debriefing."

Angus was only daunted for a second. "And while I'm on the subject, next time give us a little more warning before yanking crew, hey? They lost six at one go over here, and we lost four. If it hadn't been for Science being way ahead, we'd all be in deep shit."

"I understand your frustration, Angus, but I can't do a thing about how fast the storm travels. Some of the less essential Phase II tasks are simply going to have to be dropped."

"Yeah. I know. But it's moving in too damn fast. It's messing with the schedule." Then he coughed. That was about as close as Angus ever got to an apology. "We're almost done with battening things down and divvying up supplies. We'll be distributing food and toiletries in a bit, and then Gene and me will head back to wrap things up in Mariculture."

Gene and *I*, Emma thought. She propped the clipboard against her hip and scribbled notes. "Who's in Mariculture now? How much more prep time do you need there?"

"We need another couple hours to finish up. And

nobody's there at the moment. But it's not a problem—me and Gene are both on the Phase III list. We can finish up after last dust-off.''

Gene and *I*, damn it. She ran through the Phase II task checklists one more time, chewed on the end of the pencil with her eyes narrowed. Flo met her gaze: they had the same thought. Emma nodded at her and pressed the talk button. ''Flo's on her way to Mariculture now. I can lend you Rob, too, after we dunk the reef and the power plant.''

''Oh, goody.'' Rob rolled his eyes, but his tone was good-natured.

Flo picked up another two-way radio from the office and left through the outer door, pulling it shut against a cooler, now more urgent wind that disrupted papers and blasted hair from about Emma's face. Ambient temperature was dropping. She depressed the talk button again.

''Gloria get there okay?''

''Ten-four. She's being a real pill—talking about a macrobiotic diet for the storm crew.''

Gloria's voice rose in the background, objecting loudly. A grin tugged at Emma's mouth. ''A little broccoli never hurt anybody.''

Angus made a rude noise. Or perhaps, she thought in a spirit of generosity, it was just the radio making static.

''The storm still looks like it'll hit between midnight and two-thirty A.M.,'' she said with a glance at the displays. ''Final dust-off for Phase II personnel looks like it's going to be in about two and a half, three hours, so tell your people to be prepared to wrap up before then.''

''Ten-four.''

As she was speaking, she caught movement out of the corner of her eye, and squinted at Mariculture, a stone's throw across the churning waters. Mariculture's yellow crane dropped a cylindrical machine about the size of a large dog from beneath the utility deck. The wind hit it and it started swinging. At the machine's head were mounted a set of floodlights and a hemispherical camera port. The body casing had a painted dog face resting on huge paws: fox-red fur, blue claws, big brown eyes, and a doggy smile showing sharp white teeth and a crimson tongue. Mounted on each side, where the dog's ears would be, were pivotable, ducted propellers.

As she watched, the utility door opened and Mac walked out, holding on to an orange box that hung from inside the door. He leaned over the railing, checking for obstructions that wouldn't be visible through the utility deck floor opening inside. Then he gave a wave, which Rob returned, and went back in.

"Engineering, you copy that on the final Phase II dust-off?" she asked.

"You bet, chief. Nine P.M., EDT. Flo and I've got a seat on that flight."

The little grin spread into a full smile at the sound of her chief engineer's voice. "Ben. Glad you stuck around for Phase II after all."

"Leave and let Flo have all the fun?"

Flo glanced over; Ben's remark briefly erased the hint of worry in her eyes. She exchanged a smile with Emma.

"These professionally competitive marriages. Tch. Who took Veronica ashore? When I heard Flo was the coordinator on call, I assumed you'd be ashore with Ronnie."

"I couldn't leave with you gone, chief. Veronica went ashore on the first flight back. She'll be staying with the Wilsons and their two kids tonight, till we hit shore."

"Well, I'm glad you're here. Status report?"

"We're right on schedule. But I've got Keith here

with me and he has some new items that need attention.''

"Keith." Then she remembered. "Right. Put him on."

Keith's voice came out of the speaker. "I've finished in Mariculture and started in Engineering."

"What have you found?"

"Two problems. The fuel distribution area over in Mariculture has no containment—no berms, no catchment sumps—and the drums are only secured by a single lightweight chain. If the module takes any kind of beating a spill is likely, and you're going to have flammable, toxic liquid spreading all over the utility deck."

"That's right." Emma ran a hand over her mouth and chin. "The old storage area in Engineering *did* have a containment sump, but we moved the drums last week to make room for storage of hydrogen cell membranes. It was supposed to be temporary."

"That's not going to do you much good now."

No, really? she thought, grinding molars. "How about moving the drums back over to the Engineering containment area?"

Ben responded. "There are too many to move before the storm hits."

"Any way you can set up a temporary berm?"

Keith sounded reflective. "I could use some of the spill response equipment, the booms, the kitty litter and absorbent pillows, I guess. Secure them with pallets or heavy equipment so in case there's a breach during the storm they don't blow away. It won't be ideal."

"Unless you can think of something else, it'll have to do."

"There's probably a way to secure the drums better, too, so a spill is less likely."

"Good. Ben can assign one or two of his techs to

you. You can get them started and then finish checking the other modules. Okay?''

''Yeah. Okay.''

''You copy that, Ben?''

''Affirmative, chief. But we may have a scheduling conflict. Keith has also identified a problem with the sewer lines.''

Keith came on the radio. ''There'll be a lot of stresses on the intermodule sewer lines, the ones that run beneath the catwalks, during the storm. If any one of them ruptures you'll have a raw sewage release.''

''Not a big one,'' Emma said, ''if they've sealed off both ends like they're supposed to.''

''Oh? What's your definition of big?''

She ground her teeth together again. At this rate, I'm going to need a bite guard, she thought.

Ben cut in, ''I estimate that if one of the lines goes we'll probably lose either two or four hundred gallons, depending on which line.''

She looked out the window in time to see Bowser splash into the churning water. Twined fiber-optic and power cables, strung from inside Mariculture, uncoiled into the water.

''We're ready for the dunk,'' Rob said, looking up from his console, ''whenever you are.''

''Take him over toward the reef. I'll be done in a minute.''

''And why risk spilling any,'' Keith was saying, ''when we can purge the lines with salt water before blocking them off?''

''The problem is,'' Emma said, ''if I'm remembering right, there aren't any water lines hooked directly to the sewer. They'd have to hook up special lines and that'll take a while. Not to mention potential corrosion problems. And we're short personnel. I'm no toxicologist, but wouldn't a gasoline spill be a lot more dangerous than sewage?''

"Of course. That doesn't mean raw sewage is okay to dump into the ocean." A pause. "The reef is downstream, you know. The sewage could harm some of the more sensitive species."

Emma remembered the look in Flo's eyes; she glanced at her watch, grimaced. "Ben, can you do both, and be done in time for the final dust-off?"

"I've already figured out a way to get the sewer system purged, Emma. We can use the fire hoses. They use salt water and we have to check them anyway; we can do both tasks at once and cut down on our total response time." Ben sounded confident. "I think we can do it."

Emma tugged her lip, nodded to herself. "Then do it. But the gasoline problem comes first. Send two of your crew with Keith to berm the storage area. Have the rest of your team start with the largest sewer line. If it looks like you're not going to be able to get all four lines purged in time and still complete the rest of your Phase II checklist, I want you to abort the purge and seal them off unflushed. You copy?"

"Ten-four."

"Keith, get them started berming and stabilizing the drums and then finish your inspection. Once you've reported on the rest of the modules and the power plant, I'd like you to head back and check their work before dust-off."

There was a brief pause. "Right," he said.

"Ben, you got that?"

"Ten-four, chief."

"Oh, and Ben."

"Yeah?"

"Stop calling me chief."

Ben laughed. Smiling, she depressed the talk button again. "Science, come in."

No answer. She repeated herself. Still no answer. She frowned and flipped through the pages of the checklist with her pencil eraser, then lifted the radio back to her mouth. "Anybody out there know what the Science team is up to?"

"Emma—Flo." On the catwalk below, outside the window, Flo had paused, radio at her mouth. She was looking up toward the control room with her hand on the rail, braced against the wind that whipped at her shirt and shorts. "They got done early with their Phase II checks in Science. It should be marked on the roster. I sent most of the the team with the recent dust-off."

"I see that. But Michael, Jess, and Nikki should still be over there, wrapping things up."

"Oh yeah." Flo sounded embarrassed. "I moved Nikki and Jess over with Ben's team, and Michael to help Terri in Residential. You arrived right then—I got distracted and didn't get the changes marked before you took over. Sorry."

"Don't sweat it. Long as I know." Emma scribbled the changes on the personnel roster, then stuck the radio in her belt.

Flo's voice issued from the radio again, this time asking Angus for a rundown of what was left to do in Mariculture. Outside the window, she hurried toward Residential, leaning into the wind, head down, shoulders squared. Angus replied. Emma turned the volume down and stuck the radio in its holster at her belt.

The sky had darkened, due to the impending sunset rather than the storm. But beyond Mariculture, to the south, massive thunderheads were piling up. Sunset stained their westward faces brilliant and beautiful—a palette in hues of pale buttercup, tangerine, and violet—but their eastward faces were as violent and purple-black as bruised fists.

Against the clouds and dark blue sky and the first of the evening's stars, pale gulls and albatross sailed above the modules, tipping left and right, rising on the wind, then dropping as they cocked their heads back and forth to study the water for stray surface feeders. Emma wondered how long they would hang around before fleeing Sophronia.

Beneath the intense white navigational strobes on the modules' roofs, lights were appearing in the windows and on the balcony walkways of the other three modules. Along the catwalks, fluorescents lit up on the undersides of the midlevel railings: strands of glowing liquid that turned the grating underfoot an eerie blue. Over at Mariculture, the crane had been pulled back up through the hatch, though the twined cable still hung down, an umbilical stretching from beneath the utility deck to the water. At Residential, two figures knelt near the catwalk before a large red box with an open glass front—the sewer line crew, uncoiling fire hose. A couple of others carried boxes along the catwalk from Residential toward Mariculture, leaning into the wind.

The sun had dropped low enough to turn the water dark and rob it of color. The ocean's undulating surface cast reflections of the lights and surfaces and people that shifted and distorted them, creating from Gulf Stream's cast-off energy a glistening, chaotic abstraction.

She noted that many of the swells were capped with white, and checked wind speed. Just under twenty-seven knots.

"We have Bowser positioned at the reef," Rob said.

Emma sat back down. The TV mounted above the console screens had been switched over from *NBC Nightly News* to a Bowser's-eye view of the reef. Bowser was looking up from below.

The habitat, surrounded by murk and darkness, hovered overhead in the middle distance: a dim, whitish-green grid with odd shapes attached or hanging from it that appeared out of nowhere when Bowser's flood-

lights shone on them and faded like ghosts when the
lights moved away. The seaweed, clumps of brown
and red algae, clung to the grid, moving in the surge's
rhythmic pulse like a mermaid's hair. Miniature bubbles trickled upward from air hoses, seaweed, and the
hanging structures. In the foreground, blurred silver,
white, and dark brown shapes—schools of fish—
flowed and flicked amid a drift of pale, snowlike
specks: plankton, a bloom of microscopic life in the
nutrient-rich spillway discharge, drawn like moths to
Bowser's lights. The reef and its inhabitants shifted up
and forward, down and back with the surge.

It certainly didn't *look* like the facility's single most
important, most fragile, structure.

Accompanying the soprano hum of Bowser's motor
were the deep, steady tone the chill seawater played
against the walls of its pipes as it hurtled up from
fifteen hundred feet, and the throaty counterpoint of
the power plant's turbine generators.

She realized she'd been smelling fresh coffee, and
turned. Rob was over at the snack nook filling a mug
with fresh brew. He poured a dollop of evaporated
milk into the mug and handed it to her. The mug had
a caricature of a woman with her hair standing out and
a wild expression. The caption read, "I'm 51% sweet-
heart and 49% bitch. DON'T PUSH IT!"

On reading this she cast a look at Rob, who returned
a big, innocent grin.

"Very funny," she said.

"Couldn't help it. You should have seen your ex-
pression when you were talking to the new guy."
Emma made a face. "And anyhow, it beats Hagar the
Horrible." Rob handed said mug to Lee.

"It's a good thing you're so damn good at your job,
Kling," Lee muttered.

Rob wiggled his eyebrows at Lee, still grinning.
Emma took a sip, inhaling the pungent aroma at the

same time. World-class arabica it was not, but Rob had made it strong, the way she liked it. Hot liquid trickled down her throat.

Emma pulled a rolling chair over from against the wall by the laser printer and sat down at the console, setting her cup on the ledge atop a field of mug-sized, ring-shaped stains. Then, with the idea of hazardous spills fresh in her mind, she moved it down to between her knees. No food or liquids on the console was the rule, but she violated it as often as anyone. With glances at her and each other, Lee and Rob followed suit.

"Take Bowser in closer," she said.

Rob twitched the two joysticks set into the console; on the TV screen the reef tilted and loomed larger, still advancing and retreating as the surge shoved Bowser around. Schools of fish parted to let Bowser pass, exposing and obscuring the reef.

The hanging shapes resolved into empty plastic milk jugs, old tires, or other things less mundane: boxes of Plexiglas, wood blocks with tunnels in them like chunks of Swiss cheese, weird knots of twisting PVC tubes. Barnacles and algae coated many of the objects, which swung back and forth with Bowser and the sea life.

One strong surge carried Bowser up high enough to bump a tire. It spilled tiny, panicky crabs; an octopus tumbled out in a wheel of tentacles and rocketed away, spurting a jet of black dye. Poor Louie. With a reddening neck and muttered apology, Rob backed the camera down a foot or two.

Lee had brought up two schematics of the reef— one a 3-D projection and the other a split screen, a view of the reef grid from the top and a view from the side. The graphics displayed key data, most of it live.

"Accumulators at one hundred ten percent," Lee

reported. "Compressors are on-line and ready. Reef set point at eight-point-two psi; actual is ranging plus or minus two psi with a mean of eight-point-one-nine. Depth averaging nineteen-point-two feet."

Emma took a gulp of coffee. "Let's take it to eighty feet. Slowly."

"Two foot a minute slow enough for you?" At her dubious expression, Lee added, "It works okay in the drills."

"Yeah, but we've never taken it that deep. I want to go nice and easy and give the free floaters a chance to keep up." After a pause, "And the surge makes me nervous. Let's stay well within the design limits of the microcontrollers, okay?"

"How well within the limits, then? You tell me."

Emma rubbed her chin and mouth, checked her watch, gulped more coffee. It was 7:16 P.M. and they still had the power plant to do.

"Let's make it a foot a minute."

"Foot a minute," Lee repeated. His fingers flew over the keys.

"Rob, take Bowser up above the reef. Keep a close eye on the inhabitants, and if you see any reason to be concerned, make a loud noise." Emma exhaled. "Damn. I wish Flo were here. She knows the reef better than anybody."

Lee frowned at her. "I've done this a hundred times, chief. Relax!"

He typed in the new depth and rate of descent and, once Bowser had cleared the edge of the reef, began bleeding air from the buoyancy tanks. Emma got on the radio to Mac and sent him back to Engineering to monitor the reef's buoyancy manifold. Meanwhile Lee switched the intercom over so they could hear what was happening in the compressor room on the deck below. The sound of escaping air reached their ears: air rushing from the escape valves in the manifold.

They all stared at the TV screen. Little seemed to be happening. But it soon became clear that the reef was receding into the murk. Rob coaxed Bowser after it in a slow spiral.

Lee still looked a little surly. Emma slurped down the last of her tepid coffee, took Lee's cup from him, and came to her feet in a quick, restless motion to pour them both another cup of coffee. She offered it to him.

"I know you'll do fine. You're the best." She rubbed the back of her neck. "It's the surge. It could take the reef down like a brick if the computers don't keep up with quick buoyancy changes. I know," she added as he opened his mouth. "Not bloody likely. But possible."

She paced, sipping at the scalding coffee. Lee knew as well as she did, Gulf Stream floated or sank along with that habitat. Lose a couple of their major marine products, or one of their major science grants, and the facility would close in six weeks.

Emma let out her breath, slowly, and set an alarm on her watch. It'd be an hour and ten minutes, more or less, before the habitat reached its new set-depth, and she wanted to check the power plant before they dunked it. Lee was more than competent to implement her instructions. And he would probably appreciate it if she'd stop hovering and let him do his job.

"I'll be below. Page me if there are problems."

Chapter 8

After their hike, Gabriel and Boadica headed up Route 14 to Madrid, a tiny former-mining-town-turned-old-hippie-haven northeast of the Sandias. A dirt alley between two houses became a meandering "road" that wandered out of town down a hill. The road consisted of two rocky tracks, barely visible in the desert grasses, that wound amid piñon shrubs, blooming cacti, and yuccas. After several miles of this— lurching, heaving, and bumping over rocks and across dry arroyos—by the time the sun perched on the shoulder of Sandia's northern peak, they reached the cabin.

It was built at the base of a hill. A windmill next to a water reservoir turned, creaking, in the brisk breeze, and in a nearby corral were two burros, who cocked their ears as the Jeep approached. Hens pecked at the dirt near a small chicken coop. The smell of animal dung mingled with the wind-borne scents of sage and pine. A car sat beside the house.

Gabriel jumped out of the Jeep and gave three short, sharp, rising whistles. Mark and Jax, wearing full desert camouflage, stood, resolving slowly into visibility among the shrubbery beyond the house.

"Hey!" Gabriel ran up, and they hugged, pounding each other on the back.

"We read in the papers that you were arrested," Jax said. "We were worried."

"They didn't have anything on me. I was released yesterday."

"Who's she?" Mark asked, gesturing with his chin at Boadica.

"A kindred soul," Gabriel said. "She's cool. Meet Boadica. Bo, this is Jax, and this is Mark."

They shook hands with her.

"She knows everything," Gabriel said. Mark and Jax lifted their eyebrows, eyes widening, and Gabriel nodded. "*Everything*. Now, Mark, *compadre*—" He put his arm across the young man's shoulder. "Did you go out drinking sometime, perhaps, shortly after the hit?"

"We had a couple of drinks with some buddies," Mark said, with a confused glance at Jax, "with dinner. In Santa Fe last week, on our way back from the Jemez. Why?"

"Apparently you were a little too talkative to the wrong person."

A frown gathered between Mark's brows. "But I didn't say anything about the hit. Right, Jax?"

"Not while I was there, but you and Rachel went out to a bar after dinner. Remember?"

Mark looked shaken. "You're telling me Rachel . . . ?"

Gabriel glanced at Boadica, who nodded. "Rachel Morán. That was where the leak was. She apparently tipped the police off."

Jax gave Gabriel a cocked head and an intent look: *Who* is *this woman*? Gabriel raised a finger: *I'll get to that in a minute.*

Meanwhile Mark rubbed at his face. "I don't really remember what I said. I stayed the night with her. I guess I drank too much and got carried away." He gave Gabriel an anguished look. "I really blew it. Jesus Christ. I'm sorry, Gabe. If you want me out, I'll understand."

Gabriel gave Mark a little shake, then let him go. "What I want is for you to stop blabbing. And that means no more getting drunk and telling secrets to women. Or anybody. No serious harm was done this time, but if it happens again you could get us all into deep shit."

Mark's face hardened as he thought about it. "I thought I could trust Rachel. I've known her since elementary school. Oh, man. She screwed me but good."

Boadica said dryly, "In more ways than one, apparently."

Gabriel shrugged. "Hey, man, at least she didn't give them *your* name. If she'd told the cops everything she knew, we'd all be sitting in jail right now. So count your blessings, *ese.*"

"It's getting dark," Jax said. "Mark—critter duty or dinner duty?"

"Dinner duty."

"Why don't y'all go on in, then," Jax said. "I'll join you in a bit."

Gabriel and Boadica followed Mark into the cabin. It had a large front room with a fireplace and two bedrooms on the lower level, plus a ladder up to a loft. A big pine table with wooden chairs sat on one side of the room, near the cabinets and sink. The faucet was a hand pump that pulled water from the reservoir outside. A big sheepskin rug lay by the fireplace, with an old, frayed couch and an easy chair framing the rug.

Mark lit the storm lantern and the room filled with dim gold light; shadows sprang up in the corners. He added wood to the fire in the fireplace and hung a pot of water over the flames, then poured them some coffee from a large thermos.

"Thanks," Boadica said, and touched his hand with a reassuring smile. Mark gave her a grateful look. The three chatted about inconsequentials till Jax came in. While Jax cleaned up in the sink, Gabriel said, "Did you hear about the other two bombings?"

They shook their heads, eyes wide.

"The other two Woodland Products plants were hit, one two days ago, and the other one last night." Gabriel spread his hands. "They're out of business."

Mark made fists and whooped. Jax came over, wiping his hands on his camo pants and frowning. "That's great, but . . . who did it?"

Gabriel gestured at Boadica, who nodded at their incredulous expressions.

"Gentlemen," Gabriel said, "as of today, Wild Justice has a new member. And a new target. A big one. Let's eat first, and then we'll talk."

They enjoyed a simple meal of beans with green chili, vine-ripened tomatoes, whole wheat bread with butter, and fresh, cold well water in tin cups. Once they'd finished, Gabriel said quietly to Boadica, "I wonder if you could give us a few minutes."

"Sure. I'll take the loft, if it's all right with you guys, and get it set up for the night."

Mark got her some sheets and a blanket and pillow, and she headed up the ladder.

Jax leaned close. "Is she for real?"

Gabriel shrugged. "Everything she's done has checked out. And a fed wouldn't blow up a couple of plants to prove herself."

"True."

Mark said, "I trust her."

"I don't like it," Jax said. "I wish you would have consulted us before bringing her here, Gabe."

"I've got news for you. She already knew about both of you guys, and your connection to me. If she had wanted to turn us in, all she had to do was phone in a tip once you two were back in town."

Jax and Mark gaped. "You're kidding," Jax said. Gabriel shook his head.

"Where does she get her information?" Mark asked.

"She's got her sources."

Jax shook his head with a sigh. "Women and combat are a bad mix." He held up his hands when Mark started to protest. "I know. It's not PC. But someone's got to say it. For all intents and purposes, this is a military operation. And I don't care what they say; women aren't cut out for it. She's going to get us into trouble."

"What kind of trouble are you afraid of, exactly?" Gabriel asked.

"I don't know. She could fall apart under the stress and give us away. She could chicken out at the last minute. She won't have the physical strength a man would, and that could spell trouble all by itself."

"Yeah, but did you get a look at those biceps?" Mark pointed out. "And her thigh muscles. She's no pansy-ass."

"And she won't flake out on us, either," Gabriel said, "if her past behavior is any guide. She's shown real guts and ingenuity. Christ, can you imagine what kind of security that Ruidoso plant must have had? And still she got through."

Jax gave a grudging nod.

"And, frankly," Gabriel went on, "this is *my* group, boys. You agreed to that right from the start. I appreciate your input, but I'm the one who defines the mission, and I say who's in. She's in. If you don't like it, I respect your right to your own opinion, but you're just going to have to live with it."

Jax blew air out explosively. "All right, all right. I've had my say. She's in."

"She's in," Mark said, with a firm nod.

They called Boadica back down, and they all arranged themselves around the fireplace.

"Why don't you fill them in on our next target?" Gabriel said. And she did.

To Gabe's surprise, they voiced none of the objections he had. She easily persuaded them that Gulf Stream I was an appropriate target, and they were completely unconcerned about the potential risks. They had a frightening degree of confidence in Gabriel's ability to come up with an airtight plan, or—more likely, since they were still in their twenties—in their immortality. Ah, youth, he thought. How overrated it is.

Gabriel remained mostly quiet during the exchange, watching Boadica's rough charm work its magic, thawing Jax's skepticism about her competence. Mark was already half in love with her.

For that matter, so am I, Gabriel realized, disturbed at the tinge of jealousy he felt. Maybe that's the real danger of having a woman member.

"What are the next steps?" Mark asked.

"It'll take a couple months to gather information," Gabriel said. "Then we come up with a detailed—"

"A couple months?" Boadica repeated. "Uh-uh. We can't afford to wait that long. Besides which, I've already got a lot of information on the facility. The rest we'll get when we get there."

"What's the big hurry?"

"A hurricane is moving in. It'll hit the facility by tomorrow morning. My sources believe Gulf Stream will survive the storm, but it'll almost certainly sustain damage."

"Meaning . . . ?" Jax said.

"Meaning they'll be bringing in contractors for repairs over the next week or so. If we move now, we can hit them while they're still disorganized—recovering from the storm. With a lot of contractor personnel on site, we'll be able to move discreetly, if need be, without raising questions among the regular staff. But that only gives us about a week. Two at the outside."

Gabriel rubbed his mustache with a thumb. "The last thing I want is for us to rush in without a sound plan that has considered all the contingencies. It's a surefire recipe for disaster."

"He's right," Jax said. "We need to know a lot about them. It'll take time to find out everything we need."

"I agree we need careful planning. But as I said, I already have access to a lot of the information we need. We can get the rest there, while gathering materials. I suggest we leave for Melbourne, Florida, as soon as we can get a flight out there." She sat back, cross-legged, on the sheepskin, leaning on her palms, and looked right at Gabriel.

Gabriel looked into the flames and thought it over. I'm sure having to place an awful lot of trust in this woman and her mysterious sources, he thought.

"I have no doubt that I'm on all sorts of FBI and criminal investigation lists," he said. "If I show my face there, and I'm recognized, it could screw the mission."

Boadica nodded thoughtfully. Then she smiled. "So we'll give you a makeover. You, too, Mark and Jax. Leave that to me. That is one of my specialties."

"There's another factor. I . . . happen to know the engineer who designed the facility. Emma Tooke. Or I used to, fifteen years ago. I don't know if she's still there or has moved on—"

"She's still there, I believe." Boadica's eyebrows shot up. "You know her?"

"Whoa, what a stroke of luck!" Mark said.

Gabriel shook his head. "Well, but we can't have

it both ways. We can't disguise me from the feds but not from Emma.''

"Sure we can," Boadica said. "Any pictures the feds have on you will most likely be recent. Tooke won't have see you for years, right?''

"Ri-ight," he replied slowly.

"People change a lot in fifteen years. Don't worry." She flashed him a sudden smile. "It'll work out. You'll see.''

Chapter 9

EMMA: **Thursday, 1 October, 7:34 P.M. EDT**
Gulf Stream I

Spray splashed up through the grating onto Emma's jeans and spattered water onto her face and arms as she stepped out of the antechamber onto the dock deck. The wind, strong and steady, made her eyes sting.

She licked salt from her lips and grabbed her hair, which was coming loose from its braid and whipping at her cheeks and eyes. Holding her hair captive at the base of her neck, she gripped the dock railing.

Her power plant lay just below; she could see it over the railing and through the grating between her feet. Mostly submerged, its dull grey roof was barely visible in the twilight, only in the troughs of the waves that broke themselves over it. The swelling baritone hum of its compressors and power generators, which carried even above the rush of the waves and wind, made her smile.

Rhythmic waves slammed against the plant's raised

deck, which was lit by the dock floodlights. It was
dark and wet down there, and water churned, billions
of tons of angry water. Maybe it was the approaching
hurricane, the possibility of loss—she looked at that
water and was afraid for her plant. And for herself.

She was alone; it'd be so easy to slip, or lose her
grip, and sink like a stone, down, down, thousands of
feet into unimaginable pressure and cold—of course
she'd be dead long before then, long before anyone
knew to look for her or wonder where she was. She
grimaced. Cheery notion, Tooke. But she really should
have grabbed a life vest. Sometimes she was in too
damn much of a hurry.

She backed down the ladder, and cool water sloshed
against her legs and back, dousing her jeans and
blouse. Emma gasped. As the water receded she
splashed across the raised deck and grabbed the door
hatch, yanked it open, and jumped over the threshold.
As she shoved the door closed a wave broke across
the deck and seawater cascaded down through the narrowing crack, drenching her. She shut the door with a
clank. In that instant she heard a shout.

Beyond the small glass port in the door, a figure up
on the dock signaled her. Keith Hellman. He backed
down the ladder, waited for a trough—Emma opened
the hatch as he splashed across and scrambled inside
onto the cramped landing. A second wave slammed
the door open and drenched her again; Keith and she
pushed the door closed and cut off the deluge.

Then Emma turned to eye him. He actually had the
good sense to be wearing a life vest, she noted. He
returned her stare. She turned, discomfited, and opened
the inner hatch. Sound filled the air around them: the
fast-paced pounding of the compressor engines and the
power generators, the scream of fluids against pipe.
The air smelled faintly of sour-sweet lubricants, of ammonia and ozone.

"They told me I might find you here!" he shouted.

Emma opened the locker behind the inner hatch and pulled out headphone/mike sets for them. The noise receded to a more muffled, tolerable level as she fit the headphones over her ears. She adjusted the mike in front of her mouth and then started down the spiral staircase. "Come on."

On the mezzanine landing that wrapped around the beanpole, she watched as Keith descended toward her, looking around at all the equipment with a rather grim look on his face. Emma felt a twinge of guilt. It wasn't strictly his fault Pendleton had forced him on her; she really should try to make him feel welcome.

Once he'd caught up, she pointed around. "Those are the power generators, on the mezzanine. Directly below us are the primary condenser heat exchangers."

He said, "I smell ozone and ammonia."

Emma nodded. "The ozone's ionization from the electromagnetic field that surrounds the generators."

"What's the EMF exposure like down here?"

"Down by the generators, it's pretty hefty. We don't keep operators in here, though, when we're operating, and we have strict exposure limits for personnel who have to come down for maintenance."

"Good."

"The ammonia you smell is trace amounts from the closed-circuit power loop down there. The detectors say it's way below OSHA standards and we monitor it continuously.

"We use mostly silicone lubricants, which are more inert than the petroleum-based stuff. The most toxic substance we have in any quantity, other than gasoline and diesel, is the ammonia, and even that wouldn't be too big a disaster in a spill; it'd be quickly consumed by the nitrogen-eaters in the water. And the spills are easily neutralized with acid. So the chemists tell me."

Keith lifted eyebrows. "Don't underrate ammonia.

It's highly corrosive and it's gaseous at room temperature. You industries that deal with toxic chemicals consistently underestimate the risks. And it's not just your own life and safety you're risking, you know.''

Emma felt her hackles rising again. "Give me a break. Our ammonia storage tanks have full containment systems and emergency water curtains in case of a release. Do you think we're idiots, for Christ's sake? I may not be an environmental expert, but I know how to engineer a safe structure, and I know how to minimize risks of spills.''

His expression didn't change; he shrugged. She frowned at him. How had she ended up on the defensive?

''And on top of that we have a technician dedicated full-time to sampling our fugitive air emissions and water discharges, maintaining the spill equipment, and collecting hazardous wastes. As a matter of fact, he'll be reporting to you. So once we get past the storm you can get him to explain our systems to you and verify our methods to your heart's content.''

Again, he said nothing. What the hell are you doing here? she thought. He sure didn't act as if he cared one whit about Gulf Stream or what they were trying to accomplish.

She took him out onto the mezzanine catwalk; he snooped around the generators, inspecting the coolant seals, valves, and containment structures, and then they went down to the main level. As they moved among the huge pipes and turbines, the floor trembled so and the sound so battered the air that it affected the rhythm of Emma's speech, set the bones and muscles in her legs to quivering, made the air flutter in her lungs.

She watched Keith's back for a moment as he bent over, inspecting a series of seals, and then turned her back on him and looked around at her great, graceful machines, matte-blue and -green and -grey. She thought of them as creatures, sometimes: elephants, or dinosaurs, or maybe whales, drinking water from great depths and producing power. She knew them intimately, more intimately than she knew any human, knew their quirks and foibles, knew what they could and couldn't do.

She couldn't bear it if her plant went down with the storm.

"I'll keep you safe," she said softly, laying a hand on a compressor.

Then Keith was standing in front of her again.

"I beg your pardon?"

She shook her head, instead of replying, and hoped he'd attribute her words to his imagination. "Find any problems?"

He shook his head. "Everything looks fine."

"Then let's get out of here."

She dogged both hatch doors on her way out, spinning the locking wheels to their fully latched, pressure-containing positions.

She got very wet sealing the outside hatch. Keith stayed with her the whole time—not touching her, but close, ready to grab if a wave took her. She appreciated it.

They splashed across the deck in the next trough and climbed the ladder.

She left Keith off at the catwalk level, to finish his inspections with a tour of the Science module, and headed back up to Control. By the time she'd checked the wastewater and the hydrogen generating plants it was after eight o'clock.

She entered the control room to find the coffee all gone and the reef safely at its eighty-foot depth. Lee reported they had shut down the desalination plant and finished purging the hydrogen plant, and were ready to bring the modules' diesel generators up, shut off the power plant compressors, and drop the power plant.

"But you'd better get ahold of Freddy first," he said. "The thirty-knot alarm went off a few minutes ago."

"On his way," Rob reported after radioing York Aviation. "He'll be here in about forty-five minutes."

Emma wiped her palms on her jeans and picked up the radio. "Attention all personnel. Final Phase II dust-off will be in fifty minutes. That's *fifty minutes*. Give me a roll call, by module. Over."

Voices issued from the radio; Emma checked them against her list, asking for repeats and verifications. Finally: "Flo, come in."

"Flo here."

"Before you dust off I want you to report to Control and check reef systems. Okay?"

"You got it. We're in good shape over here; it doesn't look like we'll need Rob after all. Give me a half hour or so."

"Ten-four."

"Thank you, Jesus," Rob said behind her.

She lifted the radio again. "Angus, come in."

"Yeah?"

"I'm going to take you up on your offer to stick around for Phase III. You and Gene are the Mariculture Phase III team."

"Right."

She checked the Engineering roster. "Nikki, come in."

"Nikki here. We're nearly done with the fuel drum containment."

"Good. As soon as you get finished and Keith checks your work, report to Science. You and Jess will be Science Phase III."

"Right, then."

"Terri and Michael, you're Residential Phase III. Copy?"

"Ten-four."

"And Lee, it's your lucky day," she said, lowering the radio. "Engineering will be Rob and me, and Mac down below." Lee raised his eyebrows, then dropped them.

"Can't figure out whether I like that or not," he said.

"Can't be helped; you've got children. That puts you lower on the list than us single folk."

"Teenagers. The oldest is practically in college. And they live with my ex-wife anyhow."

"Are you insisting on staying?"

He harrumphed and didn't reply for a moment. "Nah, I guess I'll go. But take good care of the plants while I'm gone, will you?"

"You bet."

She leaned forward. "Ready to bring up the backup generators?"

Lee swung back to his station. "Ready."

"Do it."

They felt a slight change in the floor vibration and Lee said, "Engineering on-line. Mariculture on-line. Science on-line. Residential—uh . . . Residential didn't start. Hmm. Let me kick it over again. That's got it. Voltage stable on all four units."

Emma frowned. "Are we up-to-date on the scheduled maintenance for that generator?" She threaded her way through a maze of screen menus to call up the generator maintenance logs. "Hmmm. Well, we're due for a tune-up on all four units next month. We should make it a priority." She quickly edited a note to that effect and E-mailed it to herself and Lee. "Let's give the generators a few more minutes to warm up."

They sipped coffee in silence.

"Okay. Let's switch the busses. Engineering first."

There was the slightest flicker from the lights and Lee reported, "Engineering on backup."

They repeated the process for the other modules. "Voltages steady, chief."

Emma took a deep breath. "Right. Shutting down pumps One through Four and Six through Ten." On her screen, the flow meter on the cold water deep pipe dropped to a trickle. "We still have Mariculture's cold water pump on-line?"

"On-line and running under Mariculture's diesel generator," Lee said. "The lobsters are still getting their a/c."

"Okay. I'm bypassing the main generators." Emma pushed squares on the screen, then confirmed choices. Below, solenoid-actuated valves opened, equalizing the pressures between the condenser and evaporator sides of the OTEC plant's heat exchangers. The RPMs on the main generators, as well as voltages, dropped, vertical bars shrinking to zero on the screen now that there was no vaporizing ammonia turning the turbine blades.

"Locking rotors," Emma said. "Plant shutdown complete." She blew out between clenched teeth and said, "Sink her."

Rob moved over to the other workstation. "How deep?"

"All the way to the stops. Put the top forty feet under."

"Right. Slaving spillway buoyancy controls to the power plant set points. Releasing annular locks. Released. Setting descent at five feet a minute to forty feet."

Emma stood and pushed out through the door, down the hall, and out onto the walkway. The wind whipped her hair and tugged at her clothes as she walked around to the north side of the module. The spillways, a football field-sized rectangle, were already noticeably lower in the water. She leaned out over the railing and looked down at the power plant. The waves washed over the access hatch. A few seconds later and it dropped completely below the surface, the dark circle of the plant's perimeter distorted as the water depth increased. She swallowed convulsively and went back into Control.

"Watch your depth as you near the stops, Rob. We don't want to shear them off."

"Not to worry, chief. I'll drop down to a foot a minute when we get to the last five feet. Besides, the annulars will automatically lock if I overrun the limit switch."

"Which will transfer the stress to the beanpole all at once. Be careful, okay?"

"I'll float like a butterfly," Rob said.

"See that you do, or *I'll* sting like a bee." She kept herself from biting her nails as the depth increased. True to his word, Rob eased the last five feet down at a snail's pace. She wished they still had Bowser in the water to get a televised shot of the clearance between the crossbeams and the bottom of the plant.

"Buoyancy steady at thirty-nine-point-seven-five feet. Good enough, ma'am?"

"Lock it."

"Actuating annular locks," Rob said. Then, "Locked."

She breathed out. "Pressure alarms set?"

Lee said, "Yes, ma'am. Relax, ma'am. We know our job, ma'am."

Emma smothered a grin and looked out the window.

Clouds had moved in, blocking out the stars, and the wind was out of the east-southeast at more than forty knots when a bright dot appeared on the western horizon. Freddy the helicopter pilot signaled them that he'd be there in twenty minutes.

The interior door opened. Gloria and Angus came

in with sandwiches, corn chips, sliced carrots, a bunch of bananas, two thermoses, and several large, plastic mugs. Emma took the salami and Swiss on rye that Gloria handed her, and set it down on the counter. The thought of eating made her queasy.

"All personnel," she said into her radio. "Final Phase II dust-off in twenty minutes. Repeat, final Phase II dust-off in twenty minutes. Non-Phase III team members, finish what you're doing and report to the helipad ASAP. Repeat, Phase II personnel report to the helipad for dust-off in twenty minutes. Acknowledge."

She checked the names off against the roster. Everyone accounted for. Sixteen minutes to go. Her head hurt; she rubbed her neck again, and rubbed at her mastoids.

Then Gloria was there, expertly kneading the knots in her shoulders. She smiled down at Emma from overhead.

"I'll be sending positive energy from Melbourne," she said. "We all will. The facility will do fine."

"Yeah." Emma closed her eyes, breathed slowly, and relaxed into the pain, and release from pain, Gloria's fingers brought.

◆

Chapter 10

KEITH: Thursday, 1 October, 8:44 P.M. EDT
Gulf Stream I

Keith stopped on the catwalk between Science and Engineering, turned into the wind, and gripped the railing. It was heavily overcast and well after sunset, but the lights from the modules lit the big waves rolling up from the south. He stared out into the formless sky beyond the lights.

He was angry and he didn't want it to show when he went into the control room. He was also afraid that the FBI might be right—that there might be a saboteur on Gulf Stream.

He'd expected relatively minor things, like the gasoline storage area and the sewage left in the lines between the modules. All and all, though, he'd been moderately pleased with how environmentally friendly the facility design was. The power-generating technology was a perfect example of what could be done to clean up an industry that produced far too many pollutants, far too much CO_2. The sewage treatment plant was excellent, rated for twice the amount of sewage.

Then he'd hit the Science module.

He released the railing and spread his fingers. Breathing calmly, in measured breaths, he walked on.

The control room door to the inner hall was propped open and Keith paused for a moment to study them before they saw him.

Lee, frowning at Emma so hard it was almost a scowl, was putting on a jacket. Gloria was rubbing Emma's shoulders and smiling. Rob, off to the side, was watching Emma, his face unguarded, unaware that anybody was watching him.

Rob adores her, Keith realized. He studied the way they stood, their attention focused, in one way or another, on Emma. They all do.

He stepped from the shadow of the doorway into the room. Rob's face closed suddenly, Gloria's hands dropped from Emma's shoulders, and Lee stopped frowning.

Emma blinked. "You should be over at the helipad—oh, you came back for your jacket."

Keith started to open his mouth, then shut it. He paused, marshaling his thoughts.

"I'm afraid there's a problem in Science."

Emma frowned. "Is it something we need to fix before the storm?"

"Only if—" He heard movement behind him and glanced over his shoulder. Flo and Ben entered from the hallway.

"Just sticking our heads in to do a quick check of the reefs," Flo said.

Ben added, "And to say good luck. If it weren't for Ronnie . . ."

Emma managed a distracted smile. "Thanks. Hang on a second." She looked back at Keith. "What is it? The hazardous waste storage room? It exceeds specs."

"There's nothing wrong with *that* storage room. It's the chemical stores that are screwed up."

"In which labs?"

"All of them."

Emma stared at him. She looked as if she wanted to bite someone's face off.

Rob spoke. "So we're talking some broken glass if things get shaken? Can't we live with that?" He looked from Keith to Emma. "What's the matter, chief? You look pissed."

Emma grabbed the clipboard and turned to Flo, who was scanning the reef schematics. "Tet was in charge of Phase I for Science. He *knows* better."

Flo frowned. "Tetsuo is in Alaska, Emma, for the Prince William Sound evaluation. It's my fault. Dick Munzer was the second and I believed him when he said they were done."

"What's the big deal?" Rob said.

Keith stared at him. In six years of enforcement he'd learned over and over again that ignorance and stupidity were far more likely causes of disaster than

malice was. Still, he made a mental note to check out
Munzer as a possible suspect.

"I suppose we're looking at a potential toxic spill,"
Emma said.

"If there's any sort of major wave or wind strike
on that module you're looking at serious damage for
any of a number of reasons. In the worst case, loss of
the whole module."

Emma blanched. "Isn't that going a bit far?"

"There are bottles of potassium in kerosene on
shelves next to organic solvents. The bottle gets broken and after a while the potassium ignites. The organic solvents burn, producing dioxins and furans
which are *so* toxic that, if the structure survived, it
could *never* be occupied again. Sulfuric and nitric acid
next to cotton lab coats. Do you know what guncotton
is? Those are only a couple of the potential reactions
I noticed. I'd have to have a Ph.D. in chemistry and
several weeks to evaluate all the possible synergistic
combinations. Far too many of them are toxic, corrosive, flammable, explosive, and just plain nasty."

Emma gripped her clipboard. "Okay. What do you
recommend?"

"Give me who you can and we'll move the bottles
to the floor and secure them. Probably duct-tape them
into compatible groups and make sure nothing can fall
on them."

"Okay, we'll do it, but you're out of here in ten
minutes, on that chopper."

"I don't think that would be a good idea."

Emma frowned. "That helicopter is the last ride out
of here until the hurricane passes. You've got no
choice."

Keith knew he could override her with one phone
call to Pendleton. He also knew that would do more
damage than good. "You keep a team aboard during
the storm."

"Yes—single volunteers."

"If there's a spill and I'm not here, I won't do any good. I'm not married. I volunteer."

Emma made a sharp gesture with the clipboard. "Out of the question. My storm response team has been training for this sort of thing for over a year."

Keith crossed his arms and said mildly, "And I've been doing this sort of thing for *six* years. Have any of your people dealt with a major spill, not just a drill?"

The radio by Rob crackled and a voice overlaid with helicopter noise said, "Gulf Stream I, this is York One. I'm fifteen miles out, ETA ten minutes, come back?"

"Put that on a headset, will you?" Emma said to Rob. Rob plugged in a headphone/mike set and talked to the helicopter in a low voice. Emma looked back at Keith.

Keith kept his face blank and still. The last thing he wanted was to make this an issue of "face." If this woman turned against him, everyone would, making all his jobs impossible.

Emma looked at Gloria.

Gloria looked back and said, "Oh, I'll stay. You know that, but I think we'll need all the hands we can get. Everyone else on the evac list is married or has kids."

Emma's shoulders slumped. "Okay. Rob, let Freddy know that it's two fewer going back." She raised her eyebrows at Keith.

"How many people do you need?"

"As many as you can afford to give me." He paused while she looked at her clipboard and rubbed at her brow.

"I could make do with six," he said. "No less, or we'll be at it all night, while the worst of the storm is overhead."

She nodded. "Six I can do. You and Gloria get over to Science and get started. Nikki and Jess are already there. I'll have Michael and Terri there in five minutes. If you need supplies from Engineering, let us know before the wind gets too strong for us to cross the catwalks." She turned back to Gloria. "Before you do *anything*, though, run through the evacuation drill with him. Make sure he knows where the module lifeboat is, how to open, seal, and launch it."

"Will do."

Keith nodded. "Thanks. I'll do my best to see you don't regret it."

Emma almost smiled at that. "Too late."

After an hour of lifting, bending, and stooping, Keith regretted it, too.

"Toss the tape, please."

"Sure." Gloria rolled it across the floor. "So you were in Greenpeace. For how long?"

Keith wrapped tape around an island of grouped bottles. "Four years. After college. I was going to finish grad school, but . . ." Keith rolled the tape back to Gloria and began shifting the contents of another shelf.

"But? But? But what?"

Keith gave Gloria a shrug and a smile. "I decided to try to save the world instead." He stood and straightened, ignoring her quizzical look. "What's next? Graham's Physical Chemistry lab? No, Nikki and Jess got that, right?"

"Right. Theoretically, we're done." Gloria put the last piece of tape in place and moved back, remaining on the floor. She stretched her legs out and began doing yoga-like stretches.

Keith picked up the radio. "Terri, Michael, come in."

"Michael here. Terri and I are just finishing up in the biology labs. We need to get back over to Resi-

dential and get some more tarps laid over the gardens
if it's not too late. Do you want to give our work a
look before we head back?''

Keith thought it over. ''No. We're done up here. If
there's any more to do Gloria and I can handle it. Go.''
He remarked to Gloria, ''I doubt if they'll get much
more tarping done.''

They both listened to the sounds of wind and wave
outside, and Gloria gave him a somber nod.

''You want to come with me for a final inspection
of the module?'' he asked. ''We'll work our way up.''

''Sure.''

They headed for the elevator.

She asked, ''What did you do for Greenpeace?''

''I worked for the ocean ecology branch, doing ed-
ucation and community organization. Mostly ocean-
dumping issues, but I did a stint running interference
on some drift net operations in the Pacific.''

They stepped into the elevator. Keith pushed *Main*,
and the cage started down.

''Oh, really?''

''Yeah. We hounded the Japanese fishing fleet, running inflatables out when they tried to deploy their
nets. We worked on educating Pacific Rim governments about the ecological and economic damage being done in their coastal waters. The economic
argument always worked better than the ecological
one.''

''Did you cut nets? Ram ships?''

Keith shook his head. ''You're thinking of the Sea
Shepherds, Watson's old group. Greenpeace doesn't
damage property. Watson was a founder of Greenpeace, but he wanted to push things farther. They
kicked him off the board.''

The elevator came to a halt, and they stepped out
and went to the left. The main biology storeroom was
next to the elevator: a windowless, interior room lined

with shelves that housed dozens of jugs and carboys of chemicals. It looked, smelled, sounded, and felt like any storeroom in a commercial laboratory Keith had ever been in—the whiff of assorted chemicals and preserving solutions, the boxes and glass and plastic containers stacked all around—until he concentrated on the vibration. Part of it was the module's diesel generator. Part of it was the rising wind. The floor was still steady—no appreciable motion yet evident—but Emma had said that was likely to change.

They checked cabinets and shelves. All was in order.

Next door was a marine biology lab whose shelves housed aquariums, lit with fluorescents, with tiny fish flitting about in them. The aquariums were all now taped to the shelves with packing tape. Other shelves and cabinets housed jars and boxes of various sorts, and a thicket of glassware. Again, all sound.

They worked their way around the rest of the labs, offices, and storerooms in the head section and then covered the labs in the tail, inspecting cabinets and shelves and hoods, verifying that equipment and glassware were stabilized and staged properly. It didn't take long; Michael and Terri had done a good job. Then they went up a level to check on Nikki and Jess.

The storm had grown noisier in the past few minutes, its wind rattling the windows' storm shutters. Reynolds's Chemical Oceanography lab smelled faintly—sweet? sulfurous? sour?—to Keith's nose. Two gas chromatographs were bolted to one work bench; a mass spectrometer and data collection computer stood beside the door, their red LEDs flickering. Taped bottles and flasks were arranged in groups, strapped inside the hoods, and Jess and Nikki were emptying a set of shelves.

"Going okay?" Gloria asked.

"Tip-top," said Nikki. She was a pretty young

woman from England with brown eyes and wheat-colored hair, and her voice reminded Keith of BBC shortwave broadcasts.

"Need any help?"

"Don't think so," said Jess, a young, dark-haired man, stocky and ruddy complected, with an amiable face. "This is the last cabinet. We'll be done in another few minutes."

"Okay," said Gloria. "See you in the conference room. Last one in has to make the popcorn."

"Popcorn?" asked Keith, as they continued down the hall.

"Angus threw a couple of bags of microwavable popcorn and some videos in with the supplies. There's a VCR in the conference room."

"Are Jess and Nikki permanent staff?"

Gloria shook her head, then said, "Jess is, now. He used to be an intern but came back permanently a few months ago, after he got his master's. But most of our researchers are actually here on a temporary basis, working on a particular study. Their universities or institutions rent space and they work at Gulf Stream as visiting faculty."

She stopped at the end of the hall. An armored glass window set into a door gave them a view of the walkway. They looked out. Across the way, the Engineering module's lights were dimmed and diffracted by rain falling at a forty-five-degree angle.

The door vibrated slightly and, despite heavy weather stripping around the door, slight fingers of wind stirred against his skin. But the structure seemed solid, unmoving. For a second Keith wondered if all their work in the storerooms was unnecessary. Well, the storm was just beginning.

He asked, "And Nikki?"

"An intern." At Keith's querying look, she elaborated, "A volunteer. We have agreements with several

universities and technical-vocational institutes. Nikki,
for example, is an engineering major at MIT. She gets
credit hours for her work here, and job experience, and
we get cheap labor.''

They turned aside and went into the conference
room. It was one of the largest rooms he'd seen at
Gulf Stream, rivaling Control. A table with twelve
chairs dominated the room. A couch sat against the
wall by the door, with a projection-screen TV opposite
it, across the conference table. A rack with books and
magazines and a kitchenette were on the other wall.

''You were talking about the Sea Shepherds,'' Gloria remarked. ''Do you approve of those guys?''

Keith studied her for a moment, wondering about
her motives, trying to figure out how he should portray
himself.

''Yes and no,'' he said finally.

''Nothing like a straight answer.'' She went to a
small refrigerator in the kitchenette and looked inside.
''Coke? Mineral water?''

''Mineral water, please.'' He waited for her to pour
it. Why was she asking him about the Sea Shepherds?
Should he play the radical? He shook his head with a
frown. He was seeing a terrorist behind every face.
''It's a hard question. I don't approve of the Sea Shepherds, but they've accomplished some things. Iceland
no longer hunts whales. Was it because the Shepherds
trashed the whaling station and sank two of the whaling ships in Reykjavik harbor, or was it because
Greenpeace organized a boycott of Icelandic fish almost immediately after the sinking? I'd say it was
both.

''I don't approve of violence, even against property,
but it's always the radical extreme, the groups like the
Sea Shepherds and Earth First!, when they were still
active, that pushes the 'middle' into the public con-
sciousness.''

He accepted the glass from her and eased down into one of the conference table chairs.

She rummaged through a box set on the end of the table and pulled out a stack of video tapes. "Let's see—we've got *Indiana Jones and the Temple of Doom, Silent Running, Never Cry Wolf,* and *Key Largo.*"

"Which *Key Largo*?"

"What do you mean?"

"The black-and-white one with Bogart and Edward G. Robinson or the later one?"

Gloria examined the box. "Bogart. Didn't know there was a later one."

While Gloria queued up the tape, he sipped at his mineral water, his thoughts wandering. She came over and said, "Where are you?"

He smiled. "Last hurricane I had anything to do with wasn't even called a hurricane."

"What? It was a hurricane or it wasn't."

"Well, wrong ocean. In the Far East they call them typhoons. Okinawa. We ran the ship into their major port, Naha, for shelter. After the storm the authorities refused us clearance while the Japanese fishing fleet got underway. We picketed and complained. Then one of our crew members was accused of bombing a local cannery."

"I thought you said Greenpeace didn't do that sort of thing."

Keith shook his head. "I did and he didn't. It was a setup. A frame. And if it weren't for one piece of luck, it would've worked, seriously damaging Greenpeace's reputation."

Gloria leaned forward, elbows on table, eyebrows raised. "Go on."

"There isn't much to tell. We held a reception aboard for some local environmental groups. Some of the consulate people and the international community also came. Early the next morning, a bomb went off at this cannery along the waterfront—it started a fire that gutted the facility. Fish oil, don't you know.'' Keith paused, his mouth setting in a thin line. "The fire also killed the night watchman.''

"How awful.''

"Yeah. Anyway, there was an anonymous phone call to the police and a dock worker came forward to testify that he'd seen our first mate leaving the cannery. The police searched his cabin and found plastic explosives and detonators hidden under his berth.''

Gloria grimaced. "Jesus. Sounds pretty damning.''

"Yeah . . . except for two things. First, Joseph, the first mate, was taken to the hospital with acute appendicitis right after the reception. So at the time the dock worker claimed he saw him leave the cannery, Joseph was on the operating table surrounded by a doctor, an anesthesiologist, and two operating nurses—all local, impartial witnesses.''

"What a way to get an alibi.''

Keith snorted agreement.

"What was the other thing?''

"Well, when it was clear that the dock worker was lying, the police charged him as an accessory to murder. It didn't hurt that he'd been involved in some minor extortion locally. He confessed that he'd been given Joseph's picture and a hundred thousand yen by an American man. He didn't know anything about the bomb or the planted evidence.''

"Did you ever find the American who paid him off?''

"The dock worker *supposedly* recognized him in a picture taken at the reception, but the person he identified was female. He may have just been confused— the picture quality wasn't great.''

"Or maybe he was lying to protect someone.''

Keith pursed his lips. "It's certainly possible. The

local authorities wanted the culprit to be a foreigner—they were clearly relieved when he said it was an American. So who knows? Maybe they pressured him to come out with that story.

"Anyhow, suddenly we were cleared to leave, all the red tape cut away. I like to think it was because the authorities were outraged at the frame-up, but it's just as likely they were afraid another attempt would be made and they didn't want any more bombings."

The radio crackled and Emma's voice said, "Wind speed is gusting to fifty-five knots. The barometer is down to twenty-eight-point-four. Give me a status, guys. Mariculture first."

"This is Angus, Emma. Everything's okay so far."

"Good. Science?"

Gloria picked up the radio. "Jess and Nikki are finishing up right now. We'll be secure in less than five minutes."

"Good. Residential?"

"Terri here. We didn't get finished with the tarping, I'm afraid."

"Too bad."

"Yeah. Sorry."

"Not much you could do about it. Don't sweat it."

Angus interjected, "The TV reception is breaking up."

"Yeah. The wind is shaking the satellite dish something fierce. I suspect that the entire complex is also swinging a bit on the main anchor tether."

"Ah. Well, it's screwing up our movie."

"Shocking. Watch a tape," Emma answered. "We'll be updating the weather conditions every thirty minutes. More if something weird happens. Report anything unusual."

Keith took the radio from Gloria. "Keith here. Am I remembering correctly that the NPDES compliance records are over here in the Science module?"

"Uh, refresh my memory."

"National Pollutant Discharge Elimination System."

"Ah, the wastewater outflow analyses, right?"

"Yes."

"Well, they're not NPDES records; we're not really covered by U.S. regulations. They're based on a consent agreement. But yeah, there's a closet in the analytical lab that has the samples and a file cabinet with the records. Why?"

Keith tried to make his voice sound relaxed. "Just thought I'd familiarize myself with the records, as long as I'm stuck here." He paused. "If that doesn't tread on anybody's toes."

"Considering that your first day on the job has lasted almost thirteen hours, so far, you certainly don't *need* to. But it's your responsibility now, so you're certainly free to have a look."

"Right. I just thought I'd see what they say."

"Whatever. Don't wear yourself out, though. If we have any problems during the storm I need everybody fit and rested."

"Understood."

"Anything else? Anybody?" A chorus of nos. "Emma out."

Keith passed Nikki and Jess in the hall. "Start the popcorn," he said. "Just getting some paperwork."

He found the racks of postanalysis samples with their dates carefully marked, and the analytical logs. The preanalysis samples were probably kept in the cold room across the hall, at four degrees centigrade.

The analytical results, along with the quality control printouts, were collected in three three-inch loose-leaf binders. Keith gathered them and a separate file of quarterly summaries and took them back to the conference room, where popcorn rattled in the microwave. The smell of popcorn made his mouth water.

"A little light reading, there," Gloria said.

"That should put you right to sleep," Jess remarked, and Nikki laughed, curling up on the couch next to him.

Keith smiled. "Uh-huh."

He took over one end of the table so he could spread the effluent reports out. The wind was shaking the storm shutters hard enough to be heard above the movie's opening credits. An extra large swell, passing under the module and slapping against the beanpole, sent a strong vibration through the floor.

He took lots of notes.

Chapter 11

EMMA: **Friday, 2 October, 6:15 A.M. EDT**
Gulf Stream I

Emma was looking right at the control panel when it happened, so she knew wind speed had just hit a new high of 132.6 miles per hour when the wind snatched the pitot tube off the roof. On her meteorological display screen, the wind speed line plummeted and zeroed out.

That made the third weather measurement device to go so far, after the anemometer and the wind vane, which had gone together early on.

The floor vibrated, rising and falling in a slow roll. Wind pounded at the battened door. Its rage-filled screams made her neck hairs stand on end. Behind her, Mac paced back and forth across the control room. Every few moments he stopped and she sensed him behind her, looking over her shoulder at the displays.

Several alarms on the main display were flashing—lost instrument warnings, mostly, though at odd moments the structural stress or buoyancy alert indicators would flicker on for one module or another, or for the spillway or reef. The catwalk strain gauges chimed more insistently, until she reset the alarm to a higher set point. But with the plants purged and shut down, and the fact that the diesel power generators weren't wired into the main process control system, most of the indicators were dead.

When the heavy rains had hit, rather than closing the opaque shutters, Emma had lowered the clear polycarbonate storm shield over the control room window. Floodlit blasts of water and debris smashed against the polycarbonate. Emma shivered and folded her arms across her chest, more a reaction to the spectacle outside the window than the chill humidity of the air-conditioning.

Whenever a gust of wind swept the rain aside, she caught a blurred glimpse of one of the lighted catwalks and the aircraft warning strobes on the roof of Science. The catwalks and lights were moving around a lot, and Gulf Stream complained about it, too, not only with its alarms, but with quiverings, creaks, and groans. Between those rare glimpses, the notion would start to nag Emma that the others had already broken loose and gone down.

Of course no such thing had happened. Even if what she'd just seen was a hallucination, all the other modules showed up, intact and functional, on the displays. And she had just checked in with everyone twenty minutes ago, before calling Pendleton in Melbourne. Besides, if any of the modules went it'd probably be Engineering, which operated closer to its lift tolerances than the others.

And for that matter, if one went down it would almost certainly take the rest with it.

Mac started pacing again. Emma sat back, rubbed her stinging eyes. She eyed the cold dregs of coffee in her mug and then took a slug, wincing at the bitter taste and wondering why she was drinking it. Then she looked out at the water splashing against the window and wondered what else was going to give before this was over.

"Maybe I should take a walk around, down below," Mac said.

Mac was a short, muscular man in his mid-forties. The air-conditioning didn't seem to bother him; he'd peeled off the top of his grease-stained coveralls and tied it around his waist by the sleeves. The red T-shirt underneath had a Grateful Dead logo on the chest and a pack of cigarettes rolled in the left sleeve. He had two tattoos from his navy days—a blue-and-green snake coiled around one biceps and a red-and-black heart pierced with a vertical arrow riding his other forearm. A two-day stubble shadowed his chin, and fatigue shadowed his eyes. He smelled faintly of old nicotine, coffee, and bearing grease. The cuticles, fingernails, and creases in his palms were stained black.

Mac was relatively new to Gulf Stream. He was one of the best mechanics Emma had ever known and, unlike some of the gays and lesbians on the facility, didn't pull any punches about his sexual preference; from the start he'd billed himself as the Gay Grease Monkey. It was a risky tack. His first few weeks at Gulf Stream had been rocky—some of the other technicians had beaten him severely early on.

Emma wanted to fire the offenders, but Mac refused to identify them—though she had her suspicions.

"I'll handle it," he said. A month later, Emma saw him off-duty, laughing and drinking beer with one of her suspects. There'd been no more incidents, and Emma didn't know whether Mac was a Gandhi or had beat the shit out of his attackers some landside week-end. Mac never talked about it.

He'd been below two dozen times since the full force of the storm had hit.

"Go to bed," she said. "Everything's fine below. I'll wake you if there's trouble."

"Why do these damn things always happen at night, is what I want to know. Either on your day off, or the middle of the night. It never fails."

A tired smile came onto Emma's face, sagging under the weight of her cheek muscles. She gave his arm a slap. "Go to bed."

"Nah. I couldn't. I don't see how Rob can be sleeping through all this."

"Maybe he's been learning relaxation techniques from Gloria."

Mac snorted. "Is *that* what it's called now?"

Emma gave Mac a surprised look. "Do you know something I don't?"

Mac shrugged, a deadpan expression on his face. "I don't know nothing."

"Come on, Mac. Spill it."

But he shook his head, stubborn. Emma frowned.

"You're imagining things," she said finally.

"Like I said. I don't know nothing."

Emma turned back to the controls, still frowning. Rob and Gloria? Surely Gloria would have said something. Wouldn't she?

Why would Gloria, or Rob, tell Mac—whom neither was especially close to—that they had a thing going and not tell Emma? When Gloria was in many ways Emma's closest friend on Gulf Stream? And Rob was like a little brother to her.

But of course, if anyone knew Mac would: Mac and his partner, Charles Lawson's, quarters shared a bath-room with Rob and his roommate's.

Emma gave it some more thought. Rob and Gloria.

An odd couple if ever there was one. Though she supposed odder matches had worked before.

While she pondered this, Mac paced another circuit. After a minute or two he came to a stop behind her and asked, "So, what's the wind speed now?"

The same question he'd asked every ten minutes for the last couple of hours. Emma rubbed the back of her neck with a sigh.

"Don't know. We lost the anemometer a few minutes ago."

"I know," Mac said, "but what do you figure it is? A hundred? Hundred twenty?" He squinted at the blasts of filthy water. "Jeez, would you just look at it."

"Sit down, would you? Your pacing is making me nervous."

He dropped into a chair next to her. "Jeez, I really need a smoke."

She gave him a look that meant *don't even* think *about it*. He slumped back in the chair with a sigh.

"Guess I'll head over to the conference room for a smoke. Maybe watch a movie."

He didn't get up. He probably wanted the company. God knew she did, even with his pacing and restless, repetitive questions. The book she'd tried to read earlier lay facedown on the console, neglected: she couldn't bear to take her attention off the controls.

With a crack of thunder, lightning strobed a wave descending on the windward catwalk. Emma came half out of her seat in alarm. She didn't see the wave strike, but in the next flash the catwalk was awash in swirling foam and green water.

The waves had gotten a lot higher than she'd realized. Early on, she'd taken Gulf Stream high enough—twenty-four feet above mean sea surface—that even forty-foot waves shouldn't reach the catwalks. Much less crash down on them.

Emma called up the beanpole graphics and tried to make some sense of the wild fluctuations on the water level indicators. The readouts were all garbage, really; the seas were too confused to get a good measure of wave height.

Tugging her lower lip, Emma called up the buoyancy control screens. Air accumulators showed 70 percent, 72 percent, and 89 percent of capacity. Compressors were on standby, the controls set low to conserve diesel. All but two of Engineering's beanpole buoyancy compartments were filled with air, and the module lift indicator reported that Engineering was using 87 percent of design lift capacity just to stay afloat. Mariculture was creeping up to 81 percent of capacity, and Science and Residential both hovered at about 70 percent.

Taking lift capacity above 90 percent was forbidden except in emergencies.

If this wasn't an emergency, the operating procedures needed a rewrite.

She turned the compressors on manually, overriding the control. The storm's roar and the groaning structure masked the engines' noisy vibrations. As the accumulators began to fill, she brought up a detail of the buoyancy control schematics.

"What are you doing?"

"The waves are threatening the catwalks. I'm going to buoy us up some more."

"You sure you want to do that? We've already got an awful lot of bobbing and rolling. It'll only get worse."

"It'll be okay. She's bottom-heavy enough to take a little more height, and we have a few tons of lift to spare. I'm only going to take us up a little. A few feet at most." Emma changed the buoyancy set points to lift the catwalks another five feet.

On the module schematic, the second-from-the-bottom buoyancy compartment on the Engineering beanpole started to turn from blue to white. As the beanpole compartments filled with air and buoyancy pressures tumbled upward, the height indicators told them that the modules were creeping up on their beanpoles: a few inches, a foot, two, three feet, four, a few inches more.

An alarm trilled insistently; Emma acknowledged it and the beeping stopped, though a light continued to blink both on the buoyancy screens and on the alarm master screen over at the left end of the console.

"What? What was that?"

"Engineering has exceeded ninety percent of its lift capacity."

"Christ." Mac rubbed at his face, eyeing the screens. Emma dabbed at the sweat that had gathered on her lip.

After five minutes that took an hour to pass, the air flow to the lower beanpole tanks tapered off. Engineering buoyancy had stabilized at 95 percent of lift capacity, Mariculture at 89 percent, and the other two at just over 80 percent. Storm-caused fluctuations made it hard to tell precisely when, but shortly after that, the pole heights maxed out also. Mac noticed it, too. He pointed.

"Pole heights have stabilized."

Emma gave Mac a wry look. " 'Stabilized' isn't exactly the word I'd choose."

While the accumulators refilled, Emma switched the screens back over to the main systems displays and put the compressors back on automatic. The pitch and roll seemed worse; she hoped that was her imagination. It probably wasn't.

The readouts showed that the catwalks had risen by several feet. A little better. She slumped in her chair with a sigh.

Wind clapped at the door, making Emma's ears pop.

A moist draft stirred in the room; she slipped on Lee's tweed cardigan, which he'd left draped over the back of his chair. By the door, a pool of water had collected. She eyed it with a frown.

Mac sat slowly up and cocked his head, looking thoughtful.

"What?"

"You know . . ." He raised his eyebrows. "I think she's slacking off."

Emma listened. Gusts and water still blasted the windows; she couldn't tell any difference.

At her dubious look, Mac said, "I've been through a few. I can tell. She's not as strong. Listen."

Emma listened again, and after a few moments she could hear it. The storm's fury was slackening.

They both looked out the window. Winds were still fierce, but the other modules were now visible— bleared shapes and haloed, strobing lights amid the rain streaks. A hint of early morning light revealed numerous shapes: the orange lifeboats that clung like barnacles to the edges of the modules, turned a dull umber in the predawn; the grey, drenched shutters and walkways and battened-down lockers and cabinets.

"It's happening fast," Mac said. "It's the eye coming over."

Emma's fatigue vanished. She came to her feet, snatched up the headset.

"Get below," she told him. "Do a thorough check. If anything's amiss that we'll need extra muscle to fix, I want to know in time to get people over here and back during the eye."

She got on the radio and alerted the rest of the team, and had them run checks of their modules. "I want a full report of conditions as soon as you can get it to me."

Then she started a new pot of coffee, removed the pot and placed first one cup, then another, under the

stream of fresh, brown brew, and doused both with
evaporated milk. Mugs in hand, she hurried to the Engineering bullpen.

It always surprised her, faintly, how large and hollow the bullpen became when deserted. Dim fluores-
cence, the night lighting, made the white surfaces
glow. Even more so than usual, with the wailing wind
and Gulf Stream's creaks and moans underlying them,
the debris left by her engineers' hurried departure—
the half pot of cold coffee and calcified doughnuts on
waxed paper, the bits of litter on the floor—made the
place seem more empty, somehow. As if they'd never
be back.

She wound her way through the labyrinth of cubicles toward the back. Blueprints and posters of various
sorts—aircraft, a photograph of a space shuttle, mechanical mock-ups, a photo collage of the Everglades,
a wall covered in tacked-up cartoons, with the original
names whited out and Streamers' names filled in—
cluttered the cubicle walls, inside and out. Several cubicles had been left neat; others looked as though
they'd been ransacked. Though time was precious she
took a second or two to turn a desk light and computer
off, picked up and shelved a reference book that had
fallen to the floor.

Rob lay curled up on a cot next to one of the drafting tables against the front wall, snoring lightly with
his mouth open. Asleep he looked even younger than
when awake.

Rob had the tall, lanky look of a man barely out of
his teens, though in fact he was in his mid-twenties,
two years out of MIT's electrical engineering program.
His hair was ash blond, his complexion fair, his cheeks
wind-chapped. One arm hung limp over the edge of
the cot. He and Gloria, Emma thought. For how long?

"Rob?" Emma said softly. "Rob, wake up."

"What?" He woke with a start, skewing covers and staring at Emma in vague alarm.

"It's okay. The eye's about to pass over. I need your help in Control."

He grunted something, swung his legs off the cot, rubbed his eyes. "What time is it?"

"Almost seven. Here." She handed him the cup of coffee. "Why don't you hit the showers and freshen up? I'll meet you in Control in a few," she said. "Don't dawdle."

"Right." He stared blankly down at the coffee. She wasn't entirely convinced he knew what either of them was saying.

Back in Control, while she waited for Rob, she ran checks on the module rotation systems.

She was almost finished with her instrumentation checks when Rob showed up. He poured himself some more coffee and then dropped into the seat next to hers, puffy-eyed, wet-haired, and smelling of soap. Emma followed his gaze as he looked out the window.

The sky had cleared. Stormward, in the south and east, dark clouds piled high into the upper atmosphere, capping evil, impenetrable shadows. Below, all about them, violent white swill hurled itself into the air in gouts of spray, bashed at Gulf Stream's beanpoles, and tossed debris up onto the catwalk gratings. The floor pitched and rolled almost as much as it had during the storm. But overhead the predawn sky was calm, virtually cloudless: a gorgeous, raw, morning blue. All the visible ties and mooring cables hung slack.

"What would you like me to do?"

"Give Melbourne a call. We need a weather report; I want to know how fast the storm is moving and how much eye we're going to get. And once you finish that"—she handed him the headset—"check in with everyone for damage reports on the modules while I finish these rotation checks. With our wind instruments gone, I'm having to do everything manually and it's a pain in the butt.''

Rob donned his headset and muttered into his mouthpiece while Emma finished her checks. After a moment he moved the mike down away from his lips and reported, ''Satellite pictures show the storm moving due north at twelve knots. Gulf Stream is just now moving into the eastern fifth of the eye. Or rather, vice versa.''

''I get the idea.''

''Their best conservative estimate is that we have about twenty-five minutes of calm before the wind and rain pick back up.''

Emma nodded. ''Let's make the minutes count.'' She activated the module rotors. ''Ready to turn.''

''It's going to be a crude adjustment without our wind instrumentation. Maybe we should get more data from Melbourne.''

''Wouldn't do any good. They can't give us that level of accuracy. We'll just do a straight one-eighty and leave the modules unlocked to correct themselves as the winds pick back up. All hands,'' she said into her radio, ''prepare to come about.''

Emma repeated the alert. Then she typed in the commands that brought the modules around. With a reverberant ka-*chunk* that carried up through the soles of her feet, the module's locking mechanisms disengaged from the beanpole. A hum swelled up, and the other modules, also turning on their poles, began to creep clockwise into view. Meanwhile Rob switched to a local frequency on his console. ''Mariculture, give me your damage report.''

A grin broke on his face as he listened; he turned to Emma, a finger over the end of the mike.

''Gene says some of the northern lobsters have somehow gotten out of their tanks and are crawling all over the main deck''—Emma laughed—''and a few nonbreakables have fallen over in scuba storage on the utility deck. But it's nothing serious. No assistance needed.''

"Great."

"Science, damage report please?"

A moment later, "Gloria reports the last-minute battening-down job in Science held up beautifully. No problems there.'' He paused, listening, then covered the mike with his finger again. "Gloria gives the new guy high marks.''

"That's nice."

Rob looked at her, eyebrows high. "You really don't like him, do you?''

"What I *don't* like is the way we were saddled with him without my being involved in the interview process. It was a shitty thing for Pendleton to do.''

"I thought you got along okay with Pendleton.''

"So did I.'' She shrugged. "Maybe he just got a wild hair up his ass over this guy—or Hellman has an in with one of Pendleton's cronies. Though that's not really his style.''

"Maybe it's male menopause.''

Emma burst out laughing. "That sounds more like Dennis.'' After a pause she said, as her fingers played across the control keys, "I'm probably just going to have to be pissed about it for a while, till I get over it. But I guess I shouldn't take things out on Hellman. He's just trying to do his job.''

Rob gave her a sympathetic smile and said into his mike, "Engineering, damage report, please.''

A moment later, Rob said, "Emma, Mac says a solvent feed drum in the machine shop overturned. He's got it contained, but the fumes are really bad. He figures we should get it cleaned up while we can still ventilate the area. You want I should go give him a hand mopping it up?''

"Yeah. Wait, no. First get Residential's damage

control report. I want a complete picture before I start allocating resources.''

He got on the radio to Residential, then turned to Emma, his lips pulled down. "No interior damage, but some of the tarps got torn off the roof gardens and the plants are damaged. The storm has shredded or torn away a lot of the plants and stripped off some topsoil.''

Damn. Emma pinched the bridge of her nose. "Are any of the torn-off tarps still usable, or did they all get carried away?''

He spoke into his mike. Then, "Some are usable. Not nearly enough.''

"Tell them to use sheets and blankets if they have to, and retarp as best they can.''

"Shall we send somebody else over?''

Emma winced, shook her head. "Uh-uh. I don't want people moving back and forth out there unless absolutely necessary, and the gardens just aren't a high enough priority to risk lives for. Get me our spill expert.''

She picked up her handheld radio as Rob paged Keith. When he responded Emma said, "We have a drum of spilled solvent over here. Mac, you there?''

"Ten-four. Keith, it's a fifty-five-gallon drum of solvent we use in our tool-rinsing sink. Looks like a ladder that wasn't tied down toppled against it.''

"What's the material?'' Keith asked.

"Hang on.'' After a pause, "The drum says Alcomax Three, but I don't think the material is the same as the drum it's in. We switched solvents a while back, as I recall, but we've been reusing the drum as a reservoir because we had all the fittings set up just right. It stinks something fierce.''

"How much spilled?''

"The whole drum, almost. At least forty gallons, maybe more. It's all over the damn place, too.''

"Any drains for the stuff to go down?"

"Nah, I plugged the one drain in the area with a cork and a rag, so we're okay for the moment. We lost some of the stuff down it before I got to it, but probably not much. There was only a trickle when I got there. It's a long way from the sink."

"What is the drain for? Where does it go?"

"It's the drain for our steam clean unit. Usually it's just hot soapy water with a little grease. It goes to the wastewater treatment plant."

"Keith," Emma broke in, "what do you think?"

"I'd better come have a look."

"Ten-four," Emma said. "And hurry; we only have twenty minutes of calm."

"Emma," Mac cut in, "I still haven't checked the tanks and flare on the roof."

"Well, you wait right where you are till Keith gets there. Rob'll take care of checking the roof."

She gave a nod to Rob, who nodded back, grabbed a radio out of the office, and left.

Keith was telling Mac, "While you wait, I want you to shut off all ignition sources and stay out of the fumes. Okay?"

"You got it, Kimosabe."

Knowing Mac, Emma couldn't resist adding, "Which means don't light up around there, either."

"Of course not." Mac sounded insulted.

"And see if you can find out what material was in that drum," Keith said.

"Check Product Storage, Mac," Emma said.

"Where do you keep your MSDSs?" Keith asked.

"Our what?"

"Material Safety Data Sheets. They have the product safety and environmental information on them. You should have a file on it somewhere, I'd guess."

Emma snapped her fingers. "Right, I didn't know the acronym. There's a three-ring binder in the office here. I'll bring it down. I don't know if it's completely up-to-date, since Franz left.''

''Franz?''

''Our former environmental compliance person. I'll explain later.''

''Mac, I want you to go to the spill response closet,'' Keith went on, ''and load up the handcart with the following items. The explosimeter, the *large* wet-dry vac—the eighteen-gallon one. An open-top drum, a large crescent wrench—am I going too fast?''

Emma's eyebrows went up as he spoke. Not a bad memory of the spill response closet, for one walk-through.

''Nah, I got it. The big vac, an open-top drum, a crescent wrench. You want a bung-top drum for the stuff we get with the vac?''

''If there's room. If not, we can use the reservoir drum as a temporary measure. And also bring shovels and kitty litter. Plus two PPE kits.''

''PPE kits?'' Mac repeated, sounding confused.

Keith sounded amused. ''Personal Protective Equipment. More acronyms. You'll recognize them. They're black plastic suitcases with 'PPE' written on the side with red electrical tape.''

''Got it. I'll meet you with the elevator down at the catwalk.''

''On my way.''

''Keith?'' Emma cut in.

His voice came back, a little wary. ''Yes?''

''Wear a life vest while you're outside. We've got a lot of pitch out there.''

A hint of surprise colored his voice. ''Right.''

The modules had finished their rotation; Engineering now faced due west, where another distant pile of storm clouds climbed high into the sky.

Emma stuck her radio in its holster and went into the office to grab the black three-ring binder above the

super's desk labeled *Material Data*. Then she pulled
the outer door open and followed the walkway around
to the back till she could see the catwalk leading from
Science. Without the wind to mute it, the ocean's noise
was overpowering. She looked down.

The sea's surface *moved*. It heaved, coiled, whirled
into great peaks and valleys. Water rode the surface
of the waves like a confused, slickened sheet—sliding
across the surges, it struck bumps and sprayed outward—leapt up, then dropped in a cascade of white
collisions into the bucking, swirling morass.

It gave her vertigo.

Though the morning air was moist and still, it
seemed to hang close, filled with an oppressive patience: a promise of further violence. She hung on to
the rail, riding the slow rise and fall of the module,
and licked her lips, which tasted of salt. Her eyes
started to sting.

The Science elevator door opened then, down at the
catwalk level a few feet above the waves, and Keith
stepped out, decked out in an alarming orange life
jacket. He had rolled up the sleeves of his white
button-down shirt. She guessed that his black dress
slacks and expensive cowboy boots would be the
worse for wear, after this crossing and the spill
cleanup.

As the elevator door closed behind him he turned
his head and lifted his arm against a spray of seawater
that leapt up, spattering him. He hesitated at the brink
of the catwalk, looking down at the violent water.
Then he stepped out onto the grating.

Emma watched the crossover. Though he got quite
a soaking, Keith made it safely. He waved up at her
before stepping into the Engineering elevator and she
waved back, realizing only then how nervous she'd
been. Releasing her breath with an explosive *whoosh*,
she went back inside, binder under her arm.

*   *   *

She found them suiting up in the loading area of the
utility deck.

"Thanks," Keith said, taking the binder from her.
He set it on the floor next to him and finished taping
the cuffs of his Tyvek coveralls to the plastic booties,
while Mac struggled into his coveralls and zipped
them up. Emma squatted and helped tape Mac's cuffs
while Keith flipped through the pages.

"There," he said, pointing to a sheet labeled *Material Safety Data Sheet—OSHA Form 2010/Grease-
A-Way.* "Is that what you use?"

Mac squinted at the sheet and nodded. "Yep. That's
it."

Keith studied the ensuing several pages. "Mostly
toluene with ten percent phenol." He whistled.
"Yuck. Nasty stuff."

"It cleans the parts real good."

"So do a number of much less toxic compounds. I
hope you guys use gloves with this stuff. Oh, well."
He stood, pulled on his green neoprene gloves, and
studied the canisters on his full-face respirator. "Organic vapor and acid gas. These should do fine. We
really should have been fitted for our own respirators
ahead of time, but I'll show you how to do a quick fit
test. Then we can tape each others' gloves on and get
started."

Emma stood as well. "Keep me posted on your progress."

"You ain't going to hang around? It'll be a great
show." Mac brandished his respirator. "The 'Waste
Busters' in action. Live and in person."

Emma gave him a little smile. "I'll catch it on
video."

Exhaustion had seeped back into her muscles and behind her eyes; she decided to take the outer stairway

up instead of the elevator, to get her blood circulating again. It surprised her, how hard it was to climb the stairs.

The sea had gotten rougher, wind was picking up, the clouds had neared and grown more threatening. A drop or two of rain spattered her shoulders and head. She paused after only a few steps and lifted her radio.

"Residential, come in."

"Michael here."

"Status report."

"There's just too much damage, chief, and not enough cover. I gotta go; Terri needs a hand."

"Ten-four. All hands." Several droplets struck her in the face; she wiped the wet away, looking resentfully at the boiling vapor cells overhead. "All hands, the storm's moving back in. If you need to do anything outside, do it now and make it quick. I want everyone back inside in five minutes, max. Michael and Terri, that includes you. Copy that?"

The acknowledgments came in, one by one. Emma tucked the radio back into the holster, a little dejected herself.

She heard something and looked behind her. The wave had to have been eighty feet high, trough to crest. A great wave. A cliff of water. It was the pale green of antique jade. The morning light passed through it all but unimpeded; foam draped over it like fine lace; its tip glistened, curling as it raced toward Gulf Stream I.

Emma's knees went weak. She gripped the railing, staring. Then she started to run.

There was no way she could have gotten inside, or above its crest, in time.

It struck Gulf Stream, halfway up the windward sides of Engineering and Science, and water cascaded over their roofs. Metal screamed as the water crashed onto the catwalk, and it struck her, a slab of concrete smashing against her head and back. She flailed, weightless in a tepid green blur—choked on fishy, salty water that forced its way up her sinuses and down her throat.

Something hard struck the back of her arm. She jackknifed and grabbed it—a catwalk? A walkway stanchion? Wrapping an arm around it, she hugged it to her chest. Gravity grabbed her then and she dragged air into her lungs, coughing.

All her weight hung from that elbow joint—she dangled from the outside of the walkway railing, almost a full floor up from where the wave had struck her.

Emma swung a leg up and struggled back onto the stairway. There she lay, panting, dripping, and trembling, and stared down at the water below. I nearly died, she thought. She rolled onto her back, hands pressed hard against her face to force down the nausea. Not now, she thought. I'll come apart later. Not now. She pulled herself to her feet.

The catwalk between Science and Engineering, she saw then, had been shorn loose at Science by the wave's impact. It hung down into the water, attached at one connector: a hundred-fifty-foot steel saw, wielded by wave action, pointed straight down at the power plant. With the loss of the catwalk support, the bob and pitch felt more like that of a ship in rough seas now than a massive, stabilized, off-shore facility. And a slow *thump-gri-i-ind, thump-gri-i-ind* made the grating shiver beneath her hands. The edge of the catwalk was dragging across the power plant.

Emma grabbed for her radio. It was gone. With a curse, she ran back down the stairs to the utility deck, dodged around the carboys and crates and moving equipment to where Keith and Mac had last been. An intercom phone was mounted by the equipment cabinet. She snatched it up and dialed the control room.

"A wave——," she started, but Rob interrupted.

"I know. Everyone has checked in but Mac and Keith."

"Thank God. I'll check on them now and be back to you in a minute."

The door to the maintenance shop had been propped open, and fumes emanated from inside. Emma held her breath and went inside.

Keith and Mac, unrecognizable in papery white suits and black insectoid masks, stood at one end of the room, amid dikes of cat litter, looking around.

"Hey!" They looked up at her. "We have an emergency. Come outside *now*."

Then she stepped back outside, and bent over, panting, coughing.

Keith came out and stripped off his mask. Mac followed suit.

"What happened to you?"

"What hit us?"

She brushed their questions away. "Listen to me. The Science-Engineering catwalk. A freak wave struck it and it's broken away at the Science side."

"We wondered what the hell was going on," Mac said.

"The storm's coming up. We've got to get that catwalk out of harm's way. It's still attached at the Engineering side and pounding away on the power plant. Listen." She raised a hand. They heard it: the steady pounding and grinding that carried up into the soles of their feet.

"Mac, you'll have to get a cutting rod out there somehow, tie a line to the catwalk, and cut the walk loose so we can lower it beneath the water. Keith, I need you to help him."

A thoughtful expression came onto Mac's face. "That'll be tricky, chief."

Keith frowned. "Can't it wait?" He gestured toward the maintenance room with his mask. "There's a good thirty gallons or more of toxic spew in that room, swirling around in this pitch and getting all over everything, ruining valuable equipment. And there may be other drains we haven't located—which means your wastewater treatment plant bugs will all die. All I need is another fifteen minutes and I'll have it completely contained."

"Keith, we may not *have* fifteen minutes. That catwalk could put a hole in the power plant. If the power plant fills up with water it's going to act just like a lead weight—"

Mac went ashen. "Oh, my God."

"Can't you compensate for it?"

Mac answered the question for her. "Hell, no. We're almost at maximum lift now. We'll sink like a stone."

Keith looked back at Emma. She nodded.

He started stripping tape off his cuffs. "Tell me what you need me to do."

Chapter 12

The storm regained its full strength in the few minutes they spent gathering tools. Keith heaved a coil of wrist-thick rope over his shoulder, straightened with a grunt, and made his way across the quaking metal floor toward the elevator. The utility deck's main section tossed the storm's sounds, and its own structural groans, back and forth off the walls, crates, and machinery, in a deafening chorus of echoes.

The beanpole rose like a concrete tree trunk from the floor several yards away, disappearing through the ceiling fifteen feet overhead. He dragged the rope toward it. The rope rivaled his forearm in thickness and smelled faintly of fish. It took him three trips to lug the several hundred feet of coiled, dirty, algae-covered rope over to the elevator door set in the beanpole's interior.

Finally he dumped the last of the coils on the floor of the elevator and came back out. Mac, who was over near the mechanical room, choosing tools from shelves and putting them in a white plastic tool kit, pointed toward the narrow end of the deck as Keith approached, and shouted.

"Safety harnesses, there. Grab four."

They hung on hooks beneath the crane pulleys: shoulder- and seat-harnesses combined, made of orange nylon webbing. Keith turned one over in his hands, inspecting it. The harness appeared to be one-size-fits-all, with straps and buckles for adjustment. A stout brass ring rimed with pale, green-blue copper rust dangled from the belly clip that secured the harness, and a locking carabiner, also made of brass, grasped the ring. The carabiner was secured to a fifty-foot coil of 9/16-inch, high-visibility-yellow nylon rope. At the other end of the rope dangled a second locking carabiner.

He took four from their hooks—harness, rope, and all—and dumped them in the elevator, then ran back to help Mac carry the rest of the tools into the elevator, then wheel the dolly with the oxyacetylene rig. The storm's noise receded when Keith closed the beanpole door. He stepped aboard and the elevator started down. The rhythmic thumping and grinding of the catwalk on the power plant became more audible, ringing the beanpole walls like a bell and making the elevator shiver. Keith and Mac exchanged a look.

With an anxious intensity, Mac inspected the brass regulators on the oxygen and acetylene bottle heads, and then the hoses and the torch. He shook his head with a sigh.

"I knew it. Criminently. I wish those morons over in Mariculture would put things back the way they found them." He pulled a set of wrenches from the tool pouch hanging at his belt and took hold of the torch at the end of the oxygen and acetylene hoses. "They left the welding tip on. Call Emma for me, would you? Tell her we're on our way down. We're going to need Rob's help."

Keith passed the message along via his radio. Emma asked, "Why?"

The elevator settled with a lurch, and the door slid open on the crescent-shaped antechamber. The storm made plenty of noise down here, though not as much as in the echo-chamber utility deck. By speaking loudly and slowly, they could hear each other. Keith could also still hear the thumping of the catwalk on the power plant. The elevator door started to close; he found and flipped a toggle and the door reopened.

"She wants to know what we need Rob for," he said.

Mac stood, brushing off the knees of his coveralls, and dropped the welding tip into his tool pouch. "To belay us. We need someone inside while we're out there." He picked up two four-foot, inch-thick rods leaning against the wall, then grabbed the handle of the dolly and tipped it with a grunt.

Keith eyed the door opposite the elevator entrance: a gasketed metal door with a red neon Exit sign posted above it. The grey rubber seal flexed at each blow of wind and rain; water pooled on the floor. They would be within feet of the wave crests out there—or beneath them.

Mac read his expression and grinned. Tobacco stains tinted his teeth. "Nothing like a little excitement to liven up your day, eh?"

Keith grimaced. "I sure am glad of one thing. Make that two things."

"Oh yeah?"

"Yeah. It's a good thing this is an oxyacetylene rig and not an electric arc cutter."

Mac chuckled. "Well, we won't be using the torch to cut, but we're not using electricity, either. What's the second thing?"

"Sure am glad it's you doing the cutting and not me."

The radio crackled. "Keith, you still there?" It was Emma.

Keith relayed Mac's reply to her. Emma made a noise. "Rob weighs a hundred thirty-five pounds, max. I've got a good five inches and ten pounds on him. I'm coming down."

Keith heard Rob's voice in the background, cut off as Emma released her talk button. Mac sighed. "What a woman. If she had a dick, she'd be perfect."

Keith noticed Mac eyeing him as he said this, looking for his reaction. Odd time for a come-on; maybe it was just a statement of identity.

Keith raised his hand, like a kid answering a question in class, and said mildly, "I'll lend her mine."

Mac laughed, a short bark. Message received.

They began moving the equipment out of the elevator.

Emma brought foul-weather gear: waterproof jackets, pants, rubber deck boots, hats, and goggles.

"It'd be a shame to ruin those cowboy boots." She tossed Keith a bundle.

Keith followed her gaze toward the door and around the room. She appeared to be calculating something.

He lifted his eyebrows, and she answered the unspoken question.

"The door faces almost directly into the storm. We're going to get some serious flooding in here." Then she shrugged. "Can't be helped—the sump pumps will handle it."

Keith strapped the cutting rig to the elevator cage while Emma secured her own safety line and then drew Mac and Keith's lines around a pipe and secured the ends to some pipe clamps. Keith started putting on his rain gear. Getting the safety harness on over the raincoat gave him some difficulty.

Mac had already suited up and put on his safety harness, and was now checking the pressures on the tank regulators. He cranked the regulator second-stage valves farther open, then pulled on heat-resistant gloves and slid his welder's face shield on with the darkened plastic tipped up. His flint in hand, Mac turned a valve on the hose fitting to start the acetylene flow to the tip.

He struck a spark in the gases' path and a sooty, candlelike flame flowed out and up, billowing in the faint draft. Mac's hand moved across the valves on the hose fitting; the flame shot forward, blue-white and clean. Keith felt its heat on his cheeks.

Keith measured out about sixty feet of the big, smelly rope, using his arm length as a measure. He tied the end around his waist and secured it with a bowline, then coiled the remainder of the sixty feet up and hefted it over his shoulder. The rest of the rope he left in a mass of coils near the door. Then he pulled his goggles down.

"One tug for more slack," Mac told Emma, "two for you to reel us in, and three to take up slack and hold steady. Okay?"

"One for more line, two for less, and three to take up slack and hold," Emma said. "Got it."

At Mac's insistence, Keith repeated the signals also. Mac lowered his face shield and braced himself beside the door. They both looked back at Emma, who was braced between two pipes near the elevator.

"Keith," she said, "it'd be great to get the catwalk secured so we don't have to salvage it from the ocean floor later. But the most important thing is to stop it banging on the power plant. If Mac gets done cutting before you get the rope secured around the beanpole and tied to the catwalk, you're to abort and let it go down. Got that?"

"You don't care if you lose the catwalk?"

"Nah." She grinned. "We won't lose it. We'll just send Mac down in the sub to fetch it."

Mac rolled his eyes. "I hate that damn thing. Makes me claustrophobic. Make Rob go this time, or Oleg or Steve."

"We'll discuss it later," Emma said.

Mac nodded. "Fair enough. Ready?" When Keith and Emma nodded, he pulled one of the rods over and said to Keith, "You get the door open the minute this thing ignites or we're gonna choke on the fumes."

"What is it?" Keith asked.

"Mostly magnesium, part rocket fuel. It's a cutting rod. Once it's lit, it doesn't go out. We use 'em underwater. But a wind this strong could blow out the welding torch, so first we light the rod—then we open the door. Got it?"

Keith rested his hand on the latch. "Let's do it."

Mac put the torch to the tip of the rod. It slowly turned red in the dim antechamber. Keith was about to ask Mac if he'd picked up a piece of steel rebar by mistake when the tip suddenly lit in a flash of brilliant white light.

Keith disengaged the latch, and a blast of water and wind forced the door fully open, yanking it out of his grasp. Keith went to his knees. By the time he had regained his feet Mac had already gone out; his safety line disappeared out the door. Keith grabbed Mac's safety line and fought his way out.

Vision vanished in a grey blur; the shrieking stole his hearing. The wind slammed him back against the outside wall by the door and rain bullets peppered his face and hands. The wind's force made it hard to breathe.

Keith gripped the edge of the door and gave one sharp tug on the safety line at his belly. As the line slackened he bunched his leg muscles and threw himself in the direction he knew the railing to be.

Metal struck him in the chest, knocking the wind from him. He gripped the railing. A faint shape, barely visible, appeared when he lifted his hand before his face. He began to fear Mac had been swept over the side.

Then he spotted a white light, off to his right. He ducked under Mac's lines, and stumbling past what must have been Mac's hunched shape on the pitching deck, he let out lengths of the heavy rope. Suddenly the wind lifted him off the ground—he whipped around, suspended kitelike on his safety line. Somehow he managed to shove another couple of coils of rope off his shoulder, without dropping the whole mass, before his calves struck the downwind rail.

Keith climbed down and hung on. Three sharp tugs jerked at his belly; Emma wanted to know if he wanted her to hold steady. Keith fumbled for his safety line, tugged three times. *Hold steady*. The line tautened, stabilizing him.

He tried to catch his breath. Two-thirds of the beanpole's circumference to go—and he'd done most of the easy part already. He should have gone in the upwind direction first.

Keith tugged once and his line loosened; he proceeded to pull himself along the railing, across the wind and then into its face, letting out rope. His footing slipped; he grabbed at the railing and spent a handful of terrifying seconds clinging to it, airborne, feet straight out behind him, till he could hook his legs around the rail and climb back down. Then he dropped the coils of rope. He tried to scoop it back up using his feet. No luck. So he went to his knees, then his belly, and pulled himself and the rope along the metal grating. The going got a little easier then, but it seemed hours before he saw the dark hole in the beanpole that told him he'd made it all the way around.

Keith splashed inside on his hands and knees, dragging the last few feet of the heavy rope. He had circumscribed the beanpole.

In a comparatively calm space beside the door, he climbed to his feet, wiped water from his face, and heaved great breaths. His arms burned from the toxins produced by overexertion; his cheeks and forearms were numb from the rain's pounding.

Emma stared at him. She was a sight: drenched head to foot, eyes so fatigue-sunken the skin beneath them looked bruised, ropy hair tendrils in her face, a shoulder and both feet braced against pipes, hands clutching yellow nylon line. The sight of her burned into his mind in a way that disturbed him.

Rain flew in through the door, and waves spilled more water over the threshold. Keith was amazed he'd been able to breathe at all out there.

"Okay?" she shouted.

He was too exhausted to shout. He gave the *okay* hand signal, then pointed at the carabiner at his belly and made a horizontal circle in the air with his forefinger. Emma looked confused—then nodded as he unhooked the carabiner. She hauled his line in one-handed, and as it came back in from its reverse trip around the beanpole he snatched it up and reattached it.

Keith made a bowline knot in the heavy rope, attaching the end he'd taken around the pole and the portion that led outside from the coils piled on the floor. He then rooted under the coils and found the other end of the heavy rope. He coiled up another fifteen feet over his shoulder.

"Hurry!" Emma shouted.

He gave her an *okay* signal again and plunged back out into the storm.

Mac squatted at the railing, an outline silhouetted by the harsh light of the cutting rod. Keith swiped vainly at his goggles and crouched behind Mac to see how much progress he had made. A wave struck and steam exploded in Keith's face; he flinched with a yell of surprise and pain. How could Mac work in these conditions?

He leaned forward again, more cautiously. Mac hung on to the railing with one hand and wielded the rod with the other. The flame seemed to be moving around an awful lot.

Mac squinted up at him. His face shield was gone, as was his rain hat. Keith saw his mouth move but couldn't hear a word. Clearly, though, things weren't going well. He hadn't even gotten through the first strut.

Another wave struck, releasing a steam blast. Keith dodged and swore. He'd just risked his life getting the big rope around the beanpole. But Mac needed both hands free. Which meant Keith had to stabilize him, which meant securing the catwalk with the big rope had to be aborted.

He tied the big rope to the railing—maybe they'd get a chance to use it later—and gave three tugs on his safety line. The slack was drawn up. He swung around behind Mac, who lay down and stuck his head out beyond the railing. Keith crouched and sat down on Mac's lower back, grasping the deck beneath Mac's arms.

Mac started cutting. Steam and flecks of molten metal seared Keith's unprotected arms; he hung on and tried to distract himself. The image of Emma holding the lifelines floated into his mind.

Then the deck shuddered. Mac made an *okay* signal in front of Keith's face. One strut cut free. He expected Mac to move over to the other strut, but Mac slapped his arm and pointed at the big rope knotted on the rail. Mac was offering to stabilize him while he secured the catwalk, before starting on the remaining strut. Keith grimaced, remembering what Emma had said earlier.

He tugged once on his line, then groped for the big rope, and untied it. Mac pointed the flame away and shifted around behind him as Keith moved downwind. Clinging to the rail with one hand and supported at the waist by Mac, he stuck his head and arm out beneath the railing and felt around.

He got a noseful of water as a wave struck. His hand found the still-warm stump of the cut-away hinge. He wormed his way over till his hand touched the other strut, hinged about six inches below the deck level. Then he tugged three times on his line, slapped the backs of his legs, cueing Mac to hang on, and, once supported, stuck his head, both shoulders, and both arms out beyond the railing.

Getting the rope around the strut and knotted came surprisingly hard. Muscle fatigue, the awkward angle, and the wind and waves conspired to make him clumsy. He swallowed salt water and his back banged the rail with every wave. A large D-clip would have made the operation much simpler; they'd needed more time to prepare.

Finally he got the rope looped in a figure eight around a vertical and horizontal support, below the hinge. He knotted the thick rope and pulled it as taut as he could: a sloppy-feeling bowline knot. He hoped it would hold.

Then he crawled out of the way and Mac moved in again, wielding the torch.

Moments later, another shudder shook the deck, and Mac shoved him back as the big rope snapped tight between their feet, nearly tripping them. They fought their way upwind to the door with help from Emma, stumbled back inside, and fell against the wall by the door. Keith doubled over, blowing salt water out his nose.

When he looked up Emma gave him a brief smile, but her attention was on the coils of rope. The rope was unfurling fast, coil by coil like a snake, and tumbling out the door. The last coil slipped out finally, yanking Keith's knot out across the threshold. The floor took a shock as the falling catwalk reached the end of the rope.

It took all three of them to close the door.

Rob was standing by when they entered the control room. They hung their rain gear on hooks along the wall and pulled off their deck shoes. Rob handed them beach towels and brimming mugs with buttery, alcoholic, sweet-smelling steam rising from them.

Keith's towel had Roger Rabbit on it. He set his mug down and buried his face in Roger's chest. His muscles had turned to Jell-O during the ride up in the elevator; he'd started to tremble and now couldn't stop. His ears were ringing.

The storm seemed so much quieter in here that he began to wonder if it was dying down. But no, it was too soon.

"Hot toddies," Rob said, when Mac took a whiff and raised his eyebrows. "With a splash of Cuervo Gold, from my private stock. I figured you guys could use it."

"The emergency's not over yet." Emma set her mug down, dried her hair vigorously, and went over to the console with her towel wrapped around her head. "Hold off for a bit, guys."

"I only used a dash," Rob said. "Honest."

Emma still looked dubious, but that was enough for Keith. With shaking hands he took as big a gulp as the near-scalding temperature would allow. Warmth spread down his throat.

Emma looked at Keith, then at Mac, who was slurping from his cup. Then she said, "What the hell," took a gulp of her own toddy, and sat down at the console.

Mac sank into a chair and slumped over his arms. Keith took another gulp of the hot toddy and felt his body relaxing; his trembles grew larger and looser, like the vibrations in a slackening wire. He sighed.

"Why are the sump pumps running?" Emma asked, then swore.

Mac croaked, "We took a lot of water through that door."

"Not the dock level sump pumps—the *plant* sumps. We have a leak!"

Keith and Rob came up on either side of her, and Mac lifted his head.

Rob said, "I was about to tell you. It's not serious."

"Where is it?" Keith asked, sitting. A graphic sketch of a rectangular torus in blues and purples turned slowly on the screen, filled with arcane engineering symbols, geometric shapes, and a network of lines: the OTEC plant. Alarms blinked red. Emma froze the perspective and tapped keys; the colors grew muted. With a few exceptions—at an upper corner, a box blinked bright red. Other red lights flickered lower down.

"The leak is up here, at the top edge." Emma pointed. "These lower red lights are alarms being triggered as the water flows down the inner wall. This readout down here is the sump level indicator.''

"I've got both sump pumps operating at full capacity," Rob said. "They're emptying it out."

"But they're not! Look. The sump is filling. Slowly, but it's filling."

Rob frowned at the screens. "It's gotten worse. I swear I just checked it a few minutes ago and it was practically empty."

"Hang on." Emma called up a few screens, ran her finger like a wand across the schematics. "You're right—it *has* gotten worse. Right about the time we cut the catwalk free."

"You mean cutting the catwalk free made things *worse*?" Keith asked.

Emma gave him a pained glance over her shoulder. "It went down hard and fast. Maybe it banged things up on the way down." She jotted down some numbers from the screen and scribbled some calculations on the back of one of the pages from the clipboard. "It leaked for twenty minutes at a slow rate and about nine minutes at this faster rate; let's see. You say the sump was actually emptying on your last check?"

"Absolutely." Rob's tone was anxious. "It was down to an inch at the drain end, at most."

"Then we'll assume it was empty when the larger leak started. The sump has about eight inches of liquid now, and both pumps are operating at their full capacity of one hundred GPM—do you remember offhand what the sump capacity is?"

"No. I could go look it up; we have the as-builts in the bullpen."

"Do that."

"It's seven hundred forty gallons," Mac said, lifting his head. "I counted every goddamned gallon, last year, when I was having to manually empty that sucker with the diesel pump, before we got the new sump pumps in."

"Thanks." Emma scribbled some more. Meanwhile Mac gave Rob a questioning glance; Rob only shook his head, looking miserable.

"The plant is taking on water at about two hundred fourteen gallons a minute," Emma said. "The pumps are taking care of two hundred of that, so we have a net intake of fourteen gallons a minute."

"That doesn't sound so bad," Keith said.

Emma didn't look happy. "It means the sump will be full in less than twenty minutes, and the plant will start taking on about four feet of water every hour. That gives us about eight hours before the loss of buoyancy puts the facility at risk."

Rob groaned and buried his head in his hands. "The power plant will be ruined. We're shut down."

Emma punched him, gently. "Relax. It's not *that* bad. The power plant has plenty of spare buoyancy for now, and we have a few hours before the equipment will begin to be seriously affected. The more water-sensitive, specialized equipment is up on the mezzanine. And if the storm keeps moving at its current pace, it should blow over in the next three to four hours. At that point we can bring the OTEC plant up above sea surface, and we'll have all the time we need to find and repair the leak."

"*If* she doesn't stall overhead," Mac said in a morose tone. "And *if* one of the pumps doesn't suddenly make up its mind to quit working."

"You're starting to sound like Lee," Emma said. "If we have to, we'll bring the plant up before the storm passes over. Let's not manufacture more bogeys for ourselves." Emma massaged the back of her neck. "For now we have a problem that isn't life-threatening yet, and a little time before we need to do anything about it. Mac, check the as-builts, anyhow, to make sure we have the sump capacity and pumping rates right. We can't afford to be wrong in our calculations."

"Right."

"And Rob, give us a countdown clock on the right-hand screen. Start it at eight hours and zero minutes."

Rob's hands moved over the keys, and a big graphic of a watch appeared on the far right screen, with a digital readout that immediately changed from an 8:00:00 to a 7:59:59, and continued down from there.

"And maybe—" She frowned at Rob. "Do we have enough diesel to run the air compressors continuously for at least eight hours?"

He seemed surprised. Keith and Mac exchanged glances.

"Would it help?" Keith asked.

"Sure," Rob said simultaneously. "No prob. But why?"

"We could maybe slow the leak a little by pressurizing the plant's interior."

"Or by raising the plant a ways," Rob said. "But it's not going to make any real difference. The plant's going to take on water till we can raise it above water and repair the leak. It'd be a waste of fuel and air to pressurize, and it'd put the plant at more risk from the storm if we raise it. I think we're just going to have to wait."

Emma nodded. Her shoulders slumped and she rubbed her face. "I feel helpless."

Keith had a sudden urge to put an arm across her shoulders. Instead he inspected the angry red sores and blisters, weld and steam burns, that dotted the backs of his hands and forearms. They were starting to throb and sting.

"Do we have any antiseptic?"

"Jesus," Rob said, eyeing Keith's arms with a look of dismay. "Come on, the first-aid station's in the head. How about you, Mac?"

"What?"

"You have any burns you need treated? Or anything else? We have a special on fractured tibias."

Rob's joke didn't even raise a smile; they were all too exhausted. Mac inspected his arms. "Nothing worth bothering with. I had gloves on." He shoved himself to his feet. "Listen, chief, I'm going for those as-builts, and then I gotta get some sleep. I'm dead."

"Mac"—Emma turned, a thoughtful light in her eyes—"I hate to do this to you, but . . ."

"But?"

"Would you be willing to give me twenty, thirty more minutes?"

"For what?"

"It occurs to me. If we cross-connect one of the nitrogen purge mains in the hydrogen plant with the air line that goes down into the OTEC plant—"

"—we can put a nitrogen blanket on the plant and stop rust damage to the equipment. Yes." Rob looked pleased. "It doesn't help with buoyancy, but at least it buys us more time from the standpoint of preventing saltwater damage." He called up the storage tank schematics, ran a finger across the screen. "And we've got plenty of nitrogen—one hundred and eighty thousand standard cubic feet. Except it won't be perfect; we can't eliminate *all* the oxygen."

"But we'll slow oxidation down." Emma looked at Mac again. "I know you're beat. I promise this won't take long. If you'll just show Rob what to do, he'll be your muscle."

"I'm game," Rob said. "*I* got four hours of sleep last night, unlike you two."

Mac made a face. "Hell, I can do it, myself, if Rob'll help me out. I'm not that big a feeb. Come on, kid."

Rob caught a glimpse at Keith's burns again. "Shit. Your arms."

"I'll take care of Keith," Emma said, waving Rob and Mac out the door. "Go."

Keith followed Emma out the door, but stopped at the threshold to the corridor. "The spill. Damn. I've got to clean it up."

Emma eyed him, cocking her head back and forth; a gesture he was coming to recognize. "First aid, first. Come on." She gestured for him to follow her to the lavatory down the hall.

While washing her hands, she asked, "How long would the spill cleanup take?"

Keith hesitated, resisted the temptation to underexaggerate. "A while. Couple hours, maybe."

"And how much sleep did you get last night? Here, sit." She put the lid of the toilet seat down. He sat. She put a basin in his lap and pulled the first-aid kit down from a cabinet by the sink.

"Some." Two hours, maybe; he'd tried to sleep for a while, but had gotten up finally and spent most of the early morning hours going over the sample logs. Some odd anomalies had started to turn up.

"How much is 'some'? You look like you just stepped out of *Night of the Living Dead*."

"Thanks a lot."

"No charge." She poured Betadyne over his sores and scrubbed gently with gauze; it smelled like chemicals but looked like blood, or burgundy, and left a yellow residue. He maintained a stoic expression against the sudden stinging.

"The spill is contained, isn't it?" she went on, and looked up at him. "You should see yourself, Keith. You really are a mess. Fifteen, twenty minutes I could see, but two hours? And I may need you later, as rested as possible. The emergency is far from over."

Keith pursed his lips. "You're going to lose equipment and supplies, then. The organic fumes are going to render any plastic and rubber parts in that room useless. And you may lose use of the room for a while.''

Emma nodded. ''And space is at a premium.'' She pulled out a packet of antibacterial ointment and clipped off a corner, looking thoughtful. She tore open another gauze packet and squeezed a glob of clear gel onto the gauze. ''But no one is in danger from the spill, and the solvent isn't going anywhere. I think you should leave it till after the storm, when you're better rested and have some trained backup.''

Keith frowned. Leaving a toxic spill uncleaned rubbed him the wrong way. He thought about the open sores on his arms, the tremors in his muscles, the ache of fatigue behind his eyes.

''I want to at least check it out and see how the containment is holding.''

''All right. You can radio me from there with a status report.''

He watched the top of her head as she dabbed ointment onto his hands and arms, surprised at how light and sure her touch was; her manner had always been so brisk, almost rough.

The touch felt good.

''That was fine work you did out there, Hellman,'' she said as she worked, and looked up. ''And before, catching the problems in Science, and the sewer line problem. If we hadn't had you here, things could have been pretty bad. A lot worse than they are.'' She paused. Color came into her cheeks. ''Sorry I was so rough on you.''

Keith smiled at her, reflecting that, on the whole, things might have been a little easier if she'd kept on hating him.

Keith stood at the door to the maintenance room. The spill had spread all over one end of the room. Shiny brown liquid pooled at the vermiculite dikes he and

Mac had laid down, and at the bases of work counters and equipment. A pungent, gluey-sweet smell seeped past the rubber seal of his respirator.

He hated to admit it but Emma was right: the spill wasn't going anywhere. And he was in no condition to remediate it.

Outside the room, he stripped off his respirator.

"The containment is holding," he radioed Emma. "It can wait."

He barely remembered stumbling up to the bullpen to fall onto a cot before he was out.

Chapter 13

GABRIEL: **Friday, 2 October, 9:00 A.M. MDT**
Airport La Quinta Inn, Albuquerque

They arrived, per her instructions, at the La Quinta on Yale near the airport. She had rented the room the night before and cautioned them about being seen when they came into town.

They entered the room and blinked in the comparatively dim hotel room, waiting for their eyes to adjust. She had spread towels on the counter by the sink and the floor. On this surface were dozens of small bottles, jars, tubes, and plastic Baggies.

"What's going on?" Mark asked.

"Time to change your looks, and your IDs."

"Even Jax and me?"

"Even you two," Gabriel said. "Let's not take any chances."

Boadica pointed at Jax. "How long have you had that beard?"

Jax stroked it with his fingers. It was thick and bushy, and covered his face all the way up his cheekbones. "Since '92,'93, I guess. Shortly after I got out of the service. I shaved it off for a while last year—not for long."

"Good. Off it comes. Use the bathtub; I'm going to need the sink." She tossed him a can of shaving cream, scissors, and a pack of disposable razors. "Be sure to clean up after yourself."

He had a frown, and looked like he was going to argue, but Gabriel's glance silenced him. He squeezed past her into the bathroom. Meanwhile, Boadica scrutinized Mark. "We're going to put a few years on you, and add a mustache. Sit down. For the flight we'll use a false one, but stop shaving the lip. We'll see if we can have the real thing by the end of the week."

While she worked on Mark, Gabriel started going through the national papers he'd picked up at a university newsstand, looking for environmental articles, and collecting the reporters' bylines in a notepad.

The room soon reeked of chemicals.

After a bit, Mark said, "How do we look?"

Gabriel set the paper he was reading aside and looked them over. Jax without a beard—and she had trimmed his hair and added a few streaks of grey—looked like someone else entirely: someone ten years older. The beard had hid a square jaw with a cleft chin and thick lips. She must have stained the lower part of his face somehow, too, because the lower half of his face appeared as tan as the upper. He gave Gabriel a big grin and wiggled his eyebrows.

Mark, too, looked older. His hairline had been shaved back and touches of grey added to the hair that remained. His eyebrows were also streaked with grey, and he now sported a mustache like a big Brillo pad on his upper lip that changed the lower half of his face.

Their families might recognize them, but strangers working from photographs and verbal descriptions wouldn't.

"Have we met?" Gabriel asked. They both laughed.

Boadica stood them up against the off-white hotel wall and took pictures.

"What are those for?" Gabriel asked.

"Your new IDs."

Then she cocked a finger at him. Gabriel came over and sat down in the chair she had set up before the hotel room mirror. On the counter before him were all her makeup tools—brushes, spatulas, sticks, and assorted pots and bottles of goop and dye. Then she studied his face, tilting his head this way and that. She took hold of his ponytail and fingered his hair; he was suddenly, unaccountably nervous. He hadn't cut his hair since college. Samson and Delilah, Cervantes? he thought scornfully. How vain.

"I'm going to change your face a little, shave off your mustache, cut your hair, and bleach it from black to brown. You're fair-skinned enough we can make you an Anglo."

Gabriel scoffed. "With my accent? I'm Chicano. No way anyone will think I'm a *gringo.*"

"So disguise your accent."

"We're going over to Goody's for some breakfast," Jax said. "No way we'll be recognized, right?"

"Go," Gabriel said. "I'll be there in a while."

She got to work, while he muttered assorted phrases, talking like an Anglo. In fact he had always had a pretty good ear for dialect; with a little practice, he could probably pull off a twang that a Texan might guess was false, but not many others.

First she had him shave off the mustache. Then she cut his hair, wet it, and put a strong chemical on it that made his eyes sting. She wrapped his head and had him leave it on for a while; he went back to reading the papers. Then she had him rinse out the chemical in the shower and applied a brown dye to his hair. More waiting, more reading.

"I can't believe women pay to have this done to them," he said, though he was enjoying her touch, her proximity.

Finally she had him rinse out the dye. Cool water poured over his head and, brown-stained, swirled down the drain. Then he returned to the chair and sat down.

Boadica held his right eye open—"Hold still"—and put a contact lens in it. He yelped. "One more." Deftly, swiftly, she popped another into his left eye. He doubled over; she grabbed his wrists before his hands made it to his face. "Don't rub. They'll come out."

"Jesus, Mary, and Joseph! *Take them out!*"

"Relax. You'll get used to them in a few minutes."

While he held on to the chair arms, gritted his teeth, and cursed—vision blurred, eyes insulted, watering and burning, as if invaded by sand—she applied some putty to his nose and inserted shaped rolls of wax between his upper teeth and gums. By the time she was done the lenses had ceased bothering his eyes quite so much, and his vision was stable, unless he blinked.

"There." She stood back and looked at him, fiddled with his nose a bit more and, finally, nodded. "That'll do." She stepped out of his way and he saw his reflection.

It was a shock. The man looking back at him bore a strong resemblance to Gabriel Cervantes, but was definitely not the same man. The hair was very short now, and dark brown rather than blue-black; eyes a lighter brown—closer to hazel; cheeks and nose all wrong.

He rubbed at his hair. To his surprise it felt good—cool and lightweight. He hadn't been aware just how heavy all that hair had been. "Jesus. I'm practically bald. I look so . . . so straight. Next thing, you'll put me in a business suit."

A smile flitted across her face. "Not a bad idea—maybe later."

"No way." Gabriel touched his face and leaned close, examining the false contours of his nose. He touched his cheeks where the wax pushed his rather narrow face out. It was slightly uncomfortable, but the effect looked natural. He just hoped he wouldn't cough a roll of wax in somebody's face. He tried the Texas accent. "Not bad. Not bad at all, little lady."

She nodded once, smiling, accepting the compliment.

"But what will Emma think?" he added. "I don't know . . ."

"She'll attribute the changes to time," Boadica said, "or her faulty memory. Don't worry about it. I have lots of experience with this sort of thing and have never had a problem."

He took his turn in front of the camera. Then, while she cleaned up the counter, he gathered up his papers and watched her for a moment.

"Bo . . ." he said.

She stood and turned around. Neither said anything for a moment. But she felt it, too; he was certain.

I don't even know your real name, he thought. I don't know who you are. He put his hand on the door. "We'll be waiting."

She hesitated. Then looked down at her watch. "Three hours, Gate Six-B. I'll have the IDs and the plane tickets. Everybody's packed for carry-on, right?"

He nodded.

"—so we won't have to use the ID until we check in at the gate after we rendezvous. Got it?"

"Claro que sí."

She smiled. *"Bien."*

Chapter 14

"Wake up, Hellman." Someone jostled his arm. "Come on, rise and shine."

Keith forced his eyes open. Mac stood over him, looking like he felt: eyes bloodshot and puffy, his bristly salt-and-pepper hair sticking out all over his head.

"Emma needs us in Control."

Keith dragged himself upright, groaning, and ran fingers through his own tangled hair. His muscles had stiffened to the point of rigor and his mouth tasted like a sewer. Something else seemed wrong, too—something he couldn't quite finger.

Then it struck him. Stillness. He wasn't hearing the storm's roar outside the walls. The floor wasn't trembling. He looked at Mac. "The storm?"

"Passed over."

Keith slumped with a sigh. "Thank God."

"We've still got problems. You better hurry."

He turned and headed out. Keith glanced at his watch: two hours and fifty minutes' sleep. As he zipped up his slacks he thought, I deserve a raise for this. He made a mental note to bring the subject up with Jennifer when next they spoke.

Emma paced the control room with the restless energy of a pent-up cheetah. Her eyes were red-rimmed and a bit wild. He doubted she'd gotten any rest yet. Rob sat at the console. Keith glanced at the clock on the far right screen; it read 5:42.

"Status?" she asked.

Keith followed her gaze out the window and had a shock. The other modules were gone. As he neared the window, he spotted Mariculture at the extreme right. The clusters of orange buoys bobbing on the swells in the window's left quadrant, with greenish blobs beneath them, had to be the reef; the modules had been rotated to face east.

Soggy sargasso weed the color of brown mustard was strewn across the deck and railing. Beyond, mid-day sunlight drenched water blue as sapphires, creating a vast field of sparkles. Cotton-puff clouds floated in an astonishing turquoise sky; gulls, terns, and albatross circled overhead a few hundred feet out, dipping down to skim the water's surface. One big tern rose with a fish struggling in its beak. Near the birds, curved grey dorsal fins rolled across the big, foamblanketed swells: a pod of porpoises, making a meal of whatever school of fish the birds were feasting on.

The sunlight, and sea life, lifted his spirits.

"Still jammed," Rob said to Emma.

Keith limped over to the coffeepot and poured himself a cup. He took a slug. It smelled vile, tasted hot, strong, and bitter, and cut through the gluey residue in his mouth. He swung and flexed his arms, trying to loosen them up.

"Try resetting the pistons one more time," Emma said.

Rob turned back to the controls and fiddled around.

"Damn it. This is driving me crazy. I've got to know what's going on down there." Emma turned. "Mac, head over to Mariculture and get Bowser into the water."

"You've still got fifteen-foot waves out there. I don't think it's such a hot idea—"

"I don't feel like arguing about it!"

Mac's jaw set. Emma sighed and tugged her hair back, which had fallen into her face.

"Just do it," she said.

Mac looked sullen. "Don't blame me if we lose him."

"Nobody's going to blame you."

With a sigh, Mac pulled the door open. Through it Keith glimpsed seven people approaching on the Mariculture-to-Engineering catwalk. He recognized Gloria, Jess, and Nikki. The door slammed.

Emma gave Keith a wry smile. "Mac's never been the same since we lost our other ROV last month."

Rob burst out laughing. "That's not the problem. When it comes to his job he's an opinionated son of a bitch. But a good mechanic." Then he said, "No. Still jammed."

"Damn it!"

"What's going on?" Keith asked.

"We think the catwalk may have damaged one of the OTEC plant's buoyancy tanks," Rob said. "It's not filling when we try to blow ballast. All we get is a lot of bubbling at the surface."

"A tank leak," Keith said.

Rob nodded. "It looks that way."

"You don't have enough spare buoyancy to bring the plant up without that one tank?"

"The problem isn't buoyancy—not yet, anyway. It's uneven lift. With one ballast tank failing, the plant rises higher on one side than the other, which makes the annular locks jam on the beanpole."

"Annular locks?"

"They're large O-rings—more like a solid giant tire thirty feet in diameter—set in the throat of the power plant," Emma told him, making a circle with her hands, "and they extend into the annulus between the plant and the beanpole. They're for locking the plant in place. There are pistons above and below them, and when the pistons compress them, they expand sideways and grab onto the beanpole. And there's not a lot of clearance between the locks and the beanpole, even when they're disengaged. When we try to lift the plant"—she tilted her ringed hands—"the tilt makes the locks jam against the pole, even when they're supposedly disengaged."

So the plant was stuck down at forty feet, slowly filling with water. At four feet an hour, that meant twelve feet of water in there so far. Hundreds of thousands of dollars' worth of machinery had to have been ruined by now. Though—he glanced at the clock—they still had five and a half hours to figure out what to do about it.

The bigger problem was that they were slowly losing the buoyancy the submerged, airtight plant provided. And she'd said earlier that a water-logged OTEC plant could take the entire structure down.

No wonder Emma looked like an explosive charge about to go off.

"Give me a report on wind, wave height, and current flow," she said.

"Wind is a steady twenty-seven knots, currently out of the east, east-southeast. Wave height ranging between fifteen and sixteen feet. Current is four-point-two knots." Rob looked at Emma. "It's diveable, you know. We can descend on the catwalk line and moor ourselves to it while we do repairs."

Emma looked dubious. "Is that safe?"

"No!" Keith broke in. "First of all, you can't go down the catwalk line unless you want an embolism when the first wave trough passes overhead. With those waves there'll be significant pressure changes, even at depth. A diver draws a lungful of air during a wave peak, in the next second he'll be beneath a trough. Instant depth change. The volume of air in his

lungs will increase like that." He snapped his fingers.
"Ruptured lung tissue, blood in the lungs. Embolisms
are usually fatal. Or he'll end up with ruptured eardrums or sinuses."

Rob shook his head. "I didn't mean we'd physically
go down the catwalk line. We have plenty of DPVs.
We can free-float down on those, following the line.
The wave action will carry us with it, so we won't be
at risk in the shallow depths. And the volume change
effect decreases with depth. Once we're down at forty
feet, the effects will be minimal. And I've done repairs
on the plant in ten-foot waves. All I got was a little
ear popping and a squeeze in the sinuses."

"Don't dive SOPs specify a maximum wave height
of six feet for routine work dives and ten feet for emergency dives?" Emma asked, frowning.

Rob shrugged. "Well, yeah, but they're mostly intended for reef work, at twenty to thirty feet down.
We're talking forty feet. It makes a big difference."

"I still say a fifteen-foot depth change at forty feet
isn't minimal," Keith said. "I grant you it may be
manageable, with experienced, careful divers."

Rob turned to Emma. "Like I said. It's doable."

Keith nodded thoughtfully at Emma's questioning
glance. "It's doable. With experienced divers. *If* we're
all very cautious. How many hours have you logged?"
he asked Rob.

"A hundred hours or so."

"Work dives?"

"Mostly. You?"

"I guess around fourteen hundred."

Rob whistled. "What are you, part fish?"

Keith suppressed a smile. "Something like that."

Emma pursed her lips and nodded. "It sounds like
we have a plan, then. The dive team will consist of
you two and Angus. But I expect you to take plenty
of precautions," Emma said, looking at Rob. "I don't

want to have to medevac you guys. Or call your loved
ones with the bad news.''

The rest of the Phase III team crowded through the
inner door as she spoke, talking noisily: Nikki, Jess,
Gloria, and four others Keith hadn't met.

The oldest of the strangers, a man with a weathered,
bassetlike face and one big caterpillar eyebrow said,
''Someone using my name in vain?''

Gloria went over to Emma.

''You need sleep,'' she said. Emma gave her a tired
smile. Gloria pulled a glob of seaweed from Emma's
hair and gave her a quizzical look. Emma shook her
head.

''Later,'' she said.

Rob was shaking his head, also. ''Angus isn't diving anymore, remember?''

''Heart condition,'' the older man said. He put his
hand on his chest. ''My doctor says no more dives.''

''Right. Hmmm. Who else here dives?''

Jess raised his hand. ''I'm certified.''

Keith asked, ''How many hours, and what kind of
diving?''

''Around three-fifty. Research dives, mostly. And of
course as much recreational diving as I can squeeze
into my schedule.''

Keith gave Emma a nod.

''You're volunteered,'' she told Jess.

''We'll need a chase boat, too,'' Rob said, ''with
snorkelers, spare equipment, and extra tanks.''

''And a radio, of course,'' Angus added.

''Agreed. Angus and Nikki, you handle the chase
boat, and give me regular updates.''

''Right-o.''

''Rob,'' Emma said, ''you'll direct the repair work.
Keith, since Sean is still on the mainland and you have
the most dive experience, I'm appointing you divemaster.''

''You got it.''

*   *   *

Keith picked up his own dive gear from the Mariculture conference room and met the others down at the
dock level antechamber. Both Rob and Jess had suited
up in quarter-inch wet suits. Rob was attaching regulators to his and Jess's air tanks; a third tank sat
nearby. The underwater scooters were lined up against
the wall.

"That one's yours," he said, pointing at·one of the
scooters, and then at the third tank. "And so's that."

Keith set his bags down. "Thanks." He opened up
the soft-sided bag and pulled out his diving equipment:
weights, a belt, swimsuit, quarter-inch farmer johns
and pants, his work gloves, diving boots, mask, fins,
snorkel, and diving knife.

Rob asked, "Do you have a slate and pencil?"

"Well, once. Lost it on a dive." He didn't want to
say that on a lot of his inspection dives, a slate
would've been useless because of zero visibility.

"Here." Rob tossed him an underwater slate with
an attached pencil, and a coil of nylon line with clips
on both ends. "I'm going to assign you the underwater
light." He handed Keith a large underwater spotlight.
"Your job is to keep it pointed at wherever my hands
are working, okay?"

"Got it." Keith switched it on. The light was blinding. He turned it back off.

"Jess, here's your slate and pencil. And you'll carry
this bag." Rob pulled the parts out and laid them out
on the floor. "These are the plugs. Several sizes. I'll
just signal the size I want"—he held up one hand as
if he were holding a ball—"and we'll wing it.
Wrenches, pliers, metal shears, file. You get the idea.
Why don't you pack them up so you know where
everything is."

"Right." Jess went over to the bag. "Hey!" He

held up an umbrella with a circle of rubber-impregnated canvas draped over it. "What's this for?"

Rob shrugged. "You never know. We wouldn't want to get wet."

Jess and Keith stared. Rob grinned. "You'll see."

"You really want me to bring it?" said Jess.

"You bet."

"What's the water temperature?" Keith asked.

"Around the beanpoles, about seventy-eight," Rob replied. "Normally, it's a lot colder over at the spill-ways and reefs, from the cold water discharge, but the pumps are shut down. Besides, we're not going over there anyway.

"Usually we have a thermocline around forty to forty-five feet, but with the storm stirring things up, I don't know. Even if there is a thermocline, though, I don't expect it'll be much colder than seventy or so beneath it."

"I'll skip the pants and just go with the jacket, then," Keith said, and put the pants back into the bag.

He sorted out and threaded eighteen pounds of lead weights onto his belt, then stripped and put on his swimsuit. After donning his wet-suit top and strapping his diving knife to his calf, he went over to examine his scooter, an Aqua Zepp. It was similar to ones he'd used, but not identical; a cylinder about two feet long and eight inches in diameter, ending in a ducted pro-peller. Two pistol grips stuck out from the fan cowling and a headlight was set into the front end.

"This is the trigger for the fan and this thumb tog-gle is the front light, right?"

"Right." Jess came over and pointed to a ring set in the bottom of one of the pistol grips. "Snap onto that when you're not using it." He picked up a spring-coiled snap line from the dock. "We tend to leave it off the unit while operating. We've had trouble with the line getting sucked into the propeller."

"What's your procedure for getting them into the water?"

Rob hefted up his tank and BC and strapped the jacket in place. "Usually the divemaster hands them down once the other divers are in the water, but with those waves out there we're not going to be able to. What do you recommend?"

"We can hold them to our chests," Keith said, "and do a large-stride entry at a wave peak. Hang on to the scooter with one arm and your mask and regulator with the other."

"That should be interesting," Jess remarked dryly. Keith gave Jess a hand with his BC and tank, and then hooked up his own regulator and BC to his tank.

Keith opened the valve on his tank. The air gauge read an even three thousand psi. He clipped the slate and nylon mooring line to his BC.

Rob helped Keith lift his tank, and held it while Keith slipped it on and secured the straps. While Keith put on his weight belt, work gloves, and mask and snorkel, Rob opened the outer door; he and Jess carried the scooters and other equipment outside. A stiff breeze instantly cooled the sweat from Keith's neck and forehead, which putting on the thick rubber and lifting his equipment had worked up. Outside, large waves surged against the dock, boiling up through the deck grating and washing around their ankles. Water splashed through the open door.

Keith went through the door and shut it behind him before more water washed in. The water swirling around his calves felt good.

Jess and Rob were eyeing the empty space between Science and Engineering where the catwalk used to be. Rob whistled.

"Awesome." He turned to Jess. "Did Science take much of a jolt when the great wave hit? We sure did."

"You better believe it. Felt like an earthquake."

That reminded Keith. "How did our last-minute taping and tie-downs hold up to the shock?"

Jess shrugged. "We lost some glassware and a couple of containers broke. Nothing toxic," he added at Keith's questioning look, "or I would've told you. A carboy of ethylene glycol that wasn't secured, is all. Nikki and I already cleaned it up."

They quickly reviewed dive signals and procedures; Keith reminded them again about shallow breathing and not holding their breath. About forty feet away, through the open Mariculture trap door, a hard-bottomed Zodiac inflatable was being lowered on the crane, directly next to the underwater camera lines.

Angus whistled sharply. He and Nikki, inside the boat, waved. The crane lowered them till they were just above the wave crests, and then, when a peak was just beneath them, the boat was released and dropped into the water. The engine sputtered to life; the boat swung around and splashed across the waves toward Engineering.

"Meet you at the catwalk line!" Nikki shouted as they passed. She wore a swimsuit, T-shirt, and visor. White zinc oxide streaked her nose and cheeks. Angus, at the stern, wore a golf cap; they both had dark sunglasses on.

Keith picked up his scooter. He heard a splash and turned; Rob, in the water, signaled *okay* with an arm on top of his head and then turned on his scooter to hold station against the current.

"You want to borrow my drops?" Jess held out his antifogging drops.

"Nah. Don't need them." Keith spat into his mask, rubbed the spittle all over the lenses, and when the next wave struck, dipped the mask in the water to rinse it.

Jess grinned and tucked his drops into a pocket of his BC. "You *are* an old-timer, aren't you?"

Keith grinned back. "Old habits die hard."

Jess stepped out onto the peak of the next wave.

Pushing his hair back, Keith slipped the mask on and adjusted the snorkel. Then he slipped his fins on, picked up the scooter, and put the regulator mouthpiece in his mouth.

The water surged and receded once. As the wave beneath his fins neared a second crest he took a giant stride and sank into a cushion of liquid. Cold wet trickled beneath the suit, down his neck, up his arms, around his waist. Jess and Rob, clinging to their scooters, waited, bobbing on the surface.

Keith signaled *okay* and triggered the scooter motor, not against the current, but across it, letting the combination of the two propel him across the pitching surface of the water toward the Engineering beanpole. Rob and Jess were right behind him.

It only took a few minutes to reach a point upstream of the Engineering module. Keith shut off his DPV and looked back toward Rob and Jess.

Rob held his hand out of the water, thumb pointed down.

Keith took his regulator out of his mouth and shouted, "Shallow breaths, right?"

The other two divers nodded.

Keith put his regulator back in his mouth and pointed his thumb at the water.

There was plankton at the surface, a thick fog that made visibility poor, and Keith concentrated on keeping his eyes on the other two divers. Then they dropped below ten feet and the visibility increased, though the storm's turbulence had muddied these depths somewhat.

Keith could feel the swells overhead, lifting and dropping him as the water passed overhead. Salt stung his sinuses. He could feel the pressure fluctuations in his ears, but so far, it wasn't a problem. The corners of his mouth curved up around the regulator.

It was good to get back into water again.

Keith saw Rob point at something downcurrent and turned his head. The dark mass of the beanpole, with the larger mass of the power plant below, loomed out of the murk, rushing toward them at four knots. He kicked in the scooter, pointed upstream, to slow the approach, and checked to make sure Jess and Rob had, too.

They sank slowly, carefully, using a downward angle with the scooters to pull them on down to forty feet.

As they approached the roof of the power plant, it became obvious where the problem was—a plume of air bubbles, bent over at an angle from the current, poured from the top outer edge, where the edge of the catwalk had pounded repeatedly. If the rupture had happened just a bit more upstream, it would've crumpled the skirt on the surface water intake vent, but left the buoyancy tank intact. As the divers got closer, going cross-current, the bubbles from the tank resolved into two separate streams.

The outer one—the breach in the buoyancy control tank—was a jagged tear in the rounded outside corner. It was over eighteen inches long and six inches across at its widest. Some part of the catwalk had torn across it and one edge was curled in while the other was curled out.

The second tear, the one that opened onto the interior of the plant, was a sprung seam stressed by the other rupture, a thin line over two feet long.

Rob drifted in, letting the current carry him to the breach, then caught the edge of the outer tear with one of his gloved hands. He felt carefully around the edges of the cut with his free hand. Bubbles poured around his hands.

Meanwhile, Jess caught the grid at the intake screen

and clipped a line to it, letting the line flow downstream to Rob, who tied it to a clip on his weight belt
and then moored the DPV to his belt. This let Rob use
both hands to explore the tear.

. Keith pointed the floodlight at the tear and turned
it on but couldn't see what good it did—the bubbles
reflected the light back brilliantly, making it harder to
see the tear than before. Rob held out his hand and
shook his head. Keith turned the light off, then joined
Jess at the intake screen. Jess was rigging another belay line for himself, so Keith did likewise.

Once in position on both sides of Rob, they started
working on the hole. Rob used the metal shears to cut
away some jagged corners on the inside edge, working
by feel. Then he used the file, filling the water with
loud grinding sounds that startled nearby fish.

The plugs were cylinders of rubber four inches thick
in varying diameters. They had washers on both sides,
with a bolt running through the middle and into a nut.
Once positioned in the tear, Rob cranked down on the
bolt with a wrench. The washers compressed the
rubber cylinders, expanding their sides into the metal
edges of the tear, and wedging the plugs in place.

Keith could see how this would work well for a
circular hole, but the tear was nowhere near circular.

Rob placed four of the plugs in—two small ones
near the narrow ends and two large toward the middle—leaving a six-inch, irregular hole in the center.

. Bubbles still poured forth around all the plugs and,
though the flow was probably diminished, Keith didn't
see that it was good enough. He was expecting Rob
to place a last plug in the middle gap when Rob motioned for the umbrella, instead.

Jess pulled it out of the bag and handed it over.

Rob smoothed the rubberized canvas down over the
outside of the umbrella where its loose folds flapped
slowly in the current; then he tipped it down and

pushed it into the gap. As soon as it was all the way in with only the curved handle sticking out, he pushed the release button for the spring-loaded opening mechanism.

Keith didn't see any difference. The bubbles still rushed out around the plugs.

Rob pulled the handle back; suddenly, the handle jerked out of his hand, pushing up hard and fast, out of the crack. Keith heard a thud and the geyser of bubbles stopped, reduced to the tiniest trickle in seconds. He turned on the flashlight again. In the gaps between the rubber plugs and jagged metal edges he could see the black umbrella fabric and mangled umbrella ribs, pressed tight against the hole by the air pressure within.

Jess gave an okay sign with his thumb and forefinger, then wrote on his slate with the grease pencil. *Other leak?* He pointed at the slit seam farther in, still streaming air.

Rob wrote, *Wait*.

A deep groaning sound seemed to come from everywhere. The power plant shuddered, then slowly began rising.

Keith hand-over-handed up his belay line against the current and unclipped himself from the intake grid. Rob and Jess followed.

When they were unclipped and holding on to the grating, Keith got their attention and wrote on his slate, *Blow hard, blow long*. They nodded and he gave the signal to surface.

They went up fast, just slower than their bubbles, caught in the surge of the swells and swept away from the facility by the current.

Nikki and Angus picked them up seconds later, above the slowly rising spillways, hauling their equipment up and then helping them squirm over the inflated sides of the pitching Zodiac.

The plant broke water as their boat passed Engineering. Keith could see the umbrella handle sticking out of the water as they went by. Jess pointed up, at the module side, and Keith tilted his head back.

Emma Tooke stood at the railing of the utility deck, one arm extended, with a thumb up. In her other hand she held a radio to her mouth. The radio in Nikki's hand spat static and then Emma's voice saying, "Good job, divers."

Keith held out his hand for the radio and Nikki handed it to him. "Hail Caesar. Does the thumb up mean we get to live?"

Emma laughed. "I guess. This time." She paused. "It means Gulf Stream lives."

PART TWO

WATER

Chapter 15

"Stop there, at the bend."

Boadica stabbed a finger at an unprepossessing stretch of road alongside an orange grove, and some faint scent, cinnamon and musk, touched Gabriel's nose.

They were several miles north of Melbourne on Route 1. Gabriel drove the rental car they'd picked up that afternoon in Orlando. He gave Boadica a surprised look and slowed down, letting the cars behind him pass. He caught Mark and Jackson exchanging puzzled glances in the rearview mirror.

"What's going on?" Gabriel asked.

"A rendezvous. I'm picking up a few things we need."

"Why didn't you tell me ahead of time?"

Boadica didn't reply, merely dabbed at her lipstick. Her focus was inward, as if she were rehearsing. Preparing for something. She had dressed up, with eyeliner rimming her black eyes, scarlet lipstick and nail polish, very dark, cat-rimmed sunglasses, a white silk tank top, black silk shorts down to her knees, pantyhose, and a long, sheer, red scarf tied in her hair.

"I'll explain later," she said. "Just get a room at the Holiday Inn and check out the commercial docks at Port Canaveral tomorrow before six-thirty A.M., and I'll meet you in Melbourne later in the morning. All right?"

Gabriel scowled. She touched his knee.

"All right," he said. It came out a growl.

"We're low on cash," Jax said, gripping the seat. "Why the Holiday Inn? Why not stay at a dive?"

Boadica shook her head. "Uh-uh. It wouldn't fit our cover. Why would we stay at a dive and then rent a lot of expensive sport fishing equipment?"

She stepped out of the car and started to slam the door. Gabriel leaned over and caught it with his hand. She hadn't said so, but he sensed she was about to do something that was, in some way, dangerous. He sensed that she was scared, or excited. Or perhaps both. Adrenaline junkie, he realized suddenly. That explained a few things.

"Be careful," he said.

Boadica gave him a long look, but he couldn't see her eyes through the sunglasses. Then she gave him that little smile. It made the hairs stand up on his arms and neck.

"Check. Thanks."

Boadica slammed the car door closed, jumped the fence, and made her way into the orange groves. Another shiver ran up his back and made his hands tremble on the steering wheel. Damn, I want her, he thought.

They checked into the Melbourne Holiday Inn on Route 1 a few blocks north of NASA Boulevard. It wasn't as nice as the Albuquerque La Quinta, but it wasn't bad. Room 146 was comfortable and clean. And the dresser sported a color TV—the most prominent colors of which, at the moment, were bilious green, siren red, and lavender. The window sported a view of the hotel Dumpster.

"We're paying seventy-two fifty a night for *this*?" Mark demanded. He banged a hand on the TV set. The picture improved, then reverted.

"Who cares?" Gabriel said. "We're not here for the accommodations."

"How are we going to afford this?" Jax asked, sitting on the bed. The $200 cash deposit the hotel management required since they didn't want to use a credit card had cleaned them out.

"Bo's taking care of that right now," Mark said. "Just relax."

"I'm going out," Gabriel said. After seven hours crammed into a plane seat, fighting his way through the crowds at Houston Intercontinental and Orlando International, and shut up in a car, he couldn't stand to spend another minute cooped up. He needed time alone.

Mark asked, "Where?"

"I don't know. Out. I'll be back in a while."

He wandered aimlessly around town: visited the mall and the downtown historical area. Melbourne, Florida, could hardly be called a teeming metropolis, but the clusters of people on the streets and in the shops, the buildings and concrete and cars, made him claustrophobic. He went back to the car, dug a road map out of the glove compartment, and studied it for a while.

He wanted trees, animals, open sky. He wanted space not populated by other humans. Sebastian Inlet State Park sounded interesting, but he didn't feel like driving all the way out there just to discover more crowds. Instead he drove over the 192 causeway to the beach, where he found a secluded area and jerked off, thinking of Boadica's nipples moving under the silk tank top and her long, muscled legs.

Afterward he lay supine on the coarse sand, his jeans unzipped and his chest bare, warmed by sun, speckled by cool salt water, and with arms beneath his head he watched sandpipers cruise overhead.

Is this lust or love? he wondered.

He propped himself up on his elbows and looked out to sea, wondering where out there Emma was.

Another *gringa bruja*. He should know better. When they were young, Emma had ripped his heart out whole and handed it back to him. And Boadica would do the same. All unknowingly, perhaps. She, like Emma, had a touch of the *bruja*, the sorceress, in her. When she wanted something for herself, nothing— not love of a man, not fear of failure, not death itself— would turn her aside. Why did such potency always draw him? Like a moth to the flame.

Then he lay back down and let go of the Earth, fell slowly into the endless blue sky, while beneath him circled coastal gulls' cries and the wind's dry rustling through dune grasses. A single human's pain could get swallowed up by such vastness of sky and sea. He found it comforting.

Which brought him back to Emma, and their second-to-last big fight. Her mother had just died of cancer and he'd gone with her into the Capitán Grande wilderness, losing themselves in its sere beauty, its air rich with spring pollens.

How quickly human problems shrank to specks in that vast wilderness, he'd said, and oh, but she'd been angry. The quiet beauty affronted her, she'd said. How dare the universe not reel?

She wanted violence. Calamity. Destruction. Earthquakes, hurricanes, tornadoes. She wanted the universe to scream. To rend itself apart over the outrage of her loss. And *he'd* been outraged at her arrogance—how dare she wish destruction and loss on that scale—on any scale—simply because *she* suffered?

He wondered if he would still hate her as much as he had after the breakup . . . wondered if he had any feelings for her at all. And somewhere, way in the back of his mind, he wondered what would have happened if everything hadn't gone to hell the way it had—what it would have been like to raise a family with her.

Perhaps, he thought, with a trace of old sadness, such questions were better left unanswered.

Chapter 16

EMMA: **Friday, 2 October, 7:50 P.M. EDT**
Gulf Stream I

Emma snatched a few hours' sleep that afternoon, while Rob baby-sat the pumping of the OTEC plant and the rest of the Phase III crew either slept or, if they'd gotten sleep the night before, did damage inventory. Her sleep was punctuated by sudden awakenings with her heart pounding, watching the great wave descend.

It probably had as much to do, she thought, with the fact that she was too tired to sleep as with fear of the wave. It had been a problem ever since college: when severely sleep deprived, her body had a hard time believing it was time to slip out of high gear.

That evening when she awoke and stepped out onto the top level deck at Residential, two cells of turbulence still smoothed the swells at the base of the OTEC plant's raised deck. The plant hadn't finished disgorging its salt water yet. She glanced at her watch. It should be soon. Blue brilliance flickered at one edge, where a human shape crouched next to two cylinders: Mac, welding the torn metal.

She yawned and scratched her head, and then stretched carefully, wincing at the pain that shot along her arms and across her shoulders and back. She needed a shower, and a lot more sleep; the world seemed packed with invisible cotton wadding and her feet and hands were yards away. But the fresh air felt good on her face. She drew a deep breath.

At the beat of helicopter blades she looked up. A helicopter neared, its lights playing across Mariculture's roof. Emma went into the lounge and called Rob on the intercom.

"Flo and Ben are back," he reported at her query, "and one of Flo's people; I can't remember who. For the Sciences it's Reynolds, Tetsuo Hiro, and Dick Munzer, and for Residential it's Charles Lawson and Vince di Angelo. Oh, and two other Engineering staff besides Ben. I sent for Oleg Tashkovich and Steve Padwick to help Keith with that spill in the maintenance shop. Franz always used them for that. If you're headed over that way, tell them Keith is waiting for them."

Emma's eyes narrowed at the mention of Munzer and Reynolds. "Will do. Thanks."

By the time she reached Mariculture's catwalk level antechamber, the cage was descending into view, with everyone aboard but Flo and whichever of her people had returned with her.

Everyone crowded out of the elevator, including, to her surprise, Freddy. He jerked his thumb upward.

"Looks like you took some damage up top."

"What are *you* doing here?"

Freddy shrugged with a grin. "Flo and Charles promised me all the lobster I could eat tonight, if I'd hang out long enough to let you storm watchers fill in your replacements, and then take y'all back to the mainland for a furlough."

"Great. Oleg and Steve, Keith Hellman is in the Engineering maintenance room waiting for you. A spill needs cleaning."

They left. Emma turned to Ben.

"I'll meet you in Control in fifteen minutes. The power plant took a lot of water. I'd like you to do an inspection with me as soon as it's emptied."

"Right."

"And Ben—we'll need self-contained air; the plant has been purged with nitrogen."

His eyes lit in appreciation. "Smart. I'll prepare us a couple of tanks." He left.

"Charles, why don't you and Vince head over to Residential and get a late meal ready?"

"Lobster Parmesan coming up."

As they started toward the door, she added, "You probably noticed on the way in—the gardens took a lot of damage."

"We noticed," Charles said. They both looked distressed. Charles relied on the gardens for fresh fruit and vegetables; the tending of them was mostly Vince's job.

Vince sighed. "I suppose it was inevitable."

Hardly that, Emma thought.

"Where's Mac?" Charles asked.

"I don't know," she said, "but he's fine. Give Rob a call; he'll know."

She turned to Reynolds, Dick Munzer, and Tetsuo.

"Tetsuo, thought you were in Alaska."

Tetsuo Hiro dipped his head—a residual bow, as he had lived in the U.S. since his last year of high school, and his English was impeccable. "It seemed wise to return, under the circumstances. How are the reefs? How much damage to the laboratories?"

"The reefs still need to be assessed, but it appears some of the monitoring equipment took damage. The reef structures themselves appear to be fine. None of the labs took real damage, thanks to our new spill response person." She broke off and turned to Reynolds. "We need to talk."

His eyebrows arched high. "Oh? Perhaps it could

wait till after Dick, Tetsuo, and I have finished our damage assessments.''

She stared at him. "It can't. It needs to be right now. Tetsuo, Dick, would you excuse us?"

Once they were alone, she said, "Science was left in disastrous shape. Things were left totally unsecured. If it hadn't been for Hellman, you'd be coming back to a module full of toxic soup. Or gutted by fire.''

"Aren't you exaggerating just a bit?"

She threw the antechamber door open and pointed at the snarl of pipes and cables jutting from Science's catwalk deck. "Would you care to imagine just what *that* did to the module's stability? *Nothing* was secured in the labs. Flammables, toxics, corrosives—all just waiting to crash onto the floor.''

"They didn't, though, I take it."

"No. They didn't. Because Hellman identified the problem in time for me to assign him and three others to a last-minute fix. As a result of which, by the way, the gardens weren't adequately secured and took severe damage. If Hellman hadn't been here, Science would be shut down by now. Perhaps permanently.''

He said nothing, only looked at her.

"Hiro was in charge of Phase II, I believe?" he asked after a moment.

"Think again. Your man Munzer was. Hiro was in Alaska.''

"I'll have a word with Dick." Reynolds's tone was unobjectionable, but she gave him a skeptical look.

"Do that. And furthermore, his negligence is going to get a mention in my emergency response debriefing.''

"Well." Reynolds clicked his tongue against his palate. "I suppose you must. It does sound more serious than I realized.''

Emma frowned and eyed him suspiciously, but there was no more to be said.

Ben, wearing a life jacket and laden down with equipment, met her at the Engineering elevator, catwalk level. He handed her a tool pouch, a flashlight, the plant equipment checklist, and nose clips. They helped each other into the SCBAs. Then, masks and hoses dangling over their shoulders, clanking and clacking like walking percussion instruments, they took the elevator down to the dock.

The plant rode much higher in the water than usual, with the roof about five feet above the wave crests: a short hop down from the deck. Mac shut off his arc welder and came over from the weld site as they neared the hatch, removing his face shield and gloves. He took his safety lock from the hatch handle and gave them a thumbs-up. Emma turned on her air, hooked up her mask and slipped it on, and, tightening the straps, stepped over the threshold. Ben came in on her heels.

Power was out, except for two emergency lights up top. The generators had been shut off, but the deep-water pumps, still running, made a deafening roar. The weak pools of light made by the emergency lamps made the plant seem much larger. They turned on their flashlights and climbed down among the turbogenerators on the mezzanine, to look for the watermark. Shadows leapt around them as their flashlights moved. The ubiquitous smell of ozone was gone.

Emma found the watermark and Ben did some quick measurements. He wrote *17'2"!* on his clipboard. His eyes were wide.

They split up; Ben went below to check the heat exchangers while Emma checked the turbogenerators. Her own compressed-air breathing loud in her ears, she opened a panel here, a hatch there, loosened fittings and checked cables. Seawater trickled, sometimes gushed, out of the openings. Rust damage appeared minimal, water damage moderate. She pushed her dismay aside and made notes.

An hour later, when their air began to run low, they headed up to her office to compare notes. Emma had a hard time keeping her balance; she felt as if she were moving in slow motion. She sank into her chair and pushed her unread stacks of mail aside.

"We've got to get meters on a lot of that equipment before we know the full picture," Ben said, "but hell, it could be a lot worse. With the nitrogen blanket there's been very little rusting—I figure we can salvage a lot of the equipment with a good rinse. We'll have to run some new cable and we need to get into the guts of the equipment to do a thorough cleaning. I'll get more crew out here and we'll start disassembly right away."

Emma laid down her checklist as he spoke and rested her head on her arms. She barely understood what he was saying.

"I have to close my eyes for a minute, Ben," she mumbled. "Will you take over?"

"You bet, chief." He perched on her credenza. "In fact, you should get on that helicopter, when Freddy goes. Take a couple of days."

She shook her head. "Uh-uh."

Then she smelled lobster, and Gloria was saying, "Sit up, Emma. Supper."

She sat up and rubbed the blear out of her eyes. A tendon in her neck tightened—pain shot across her shoulder and she couldn't turn her head to the left. She winced and tried to stretch it out.

"Supper." Gloria set a tray in front of her. Keith and Flo stood behind her. "Eat."

Her stomach rumbled and saliva filled her mouth. As she wolfed the lobster and angel-hair pasta, Gloria went on, "Keith has a proposition for you. He can get you your certification this weekend, if you're up to it."

It took a moment to understand. Abrupt interest cleared the cobwebs from her mind. She lifted her eyebrows at him; he nodded.

"Aren't the seas here too rough to train a beginning diver?"

"Yes," he said. "We'd have to do it landside."

She caught Gloria and Flo exchanging a look. So. An attempt to get her to leave for the weekend.

She shook her head. "Maybe some other time."

Flo, who had been leaning against the doorjamb, came forward. "Ben says he can take care of damage inventories and give you a report Monday, with a first pass at estimated costs. And what about our meeting with Pendleton and all on Monday afternoon? You need to be in Melbourne for that. And you *have* to be rested for that meeting. Otherwise Reynolds will walk all over you."

Emma leaned on her desk and eyed first Flo, then Gloria and Keith. It was hard to focus on them; her eyes kept crossing.

She frowned. "I can get plenty of rest here, tonight, and be on hand to oversee repairs tomorrow." She lifted her clipboard, filled with notes and scribbles. "I have to finish these."

Flo gave her raised eyebrows. "I seem to recall some friendly advice given to me last month, about managers who don't delegate?"

"This is different," Emma said.

Flo looked disgusted. She said to the others, "Could you give us a moment?"

After Gloria and Keith had stepped out into the hall, Flo lowered her voice. "I'm going to level with you. You're so tired you're babbling. Those notes"—she gestured—"are illegible and disorganized. You've been wasting your time."

"If they're illegible, how do you know they're disorganized?" At Flo's look, Emma said, "Okay, okay, I take your point."

"Damn right. The state you're in, you'll be a liability, not an asset. It's going to take two or three sessions of twelve to fourteen hours' sleep for you to catch up. And you won't get that kind of rest here.

"Go. Now. And give yourself a good couple of days before you come back. Ben will have time to thoroughly assess the damage and prepare you a report on your return.

"You've got some of the best people there are, here. Trust them. Trust Ben."

"I do trust Ben. He's the best. I just feel—" Emma lifted a hand. She couldn't find the word. She tugged at her hair, rested her head briefly in her hands, and looked up at Flo again. "We took a lot of damage, Flo. On top of losing the GM contract—" She broke off. "I'm scared."

Flo's gaze softened. She nodded. "Ditto. But your being here won't change the amount of damage we took. We can't start making decisions about what needs to be done until we know what damage we've taken, anyway. And we need you in good shape to fight the good fight. Reynolds has had days to scheme, while we've been dealing with the storm. You and I both know he's been up to no good. Who knows what he's going to do at Monday's meeting? You're the only one he's afraid of, you know, and if you're not rested you won't be in any condition to keep him from steamrolling us."

Emma looked at Flo. She thought of trying to face down Reynolds the way she felt now. She thought of her cozy little apartment in Melbourne, of sleeping in tomorrow in her comfy bed, of spending the weekend by the pool, of—finally!—learning to dive. Her resistance caved in all at once; she raised her hands.

"All right. I give."

Flo allowed herself a smile. She raised her voice. "Gloria! Tell Freddy he's got another passenger."

Gloria and Keith came back around the corner trying unsuccessfully to hide smiles. How much had they heard?

"On one condition," Emma said.

"What?" Flo asked, abruptly wary.

"I come back with a PADI c-card."

Keith folded his arms. "No guarantees. You'll have to earn it."

Gloria and Flo exchanged a worried look that reminded Emma just how hostile she'd been. Hey, she thought. Opinions can change. She folded her arms and cocked her head, smiling. "I always do."

Chapter 17

GABRIEL: Saturday, 3 October, 8:50 A.M. EDT
Room 146, the Holiday Inn, Melbourne, Florida

She was in the room the next morning when they got back from breakfast at the Denny's that shared space with the Holiday Inn. Gabriel unlocked the door and walked in, and there she was, sprawled on the bed reading a newspaper, dressed in baggy pants and an oversized Soundgarden T-shirt and a backward baseball cap, thumping the headboard with the toe of one of her red high-top sneakers; he thought for an instant she was a teenage boy. Until she looked up at him with her dark eyes and her little smile, and the angry exclamation died on his lips.

"We were worried," he said.

Sitting on the desk was a laptop computer. The

phone line was connected to its side. The phone
nearby sat disconnected. On the floor at the foot of the
bed were two duffel bags, each large enough to hide
a body in, with stout padlocks.

"Hey, punk," Jax said, coming forward past Ga
briel with fists clenched. Then his eyes widened and
his jaw went slack. Mark, entering behind him, looked
at her and said, "Oh, wow. Cool disguise. How'd you
get in?"

Boadica smiled. In a single, smooth motion she
tossed the paper aside, got up, and closed and bolted
the door. "Let's just say we shouldn't depend on this
lock for security."

Gabriel noticed that the curtain had been taped to
the edges of the windowsill with strips of masking
tape.

"Any luck with Tooke?" she asked.

Gabriel shook his head. "Not only was she not on
the Saturday morning boat, there *wasn't* any Saturday
morning boat. We waited until noon; then Jax asked
one of the attendants at the diesel station. They evacuated most of the crew before the hurricane, then took
them back in the trawler last night. They probably
won't be making another ferry run until next Saturday
when they're back on schedule."

Boadica frowned. "Well, they use a helicopter service for emergencies. She could've come in that way."
She went to the bedside table and went through the
drawers. The phone book was in the second one. She
flipped through the Yellow Pages, reconnected the
phone, and dialed.

Her accent thickened from her neutral Midwest to
Deep South. "Good morning. This is Anita out at Gulf
Stream. Emma Tooke misplaced her briefcase and I'm
trying to see if she left it on the helicopter." There
was a pause. "Sorry, darling, I don't know which
flight. I'm brand-new out here and they just told me

to check with y'all. Don't you keep track of those things?'' There was another pause and Boadica's teeth flashed in a sudden predatory smile. ''Yes, that would probably be the one.'' There was another pause and then she said, ''Well, poo. We'll just have to keep looking around the office. Thank you so much.''

She hung the phone up. ''She flew in last night. So she *is* in town. Try her at her apartment?''

Gabriel nodded. ''Yeah. I could've gotten the address from Tina—she's about the only one of our old crowd who we both still talk to.'' He went to the computer, sat down, and turned it on. The Windows 95 display screen came up, and he noticed that there was Internet mail and Web browser software on it. ''I should check my E-mail and newsgroups.''

Boadica shook her head. ''Forget it. We should all stay off the public boards. We have to act as if they've put a tap on our accounts.

''Disguises . . . taps . . .'' Mark shook his head. ''All these precautions seem like overkill to me. Do you seriously think we've been put under surveillance?''

Her lips thinned. ''Gabriel certainly has, after the Woodland Products bombings. And I think the rest of us had better assume likewise. It may be overkill, but it never hurts to be a little paranoid.

''I've opened a new account from a local provider under a pseudonym. It's the only one we should use.''

''You're right, of course.'' Gabriel sat back with a sigh. Being cut off from the Net felt a bit like having his hands lopped off.

She knelt by the bags. While Gabriel, Jax, and Mark gathered around, she unlocked one of the bags and emptied it. It disgorged several Redweld accordion folders filled with paper, several boxes of diskettes, a roll of maps and drawings as thick as Gabriel's waist, and at the bottom, a large Tyvek FedEx envelope.

She opened the envelope and dumped it on the bed. Five rubber-banded stacks of twenty-dollar bills bounced on the bedspread. Five thousand dollars, easy. Maybe double that. Gabriel, Mark, and Jax stared. When you've been counting quarters and trying to decide if you can afford a cup of coffee with breakfast, a few thousand dollars can make quite an impression.

She passed out two hundred dollars to each of them, "spending money," she said, and put the rest back in the envelope. She handed the diskettes, drawings, and accordion folders to Mark.

"Design details and engineering documentation on our target," she told him. "Think you can identify the locations most vulnerable to attack?"

"No sweat." Mark squatted and began going through them. Gabriel gave him a hand.

Then she knelt by the other duffel, unlocked it, and removed an olive-green cardboard box about fifteen inches long by eight inches square. Something—some hint of increased precision in her manner—drew Gabriel's attention. He paused in spreading the engineering sketches on the table to watch.

She gestured for Jax to open the box. He pulled out his Swiss Army knife and cut through the tape. The cardboard was heavily waxed—it was the extra sturdy, double-thick kind. He removed a white stick about an inch and a half square by a foot long, and nodded with a long, slow sigh, examining it with loving gaze and hands.

"Been a long time since we rock 'n' rolled," he said, softly.

Mark whistled. Gabriel leaned forward on the bed. "What is it?"

"C-4. Plastic explosive," Mark added, at Gabriel's blank look. "I haven't seen that stuff since, what, late '91, Jax?"

Jax cut open the plastic wrapping and sniffed the

stick. "Yep." He shared a grin with Mark. "Just like the good old days. This stuff is army issue. How much do we have?" he asked Boadica.

"Thirty kilos."

"Detonators?"

"Digital radio—operated. And marine packs."

"Ahhhhhhhhh!" Jax's eyes closed and his mouth parted. "You've got good connections, lady."

"Let me have a look," Gabriel said, and held out his hand. Jax held the stick out to Gabriel, then fumbled it.

"Look out, it'll blow!" he yelled.

It bounced harmlessly on the carpeting, and Gabriel, trying in a panic to catch it, landed on top of it. Jax burst into laughter. Mark and Boadica followed suit.

Gabriel picked himself and the stick up. He was not amused. Jax looked contrite.

"Sorry, Gabe, I couldn't resist. Don't worry, it's stable. Only blows with a blasting cap and a fuse. And an ignition source. We used to cook with it. You take a bit, light it, and use it to heat rations."

Gabriel turned it over, fingered the unwrapped end, pinched off a bit, sniffed it. It was moldable, like Play-Doh, and smelled chemical. A bit like packing tape. He pressed the bit he'd pinched off back onto the stick and handed it to Jax, then wiped his hands on his jeans.

Boadica glanced at her watch. "Well," she said, "are you ready to try Tooke again?"

Gabriel drew a breath and nodded. "Yeah."

"Be careful. You were in the national news; she may be suspicious of your motives."

"Right."

"Use the rental—I got another one."

"And if she isn't there . . . ?"

Boadica shrugged. "We'll deal with that contingency when we come to it."

"Fair enough."

He put in his contacts, stuffed the wax inserts back in his mouth, and then grabbed the keys off the counter by the door. Jax gave him a thumbs-up as he started to open the door.

"Be careful," Mark said.

The apartment complex was upscale—rich landscaping with lots of palms and flowering bushes. Gabriel eased into a slot in the visitor's section of the parking lot and got out of the car. The block with her unit was on the far side and he walked casually down sidewalks, smiling as people passed him, walking behind a group of two men and two women carrying scuba tanks, an ice chest, groceries, and what looked like a dive bag.

He wondered what it would be like—to just wander off on some pleasant excursion with no ulterior motives, no overriding concerns. To not have your heart rate shoot up at every passing police car. He shook his head and began checking the door numbers.

She was in 32 and he'd just passed 27. He counted ahead. That would make it that door. Shit. The group ahead of him stopped at Emma's door and rang the bell. He stepped off the sidewalk and across the grass, pausing when he'd reached the corner of another unit.

The door to apartment 32 opened and he caught a glimpse of a hand. Then the group moved inside.

Should he still try? It looked like a major outing was in store. Did he want to try a contact with all those witnesses? Would he really be able to talk to her? Even if they included him in their plans it wouldn't be private.

He shook his head and went back to the car.

"She had guests. Four of them. Looked like they were about to go diving so I aborted. What now?" He double-checked the door lock.

Boadica was at the computer. Gabriel caught a glimpse of E-mail software in front of her, as she closed it down. Mark and Jax were going over the blueprints spread out on the bed. Boadica turned.

"Maybe you could try again this evening. The CEO holds weekly meetings with his officers every Monday. She'll certainly stay landside for that. That gives us a couple of days."

And how did you know *that*? thought Gabriel. Another of your "sources"?

Boadica continued. "Let's plan for an encounter by Monday evening, and meanwhile take the weekend to procure the equipment we'll need."

"Does anybody know AutoCAD?" Mark interrupted. He had a set of diskettes in his lap. "Gabe, you've done drafting work, haven't you?"

"Yeah." Freelance drafting, along with writing articles for regional magazines, had been his main sources of income for years, helping him stay afloat enough to pursue his activist activities. "Why?"

Mark gestured at the engineering drawings. "Well, these sheets don't have everything we need."

Boadica turned, looking surprised. "What's missing?"

"All we have here are the structural drawings. To make good decisions on where to plant charges I'll want their electrical and mechanical detail, too—*and* their communications and pneumatic systems. The works. We'll need to call up those schematics."

Boadica glanced at Gabriel. "You have engineering experience?"

"You mean your sources didn't tell you that?" He shrugged with a slight grin. "Of sorts. I started out as an ocean engineering major, before I got religion."

"All right. Your main job is still to try to contact Tooke again, but in the meanwhile maybe you can help Mark with the facility plans, and Jax can come

with me to Miami to get some of the other supplies
we'll need."

Gabriel eyed her, his jaw muscles twitching. He
could find no reason to object to her suggestion, but
he didn't like it—it sounded too much like an order.
Wild Justice is *my* baby, he thought. She was making
too many of the decisions. He didn't like the idea
of Boadica going off with Jax, for other, more visceral
reasons.

Perhaps she sensed the resentment because she
looked at him and said, "So, what do you think?"

He sighed, and forced himself to relax. Don't be
petty, Cervantes. The mission is all that matters.
"Sounds like a plan."

Chapter 18

EMMA: **Saturday, 3 October, 1:04 P.M.**
The Aquarina, Melbourne Beach, Florida

Early Saturday afternoon, at the sound of the doorbell,
Emma stepped out of her shower. She threw on a robe
and grabbed a towel, and dripped water across the
marble floor of the bathroom and the ceramic tiles of
her big living room, wrapping her head, to open the
door on a mob scene.

Not only Keith, but Gloria, Jess, and Nikki stood in
the hallway. Along with Keith's equipment bag and
four tanks, they had a big cooler and two brown grocery bags stuffed with food. They were dressed for the
pool, T-shirts over swim suits or shorts.

"We thought we'd cheer you on from the pool-
side," Gloria said.

"I hope this is okay," Keith said. "They said they come over to use your pool all the time. If they get too distracting we can send them away."

Grinning, Emma stood aside.

"Nah, it's okay. Come in. Make yourselves at home. You know where everything is."

As she helped with the groceries, she saw Keith examining her shelves of seashells along one wall of the living room. The glass shelves lined an entire wall. A bar of spotlights above the shelves illuminated seashells of all kinds and sizes. He whistled sharply and went over to them.

"Quite a collection."

"Amazing, aren't they?" Nikki agreed. "Ask nicely and perhaps she'll tell you about them."

"Feel free to handle any of them except the combs—they're terribly brittle," Emma told Keith.

"You put a lot of care into your collection," Keith said as he walked along beside the shelf. "There are some remarkable specimens here. Did you collect them all yourself?"

She shook her head. "Don't I wish. I rarely have time for collecting, these days. The more recent specimens have been gifts from friends. And I have lots of marine scientist and diver friends, so I make out like a bandit."

He paused at the far end of the shelf. "Is this one your first?"

She smiled, startled, and came over to pick up the Oregon Triton he was pointing at. The whorled shell was large for its type, over six inches in length, with smooth, white lips framing an oval aperture, and a spiky, dark brown exterior. "Good guess. Because of the date?"

"Right." He flicked a finger at the card in front of it. The calligraphed card, weathered, with faint water spots, read *Oregon Triton, 6.8", San Juan Islands, July*

1974. "I don't see any earlier dates on your shelf."

He hadn't lingered all that long over them . . . or so she'd thought. "You're very observant."

He smiled back. "I'm paid to be."

She picked it up and fingered its horns and spikes. "I spent a summer with my grandparents on the San Juan Islands when I was eleven. That's when I started collecting."

She had found it on the beach. After decades of serious collecting it remained one of her finest specimens.

She remembered the trip clearly: the wild, cold ocean, charcoal-grey and nickel-silver; the rocky beach with its tide pools, its starfish and moss and mussels and barnacles, its beach crabs and driftwood; the cool, windy solitude; the boating trips with her grandfather to check the crab traps; the straight black dorsal fins of killer whales in the straits.

The islands that summer had been a badly needed escape, one far too brief. Her parents had been on the brink of divorce and she on the brink of a painful, awkward adolescence—so tall she was thought freakish, so busty at such a young age the other girls called her a whore and accused her of stuffing her bra, so smart and "scientific" she was scorned by the boys. Somehow on that beach she'd glimpsed what marvels the world could hold, marvels that could be experienced—relished and studied and, finally, understood.

Remembering, she said, "Sometimes I wish . . ." and then smiled and shook her head, placing the triton back on the shelf.

"You wish what?"

"Oh, I don't know. That I'd gone into ocean ecology instead of engineering, I suppose. I was afraid I wouldn't be able to earn a living in pure research, so I chose something more practical. And there is a lot about my career that I enjoy. But sometimes I fantasize about having made a different choice. It would have been great to have made a career of collecting shells.'' With a shrug and a laugh, Emma said, ''Excuse me for a moment.''

She left him there with the rest of the group, who were putting groceries away in the kitchen and getting settled in the front room, while she dressed—swim suit under shorts.

Then she and Keith appropriated the dining table. She handed him the three homework lessons she'd completed after breakfast, and after they'd gone over them he gave her the tests for the first three lessons, while the others made themselves sandwiches and watched a tennis match on TV. It took about an hour. She made perfect scores on all three segments.

''I wouldn't expect Boyle's Law to give you much trouble,'' he remarked.

The first hour's pool work was a stone bitch.

Keith made her swim laps till her lungs and vision burned, then—with little time to catch her breath—made her swim out to the deep end to tread water for fifteen minutes. When she pointed out afterward, hanging from the pool edge and gasping for breath, that her other instructors hadn't worked her anywhere *near* this hard (her arms and shoulders in particular had stiffened since the day before, and the crick in her neck lingered), he shrugged. His tone was mild.

''You'll be diving in a much stronger current and rougher conditions than most beginning divers. And you won't have the kind of supervision they do on their early dives.''

If he'd told her she would thank him later, she would have screamed.

Then he had her exit the pool, and the real lessons began.

So many skills to be learned. It was hard to keep track of it all. Assemble, check, and don the assortment of gear; enter the water with all equipment on, three ways: seated facing forward; big step; and squatting, head-over-heels backward to simulate a seated, backward entry.

And, once underwater, equalize pressure in her sinuses and ears; fill the mask with water and then blow it clear; replace a dislodged mask; throw away and then retrieve a "lost" regulator; use her buddy, Keith's, spare regulator, his "octopus," in a simulation that she was out of air. Practice emergency buddy breathing, where they shared the same regulator, back and forth, back and forth, arms locked together, gazes locked.

And she felt the tug of attraction, then, looking at him, with his short, cedar-colored hair waving like sea grass about his head, eyes clear and dark as obsidian, powerful cords of muscles in arms, torso, thighs, and calves, all hazed with dark hair and glazed with water, bubbles, and light.

He belonged in water. On land he moved with efficiency and competence, but his manners were too carefully managed to be graceful. Too controlled. In water, he was manta-ray lithe: floating above and watching her while she did her buoyancy control exercises, instructing her with gestures and touch. Tucking, barely kicking, he glided about her flailings in a flowing, impromptu dance.

Emma didn't like the direction her thoughts were taking. Her experiments with romantic relationships had always disappointed. Her first, college love had been a thing of passion and rage, and the parting had been nasty. And her attempts since had always left her feeling confined—caught in a complex web of rules she hadn't agreed to and didn't understand. And she'd remained distant from the process. Just going through the motions, like a smiling automaton.

She had realized finally that she was perfectly happy

alone and didn't *want* a permanent relationship, and with a feeling of great relief, had stopped pressuring herself to Find Someone. That wasn't about to change.

She reflected on this sitting cross-legged, eight feet down on the bottom of the pool, in a break between exercises, as she watched Keith move amid the bubbles of her exhalation. Above him, Gloria's passing shattered the smooth, undulating surface of the water into a crazy quilt of sky and mirrors.

Keith gestured for her to increase her buoyancy and float suspended; she added a touch of air to her BC with the rubber button on the BC hose, and her connection with the pool floor grew tenuous. Then she took a deep breath and, as she began to rise off the floor, breathed at the top of her lungs: shallow breaths that moved her hardly at all. She was suspended two feet above the floor. Exactly where she wanted to be, like a levitating fakir. She had it!

Keith nodded. His hand made an *okay*, and then, eyes smiling, he mimed applause. Sudden joy filled her to bursting. She straightened her legs and, extending arm and gaze up, her body wound slowly upward like the works of a clock, as he'd taught her, among bubbles that tickled her bare skin. Bleeding air from her BC jacket to slow her ascent, she kicked the last of the way to the surface and broke through the skin of the water.

Keith surfaced beside her. Emma tore off her mask and drew a breath.

"Nice buoyancy control on the bottom, there," he said. "Very nice. It's the thing that gives beginners the most trouble and you took right to it."

"Thanks."

"Don't surface so suddenly. You shouldn't be ascending any faster than your bubbles. And you need more practice clearing your mask. Press harder here while you're exhaling through your nose, and tip your head back farther.'' He pushed at the upper rim of his mask. ''And another thing, take your time going down. Keep pinching your nose and blowing more while you descend. Rush things the way you were doing out there and you'll have even more trouble equalizing pressure in your ears than you did today. If you're out on a dive and can't equalize, you know, there's nothing to do but abort the dive.''

''Right.''

''And next time,'' he said, shaking a finger at her, ''don't forget to give your buddy the thumbs-up before you ascend.''

''Oops.'' She gave him a sheepish grin. ''I forgot.''

'' 'Oops' is right.'' He looked beyond her, at the pool edge. ''What do you think, guys? Should we let it go this time?''

Jess and Nikki thought it over, gave grudging consent.

''What pals,'' Emma said, and splashed them both good and hard. They retreated, laughing.

She removed her tank and BC with Keith's help and handed it up to Jess. Keith slapped her on the back.

''You're over halfway there. Tomorrow morning we'll wrap up the last two lessons and give you your written and pool finals.''

Gloria had gotten out of the pool by then. The gang lifted beers, whistled, and clapped their hands. Emma blushed, grinning. She raised her mask high and gave it a victory shake.

Keith left shortly thereafter, pleading errands before all the stores closed. The rest of them went out to dinner at Samperton's, a two-story restaurant overlooking the surf that had a series of small dining rooms and served excellent steaks and seafood. Then they walked along the beach at sunset and beyond, collecting shells beneath a gibbous moon that hung above the water like a tipped-over copper bowl.

Far to the north, at Cape Canaveral, ghostly amid haze and twilight, the spotlighted shuttle squatted on its launch pad, pointed at the heavens. Emma wondered if Gulf Stream hydrogen was fueling this launch.

The moon gave them plenty of light that night, which was fortunate, since it was turtle nesting season and flashlights weren't allowed on the beach. Moonlight turned the dunes and grasses pale against the black night. Barely visible, sand crabs dashed from beneath their feet. Tinaphores glowed, firefly-green, in the dark surf.

Shells, to Emma's mild surprise, were plentiful; Sophronia had washed up some real beauties. The others came to Emma to identify their finds.

And they made some finds: bulbs, disks, and tapers; striped, solid, and spotted; shiny-smooth, ribbed, spiked, beaded. The group found baby's ears and moon shells; dove shells, ceriths, and whelks with fluted mouths; long spiky turrets and trumpets; bulbous periwinkles; tiny turbonilles, no bigger than your pinkie and translucent as glass; even a Florida spiny jewel box shell the size of Emma's palm. In the moonlight their colors were impossible to distinguish; she was anxious to get them home and examine them in the light.

The find of the night was Jess's, who stumbled on a clump of sea drift and uncovered a conch almost as big as his head. It was knobbed, milky and brown, with a large, pink mouth glossy as porcelain.

They washed their shells in the surf and then, tired and happy, walked back up the road to Emma's place. The hurricane had done little damage to Melbourne Beach: a tree down here and there, muddy streets, the vegetation all leaning southwest. Only the very eastern edge of the hurricane had grazed the greater metro-

politan area south of Cape Canaveral, leaving buildings and power and phone lines intact.

Gloria, who didn't have an apartment in town, took
Emma up on her offer of the fold-out couch that night.
After seeing the others off, they watched the news
coverage of the hurricane's aftermath, which had gone
ashore south of Brunswick, Georgia. Damage had been
extensive in the area, due to heavy flooding. Coastal
Georgia had been declared a national disaster area.
Florida north of Jacksonville had taken some damage,
too. Hundreds of homes along the Atlantic coast had
been destroyed; several people had been killed.

They were both exhausted. At ten-thirty, they
changed into nightgowns, made up the fold-out couch,
and then sipped at their Courvoisier. Gloria finished
hers and set her glass down, then grabbed a pillow and
dropped onto the bed, punching the pillow beneath her
tummy.

"You seem awfully pensive tonight," Gloria said.
"What gives?"

Emma gave her a thoughtful look.

"Something that happened during the storm," she
said. "It's sort of stayed with me, you know? I mean,
I'm fine, but . . . I can't put it out of my mind."

She hesitated again. Gloria said, "Yes?"

Emma sighed and shook her head. She didn't want
everybody making a big deal about her getting caught
in the great wave, when she was fine. And Gloria had
many sterling qualities, but keeping a secret like that
wasn't in her nature. Emma aimed the remote at the
TV set and the image vanished. Then she sat back in
her favorite, green velvet armchair, cupping her snifter
and inhaling the pungent fumes.

"Never mind. It's nothing."

"Oh, so you're going to be mysterious."

"It's nothing, really."

"Are you interested in Keith?" Gloria demanded.

Emma eyed Gloria again, startled, and wondered if she'd been eavesdropping on her thoughts at the bottom of the pool earlier. Well, it beat talking about the great wave.

"You mean romantically?" Gloria nodded. "Why do you ask?"

"It's obvious he's taken quite a shine to you. If it weren't for that, I might check him out myself."

"Really. Hmmm." Emma wondered what that meant about Gloria and Rob. "Are you sure?"

"That he's interested in you?"

"Mmm-hmm."

Gloria nodded. "Trust me—I have an eye for these things."

"I hadn't noticed his interest." Emma thought about it. "Well, you're certainly welcome to him. I'm not planning on getting involved."

"I'll consider it." She paused. "Are you so sure you don't want to pursue it?"

Emma swirled her cognac again and watched amber rivulets slicken the inner curves of the snifter. "You sound like my father."

Gloria rolled onto her back, and her braid flopped across the bed and over the side. She gave Emma an upside-down look of mock surprise. The angle made her eyes look odd. She started lofting the pillow, catching it with her palms and feet.

"I sound nothing like your father. He's a baritone, for one thing. And he has an accent."

"Har-de-har."

"I was just surprised, that's all. You seem to like Keith a lot better than you did at first. And you have to admit he's prime meat, excuse the expression."

Emma burst out laughing, shocked. "Gloria!"

"I mean it. Made my mouth water, seeing him in that bathing suit."

"I'll grant you that. But I can appreciate that sort

of thing just as much from a distance. We have a lot of gorgeous men on Gulf Stream.''

Gloria sighed. ''You just never seem to take men up on it when they express an interest. You don't even seem to notice.''

''I notice. I'm just not interested.'' Emma set her snifter down on the end table and grabbed the chair's arms, pushing the chair into recliner mode. ''I want to become a maiden old lady, like my great-aunt Nettie. She's so cool; she's never been married and she's made her life exactly what she wanted it to be. She worked as a secretary for twenty-five years and scrimped the whole time, investing her money till she could afford early retirement, and then she started to travel. All over the world. Took up photography and it turned out she had a real knack for it.''

''Sounds like a remarkable woman.''

Emma nodded, took a sip of cognac. ''At the age of seventy-eight, she's become a well-known photographic artist. Her works have been on exhibition in places like the Museum of Modern Art and Museum of the Photographic Image. People invite her to give speeches all over the world. Rutgers awarded her an honorary doctorate in Fine Arts. She's witty, and strong, and fascinating. Healthy and active. She'll probably live to be a hundred.

''And one day it dawned on me that her life is full and satisfying; she didn't need a man and children to have all that. In fact, she probably wouldn't have lived nearly as interesting a life if she had married. It looked pretty damn good to me.''

Gloria stretched out across the bed, languorous. ''Different strokes, I guess. It sure wouldn't do for me.''

''Mmm. I suppose. My dad hasn't gotten over wanting me to settle down and give him grandkids—when he bothers to return my calls—but . . .'' Emma shrugged. "I figure he'll get beyond it eventually."

"I like being in love too much to give it up. That thrill you get when you find someone new, it's like you're standing on the edge of a cliff, and you close your eyes and step off the edge, and suddenly you have wings—"

Emma gave Gloria a wry look. "So you step off before you know if you've got wings."

"That's part of the thrill."

"If you say so." There was a pause. Since Gloria had been so direct, she decided to be likewise. "But I'm a little surprised you're interested in Keith—I thought you had something going with Rob."

Gloria looked stunned. "Who told you?"

She decided to stretch the truth a little. "Nobody. I just figured it out."

"We were so careful. Did Mac tell you?"

"I told you, I figured it out myself."

Gloria sighed, a little sadly.

"It's over. It was just a fling, really. He's too—young. You know? But it was fun. He's great in the sack. A little clumsy, yet, but very attentive."

"You used condoms, I hope."

"Give me a break, Miss I'm-going-to-be-an-old-maid."

"Well, we old maids don't have to worry about AIDS and other STDs."

"True. But . . ." Gloria clutched her pillow and sighed gustily. "I like having lovers too much to give it up. I don't know if I'll ever settle down with just one person. Too many interesting men out there."

Emma finished her Courvoisier, set the snifter down, and stood. She gave Gloria's braid a tug. "So we'll both be spinsters together. You'll just be lot more sexually experienced than I will."

Gloria laughed, and launched the pillow at her.

"Good night, Gracie. Don't have too many sexually frustrated dreams."

Emma caught the pillow and threw it back. "And you behave yourself in *your* dreams."

Chapter 19

Gulf Stream Inc. had provided Keith a one-bedroom condo at Melbourne Harbor Suites, in the downtown historical district, not far from the Gulf Stream offices. A sealed envelope was waiting for him at the desk in the front office when he got back from Emma's place. *Room 210—Ramada Inn—tonight, 7:30* it said.

That morning he'd left a message at the number Gorey had given him, identifying himself as Mr. Peters and asking where and when they should meet.

Keith crumpled the note with an irritable grimace and started to toss it into a nearby trash can, then, in a fit of paranoia, thrust it into his pocket. He asked the desk clerk for a city map.

He called Jennifer when he reached the suite.

"Keith! Glad to hear you weathered the storm. I was worried."

"Aw, gee, Mom."

Jennifer laughed, a throaty chuckle.

"It's an impressive structure," he said. "I felt perfectly safe, even during the worst of it. Except while we were outside cutting the catwalk loose. I was a little nervous then."

"You'd better be joking."

"It wasn't that bad," he lied.

She sighed. "I swear to God. You and your hero complex."

"I didn't volunteer. There wasn't anyone else. No one qualified, anyhow." Keith coughed. "I gave the place a thorough going-over. Overall it seems to be a good design. Secondary containment and leak detection systems, all in great shape and well maintained. Excellent solvent recycling, and their ammonia system is a zero-discharge design."

Jennifer grunted. "Good."

"But they do have problems. And I'd say their biggest problems are attitudinal."

"You found evidence of negligence?"

"Yeah. Some." Keith hesitated. It was his job to be as objective as possible. But he found himself reluctant to paint too dark a picture of the situation. "They'd been using their chemical storage area to store a big load of process equipment that had just been shipped in, and moved all their drums and carboys of chemicals over to an unsecured location. Space is severely limited, but if environmental and safety concerns were more of a priority they would have found another location or put in some form of containment. Also, one of their people in Science signed off on the storm preparations when they hadn't even been started. And—" He hesitated again. "I'm not sure about this, but there's something funny about their wastewater analytical results."

"Like what?"

"Like, exactly the same pH, to three decimal places, several days in a row. Other, little things. I'm not convinced the guy who's doing the analyses isn't doctoring the results."

She whistled. "Not good. Criminal negligence."

"Yeah."

"This raises an interesting problem," Jennifer said.

"The FBI doesn't mind if we get dirt there in order to pursue our investigation against Pinkle at the DEP. But I had to agree—informally—not to use anything you dug up against Gulf Stream, to get you access."

Keith was shocked. "You didn't tell me that."

"Interagency politics." The words were a shrug. "I'm prepared to renege on that promise, if the crime is serious enough, and if the evidence is strong enough—and they know it. Pendleton knows it, too, which is why what's-his-name, the lawyer—"

"Evans."

"—Evans, right. Why he raised such a stink over you. If I do renege the fallout could be major, so be very, very sure of yourself, if the falsifying of records is true."

"I'll give it a close look." Keith paused. "I think the wastewater problem is an isolated occurrence, though; they lost their environmental compliance person a couple of months ago. And they're struggling, financially, right now. Everyone's so worried about keeping costs down, and so busy—sixteen-hour days must be the norm. They just haven't been focusing enough on environmental issues lately."

She clucked. "Are you empathizing with polluters?"

Keith scowled. "I'm not excusing them. Merely trying to explain why . . ."

Her tone was mild. "I was only teasing. Have you had a chance to look at their compliance agreements?"

"Only the water discharge document, so far. The air and waste generation agreements I haven't located. And I haven't found any correspondence files yet, either, so I'm not sure who they were dealing with at the DEP."

"Keep looking."

"Right. And it occurs to me," Keith said, "maybe

someone should follow up with Uhlmann. He may know something.''

"Uhlmann?''

"Franz Uhlmann. My predecessor.''

"Excellent idea! I'll get someone on it. Have you been briefed by your FBI contacts yet?''

"Not yet. I have a meeting with Abbott and Costello in about half an hour.''

She made a noise. "Don't pick a fight with them. This situation is delicate enough without sparking a turf war.''

Keith laughed—a short bark. "I'll be good. Honest.''

"Yeah, sure.''

Walking along the Indian River, parallel to Route 1, he reached Room 210 at the Ramada Inn ten minutes early. Barnes let him in. He had actually taken off his suit jacket, to Keith's mild surprise, but his yellow striped tie was snugged up tight at his throat. His sandy hair, what there was of it, was neatly parted.

Gorcy raised a hand in greeting. He looked a good deal more rumpled. He had completely removed his tie and rolled up his sleeves, and was sitting sockfooted, tailor-style, on the bed, sorting photos.

They had hooked up a VCR to the hotel room television set. Boxes of manila folders lined the floor beneath the window, crumpling the sheer curtains. The air was so damp that Keith couldn't decide whether the room was a bit too chilly or a bit too warm.

Barnes locked the door behind Keith. "What have you got? Any leads yet?''

Keith dropped into the chair at the window, by a table piled high with pizza debris and empty thirty-two-ounce Coke cups, and looked out the window. Traffic sped along NASA Boulevard toward the airport.

"One possibility. Richard Munzer, one of the permanent Gulf Stream staff. A lab technician. He failed to secure the labs and chemical stores in the Science module before the storm hit. The outcome could have been disastrous. Most likely it was just stupidity, but . . ." He shrugged. "It's worth checking."

"Great." Barnes got out a little pad, licked the tip of his pencil, and wrote the name down. "Anything else? Anyone seem suspicious of you?"

Keith shook his head and opened his mouth, but Gorey cut in, "What about Tooke? She still on your case?"

Keith shook his head again. "Nah. She's okay."

At their expressions, Keith asked, "What?"

Gorey said, "According to her personnel file, she can be bad news when things hit her wrong."

"If she takes a disliking to you it could put the whole operation in jeopardy," Barnes added. "Their general counsel, Evans, is opposed to this operation. Pendleton overrode his objections, but if his star engineer *and* his general counsel start griping about you, well—"

"I get the picture."

Gorey said, "And we have reason to consider Tooke a possible suspect as the terrorists' inside contact on Gulf Stream."

Keith gaped at Gorey, and then snorted. "Preposterous."

"Not so preposterous as you might think. We've turned up an important link to a possible suspect. And if she *is* the insider, it would be an explosive situation. We can't move against Pendleton's hotshot design engineer and operations officer without a truckload of proof."

"So we need you to play it really easy with her," Gorey said. "Stay away from her. But keep a close watch just the same."

Keith shook his head. "In the first place, you guys are off by a mile. Emma Tooke loves that plant. I watched her risk her life to save it during the hurricane. She *talks* to it, for Christ's sake! No way she'd have anything to do with damaging it. And in the second place, there's no need for me to avoid her. We're getting along fine."

The two agents exchanged a glance. Barnes said, "It may not have been made clear to you, Hellman, but the FBI has jurisdiction. Not EPA. We set the tone of this investigation. This is not some wastewater violation—*lives* are at stake. Millions of dollars' worth of property. You're going to have to follow our instructions."

Keith stared at Barnes and burst out laughing. It was not a friendly laugh. "Excuse me? Do you believe your terrorists could inflict anything like the damage done to Prince William Sound by the Exxon *Valdez* spill? What were the cleanup costs—nearing three billion? Or that they could kill as many thousands of people as the Union Carbide disaster in Bhopal did? I won't even *mention* what Chernobyl did to Ukraine."

Gorey's hands went up. "We're not saying your experience isn't useful—"

"Then let's get a couple things straight. First of all, don't make ignorant remarks about the environment. If there's one thing I can't abide, it's people who trivialize environmental crimes. And second, I'm a federal marshal with six years of investigative experience. Not some instant cop who needs his hand held by you two."

Barnes gave him a look tinged with dislike. "And let *me* set a couple things straight. We've read your file. Five years with Greenpeace doesn't buy you much credibility with me, *Marshal* Hellman. As far as I know, you'd be more likely to abet the terrorists than arrest them. If it'd been my choice you wouldn't even be here."

Jennifer's admonition to play nice with these two floated up in his memory. He rubbed at a spot between his eyebrows.

"I've never supported acts of violence. And besides, if you've read my file you know I gave up *peaceful* civil disobedience when I went to work for the government. If terrorists really are planning to hit Gulf Stream, I plan to stop them." Barnes started to speak, but Keith kept going.

"And let's get another thing straight. I'm no local cop you can intimidate with impunity—the EPA is a federal agency, too, gentlemen. I'm here as a courtesy."

"The FBI initiated this investigation. That puts us in the driver's seat."

Keith took a deep breath and reined in his temper. "Look, I'm not interested in taking over your investigation. But I'm your man in the field—I'm your eyes and ears. And I know what I'm doing. You're going to have to trust me or we're going to get nowhere."

Barnes made a sarcastic noise. Gorey glanced from Keith to Barnes and back, looking pained. "You're right about one thing—we could *all* use a little more good faith, here. Hellman, I'll make you a deal. We won't trivialize environmental crimes, and you don't trivialize the terrorism angle. Fair enough?"

"Fair enough." Keith glanced pointedly at Barnes, who said with a shrug, "Fair enough."

"Good. Take a look at this." Gorey tossed a photo onto the table next to Keith.

It was a mug shot, full-face and profile, of a man in perhaps his late twenties. The placard beneath his face said *Gabriel Cervantes—7/2/89.* His eyes were brown and his hair black, a cheap cut that hung down to his plaid collar. He was clean-shaven and had a

long, hawklike nose. Mug shots could make Shirley
Temple look like a criminal, but this man's eyes had
a look in them—something indefinable, but familiar,
somehow—a look that set him apart. He didn't look
like a garden-variety thug. Keith had a sudden insight.

"He's your eco-teur."

"A possible." Gorey handed him another photo.
The next was a candid shot of the same man on a
street corner. His hair was longer, pulled back in a
ponytail, and he had a mustache. "Gabriel Cervantes.
A more recent shot. We got a tip that he was responsible for the first Woodland Products bombing in New
Mexico. Unfortunately, he was in custody for questioning when the second plant went up and being in-
terviewed by a reporter during the third. Still, we think
he's the ringleader of a small group of eco-terrorists,
and we wouldn't be shocked if he showed up in Melbourne."

"If he's not already here," Barnes said.

Gorey continued. "His radical environmentalist activities began during his sophomore year in college, at
the University of California at San Diego in 1982. He
and several others were arrested for blocking the highway at the entrance to Sea World, in protest of Sea
World's treatment of its performing cetaceans. He was
prominent in organizing a number of other protests
throughout the eighties and nineties. Arrested a total
of eight times, always in connection with environmental issues. He had close ties with a number of Earth
First! activists in their heyday, though he was never
arrested in connection with an Earth First! action."

"Where is he now?"

"Current residence is in Albuquerque, New Mexico. He lives in the local university student ghetto and
makes a living as a writer of nature articles and as a
draftsman for various small businesses. He publishes
an on-line, radical environmental newsletter, and acts

as organizer for various environmental and NIMBY groups throughout the state. He was active in protests against the WIPP nuclear waste disposal project in Carlsbad and against various industrial plants throughout the state—including Woodland Products.''

Gorey handed him a piece of paper. It was a copy of an official UCSD transcript for Emma Tooke. ''Graduated summa cum laude with a master's degree in ocean engineering from UCSD in 1987. She and Cervantes were classmates.''

Keith gave Gorey a wry look without speaking.

''Yeah, it's a big school,'' Barnes said. ''But we know they were both members of the college hiking club, so they at least knew each other.''

Gorey showed him another photo of a page from the 1982 UCSD yearbook that showed both their names listed as members of the hiking club.

''Oh, come on. That's quite a reach.''

A frown built on Barnes's face, but Gorey spoke up. ''You have to admit, the circumstantial evidence is there. Look, Hellman, you asked us to trust you. How about a little reciprocation? Will and I have been doing this for years. You can't always spot the ringer. People can do things for the damnedest reasons. She might have a grudge against Pendleton. Or she might have been bought off or blackmailed.''

Keith remembered the look on Emma's face during the storm, her hands entangled in the lifelines. Remembered her pacing the floor of the control room, wild over the idea that something was going to take her Gulf Stream down. He sighed and shook his head again.

''Well, I don't buy it. But I'll keep an eye on her.''

He made it all the way to the door before he remembered. ''Do you guys have E-mail addresses?''

The agents exchanged a glance. Barnes looked blank, but Gorey was nodding. ''Good point. I've got a buddy who can set us up.'' When Barnes continued to look blank, he said, ''You remember Frank Wojdcek; he was on that team investigating electronic espionage at Lockheed a couple years back. He knows all the ropes.''

Barnes swiped at his chin. ''Right. Right.'' But he still looked sour. ''I don't know, Gene; there's the whole security issue . . .''

''Wojdcek will help us out there. It's a great way to stay in touch with Hellman if he has Internet-connected E-mail.'' He turned back to Hellman and raised his eyebrows.

''Not yet, but I'll get it as soon as I get back out there, and call you with my E-mail address. Preferably by early Monday evening. We'll have to work out some kind of code. An encryption program is no good if they have access to your computer.''

''Yeah.'' Gorey pinched his lip, frowning at Keith, then snapped his fingers. ''A book code.''

Barnes nodded slowly, his expression less doubtful. ''That'd take care of the security problem. But they're not exactly fast.''

''A what?''

''Don't worry about it, Hellman,'' Gorey told him. ''It's the easiest thing in the world to use. And almost impossible to decode, without the key. Or rather''— he shared a smile with Barnes—''the book.''

The next morning Keith awoke to find his message light on. He called at the front desk.

''Package for you from a Mr. Peters,'' the woman drawled. He showered and dressed, and then walked up the hill to the office to pick it up: a five-by-eight bubble-padded manila envelope. Inside he found the unabridged *American Heritage Dictionary*, 1998 paperback edition.

He leafed through it as he walked back down the

hill toward Crane Creek. It was an ordinary book, nothing unusual. Gorey had given him a quick lesson the night before on how book codes worked, using the Gideon's Bible in their hotel room, but it remained to be seen how well the code would work in actuality. Keith tucked the dictionary into the inner pocket of his jacket and walked under the Route 1 overpass, over to the manatee viewing spot.

He'd heard the river's sounds during the night, the cries of the night animals. Now, shortly before dawn, he saw no manatees, but the day creatures were out: song birds trilled amid the trees' leaves; egrets and herons glided low over the cocoa and mirrors of the water's surface; frogs and insects croaked and chattered. Dragonflies, too, skimmed its surface, and unseen creatures moved beneath the water, making mounds.

A short distance away, a bare-chested young black man in cut-offs and thongs was crabbing with a net, a line, bait, and a blue plastic bucket. As Keith watched he pulled the line up and nimbly netted the crab as it let go of the line at the surface.

"Good catch," Keith told him as he passed. The man gave him a quick nod, dropped the crab in his bucket, and swung the bait, a chicken wing, back into the water.

This side, at the viewing area, was paved, with an escarpment, benches, and an educational pavilion, but along the other sides were palms and old gnarled oaks bearded with Spanish moss, and mounds of verdant undergrowth: vinery, grasses, and tiny wildflowers bowing in the breeze atop long, slender stalks, forest-green shrubs covered in gaudy crimson and violet blossoms. Curls of fog rose, wraithlike, from the creek. The air, warm and damp, smelled of the estuary's spice and humus.

Keith sighed. The sight was beautiful, and it brought

back painful memories of another beautiful estuary. One of the posters in the pavilion, "Only 1856 manatees left in Florida," after decades of being sliced to ribbons by boat propellers and the like, depressed him further. He decided to head back.

The clouds hung so low, dark, and sullen that during the drive over the Route 192 causeway and south along Route A1A, past the bait-and-tackle shops, the resort condos and mobile home parks and vine-covered dunes, he wondered if the diving session was going to get rained out.

At Emma's place, someone shouted, "Come in!" at his knock. Keith pushed the door open.

Emma was already in her black-and-yellow swimsuit, sitting at the glass-and-brass dining room table with one long, slim leg tucked under her, scribbling notes on an engineering pad while talking on the phone. Her laptop sat open in front of her, with cords leading to an electrical outlet and the phone jack. Several engineering schematics covered the table. Off to the side were a small stack of papers and the PADI training manual. Covers and pillows made a big mound on the foldaway bed-couch.

Gloria came out of the kitchen with a pitcher of orange juice and some goblets. "Juice?"

Keith accepted a glass and sat down at the table.

"I was just fixing us some toast and eggs," she said. "Have you eaten? Would you like some coffee?"

He shook his head. "Thanks. Already ate."

Emma gave him a smile and covered the mouthpiece. "This won't take long."

"Ha!" Gloria said, back on the kitchen side of the counter. "Ask her how long she's been on already. Workaholic."

Emma stuck out her tongue at Gloria. Keith sat and sipped at his orange juice, idly watching Emma talk to one of her engineers. Help eco-terrorists destroy Gulf Stream? It made no sense. She doted on Gulf Stream the way a mother does her child.

He caught Gloria watching him watching Emma. He wanted to say, "It's not what you think," but, looking back at Emma, he realized that, in part, it was *exactly* that.

This was bad news. Keith didn't have good reflexes, even after a messy divorce, for staying out of bothersome relationships. And even if Emma *weren't* the FBI's prime insider suspect, and even if, ostensibly, he *didn't* report to her, and even if this *weren't* a temporary assignment after which, when it ended, he'd return to his home in Houston, a relationship with Emma Tooke would be bothersome. He looked at her again, rubbing at his chin.

Gloria was still eyeing him. While collecting the coffee mugs from the counter he lifted his eyebrows at her with a quizzical smile, which made her color a bit. Grinning, she came out with two plates of scrambled eggs and toast with jam, set one in front of Emma, and held her hand out for the cordless phone.

Emma took the coffee mug Keith proffered and fended Gloria off long enough to say, "Listen, Ben, I'd better go or Gloria's going to have words with me. E-mail that report to me as soon as it's done, would you? Yeah. Uh-huh. Bye."

She set the phone down and rubbed her hands together. "This is it! I'm finally getting my certification." Then she winced and rubbed at her neck.

"Still sore?" Keith asked.

"If anything, it's worse than yesterday."

"Me too." He grinned. "I know just the cure. Lots of laps. It'll loosen you right up."

"Thanks loads."

"Don't mention it. We should check the weather forecast, though. It's awfully overcast out there."

Emma scowled. "I don't care if it's another hurricane. I want my certification. It's the only reason I agreed to come back this weekend."

Keith had to smile. "I guess we'll be getting plenty wet anyhow."

Emma smiled back at him, and both the smile and the eye contact lingered. Almost nervously, he switched his attention to the papers on the tabletop. "Let's have a look at your homework, shall we?"

Gloria looked from Emma to Keith and back, and got up to collect dishes. He saw a look pass between the two women.

"I'll just do the dishes real quick," Gloria said, "and then get going."

"You don't need to do the dishes. I'll get them."

That wicked little grin came back onto Gloria's face. "I insist. You might be busy later."

Emma gave Keith a glance, ran her fingers through her hair, and averted her gaze, making a production of wrapping up the work she'd been doing. He realized she was nervous, too.

The rain started as they were finishing the underwater exercises. It was a soft rain that spread inverted globules and ripples overhead, across the water's inner surface.

Keith signaled that Emma should remove, set down, and then redon her scuba equipment at the bottom of the pool. She nodded, adjusted her buoyancy, and swam down, arms at her sides, thigh and calf muscles flexing as she kicked, hair flowing and billowing with each kick like black sea grass. Keith floated nearby and watched.

She dropped her weight belt on the floor of the pool, then unbuckled her BC and slipped it off, laying her tanks on the floor of the pool. Next she removed her fins. Then she looked up at him.

Okay? she signaled.

Keith swam down, took her fins, and deposited them some distance away. He signaled that she should throw away her mask.

They'd worked up to this; yesterday he'd had her first half-fill the mask with water and then empty it, then completely fill and empty it. Earlier today he'd had her remove the mask entirely and swim underwater the length of the pool without it. She'd done it, but he'd sensed resistance when it came to removing her mask completely.

It was natural enough. Swimming maskless made you feel naked. Exposed. On some level your brain was telling you that if you couldn't see, you couldn't breathe. A lot of beginning divers freaked out at this point—or at this same point during the check-out dive. And you could never tell which ones they'd be, either, so he felt uneasy despite the fact that she'd done so well thus far.

He gestured again for her to remove the mask. The stream of bubbles issuing from her regulator stopped. He frowned.

With a sudden, almost impatient gesture, she swept the mask off her face and tossed it away. It floated to the pool floor a few feet from her. Then she picked the BC back up and struggled into it. She did the same with her weights. Once buckled up she swam to her mask, scooped it up, put it on, and cleared it. She glanced up at him then, looking pleased with herself, as she swam over to get her fins. He nodded, and gave her an *okay*.

He broke surface seconds after she did.

"You held your breath down there, for a minute."

"Really?" She was breathless, beaming, with rain coursing down her face and pelting the water around her. The smile went straight to his heart and thawed his annoyance. "When?"

He sighed, shook his head. "You've got to be more careful. Never, ever, *ever*—"

"—hold your breath underwater while using compressed air. I know. I'm sorry." She swam to the pool's edge, and turned back to give him a look. "How'd I do otherwise?"

Keith pursed his lips. "You've passed."

"At last!"

"There's still the checkout dive."

"No sweat. Piece of cake. We'll do it at Gulf Stream sometime this next week."

Keith grimaced. "Conditions are pretty rough out there, for a checkout dive. I'd rather take you someplace inland next weekend."

She looked upset. "There are the breakwaters. And there are platforms beneath the reefs we could use. It wouldn't be so bad." She paused. "There's no way I'll be able to take next weekend off. Not after the storm, and not with everything else that's going on. It'll have to be at Gulf Stream, or not at all. At least for the foreseeable future."

Keith pulled his mask down and eyed her.

"All right, if conditions aren't too rough."

She whooped. "I'm practically official!"

As they were removing and cleaning their equipment later she asked, not looking up, "You want to go to dinner with me tonight to celebrate? I know a great restaurant on the river."

He paused and looked at her; she rocked back on her haunches and met his gaze, and a smile quirked her lips. Water coursed down her face; her eyes were red from the pool's chlorine. She'd never looked more beautiful.

"My treat," she said.

Keith smiled back. "Uh-uh. You're the practically official graduate. My treat."

*   *   *

She picked him up at the hotel at seven, waking him from a nap.

"You look great," he said. She flashed him a smile.

It was true: she wore a simple, off-white, sleeveless dress of some flowing fabric that clung to her long, lean form in a most pleasing way, with a cameo at her throat, bare legs, and leather sandals. She'd twisted her hair up onto her neck with jeweled sticks. Moonstones at her earlobes caught the setting sun's light.

He pointed at his equipment bag and overnight case sitting by the door. "Do you mind giving me a lift to Port Canaveral after dinner? I know it's a bit of a drive . . ."

"No problem."

She carried the small case and let him lug the equipment bag out to the car.

It was a beautiful evening, unseasonably cool. Moist air riffled their hair and clothes as they walked to her car. The rain had stopped. Far to the east, glowing clouds piled up on the horizon: mounds of embers and rose petals suspended between sky and land.

"I got some new dive equipment this afternoon," Emma said. "A U.S. Divers regulator, dive computer, and BC. I'd love for you to have a look at them sometime and tell me what you think. Maybe when we do our checkout dive."

Keith raised his eyebrows. She must have spent a fortune. "You don't waste time, do you?"

She looked over at him. "I have been waiting for this for so long. You have no idea."

Still drowsy, he watched Emma drive—watched her hands move on the wheel and stick shift, and the profile of her face as she gauged the traffic. He listened with half an ear, maybe less, as she talked about Gulf Stream, and meanwhile lost himself in the faint scent of jasmine from her skin or hair, in the minutiae of her mannerisms, the line of her cheek and arm, the curve of her breast under her white dress.

She glanced over at him.

"I get this sense I'm putting you to sleep."

Not all of me, he thought.

"Sorry." He rubbed his face with a sigh. "I haven't recovered from Sophronia, quite. I was drifting."

"I guess I get a little boring on the subject of Gulf Stream." She frowned and gave her head a shake. "I get a little obsessive about it."

"Not at all boring. Obsessive? Maybe a little." He shrugged. "It's quite an accomplishment. You must be very proud."

She looked at him, and her eyes glinted. "Yeah. And it was pure serendipity. Pendleton and a friend of Dennis's are golfing buddies from way back; that was how Dennis got on Pendleton's short list. And my dad is Dennis's cardiologist. And, once my name was in the pot—well, one of Gulf Stream's partners is a private trust fund that likes to see women and minorities in key positions. I think their opinion carried a lot of weight with Pendleton. I'll never again underestimate the value of luck. And having connections." She laughed and shook her head. "I was so naïve. I almost turned the offer down."

He stared at her, incredulous.

"Girl Scout's honor," she said.

"Why?"

"I didn't want to be given opportunities because I was a woman, or because my dad knew somebody. I wanted to make it on merit alone."

"What changed your mind?"

She snorted. "After watching me agonize for a couple of days, my dad asked, 'Do you want the job?' And when I said 'Yes!' and explained my reasons for hesitating, he said, 'Honey, the workplace is not a level playing field. Business is all about who you know. What do you think the old boys' network is?'

He said to me, 'It's not your job to second-guess someone else's reasons for selecting you. If you're qualified and you want the job, then take it! Prove yourself by doing the job better than anybody else could.' "

They pulled into a parking lot. The restaurant, the Chart House, was associated with a yacht club, and had a marina right outside. It had a big picture window that looked out on the river. The hostess greeted Emma by name and gave them a table next to the window. As they were sitting down, an eighty-foot yacht, white, silent, and sleek, sliced through the reflected lights that shivered across the water's surface. It was so close he felt he could almost reach out and touch its hull.

The hostess passed out menus and placed a wine list on the table. "Your waiter will be with you in a minute."

Emma leaned on her elbows and gave him a curious look. "And what about you? What made you decide to join Gulf Stream I?"

He opened his menu. "Shall we split an appetizer? I'm famished."

They discussed the relative merits of stuffed mushrooms versus the chilled shrimp cocktail, and then the waiter came. She ordered a red wine. By then she'd apparently forgotten her question.

He didn't want to have to lie to her.

The waiter brought the wine. With a flourish he opened the bottle, let her sniff the cork, and poured a bit in the bottom of a wineglass for her. With an ironic glance at Keith, she swirled, sipped, and after a pause nodded, and the waiter filled both their glasses. Keith took a sip; it was tart and nutty on his tongue.

After the waiter had left, Keith leaned forward and asked, "Would madame care to sniff the cork?"

She burst out laughing. "It is a bit silly, isn't it? If

it were a hundred-dollar bottle of wine I could understand all the fuss, but . . . oh well. I suppose it adds to
the ambiance.''

They made eye contact again. Keith gave her a
smile, which she returned, and then she averted her
gaze, looking out at the river. He followed her lead
and looked out at the twilit sky.

"It's a beautiful evening.''

"Mmmm,'' she agreed. "I'd love to go sailing—or
diving!''

"Speaking of which—'' He lifted his glass. "Congratulations.''

She touched her glass to his, smiling. "This is wonderful, Keith; I can't thank you enough for training
me. I've wanted this for so long.'' She leaned forward,
eyes shining. "Let's do the check-out dive as soon as
possible. Tuesday afternoon, perhaps, after I've had a
chance to meet with my engineers.''

"So you're not coming back with us on the boat
tonight?''

She shook her head. "Nope. Major meeting tomorrow here in town. We lost a huge deal with GM right
before you came on board, and we're having to scramble to look for other markets. It's going to be a real
battle, too; Reynolds and I are probably going to end
up head to head. Again.''

"Gloria says he's a real prick.''

Her lips twisted. "In a word. Apparently he's done
some good research in the past. But he's a liar and a
manipulator. But more importantly, he's got connections. Oh, yes.'' She sighed and looked into her wineglass. "There's that word again.''

After a pause she went on, "He brings in grants
hand over fist. Big grants. Government contracts. And
he's pressuring Pendleton to convert Gulf Stream to a
purely oceanographic research station. He wants to
push Flo and me out of the way. When our vision—

and the original goal of Gulf Stream—is to create an integrated community. Diversity. Oceanographic research, yes—but also engineering research, and marine products, and energy production and storage.''

"Really? I always thought scientific grants were few and tiny. That was certainly my experience in grad school.''

"Well . . .'' She rolled her wine around in her glass. "A stable scientific platform in deep water is a rare commodity, and there's quite a bit of money floating around out there for climate change research, these days.'' She sighed. "Apparently Reynolds knows the right people.''

She sipped at her wine and looked out at the river.

"I don't know why it matters so much to me,'' she said finally. "No matter what happens to it now, Gulf Stream I has made my career. I have all sorts of opportunities to move on to other engineering projects. Juicy ones. Chances of a lifetime. I'm a design engineer at heart, not a process engineer. Nor an administrator.'' She sighed. "I should turn in my resignation to Pendleton. Every morning I wake up and think about all the paperwork ahead, all the personnel hassles, and I ask myself why I stay.''

"And what do you answer yourself, Emma Tooke?''

She smiled briefly at his use of her name. "I don't know.''

"I bet I do.''

Her lips curved up, but her eyes held a challenge. "Oh?''

"Mmm-hmm. I have this theory.''

"Do tell.''

Keith hesitated and looked into his own wine goblet.

"There are people who aren't satisfied just to drift through life. People who are filled up with purpose—

with a need to create. To build. Pour their souls into
something larger than themselves. Something that will
live on after them.'' He gestured at her. ''You're one
of them. And Gulf Stream is your child of the mind.
You could never walk away from it, not till you know
it'll stand on its own without you. On that day, I wager
you, you'll walk away in a minute, and never look
back.'' He took a swallow of the wine and lifted the
glass. ''And give birth to another magnificent machine, in due course.''

'' 'Magnificent machine.' I like that.'' Her smile
mirrored his. ''I take it you're another of these purposeful souls who need to create.''

''Me? Nah. Haven't got a creative bone in my
body.''

He grinned at her look of surprise. She sipped wine.
''That's an odd pastime, coming up with grand theo-
ries for everyone but yourself.''

''I tried pottery. It wasn't a pretty sight.''

Emma threw back her head and laughed. It lighted
up her face. The waiter brought the mushroom appetizer and salads, and the conversation turned to food
and other trivia.

Over their steak and lobster entrees, Keith asked her
about her days at UCSD.

''I'm tired of talking about me,'' she said. ''Tell me
about you.''

He lifted his eyebrows. ''What do you want to
know?''

''Gloria tells me you worked for Greenpeace for a
while.''

''Mmm-hmm.''

''For how long?''

He gave her a wry smile. ''Four years. Just long
enough for my wife to get fed up and leave me, before
I got the 'real job' she'd always been after me to get.
Didn't help; she didn't want me back by then. Though,

to be fair, it was more complicated than that. I wanted kids, she didn't.''

''Ah.'' His answer seemed to have distracted her. ''That sounds painful.''

He pursed his lips, shook his head. ''Ancient history.''

Emma seemed pensive. ''Look, I hope this doesn't cause you to take offense, but I've never understood why people join organizations like Greenpeace. I mean, I want to see the environment protected, too—who doesn't?—but so many environmental protesters exaggerate the risks. And they get their facts wrong—to the point that it looks as if they're deliberately distorting the situation.'' She frowned. ''And half the time they don't understand the businesses they act out against. They seem to think they're dealing with a bunch of monsters, evil polluters, not other human beings. They don't understand the real issues involved. They manipulate the media.''

Keith shrugged. ''And I guess I'd have to respond that you have a pretty distorted view of environmental activists. Maybe some are misinformed, or vindictive. But there are just as many—if not more—misinformed people on the business side, who are defensive about the impact of their actions on the environment and refuse to look at the facts—to consider that maybe they're going to have to change their ways. Before it's too late.''

She studied him for a long moment. The busboy cleared their plates, and the waiter came back with an offer of coffee and dessert.

''Just the check,'' Keith said, with a glance at Emma, who nodded.

''How did you end up becoming an activist?'' she asked.

He frowned. The memory was painful, but he'd told it so many times it came out almost automatically.

"I'd just gotten my bachelor's in marine biology and was developing my graduate project with my advisor in the estuary marshes along the intercoastal waterway south of Houston. I spent three months counting in situ grass shrimp, clams, and mussels as the groundwork for a long-term study of nutrient density versus population density. Five little acres of marsh that I knew like the back of my hand."

Emma grimaced. "I'd probably quit, too, if I had to spend three months in a swamp."

"Marsh. I didn't quit because of that. One night two barges collided in the intercoastal and spilled one hundred and sixty-five thousand gallons of number two fuel oil onto my site." He paused. "They used my surveys to assess the damage, but there wasn't much left. It was suggested that I change my thesis to a long-term study of the damage done and the rate of recovery. I declined."

"Ouch."

The waiter brought the check on a plate, and Keith dropped a credit card on top. The waiter carried it away.

Emma smiled quizzically. "And what made you decide to *stop* being an activist?" She paused. "Or have you, really? Stopped, I mean."

He didn't respond. That was too close to the mark for comfort.

She poured the last of the wine into both their glasses and sat back, looking out at the lights on the river. Meanwhile Keith signed the credit stub the waiter brought him and tucked the receipt into his pocket. Emma was watching him closely.

"You have a child of the mind, Keith," she said.

"I don't follow."

She gave him an unreadable look, one that both irritated and, perversely, pleased him. Then she shook her head.

"Never mind." With a quick toss she finished her wine. "Come on. I have to stop by the office on the way to the port."

Emma pulled into the parking lot at Hibiscus and Route 1. Before them was a four-story building with a sign in front: *Reflections on the River*. The sign also said *Gulf Stream 1—Corporate Headquarters.* A well-kept lawn with flowers, shrubbery, palms, and oaks surrounded the building, which stood on stout concrete stilts. Through the stilts he could see the Indian River. It was so wide that the far bank was visible only as a dusting of lights on the horizon. A bridge—Highway 192—arced high over the river to the south: a fairy tracery of lights high above the dark water.

Keith had walked past this spot the evening before. The building was mostly mirrored glass, with a frame of steel, an apron of red brick flagstones, and a parking lot with islands of riotous, flowering shrubbery and palms. During the day the glass reflected greenery and blue sky. Now, lit and unlit offices turned the building into a patchwork of dimly lit rooms and silvery glass reflecting streetlights.

Several other cars were parked in the lot and he wondered who was working late landside.

A gangly young security guard sat in a chair by the elevators, reading a science fiction magazine. He stood, a jumble of knees and elbows, as they opened the door, and touched his hat. "Evening, sir, ma'am. May I help you?"

Keith shared a glance with Emma. She blinked and cocked her head at the man. "You're new here, aren't you?"

He smiled. "Yes, ma'am. Just started last Thursday."

"What's your name?"

"Hieronymus Sharpe. But you can call me Ron. Y'all with Gulf Stream?"

"That we are."

"Sorry for any inconvenience, but if I could just see y'all's IDs . . ."

Emma fished hers out. The guard looked at it and handed it back to her, and then glanced inquiringly at Keith. Emma jerked her thumb. "He's brand-new— hasn't been processed yet, but he reports to me. I'll vouch for him."

"All right, then. If I could just have your name, sir."

"Hellman. Keith Hellman."

He pulled out a log sheet and jotted both their names down, and touched his hat again. "Very good. Have a nice evening, now."

They took the elevator up to the fourth floor, where she had a corner office. She flipped on the light and went to her desk.

"Have a seat; I just have to check my mail and stuff."

He came in and wandered around the office. It was a good deal larger and rather more plush than her Gulf Stream I cubbyhole, but otherwise it looked similar: stacks of paper and files—a dozen or more linear feet's worth—took up most of the available desk, shelf, and credenza space. Yellow Post-its and taped memos took up the rest.

"You need a file clerk," he remarked. She chuckled and picked up the phone, punching in a number.

The wood bookshelves along one wall were jammed with engineering and materials references, but a few interesting seashells and fossils were nestled among the books and papers. Keith picked up a pink conch shell that measured maybe ten inches end to end, and walked over to the credenza to stare out the window at the lawn and the dark river beyond, thinking that

Emma's seashells were about the only thing nonbusiness about her.

A pool of light from Emma's desk lamp created a mirror in the window. The image drew his gaze. Emma and her reflection typed at the keyboards of their computers, phones at their ears. He put the conch to his ear to hear the roar of his inner ear and watched her mirror twin's big, bony, nimble hands tap-dance over the computer keys.

Emma Tooke was all long, lean lines, legs and torso and arms and shoulders—shockingly tall. He got lost tracing the lines and curves of her face. She was so breathtakingly beautiful. But beautiful wasn't the right word. Captivating. And as she worked it was as if all her being were collected together, swept inward, in a spiral of concentration as painstaking and precise as a seashell, a spiral that carried her to a blazing pinpoint of thought, deep within.

"You ready to head up to the port?" she asked, hanging up the phone. He started, coming out of his reverie, and glanced at his watch.

"I'll be awfully early if we leave now. How about a walk along the beach?"

"I have a better idea," she said. She turned off the light. "Come on."

The park outside spilled over with lush vegetation. Beneath some trees stood a picnic table. She held out her hand and Keith took it; her skin was warm and dry, and soft, like expensive silk. He stroked her hand with his thumb. The nails were trimmed to the quick.

They crossed the lawn. Crickets chirped in the flowering bushes and palm trees that surrounded the picnic table. As Keith and Emma approached the screen of trees the insects fell silent, then, after a breathless pause, resumed their raucous courting.

Emma climbed onto the bench seat and sat on the tabletop, looking out over the river. Keith sat down next to her. The evening was quite cool, and though the afternoon's stiff breeze had died down, enough of it lingered to carry the smells of fish and weed up from the river, mingled with the fragrance of the bright scarlet blossoms clustered nearby.

Emma rubbed her arms and gazed out at the river. She pulled the jeweled sticks out and her hair tumbled down over her shoulders. Keith smelled shampoo and jasmine.

"Too cool?"

She nodded. "A little. I should have brought a sweater. I'm not used to cool weather this time of year."

He put his arm around her shoulders; he half expected her to shrug it off or make a sarcastic remark. She didn't. But when she turned to look at him her blue eyes held a glimmer of fear.

"I'm relatively harmless, you know," he said. That made her smile. She shook her head.

"It's not you. It's me." She looked away again, out at the river. "I'm used to being good at what I do. And I'm no good at—" She coughed. "At this sort of thing."

"I promise not to give you a poor performance review."

She gave him a sardonic look. "Thanks so much."

"Think nothing of it."

After a quiet moment, she glanced at him again. "You've been married . . . in a long-term relationship."

"That ended in divorce. Not exactly a recommendation."

She shrugged. "I guess those things happen." A pause. "My parents divorced when I was sixteen. I know how bad things can get."

Keith sighed. "We were too young. We loved each other so much, but by the time we knew what we wanted out of life, it turned out we wanted totally different things.'' He hesitated. ''Has there ever been anyone for you?''

''One. I mean, I've had other, quote, relationships, unquote. But they just seemed like jokes. Only I'd forgotten the punch line.''

''Unlucky at love, eh?''

''I guess so.'' Again, a shrug. ''It just didn't seem so important to me. Men, that is. In college I was so determined to get my degrees—to prove myself academically—that men just seemed like a distraction.'' An inward-looking smile came and went. ''Gabe decided he wanted me, though. And he got past all my defenses. Oh, man. He got past defenses I didn't even know I'd had.''

Keith kept his expression neutral. Gabe. Gabriel Cervantes? But Keith didn't buy Barnes and Gorey's theory. Being a criminal's old lover didn't make her a criminal.

''And it was pretty bad, huh?''

She gave him a surprised look. ''God, no; it was glorious! Intoxicating. I fell so hard.''

''What happened?'' Keith asked when it became obvious she wasn't going to continue.

''Oh, I don't know.'' She hunched her shoulders up. ''I guess we were both just too strong-willed, or something. Too young. Everything seemed so clear and simple; the whole world was done up in blacks and whites. None of this fuzzy logic business—the circuit was on or it was off. You know?''

Keith nodded.

''We didn't see things the same.'' She shook her head and said with a certain fondness, ''He was so damned opinionated. The fights we had. Wow.''

''Sounds like you still care.''

She gave him a startled look, and then pursed her

lips, thinking it over. "Does anyone ever really get over their first love?"

Keith made a strangled noise. It was answer enough. Emma seemed amused.

"Maybe that's why . . ." she said, thoughtfully. He waited, but she didn't continue.

"Are you still in touch with him?" It had to be asked, but he winced internally. Conflict of interest, Hellman?

Emma sputtered a laugh. "God, no. We parted on *terrible* terms. Swore we'd kill each other if we saw each other again." A pause. "Took me a long time to get over him."

She looked rather sad. Keith thought of his ex-wife, Tricia. He gave Emma's shoulders a squeeze and she leaned into him. He breathed in her scent, perfume and skin. It was nice.

"Amazing, how much it hurts," he said.

"Yeah."

After a moment, she asked, "And you?"

"Me?"

"Yes, you." Her fingers came up and traced the center seam and buttons of his shirt. Then she seemed to notice what she was doing, and lowered her hand. "You're divorced. Didn't it make you gun-shy?"

Keith lifted a shoulder. "Nah. I always believed that old cliché; you know: ''Tis better to have loved and lost . . .' "

"I suppose so." She frowned at her feet. "For a long time I wished we had never happened. But I remember him fondly now. I saw him in a magazine the other day—he was being arrested—and it made me worry about him. Worry about what he's doing, whether he's okay. That sort of thing."

"Regrets?"

"No. I could never have been the person he wanted me to be. And I couldn't see things his way. But after that I guess, maybe, I was afraid to take any more chances.'' She gave Keith another wry glance. ''I've got the super-competent businesswoman down so well. It always seemed a shame to set her aside for some other persona I hardly know.''

''Maybe we could get to know her together.''

She smiled. ''Hmmm.''

Their faces had somehow gotten quite close to each other by this time, and her eyes seemed to draw him closer. So, it seeming like the thing to do, he leaned forward and, ever so gently, kissed her.

And she tasted so fine, it seemed like the thing to do, to kiss her again.

This led to other, longer, deeper and more lingering kisses, until he looked at his watch and realized muzzily he was going to miss the midnight boat out of Port Canaveral unless they left *right then*. Hand in hand they stumbled back to her car. She broke several traffic laws getting him up the coast to Cape Canaveral, and out to the pier at the port, and then, to his shock, walked with him to the boat with fingers entwined in his and kissed him again, just as the captain and first mate walked out on deck. They gaped.

She spotted them and made a nervous grimace. ''Oh, well,'' she said, and smiled into Keith's eyes, stroking his cheek, ever so lightly, with a fingernail.

''See you tomorrow evening.''

''You taking the helicopter back?''

She nodded.

''Good.''

He carefully placed a foot on the gangplank. When he glanced back she was still standing there, with her eyes wide and a crooked smile on her face. ''Good night.''

''Good night.''

He gave the captain and first mate a nod and went below, whistling.

Chapter 20

Then next morning Emma went to work a couple of hours early to prepare her notes for the strategy meeting. The dawn-lit greenery behind Reflections caught her eye as she slammed her car door, and on impulse she wandered over toward the little park behind the building, looked at the picnic table.

Memories lighted up along her body like a string of Christmas bulbs: Keith's deep, bark-brown eyes filling up her field of vision; his locks of curly hair entangled in her fingertips; the silk of his lips against hers, softer than baby's skin; the taste of his salt-sweet mouth and tongue and skin.

Emma slipped off her linen jacket; she'd gotten too warm and she was feeling rather dizzy. Tooke, you've got a crush, she thought. It was like being a teenager again. She hadn't thought she was still able.

When she turned to head into the building she saw that she wasn't the only early arrival. Phil's little white Lamborghini convertible was parked beneath the overhang, behind one of the concrete stanchions that supported the building, and near it sat Dennis's BMW. Pendleton's chauffeur, leaning against the smoke-and-coal-colored limousine with a lit cigarette in his hand, waved to Emma.

Ron the security guard stretched, yawned, and waved her on through. She lifted her eyebrows and glanced at her watch.

"You been here all night?"

"Uh-huh."

"What time do you go home?"

Another yawn swallowed the first half of his reply. "Not soon enough."

Emma stuck her head into Phil's office. Dennis was just standing.

"I'll catch you later, Phil. Emma." He nodded at Emma and hurried out. She looked after him, wondering if he was mad at her about their clash over Thomas. Or maybe feeling guilty.

"You're in early," she said to Phil.

His tie was askew, circles hung under his eyes, and he had a day's worth of dark stubble all over the lower half of his face. He sat back with an explosive exhalation and a smile at the sight of her.

"Emma! Come on in. Glad to see you're all right. We were all worried."

She entered and dropped her burgundy leather satchel, crammed with papers and files, inside the door.

Art— real art, paintings with a bite to them; not the costume-art most offices sported—decorated the walls of Phil's corner office. They were his personal possessions. His desktop was polished rose granite, and for all she could tell his lamps may have been gilt with real gold. His suit, though rumpled, was made of expensive wool gabardine, or some damn thing.

Phil was the primary heir to his family's fortune, and Emma figured he must work for the pleasure it gave him. It certainly couldn't have been out of fiscal need. His uncle was the other major partner funding Gulf Stream I along with Pendleton, and, albeit informally, Phil wielded a lot of influence because of it.

His office looked out over the park, toward Indian River. Emma walked over and looked out. Sunrise strung spidery emerald shadows across the park, and birds swooped from branch to branch, causing the trees' leaves and mossy beards to quiver. An egret lighted on the picnic table. Emma glanced down and brushed her lips with a finger; an embarrassed, pleased grin came onto her face again. She turned away from the window. Perching a buttock on Phil's desk, she looked down at his papers.

"Preparing for the meeting?"

"Mmmm."

"Here all night?"

"Mmmm." He rubbed at his face. "God, I'm beat."

"Is it that bad?"

He knew what she meant; he gave her a long, hard look, and then rocked back in his brown leather executive chair and looked out the window instead of answering. He asked, "How's that new fellow working out?"

"Who, Keith?"

Phil nodded, glancing at her.

"Great. I was royally pissed at first, but he's good. He's really good."

She'd been thinking of his actions during the hurricane, but her thoughts returned to the picnic table last night, and another smile threatened to break onto her face.

But Phil was looking at her with his eyebrows furrowed and his lips pulled tight. She began to wonder . . . she hadn't noticed his Lamborghini in the parking lot the night before, and the sleek little convertible was hard to miss. But she hadn't been looking closely; he might have parked in the back. And their offices were on different floors, so she wouldn't have seen him inside. They'd been right outside. Anyone working late, in fact, might have seen.

How, she wondered, could I have been so stupid? Talk about stupid; she'd kissed him in front of half the boat's crew. She avoided a groan. On the other hand, if Gloria could do it, why couldn't she? But Phil still looked grim.

"What?"

Phil sighed, ran fingers through his hair, and pushed back in his chair. He shook his head. "We've got big troubles, Emma."

She dropped into a chair. "Talk."

"Pendleton and I spent a good two hours yesterday going over the balance sheet with Dennis, and Dennis and I spent another hour this morning. Next month, unless a miracle happens, we'll have to borrow money to make payroll. If we don't come up with another major source of funds in the next two months, we'll either have to file Chapter Eleven or sell the business."

Emma gasped. "That's bad."

"Really bad." He issued a morose sigh.

"I'm working on it," she said. He shook his head.

"Be prepared for the worst. We need to take some desperate measures."

"What are you saying?"

He shook his head. "Just be prepared. Whatever comes."

On her office chair lay a plain white envelope. No name, no markings. She opened it and pulled out the piece of paper inside. A single short sentence was printed on it:

Keith Hellman is not what he seems.

Emma read it over about three times. Not surprisingly, it didn't make any more sense the third time. She turned the paper over. Ordinary 8½-by-11-inch copier/laser printer paper.

She inspected the envelope. It was a security envelope, with the blue-and-white stripes on the inside— the kind used at Gulf Stream I, which wasn't surprising since only a employee could've put it in her office.

Emma sat and thought for a minute. She got up and looked out at the cubicles. No one was in yet. Then she spotted the woman from the janitorial service leaving the bathroom, pulling a large waste can behind her. Emma crossed over to her.

"Excuse me. Did you see anyone in my office?"

The woman gave her a blank look. *"No comprendo, señora."* She hesitated, and said slowly, "No speak English."

Emma scowled, struggled to remember her high school Spanish. *"¿Usted vio . . . uh . . . alguien allá"*— Emma pointed at her office—*"antes de yo . . ."* She needed the past tense of *venir*—"to come." *Did you see anyone before I came?* The woman stared at her while she gnawed her lip. Finally, in frustration, she shook her head and turned away.

But the woman offered, *"¿Antes de que usted llegara?"*

"Yes! *¡Exactamente!* You saw someone?"

The woman gave Emma a conciliatory smile and shook her head. *"No, lo siento, pero no vi nadie."*

Emma went down to the little alcove on the ground floor. Ron's chin was touching his chest and soft snores issued from his sinuses. Emma cleared her throat, once . . . twice, more loudly. He roused and looked at Emma like a rodent trapped in her headlights. His face slowly went red.

"Ron, were you here all night?"

"Yes, ma'am!"

"And how much of that time were you asleep?"

He stared at the floor. Finally he said, "I was mostly awake. I may have dozed off once or twice, but only for a few minutes."

She pinned him with a frown, and he made an X across his chest and held up three fingers. Emma nodded, pinching her lip. "Thanks for being honest. Did anyone come through, or try to, who didn't have a Gulf Stream I ID?''

"Well . . . there was the guy who came through with you . . ."

"Besides him."

"Nope," he said. "Leastwise . . . not while I was awake.

"Ma'am?" he said, as she reentered the elevator. His face had gone completely red. "You won't tell no one, will you? I really need the job."

She hung on to the door and cocked her head at him. Not unkindly, she said, "Look. If you really need the job, you'd better get your sleep. When you're *not* on duty."

Back in her office Emma looked at the note again, then at the other piles on her desk, floor, and credenza. I don't have time for this shit, she thought, and tossed the note into her in-box.

· She tried for almost half an hour to work on her notes for the upcoming meeting but, again, unsurprisingly, couldn't concentrate. The weird note preyed on her mind.

And she wasn't prepared for this meeting. Reynolds was going to walk all over her. With Gulf Stream's money troubles, Pendleton would be in no mood to accommodate a request for more time.

Well, the worst he could say was no. And the best time to ask was before the meeting, when she could get to him alone. Emma sprang out of her chair, strode to the door, and yanked it open. Her chief landside engineer, Angelo Brucculeri, was hanging his jacket on a hanger.

"Emma, hey! Welcome back. I've got a purchase authorization form I need you to sign. I've picked out the AutoCAD station, and fax and plotter."

"What?"

"To replace the ones that were stolen last week."

She snapped her fingers. "Right. Uh, drop it on my desk and I'll take care of it later."

Angelo beamed. "Already done. It's in your in-box."

Which was six inches high. "Then I'll never find it. You'd better dig it out and put it on my chair."

"You got it, chief. Did you check out the new security setup?"

"You mean Ron?"

"Yeah. They gave us a thorough going-over and they're going to install some better alarms and stuff."

"Great. I'd like an update later." She ducked around him and into the interior corridor. Flo leaned on the counter near the pantry, dressed as close to corporate as she ever got, in a lightweight, blue linen jacket, white cotton blouse with a red-and-blue satin scarf tied like a man's tie about her neck, mid-thigh-length linen shorts, and flats. She yawned, dipping a tea bag into her mug as she stared out the waterward window with her eyelids at half-mast. At Emma's approach, she straightened.

"You look armed for bear. What's going on?"

Emma shook her head. "I'll explain later."

She crossed through the maze of cubicles and offices to Pendleton's corner office. The door to his administrative assistant Kyle's office, next to his, was ajar; Kyle wasn't in yet. Emma knocked at Pendleton's closed door.

Pendleton's voice said, "Come in. Ah, Emma." He hung up the phone and as she entered he stood, gesturing at the chairs and couch. "Sit."

Pendleton's office was surprisingly modest, given his staggering wealth. There was a large wooden desk, and a conference table set in the corner. On the wall was a large oil painting of Gulf Stream set against a gorgeous sunrise. The perspective was low, near the water, and the modules soared overhead, almost flying.

Emma dropped onto the couch against the wall. Pendleton tossed copies of the *Orlando Sentinel*, the *Washington Post*, and *The New York Times* Sunday edition onto the coffee table in front of her.

"Your copies. They're all from the same AP wire," he said. "Read the *Sentinel*. It's the longest version."

A respectable portion of the front page was devoted to Hurricane Sophronia, with an inch and a half about Gulf Stream I, complete with an aerial photo showing the facility and the damage to the catwalk. The headline read, "Sophronia's Worst Is Least of Ocean Thermal Plant's Problems." The article briefly recounted events, with a few, mostly trivial, inaccuracies. The article also quoted a leading energy sector analyst as saying that Gulf Stream was on shaky financial ground with the collapse of the GM-PG&E deal, and Pendleton was likely to declare bankruptcy within four to six weeks. Pendleton was quoted as saying, "Poppycock."

While she read, Pendleton dropped into an armchair next to the couch and rubbed a well-manicured thumb back and forth across the creases in his brow with an introspective gaze. She tossed the paper back onto the pile. Pendleton roused himself and gave her a smile.

He said, "Your design certainly withstood the acid test."

Emma couldn't suppress a smile. "I guess so."

"What can I do for you?"

She slouched on the couch and eyed him, groping for an angle that might improve her chances of getting a yes.

"Just wanted to touch base with you before the meeting. And, um," she improvised, "see if I could get your okay to make some calls to a couple of industrial and merchant banking contacts this week about some other hydrogen power ventures."

He perked up. "You have some ideas."

"Yes." She was bound to come up with *something*. "Have you spoken to anyone at PG and E? Are they still interested?"

"You bet. Rambort as much as told me last week that if we could come up with another partner on the autobuilding end of things, the deal doc was as good as signed, as far as PG and E is concerned."

"Excellent."

"What do you have in mind?"

"Actually . . . I don't want to say too much about it until I've pursued it a little further. In fact"—she decided to just dive in, banking on the good karma she'd racked up during Sophronia—"it'd work best for me if we could postpone the meeting a couple of days, so I could have some time to really prepare. With the storm and all, obviously, it wasn't possible for me to do much, and if you'll give me that time I think you'll be quite pleased with the results."

Pendleton pursed his lips. "Time is of the essence right now, but . . . I suppose that's a reasonable request." He went to the calendar lying open on his desk and flipped through the pages. "I've got other commitments Thursday and Friday, but very early Wednesday morning I've got some availability. How is seven-thirty A.M. on the seventh for you?"

"Sounds good."

"Why don't you tell Kyle to let the others know? And have him verify that my calendar is free."

She dropped by Kyle's office and scribbled a note about the meeting change.

Back in her office, Emma dropped into her chair and flipped through her Rolodex to find the phone numbers of her New York and Boston contacts. Then she went through her in-box and high-priority piles, and did up a list of everything she needed to get done.

She came across the anonymous note again; she'd all but forgotten it. After an uncomfortable moment of staring at the note, with a sigh, she added another item to her to-do list. Just what she needed—another annoying distraction.

The list was four pages long by the time she'd finished. She went through the list again and reset priorities. It was obvious she'd need to spend the first part of the week landside. Ben was doing a great job of starting repairs at Gulf Stream, and dozens of other things on her list would just have to wait.

She dialed Flo's extension. Flo picked up after three rings.

"Emma! Kyle just called. Thanks for buying us more time."

"We need it, eh?" she said. "Are any of the boats coming into port today or tonight?"

"Let me check the roster." Keys clattered. "*Ox* will be making a run down to Fort Lauderdale to pick up a couple scientists from the Florida Institute of Technology. I could have them swing by. What are you up to?"

"I'm up past my hairline in crises. I've decided to stay landside a few days. Ben's handling things just fine out at the facility, and I'm damned if I'll let Reynolds have the advantage. I need Gloria here to help me out. Could you have the guys drop her off on their way out?"

"I have a better idea. Thomas and I have booked a chopper out to the facility after the meeting. Freddy could ferry her back."

"Perfect! What's your ETA at Gulf Stream I?"

"We're booked to leave here at ten-thirty. Say, eleven-fifteen or so?"

"Great—just what I needed: Thanks."

She called Gulf Stream. The connection couldn't have been worse; it sounded like chalk screeching across a blackboard against a distant stadium full of screaming sports fans. She plugged an ear with a finger.

Lee Attewell's deep voice said, "Gulf Stream I Control."

"Lee! Glad you're back on deck."

"Hey, chief." He sounded pleased. For him. "The place is a wreck. Must've been a hell of a wave."

"It was that. Is Ben around? Can you track him down for me?"

"Let me switch you over."

After a second: "Engineering, Ben Jonas."

"Ben. I got your report from last night. Glad to hear plant repairs are going so well."

"We've been very, very lucky, chief. Interior water damage to the equipment has continued to be minimal. The last of the replacement parts are coming in on *Pesky* this morning. Things are happening fast."

"When will the main generators be back up?"

"We've scheduled a shakedown run for this afternoon. Still looking good for partial power-up tomorrow evening, and full power-up on Wednesday. We'll have the damage pretty well taken care of by Friday at this rate, other than the catwalk utility connections and the gardens."

"Fantastic." Far better than she ever could have hoped. "How about the spillways and the reef?"

Ben sighed. "Well, it ain't great out there, chief. The underwater structures took a lot more abuse than we'd hoped. I've had to turn half of my divers over to Flo's team for structural repairs."

"Damn. Any sign of Louie yet?"

"Not yet. I'll let you know."

"Thanks. How are structural inspections coming along?"

"Well . . . there've been delays. I had a crew ready to go out this morning, and Reynolds ripped me a new orifice over it. He wanted them out on the reefs."

"Why didn't you tell me?"

Silence on the line. Screaming sports fans. "You already had too much to worry about."

"I'll call him. You redeploy those divers to the beanpoles."

Ben chuckled. "Ten-four. Thanks, chief."

"Keep me up-to date by E-mail."

"Will do."

"Now. Tell Gloria I need her in Melbourne after all. Have her see Jess right away and then pack an overnight bag. Freddy's bringing Flo and Reynolds in by chopper shortly after eleven."

"Gotcha."

She called Reynolds's number.

Thomas Reynolds's voice came on. "Reynolds."

He had to know it was her; their phone system had caller ID.

"This is Emma. I understand you raised an objection with Ben over the priorities he is setting for the repair dives."

He coughed. "Well, as a matter of fact . . . I was merely expressing concern over the timing. As you know, Science is the big money-earner right now, and we can't afford to be shut down."

"You're not going to be able to earn squat if Gulf Stream sinks, and that's what could happen if we don't do structural inspections and repairs. So stop bothering my people when they're trying to do their job, okay? If you have problems with their priorities, please take it up with me."

He was silent a second. "We'll see if Pendleton shares your opinion on priorities."

"Fine, have him let me know. In the meantime, you'll have to wait your turn for divers like everyone else," she said, and hung up.

Then she swung around in her chair and looked out at the picnic table. A wave of heat spread through her

again, from the center out. But this time she didn't
smile. She eyed the note lying on her desk.

Keith Hellman is not what he seems. What the hell
was that supposed to mean?

She called Shelly, Gulf Stream's one-woman human
resources department.

"Emma! Hi, doll! Welcome back!" Shelly talked
like a roller coaster, her Southern intonation dipping,
soaring, lurching off into unexpected directions.
"Honey, we were worried sick, I can tell you. I was
plain glued to the TV set during the storm. How you
been?"

"All right, I guess. Listen, have you got a few
minutes?"

"You bet. Your place or mine?"

"Yours. We may need your files."

"Well, hie yourself on down here, hon. I'll be waiting for you."

Shelly pulled Keith Hellman's file from the big bank
of file drawers and sat down, leafing through it. She
was a pretty woman, in her forties, ample of figure,
and wore loads of mascara, powder, lipstick, curls, and
perfume, all of which should have detracted from her
beauty but didn't. Smile lines fanned out from her eyes
and mouth. She had a startling, exuberant belly laugh,
which she used often.

Shelly handed Keith's résumé to Emma, who
looked it over. Several years at a consulting firm in
Houston and before that a stint with Greenpeace; before that, graduate studies in marine biology at Rice.

"How did his background check come out?"

"To tell you the truth, doll, I haven't done his background check yet. Mr. P. told me not to bother; he
could vouch for him and that was good enough for
me. You want to tell me what's going on?"

Emma shook her head. "Probably nothing." She

handed the file back to Shelly. "Could you check his references anyhow?"

"We-ell . . ." She drew the word out, taffylike, looking dubious. "I don't know. Do you s'pose it'd tick Mr. P. off, given he's the one vouching for him?"

Emma thought about it. "I can't see why he would object. It's *his* policy, after all. He was probably just trying to save you some work, thinking it was unnecessary."

"But you don't. Think it's unnecessary, I mean."

Emma pursed her lips. "I think a check is definitely in order. Just to set my mind at ease."

"Then I suppose I'd better do some checking. I'm sure everything's fine—but I'll make a couple calls."

"Thanks." Emma got up to go. "Let me know as soon as you hear anything, all right?"

"You bet, doll."

Chapter 21

KEITH: **Monday, 5 October, 8:10 A.M. EDT**
Gulf Stream I

When *La Auxiliadora* arrived at Gulf Stream, shortly after the Streamers woke up, Keith was directed to Angus, who assigned him quarters in Residential and showed him where they were.

"Not exactly the Ritz," Angus said, opening the door.

It was a tiny room, not much larger than a walk-in closet, with two bunks against one side and a small wardrobe and six dresser drawers built into the other. A square window with rounded corners looked out

over the ocean on the narrow wall opposite the door.
Photos and postcards were tacked up in the lower
bunk's cubby hole.

"It'll do," Keith said, and tossed his overnight bag
onto the upper bunk. "Thanks."

He had two very different areas to cover: find the
on-site environmental records and search them for Pinkle's name, and look for terrorists. However the hell
he was supposed to do *that*.

The records he could do in the evening, on his own.
To hunt for terrorists, he needed to meet and observe
as many of the Streamers as he could, which he should
do while people were out and about. So that'd come
first. He'd have to find an excuse to get in everybody's
face, he supposed. Maybe a friendly introduction: Hi,
I'm the new environmental manager. But as busy as
everyone was, people wouldn't have time to chat. So
he needed some kind of excuse to meet people.

First things first: he needed the personnel rosters.

He went to Engineering and found Ben in Control.

"I'm trying to get the environmental, health, and
safety records organized," Keith said. "I need a copy
of the personnel rosters to follow up on people's training and medical records."

"No problem. See Gloria," he said. "Down the hall
on your right. Oh, by the way, I'm presuming you're
going to want Franz's post-storm checklists for the
wastewater treatment plants, chemical and waste storage rooms, and so forth."

Keith avoided a wince. Don't give me more things
to do, he thought. "Yes, of course."

"I took the liberty of assigning Steve and Oleg to
those tasks this weekend," Ben said, and Keith
breathed a sigh of relief, "so most of the checklist
items are complete, but you should have them for ver-
ification, and for your files."

"Great. Thanks."

Keith went to Gloria's office. She wasn't there. The tiny office appeared to also serve as the network server room. Five computers lined a deep shelf along one wall, crowded among all sorts of cables, router boxes, and monitors. Gloria's desk was flush against the opposite wall. Her lavender windbreaker hung on a hook by the door; papers littered her desk; all of her computers were on, with psychedelic swirls and gonzo cartoons and aquarium screen-savers swimming across their screens.

Keith spotted on her desk a small Spiderman head sitting atop a red pillar. PEZ!

Smiling, he stepped in, picked it up, and tilted its head back. There was indeed candy inside. He took a candy and sucked on it, glancing around the office.

"Help yourself," she said, leaning against the doorjamb with her arms folded. He jumped, and turned. "Oh, hi. Sorry."

She smiled. "It's okay. That's what it's there for. What can I do for you?"

He told her. She went over to one of the computers and started typing. "No problem. Give me a minute." While he waited, Keith looked around her office.

Tie-dyed African batiks and billowing muslin tapestries with scenes from India overwhelmed the walls of the tiny office. Chunks of quartz crystal and polished sedimentary rocks served as paperweights on the desk. Her phone was a complicated affair that had a liquid crystal display and dozens of buttons and lights.

And Keith laughed: pens and pencils and notepads were stuffed into a clear plastic desk organizer with so many nooks, tubes, and containers affixed that it looked like a Habitrail. The organizer sported buttons that said things such as "WAR IS BAD," "NASTY, BRUTISH, AND SHORT," "ALL MY LIFE I'VE WANTED TO BE SOMEONE. NOW, WHO THE HELL WAS IT?" and "SOMETIMES THEY FOOL YOU BY WALKING UPRIGHT."

She gave him a smile, and handed him his printouts.

"Thanks a lot," he said, looking over the list of names. Jesus. There must be several dozen names on the list. He would be at this for weeks.

"No charge."

"Is this everybody? Permanent *and* temporary?"

"Well, actually, I don't have the contractors' rosters. It includes all the permanent staff, though, and the interns and visiting staff."

Contractors. They'd be a very attractive route onboard for terrorists. "Is there a contractor liaison?"

Gloria shrugged. "I'm sure there is. I don't know who. It'd be one of Ben's people."

"I'll check with him, then." He held up a blank notepad and pen. "May I borrow these?"

"Sure—help yourself."

Rob came in. "Good, you're still here. Ben needs to talk to you."

Back in Control, Ben said, "We were just talking. Rob here tells me you have extensive dive experience. I know you've got your own work to do, but can I borrow you for an inspection and repair dive out at the reefs? I'm a little short-handed."

It was a perfect place to start meeting people. Keith folded up his list and pen and tucked it into his pocket. "Sure. And *I* have another favor to ask of *you*. Who's in charge of contractor relations? I need their rosters, too."

"Hmmm. That could be a problem."

"What do you mean?"

Ben looked thoughtful. "Well, there are some legal complications. Our contractors won't guarantee a particular roster; they'll only give us a pool of possible people, and only when pressed. This has been a point of contention for years, and we've had to do some hard negotiations on the matter. Phil has written our contracts such that they're responsible for their own health, safety, and environmental training and record-keeping, and in return, we allow them a lot of latitude in managing their personnel. They tell us that they need that latitude to effectively control costs and still keep in line with their labor union contracts.''

Keith frowned. This could be a serious impediment to his investigation. "I'd better talk to Phil.''

"Good idea. Meanwhile, let's get you out on the reefs. Rob, radio Sean in Mariculture that Keith is on his way,'' Ben said.

"Roger that,'' Rob said.

The predive briefing was rushed, and there was no opportunity to talk to the others during the dive. With the other divers he moved along the netting and structures: repairing, inspecting. Finally Jess, his dive buddy, tapped his watch and gave Keith a thumbs-up: *ascend*. He led the way up the mooring cable toward their Zodiac, a fat black bullet bobbing overhead.

Keith broke surface and touched his head: *all okay*. Sean Ellis, their dive tender and the facility's divemaster, leaned over the side.

"Ah, there you are. Ben wants a word with you.'' He was a young, chubby redhead with glaring white zinc oxide covering his freckled nose—one of Flo's Mariculture people.

Jess broke surface near him with an explosive snort and touched the top of his head. Several other grey-and-yellow, rigid-bottomed, inflatable Zodiacs bobbed in the swells all about, most clipped to mooring buoys over the reef. The boats' occupants watched the bubbles from the divers below, or scanned downstream with binoculars. At two or four divers per tender, a lot more divers were deployed now than the handful out when he'd first gone down.

He unbuckled his weight belt and then his BC, and handed them up to Sean, then kicked hard with his fins, rolled over the inflatable edge of the Zodiac, and pulled his mask and gloves off. The skin of his hands was puckered and soft. He was already chilled from working in the power plant's seawater effluent, water several degrees colder than ambient; the October wind felt colder on his hands and face than it really was. A shiver whipped up his spine.

Sean held out the radio.

"One sec." Keith wiped water out of his eyes, shoved his hair back, and pulled off his fins—awkwardly; the four-foot swells pushing at the anchored motor boat's hull made the boat lurch up and down. While Sean took Jess's equipment and helped him into the boat, Keith flexed his hands, cupped them, and blew into them.

Jess sat down next to Keith. His lips were tinged blue. "Christ. I need something hot to drink."

"Hot tea's the best I can do," Sean said, pouring from a thermos. Steam billowed downwind from the plastic mug.

"Ugh." Jess made a face, but held out his hand. "Give it here."

"Any sign of Louie down there?" Sean asked.

"Not yet."

Keith took the radio, a handheld VHF in a plastic cover, and hung on to the edge of the boat for balance. Puddles of water sloshed back and forth at his feet, amid the spare tanks, nylon rope, and buckets of tools. He slid down and wedged in the corner formed by the bench and the inflated side of the boat, then took the mug Sean proffered and sipped at the tea: sweet hot bitter nectar.

"Keith here."

Ben asked, "How's it coming?"

Keith shared a look with Jess. "Coming along. We got the leak in Number Four-A repaired. And we got started on one of the worst tears in Grid Four's primary net." He swiped at his burning eyes with a sigh. "There's a lot left to do. Maybe later today, after I get caught up on some of my own work, I can help you out some more."

"Well." Ben coughed. "That's why I'm radioing you. I'm in a jam. I still need your dive experience out there. I only have five divers available now to finish the follow-on checks of the beanpole float chambers. We had a setback earlier and I've lost the two people I had planned for that dive."

"A setback? Is everyone okay?"

"Everyone's fine; they had to go deeper than we'd planned for longer than we'd planned, rigging the second lift line for the catwalk, so I'm short four divers. It's a deep dive, a hundred and twenty feet. And with the shakedown runs scheduled for then, everyone will be tied up. Frankly, I'm getting desperate. Will you help?"

Keith frowned. He didn't see any way he could gracefully avoid it. He looked at his dive computer.

"I've got plenty of bottom time left," he said. "Give me an hour and a half for a good surface interval and lunch, and I'll go back out."

"Great! I'll radio Flo—she's inbound from Melbourne. She'll be your buddy. Meet her in the Mariculture conference room for a dive briefing at twelve-forty-five."

"Will do."

Sean handed him and Jess sandwiches in Zip-Loc bags. Keith unwrapped his sandwich and took a big bite. Fresh, grilled tuna steak with bacon, lettuce, and Miracle Whip on rye. It was amazingly good. He finished it in six hungry bites and licked the morsels off his fingertips.

Meanwhile Sean unclipped the Zodiac from the mooring buoy cable, started the outboard engine, and steered them, skipping over the swells, past the spillways.

Two workers in bright orange life vests and black rubber hip waders were cleaning one of the spillways. Keith craned to see: the spillway had maybe twenty baffled chutes, each covered with a hinged, clear plastic cover smeared with vivid green algae. One worker knelt at the head of the spillway, shoving a rectangular panel into a slot. The other stood in an opened spillway, using some sort of squeegee on the plastic cover. She stood and stretched, arching her back with her hands at the base of her spine, then pushed her hair out of her eyes and waved. Sean waved back.

Keith pointed. "What are they doing?"

"Cleaning the spillways. Harvesting algae." Jess took a slug of tea with a grimace. "It's a great system. The water we pump up for the power plant is nutrient rich, which would create a plankton bloom and disrupt the surface environment if we released it directly from the plant. And it's also a lot colder than ambient, and has a lot of dissolved carbon dioxide that would otherwise go right into the atmosphere—"

"—and contribute to global warming. I wondered about that. How much of the carbon dioxide and nutrients do the algae farms remove?"

"They're very efficient. Flo or Dr. Hiro could give you more specifics, but I know at least ninety percent of the carbon dioxide is removed, and—maybe sixty, seventy percent of the nutrients? Something like that, anyhow. Sometimes they jigger around with the flow rates, when the biologists or Mariculture want more nutrients or colder water in the reef, and then the carbon dioxide consumption drops by as much as ten or fifteen percent."

Keith whistled. Jess grinned.

"Yeah. It's a clever design. The algae eat the carbon dioxide in the plant effluent waters, and we sell the algae for guar gum and sodium alginate. The main problem with the spillways is that they're high-maintenance. We have to keep up with cleaning the algae off the spillway covers, so that sunlight can get in for the algae growing on the baffles, and it's a labor-intensive operation. So from an economic standpoint it's only a break-even. But when you factor in the environmental benefit, it's an overall gain.''

Then they were past, and nearing the Engineering module. It loomed overhead, casting a shadow across the waters. They moved into the shadow and the temperature dropped.

Keith gazed up at the module: all concrete and metal. Solid. Stable. He had a hard time, now, remembering the way the storm had dwarfed it. The sun burst over its shoulder and he shielded his eyes, blinking, and looked away.

They crossed over toward Mariculture. As they did so a helicopter rose from its roof, beating air down onto their heads, and made a big circle around the facility to head landward. They waved at the pilot.

The boat's engine shifted down from a roar to a putter as they coasted past the main dock to the smaller, circular dock girdling the module's base. Keith tied the nylon bowline to a dock cleat. He and Jess climbed out and took their equipment up from Sean. Two other divers, a man and a woman, climbed down the ladder with their equipment bags and tanks.

''Meet you and Flo in the dive locker after you get your briefing from Engineering,'' Sean told Keith.

Two young men were working at cubicles in the bull-pen, and a young woman stood at the twenty-one-inch monitors of the AutoCAD station.

''Who do I talk to about an E-mail account?'' he asked the one who sat at the nearest terminal.

The man looked up from his computer screen, a bit glassy-eyed.

"You're new, aren't you?" Keith nodded. "You'll have to get authorization from Gloria first. She's the network administrator. Down the hall."

He craned his head around the door.

"Knock knock," he said. No Gloria, and her windbreaker was gone, too. He went to Control.

"Have you seen Gloria?" he asked Rob and Lee, who sat at the console. Rob was talking into the headset and Lee was typing at the keyboard, making the screens cascade through different schematics. Next to him stood a middle-aged man Keith didn't know, with Asian features. The man was on the tall side, thin and balding, and he was staring at the console with his chin in his hand, talking to Lee about the reefs. Occasionally he took a small pad from his breast pocket to jot notes.

Nikki sat in the supervisor's office, writing at the desk. She glanced up and nodded to him with a smile as he passed the open door, and then bent back over her work.

Rob put a finger over the mouthpiece of his headset and replied, "You're in luck; I'm talking to her right now." He moved his finger off the mouthpiece. "Gloria, hang on—I have Keith here for you." He tapped a few keys and then handed Keith a hand mike with a black, phone-type spiral cord that attached to the VHF radio set in the console.

Keith pressed the key on the side of the hand mike and said, "Gloria?"

Her voice emanated from the speaker on the radio. "Dude!"

"Where are you?"

"Oh, about fifty knots west of you, I'd guess."

"Ah."

"What can I do for you?" She sounded entertained by his confusion. He realized she must be on the helicopter he'd seen lifting off earlier.

"I need an E-mail account. Hmm. I guess that'll be tricky, under the circumstances."

"Talk to Ramón. He's the assistant MIS manager. Tell him I said it was okay."

"Gotcha. Thanks."

"Anybody sighted Louie yet?" she asked, as he started to sign off.

"I don't know; you might check with Rob," he said, and handed the mike back to Rob.

" 'Fraid not," Rob said. "And he's not a benthic organism; if he got shaken lose from the reef, he's somebody else's dinner by now."

"Can anybody tell me who and where Ramón might be?" Keith asked the room at large.

Nikki came out of the office, clipboard in hand. "I'll show you."

Ramón turned out to be the other young man in the bullpen; the woman at the AutoCAD and the man he'd spoken to moments earlier, who had sent him in search of Gloria, were gone.

"Keith needs an account and Gloria is on her way to the mainland," Nikki told Ramón, jerking a thumb at Keith. "She says you should go ahead and set him up."

Ramón smiled. It was easy and wide, the kind of smile that completely disarms you. His hands were large and competent looking, with long fingers. His eyes widened at Nikki's words. "Come off it."

"Honestly. She was looking for you earlier to let you know, but Freddy couldn't wait."

"She just got here. What's the story?"

"Emma's orders. Rumor has it all hell's breaking loose on the mainland."

Nikki and Ramón shared a significant look. Ramón shook his head. "I sure hope we have jobs tomorrow."

"Emma will come through. She always does."

"That's what I like about you, Nikki. Always the optimist. What's the word on Louie?"

She shrugged. "No sign of him yet." Ramón shook his head again, ruefully, and turned to Keith. "Now, about E-mail."

"Can you set me up?" Keith asked.

"Easy. What's your name?"

"Hellman. Keith Hellman."

Ramón gave him a curious look. "Oh! I should have guessed." He extended a hand. Keith took it. "Welcome to Gulf Stream I."

Keith looked at Nikki, who merely shrugged, a dimple appearing on her cheek.

"What should you have guessed?"

Ramón glanced at Nikki. Her grin grew wider.

"I knew we had a new guy who"—he coughed—"just started." Keith thought of Emma, and the ship's crewmen last night.

"Pleased to meet you," he said.

Ramón cleared his throat. "Now, E-mail. You'll be *khellman* for internal E-mail, and your password will be *gulf-1*, no caps, until you change it. Which you should do the first time you get onto the system. Your Internet address will be *khellman@gulfstream.com*."

Keith frowned. He wanted to be able to send E-mail with a certain amount of anonymity. "Do you mind using my handle instead? It's kind of a tradition by now and I hate to change it."

"Sure; what is it?"

Keith made up something on the spot. "Kingfisher."

"You got it. *Kingfisher@gulfstream.com*. Do you know how to use Eudora?" Keith nodded. "Okay. All of our computers log onto our internal network on boot-up and load the protocols for Internet communications out of our T1 connection in Melbourne.''

Whatever that meant. "So I don't have to do anything special to connect?''

"Right. Which computer will you be using?''

"Uh, that's another problem. Can I borrow someone's for a while?''

"You should give him Franz's old computer,'' Nikki said. Ramón's eyes went wide in horror.

"That old clinker? No way. That dinosaur should be decommissioned. It's not even a Pentium. It only has a fifty-megahertz processor and six megs of RAM. Uh-uh.'' He studied Keith with the barest crease between his eyebrows. "I'll have to set you up with something temporary, at least till Gloria gets back. Are you going to take over Franz's office, over in Science?''

Keith started to reply that as far as he knew, he *had* no office; his only space was the tiny cabin that had been assigned to him.

Nikki was shaking her head. "That bugger Reynolds cleared it out last week and gave the cubicle to one of his horrid cronies. We'll have to find Keith another spot.''

Ramón really was frowning now. "That'll be tough. Unless . . . why not there?'' He gestured at a cluttered-looking cubicle across from his. "Jerry Magillicuddy has gone on a four-month sabbatical while he finishes his doctoral dissertation. The interns have been using his space, but clearly you've got seniority. We can set you up on Jerry's machine. It's much faster than Franz's and is loaded with cool software. And some great games,'' he added with a wink at Keith.

"Works for me.''

"It's settled, then,'' Nikki said. "I'm off.''

"Thanks, Nikki.'' Keith glanced at his watch and

asked Ramón, "How long will it take to set me up?"

Ramón pulled a moue. "Ten minutes, once I get done with this administrative crap I'm doing, which is going to take all damn day. Give me till five P.M."

"Right." Keith sat down at his desk and picked up the phone to leave his new Internet address with Barnes and Gorey. The woman who answered asked him no questions, simply wrote down the address as he dictated it and read it back to verify.

He pulled out the personnel roster and his pen and checked off the names of people he'd met so far. To his surprise, he'd met a couple of dozen so far. Not that he'd gotten a clue as to which of them might be in league with terrorists, but hey, it was progress.

Then he glanced at his watch, and jumped up with a muttered exclamation. He would be late.

Sean was waiting for him in the Mariculture conference room.

"Where's Flo?" Keith asked.

"She's on lunch break with her kid, Veronica, at the day care center, and she didn't take her radio. She should be back anytime, or you could go over to Residential to get her."

"What the hell, I'll head over. Uh, where's the day care center?"

"Main deck, along the port side. Right next to the medical center."

"There's a medical center?"

"You mean no one's taken you by there yet?" Sean frowned. "You should go get checked out. All staff are supposed to have a complete physical when they come aboard. Damn, I'm falling down on the job. As divemaster, I'm supposed to make sure all divers have had a physical before they start doing work dives."

"The normal procedures were a little—disrupted, with the hurricane and all."

"True. Well, I'm going to go ahead and bend the rules some more, here—clearly you're a professional diver and you know your limits. But please do drop by and see Michael as soon as possible."

"Michael—is he the same Michael as the one on the Phase III storm team?"

Sean nodded. "The very same. Michael Harriman. He's our full-time RN. He's a great guy. We have a backup physician, too, for emergencies; one of the staff scientists is also an M.D."

Under the circumstances, since he wasn't going to be here but a few more days—a couple of weeks at most—a medical exam seemed spurious. "I'm glad to hear it. I'll check in with Michael sometime in the next couple of weeks."

"Very good. Then I'll authorize you to continue making work dives in the interim."

"Now, how do I find the day care center?"

"You can't miss it; trust me."

Keith crossed the catwalk to Residential, took the stairs up one flight to the main deck, and followed the squeals to a large room that took up the back third of the tail section. Outside the room, a girl and boy about five or six years old crouched, arguing with great enthusiasm over a block construct they were making. A young man sat on the floor nearby, keeping an eye on them.

"Can I help you?"

"I'm looking for Flo Jonas."

The man jerked his thumb toward the door. "You've come to the right place. In there. Careful, Mikey—" He grabbed for the boy, who nearly tripped over his legs while chasing the girl. They fled, their shrieks of laughter trailing them. The young man took off after them, scolding. Keith stepped carefully around their complicated creation, which wandered all over the hall, and entered the room, from which other squeals issued.

The room was spacious, by Gulf Stream standards, with both a play area and a "learning" area set up with child-sized tables and chairs, science posters and experiments, and art supplies. A picture window faced northwest, mostly over open water. In the distance, beyond the orange buoys that marked the breakwater, the Gulf Stream I trawler's crane was hauling up a net heavy with fish, dogged by sea birds.

Flo and a small child sat over in the learning area. A ten-year-old girl sat at one of the computers near the picture window. An older woman—fifty or so—was standing with arms folded, relaxed but attentive, watching while three boys between maybe six and nine years old ran in and out around a playhouse-cum-jungle gym, shrieking and laughing. A boy of about three sat on the floor next to a big aquarium full of tropical fish, sucking his thumb while a young woman read a book to him.

Keith went over to Flo. She sat on a child-sized chair, her knees poking out to the sides. A two-year-old girl sat on her leg, leaning back into the crook of her arm and handing bits of sandwich to her. The little girl wore a bright red romper and miniature Nikes, and her black hair was a frizzy patchwork of barrettes and pigtails.

"This must be Veronica," he said. He wiggled his fingers at the little girl. "Hi."

Veronica grabbed handfuls of Flo's shirt and buried her face against Flo's chest, and from the safety her mother's shirt afforded, peeked at Keith. Her eyes were huge, black, and gorgeous.

"This is Keith, honey," Flo said, stroking the girl's head. "Say hi."

Veronica buried her face in her mother's shirt again.

Keith and Flo laughed. Flo glanced at her watch. "Oh, my—I lost track of time."

"Take a few more minutes," Keith said. "I'm in no hurry."

"Thanks," she said, absently stroking her daughter's back.

"Sorry to intrude."

"No, it's okay. We should get going." She picked up Veronica and tossed the remains of lunch into the trash can nearby. They walked over and Flo handed Veronica to the older woman; Veronica immediately reached for her mother, whimpering. Flo took her tiny hands and kissed the fingers.

"Shh-shhh. I'll come back for you later, honey bunch. I promise. She'll need a nap around two, Dora," she told the woman.

"Sure thing." Dora jiggled Veronica and began dancing around the room, making clownish faces and singing, to distract her. Veronica waved good-bye to Flo over Dora's shoulder. Great big tears were rolling down her face. Flo cast her daughter a last regretful look as she and Keith left the room.

"Lordy." Flo shook her head with a sharp exhalation. Then she was brisk. "Shall we go?"

Keith followed her to the beanpole antechamber. Flo pushed the button, and they waited.

"She's a cute kid," Keith said.

Flo gave him a smile. "Mmm. I love my job. My career is very important to me. But . . ." She sighed.

"But. It must be tough."

"Yeah. Leaving her is the hardest part. I wouldn't take a job that didn't let me stay this close to her."

The elevator lowered into view and the door opened. Flo entered and held the door for him.

"My wife never wanted children," he said, stepping into the elevator. "Her career was her life, and she felt kids would hurt her professionally. It was a real point of contention between us. Looking back I can understand her choice, but at the time it really hurt. I tried to talk her into letting me raise the children, but she wouldn't go for it.''

"Oh?" Flo closed the door and pressed *Dock*. "What was her profession?"

"She had—has—her own business as a travel guide. She goes all over the place. Organizes bike tours, eco-tours, things like that. Places like Antarctica and the Brazilian rain forests. It's how we met, in fact—on a tour of the Rwandan mountain apes, back in the mid-eighties.''

Flo gazed at him thoughtfully. "That would be a tough career to combine raising kids with.''

"I suppose.''

"Took me a while to get around to it," she said, "but I always wanted kids. Veronica is the single most important thing in my life.'' The elevator came to a stop, and she opened the door. He led the way into the antechamber.

From behind him she said, "Everyone's talking about you and Emma.''

He turned, surprised not so much that they were a topic of discussion but that Flo would be so direct about it.

"That's quite a non sequitur.''

"I don't believe in beating around the bush.''

"And what is everyone saying?''

Flo's hands were on her hips, and her gaze was direct. "They're curious. Maybe a little concerned. Emma is—well, she belongs to everyone, in a way, and we feel protective of her. She's a bit of an innocent when it comes to men.''

"Perhaps. She *is* an adult, though.''

Flo's lips pursed. She seemed to be waiting for him to say something more.

"Are you asking what my intentions are?" he asked finally.

"I'm not asking anything. I'm letting you know. I've known Emma a while. She's got a tough veneer, but a man could hurt her bad if he didn't treat her right. And it would be better for him not to pursue her at all than to treat her too lightly. That's what I'm saying."

Keith frowned.

"I think you're underestimating her. And me."

"I'm glad to hear you say so." She pushed the door open and held it for him. "After you," she said.

As they were walking across the catwalk to Engineering, Keith pointed at a big barge being pushed toward the facility by an oceangoing tug. "What's that?"

Flo looked. "Ah, that's the hydrogen storage barge. We have two of them. When one's about full of liquid hydrogen, a tug brings the empty back from Port Canaveral and takes the full one back. During the storm, both of them were landside."

Keith could make out the rounded shapes of tanks—double-hulled, thermos, cryogenic tanks—for the storage of liquid hydrogen. He pictured the last shuttle launch he'd seen, the flames from the main engine lighting a palpable pillar of flame. "How dangerous is it?"

"Well," Flo answered, "I wouldn't want to be near it if it went up, but we keep it moored about three hundred yards away from the facility at *that* buoy." She pointed to a large, neon-orange buoy to the northwest, bobbing near the buoys of the floating breakwater, offset from the reef's midpoint.

"How do you get the hydrogen out to it?"

She pointed down at the water. "There's a flexible pipeline—it runs down to the crossbeams at seventy feet, then over to the framework under the breakwater, then up the buoy line.''

Keith's eyes widened. "You run liquid hydrogen through a flexible pipe? Underwater?''

Flo laughed. "Oh. Not at all. The hydrogen liquefaction equipment is on the barge. We just run pressurized gas through the line. It's paired with the electrical cable that powers the liquefaction equipment.''

They walked on across the catwalk to Engineering. Ben met them in the Engineering conference room.

"We're mostly concerned with the structural integrity of the main buoyancy control tanks on this module.'' Ben spread an E-sized engineering drawing across the table. Flo automatically captured one end and held it down.

The drawing was a cross section of the entire pole, from the above-water sections supporting the module decks all the way to the concrete-filled bulb of ballast at the bottom, almost three hundred feet below the surface.

"The catwalk was hanging deep enough that it could've banged into the main tanks here.'' He pointed at the middle section of the beanpole, an almost spherical section that started below the crossbeams, seventy-five feet below the surface, reached its greatest diameter about one hundred and five feet down, and then tapered in again at a hundred and thirty-five feet. Ben tapped the midpoint of the bulge. "We don't have any sign of leakage, but that doesn't mean the end of the catwalk didn't slam into the tanks someplace along this upper quadrant.'' His finger traced along the top curve of the spherical bulge. "We want a careful look over this upper section. Videotape, too, so we can have more eyes examine it.''

Keith nodded. "Just out of curiosity, why not send your ROV?''

"You mean, since we're doing the videotape thing?"

"Yeah."

"Human eyes on location are always better. Sometimes we catch things on the video that divers miss, but usually it's the other way around—divers catching stuff that we missed with the ROV." He tapped the bulge on the pole again. "Since the buoyancy here is primary—critical—we're going with divers first."

Keith nodded again. He'd run into the same phenomenon on his own inspection dives. "Got you." He pointed at the lower curve. "You don't feel there's any need to examine this section underneath?"

Ben shook his head. "Nope. The catwalk couldn't have reached it and so there's no reason getting beyond, say, one hundred and ten feet."

"Very good. We should be able to do that without more than two decompression stops. One, if I hadn't already been diving today."

Ben nodded. "That's what I hoped. Sean will go over your dive plan and equipment check with you."

Flo pointed at the bulge at the very bottom of the beanpole. "The ballast bulb sticks out quite a bit. What if the catwalk hydroplaned over and impacted it? We lose that and this entire thing will go up like a rocket. Before flopping over on its side, that is."

Ben smiled. "Good question. I was worried until they measured the rope. The combined length of the rope and catwalk was twenty feet short of the ballast bulb. Regardless, we're taking Bowser down for a look after your dive."

Flo nodded. "Take a *good* look, okay?"

"Of course," Ben said. "And *you* be careful on this dive."

She grinned. "Of *course*."

"Any more questions?"

Keith and Flo both shook their heads.

"Very good. See Sean."

The first thing Sean did was double-check Keith's nitrogen exposure against the tables and check Keith's dive computer. "Yeah, you've got the reserves. Right, then—we're setting a hard limit of twenty-five minutes bottom time. Even if you take ten minutes to get down, that should leave plenty of time for the inspection—the area isn't that big. Because of Keith's residual nitrogen, we're going with two minutes at twenty feet and twenty-three minutes at ten feet."

He made sure they'd both written it on their slates: *Dep.110, BT:25min, 20ft:2min, 10ft:23min.* "Start the inspection at your max depth and work up. Your computer will probably give you a clean nitrogen bill before twenty-three minutes, but play it safe, right?"

"Understood," said Keith.

"Amen," said Flo.

"Right, then—equipment."

He set them up with twin eighty-cubic-foot scuba tanks and larger diver propulsion vehicles that had video cameras and heavy-duty camera floodlights mounted to them. Keith started to pick his up and Sean said, "Don't even try. The batteries are so heavy it takes two people."

"What's it like in the water?"

"A hair positive."

"So we haul them down to the dock one at a time?"

Sean shook his head. "For this sort of thing, we lower you into the water from here."

"Here" was the Mariculture utility deck, where the inflatable boats were deployed and recovered by crane through a fifteen-foot-long hatch in the floor. Sean pointed at a metal-framed platform with a reinforced steel-mesh floor already in position on the deck beside the open hatch.

Sean and Keith moved the scooters onto the platform and then Sean assisted them in suiting up. When they were ready, and beginning to sweat, he picked up his radio.

"Jess, you got those tanks in position?"

The sound of an outboard engine being throttled back came through the radio. "—finished," came Jess's voice. "We're headed your way."

"Right-o. See you soon." He put the radio back in his holster. "Jess just finished hanging a line off a float by the OTEC plant, above the side you'll be inspecting. There are two decompression stations—a tank with an octopus regulator at ten feet and one at twenty-five feet, in case you're running low on air." He tapped one of the double tanks on Flo's back. "Mind, you shouldn't, but it's standard procedure in all our decompression dives. Besides, it's a good reminder.

"Go ahead and get on the platform. I'll take you down as soon as—" The sound of an outboard engine grew louder, passed underneath the open hatchway, then throttled back to hold station in the current. "There we are."

Keith and Flo put on their fins and shuffled onto the platform, crouching awkwardly, trying to balance the heavy tank sets on their backs. Sean took the crane control, a yellow box with buttons hanging from the ceiling, and hit a button.

The platform, suspended at the corners by a four-part wire yoke, lifted off the deck. Keith dropped back onto his butt and swore. Flo lowered herself more gracefully and put a gloved hand on one of the yoke wires to steady herself. The crane moved sideways, smoothly, until it was centered over the hatch in the floor.

"Ready, guys?" Sean asked.

"Ready," said Flo. Keith nodded.

"Right-o. I'm taking it down to ten FSW so have your regulators ready."

The platform started down with a jerk, causing Keith to grab for one of the cables. "Shit!"

Flo laughed.

It only took half a minute to reach the three-foot swells running beneath the pod. They both had their regulators in their mouths when the waves began washing across the platform. Keith grabbed on to his scooter with one hand and the platform with the other as the current began pulling at him.

True to Sean's word, the platform stopped dropping when Keith's depth gauge read ten feet. He looked at Flo and signaled *okay* with his thumb. She mirrored his gesture and they both let go of the platform, floating off with the current and surfacing to get a visual bearing on the Engineering beanpole.

As on Keith's previous dive at Engineering, they used the scooters to pull themselves across the current on top of the water. Directly upstream of the Engineering beanpole they submerged, dropping thirty feet before the bottom edge of the OTEC plant rushed at them.

They used the scooters then, pointed upstream to hold them in place just before the face of the beanpole as they dropped into the depths. As they sank below the edge of the plant, they passed through a thermocline. Keith shivered as the colder water infiltrated his wet suit. He kept switching his attention between his depth gauge, Flo, and their position relative to the beanpole. A series of dark rectangular openings, spaced vertically every fifteen or twenty feet, dotted the sides of the beanpole. Keith realized they must be the vents that let water enter or be expelled from the individual buoyancy chambers.

When they passed the cross-beams running between

the beanpoles at seventy feet, Flo switched on her scooter's floodlight. Keith followed suit.

Directly below the cross-beams, the beanpole belled outward into the rounded surface of the main buoyancy tank, the upper boundary of their search area. They followed the curve down and out, toward the upstream side. Finally they reached the sphere's equator at 110 feet. Keith flashed a hand sign at Flo: okay?

Okay, she signaled back.

They filmed the quadrant in swaths, starting upstream, then letting the current sweep them across the face of the structure with their video cameras and lights activated, then running the scooters back upstream and up five feet for the next swath.

There was only one sign of any impact, a section of bare concrete, where something had scraped the algae from the beanpole. While Flo filmed him, Keith used his knife to remove algae from the edges of this scrape, looking for cracks or chips, but he didn't find any.

They finished the inspection with seven minutes to spare on their bottom time limit and ascended leisurely. At fifty feet, below the dark mass of the OTEC plant, Flo motioned him toward one of the openings to the buoyancy chambers. She let her scooter pull her in and Keith followed, curious.

The scooter's light filled the chamber and shone off a silver ceiling just a few feet above the entrance— air, held for buoyancy. Flo stood, her finned feet resting on the bottom of the chamber, and stuck her head up into the air pocket.

Keith did the same and found himself in a large cylinder with a teardrop-shaped cross section. It was lit weirdly by their lights, refracted by the water's surface.

Flo took her regulator mouthpiece out and said, ''Don't breathe too much of this air. Divers do this all the time so the CO_2 can build up." She put her regulator back in her mouth to inhale.

"Neat," Keith said. "What does our air exhaust do to the beanpole's total buoyancy?"

"The compensators take care of it, though the engineers might note the discrepancy and look for a leaking air valve. I'll tell Ben we popped in, though, so he doesn't start ripping the plumbing apart. Shall we go?"

"After you."

Flo paused by some pipes at the chamber's exit, and gestured Keith over. She shone her light, grinning, and Keith saw that a rather large octopus was wedged among the pipes, eyeing them. He wrote *Louie?* on his slate and she nodded. *How here?* he wrote—how the hell did he get here, hundreds of feet *upstream* of the reef? Flo shrugged. *We'll send rescue team*, she wrote on her slate, and they exited.

They ascended to the first decompression station and hung on to the line by the suspended scuba tank. The two minutes went by quickly.

They passed the twenty-three minutes at the ten-foot decompression stop by playing Hangman on the backs of their slates.

At the end of it, Flo was ahead, having stumped Keith with *fidelity*. She got his next word easily: *wiseass*. They were both laughing when they surfaced. Jess, in the Zodiac, escorted them back on the surface to the suspended platform beneath Mariculture.

They rode the crane up to Mariculture and sat there, on the crane platform, tired and chilled. Sean helped them get their equipment off. Then they took the videotapes up to Engineering for the debriefing.

On the way, Flo stuck her head into Control. "Rob, spread the word—Louie's hiding among the pipes in Engineering Buoyancy Chamber Three. Send a couple divers to give him a lift back to the reef."

Rob whooped. Seconds later, as Keith and Flo passed the bullpen, Rob's voice echoed on the loudspeakers announcing the sighting, and applause broke out in the bullpen; the engineers burst into a raucous, off-key chorus of "Louie Louie."

Chapter 22

GABRIEL: **Monday, 5 October, 4:59 P.M. EDT**
The Holiday Inn, Melbourne, Florida

Jax returned on Monday evening, his arms full of boxes and bags.

"How's it going?" he asked. He kicked the door shut behind him, and set down the bags. Gabriel looked up from the computer screen and rubbed at his eyes.

"It's going. Where's Bo?"

Jax shrugged. "She didn't say. She'll be back in a bit. What about Tooke? You get to her yet?"

"Not yet. I've tried a few times—keep missing her."

"You *still* haven't made contact? You've had two full days!"

Gabriel frowned. "It's not the only thing we've been doing, but as I said, I'm working on it."

"Not very hard, apparently."

"What's eating you?"

Jax's fists balled. "None of your goddamned business!"

Mark looked from Gabriel to Jax and back, and stood. "Listen, Jax, how about you watch the stuff while Gabe and I grab a bite to eat? We need a break."

Jax glared at Gabriel. Then he rubbed at his own eyes. "Sure. Bring me a burger or something, would you?" He tossed Mark a rolled-up twenty.

Mark and Gabriel walked over to Denny's.

"What was all that about?" Gabriel asked, as they studied their menus. He thumbed at his smooth upper lip, missing his mustache more than he'd expected.

Mark waved a hand. "Don't sweat it. He can be a moody cuss."

"I've never seen him like this," Gabriel said.

"Mmmm." Mark sipped at his iced tea. "You haven't known him all that long. He gets like this every once in a while. It usually has to do with women."

"You think he's interested in her?"

"I think it's likely."

Gabriel frowned. "I wonder if something happened between them, in Miami."

"She seems a little too, I don't know—careful or something—to me, to mix business with pleasure. Maybe she rejected him and he's pissed about it."

Gabriel's eyes narrowed. "Maybe."

A man was selling rosebuds outside the restaurant; on their way back to the room, Gabriel bought three. It wasn't perhaps the most circumspect thing to do, but Gabriel was getting tired of giving up ground, where Boadica was concerned. It was time to reassert control over the group. In a couple of ways.

Jax was looking over the blueprints Mark had been making notes on. Mark handed Jax his foil-wrapped take-out burger and fries, and a sweating Coke can from the soda pop machine. Jax took a huge bite and then, fist full of burger, pointed at the roses Gabriel carried. His words were barely intelligible. "What are those?"

"What do they look like?"

Gabriel carried the roses to the sink and removed

the clear cellophane, wadding it in the trash can with a frown. What a waste of a nonrenewable resource.

He filled a glass with tepid tap water, cut most of the stems off the roses, and stuck the buds into the glass. Still, the glass was too short: they leaned dangerously far above the glass's rim, a rose-tipped tepee frame.

He held it out, admiring the snug, wine-colored buds. Maybe cut roses flown in from commercial flower farms weren't great for the environment, either, but at least they were growing things. And if one needed to find a use for them, they bound up carbon dioxide, a little bit. Which was all bullshit; face it, Cervantes. But hey, he thought, sniffing their rich spice, they were pretty.

The door opened; he turned. It was Boadica. Tawny evening light streamed into the room around her.

"I've been checking out the boat rental places," Boadica said, closing the door. "I've located a couple of possibilities."

This time she looked older, almost matronly, in a calf-length floral dress, big, out-of-fashion sunglasses, and a gaudy straw hat with a sunflower on it. She swept the hat off and tossed it onto the bed. Her posture shifted and straightened; years sloughed off her.

Gabriel stared. *Bruja.* Shapeshifter.

He brought her the glass of flowers, feeling a little self-conscious.

"For you. A little welcome-back present."

She took them with a look of pleased surprise, and set them on the desk next to the computer. Gabriel glanced at Jax, who was scowling.

"Jax," Boadica said, "I'll need you to come with me in the morning to rent the boat. You'll be the captain. We'll load up our equipment and take it down with us. We should have our materials out of this hotel room by five-thirty A.M. The boat charter place opens early and I want a good selection to choose from.''

She gestured at the equipment and supplies that had piled up around the room: the cardboard boxes, the hardware store bags full of stuff Jax had brought in earlier. The two enormous duffel bags were propped up against the wall; atop and around them were wet suits, goggles, regulators, buoyancy compensators, fishing rods and nets, wire cutters, pulleys, clamps, pliers, wrenches, carabiners, and nylon line. All the papers, maps, and accordion folders were stacked on and against the table by the window. *One* person in that room would have felt cramped.

Mark said, ''Five-thirty! Ugh. What's the hurry?''

Boadica's lips thinned. ''This town is crawling with undercover heat. I've seen men in shorts and flip-flops hauling out their badges and asking questions all over.''

''Holy shit.'' Jax sat upright in bed. They all looked at the duffel bags full of several thousand dollars and thirty kilos of plastique.

''It might have nothing to do with us,'' Gabriel said. ''Let's not panic.''

''What does it matter who they're looking for?'' Boadica replied. ''We could just as easily get caught by narcotics agents looking for drug dealers as by some other group. We've spent three days on a purported fishing trip without getting out onto the water. We can make a case for needing a few days to get our act together, but any more time and we'll look suspicious.''

''Do you think we're being watched?'' Mark asked.

''I think it's possible. The minute this room is empty, to be on the safe side, we should assume it will be searched.''

Gabriel looked around at the light fixtures, the telephone, the furniture.

"Speaking of paranoid," he said, "how do we know they're not listening in?"

"We don't. But I doubt it. Today's the first day I've seen any real evidence of them, and I've been watching. And besides, I scouted around outside just now and didn't spot anything. Though I may have missed something; you can never be sure."

She pulled a strip of tape from the window and peered out.

Jax said, "Well?"

"I still don't see anything." She replaced the tape and turned. "Doesn't mean they're not there."

"We need the equipment out *now*," Gabriel said. "Let's see if we can persuade the boat dealer to open his shop after hours."

"That would be even more suspicious," Jax said. "With all the drug smuggling in this area, the boat dealer would probably call the cops. I think we should sit tight."

Boadica tapped her lips with her forefinger. "Gabe is right about the equipment, though. If we're questioned and the room is searched, the money, the non-standard diving tools, and the explosives will give them what they need to arrest us. We'll put the hot stuff in my rental trunk with the ordnance and I'll park it in the Ramada Inn parking lot down Route 1."

"But if they find it, they'll trace the rental registry and start checking all the hotels," Jax said.

She shook her head. "I didn't use the same ID to check in here. There'll be no link, and unless they're watching us right now, odds are very poor that they'll check the car." She turned back to Gabriel. "Gabe, with all this heat, I don't think we should trust in your disguise; it was only meant to distract casual observers. And you're the one most likely to be identified by the feds. I think you should stay out of sight while Jax and Mark and I load the car and move it."

Gabriel shook his head. "Uh-uh. It means postponing contact with Emma. I'm planning on trying her again this evening—at her office first, then at her home. Let Jax stay here with the stuff, you and Mark take the equipment, and I'll try again with Emma."

Boadica looked thoughtful. "I really think we should hold off on making contact with Tooke, for the time being. If the heat is on, they might know about your connection to her. Let's all lie low for a couple of days and let things cool off a bit, before we make our next move."

"I agree," Jax said. "You go out now, you could get us all into deep trouble. You should wait here."

"I think she's right," Mark said, laying a hand on Gabriel's shoulder.

"All right." Gabriel sighed, stuffing down a spike of irritation.

She shifted into high gear. "Mark, you'll help Jax and me load up my car. Jax, you'll drive the other rental. We'll go separate ways—take your time and go through a bunch of residential streets. Make sure you're not being followed. I'll meet you at that auto parts shop at NASA Boulevard and Route 1."

Jax frowned. "I thought you were going to leave the car at the Ramada."

She said gently, "I am. But *I'll* meet you at the auto parts place, right?"

"Oh. Yeah, I get you," Jax said.

Gabriel stayed away from the door while they carried the duffels out to Boadica's car. Mark came back in and said doubtfully, "Well, things *looked* clean. Hope we're not being watched, but Bo sure knows how to handle this stuff, huh?"

Gabriel grunted. He couldn't help feeling he was being shouldered aside.

* * *

While Mark went back to studying the engineering drawings, Gabriel paced for a bit.

He was losing control of the group and he didn't know what to do about it. Boadica controlled all the information, had supplied all the funds. She was deferring less and less to his authority, and now Jax, and even Mark, were defecting.

He was beginning to regret letting her join the group.

He growled and sat down on the bed, rubbing at his short hair with a sigh. Get your ego out of the way, Cervantes, he thought. You've gotten your rocks off for years playing Robin Hood, and now you've found your Maid Marian, only she isn't playing the demure groupie, and you're jealous.

Boadica had excellent instincts, had shown herself to be clever and trustworthy, and her information thus far had been impeccable. It was the mark of a good leader to let his people do their jobs. And Jax . . . he didn't know what to do about Jax, but goading him by actively competing for Boadica's attention wasn't the smartest thing in the world to do.

Thing was, he wanted her. Every bit as much as Jax did. He smiled wryly at himself; hadn't they ever heard of *le droit de seigneur*?

These ruminations weren't getting him anywhere. He started working on the speech they'd give the press when they hit the facility.

Boadica called an hour later.

He used the Texas accent. "How are *things*?"

"Couldn't be better," she said. "We're going to buy some groceries for the boat, so we'll be a while. Didn't want you to worry."

"That's peachy. Don't stay out too late. Y'all need your rest."

She laughed. "Don't wait up."

*   *   *

The toilet flushed and someone turned on the light in the nook outside the bathroom. Mark was snoring in the other bed. Gabriel lifted his head from his pillow and squinted at the bedside clock: almost 2:00 A.M.

Two A.M.? That must add up to a hell of a lot of groceries.

He lay there on his back listening to the splash of Jax's urine hitting the water in the toilet and the hum of the ineffectual air conditioner.

Well after Jax had collapsed onto the roll-out cot, Gabriel lay awake, staring at the dark ceiling. He rolled over and pounded his pillow, thinking about Boadica, sleeping alone in the next room. Jax was probably lying awake right now, thinking about the very same thing. Or maybe that was why he was so late; he'd been getting his ashes hauled.

Suddenly, he was sure of it. She was fucking Jax on the sly. Why him and not me? he thought angrily.

Cervantes, get a grip, he thought. Forget about Jax and Boadica. It's a big hit and the heat's on. You want to be leader; so, lead. Ride the wave.

Still, for the first time in his long activist career, Gabriel was scared. It wasn't just that the feds might be outside the room, watching and listening, though that was part of it. He'd never faced this much heat before, and it was forcing him to reevaluate just how far he was willing to go. But it was also the sheer size of the facility. He'd spent the better part of the past two days digging through drawings and plans for this facility that must have cost a billion, easy, trying to figure out the best way to destroy it.

Technology sucked, and big technology sucked bigtime. But. Gulf Stream I had better be a billion dollars' worth of evil. It had better be four lives' worth of evil. Because he was beginning to wonder whether they would get out of this alive.

Chapter 23

After the dive debriefing he returned to the Engineering bullpen. It was after five; where had the day gone? He had so much left to do.

"You're all set," Ramón told him. "Let's log you on and make sure everything's set up properly."

Keith sat down at his computer; Ramón watched over his shoulder as he turned on the computer and monitor.

"I put Eudora in your Windows startup list, so it'll come up automatically."

Indeed, as Ramón spoke, the Eudora startup screen flashed onto the screen and asked him for his password. He typed in "gulf-1", and the computer informed him it was checking for messages. "Getting message 1 of 2" a dialog box informed him.

"The first one is a welcome note from me," Ramón said. "Looks like you're already getting mail. Popular guy."

The mail queue showed a memo from GS1 Administrator, and one from s.purvis@netcom.com.

Keith said, "I took the liberty of letting some people know my new address."

"Ah. Well, let me know if you need anything."

Ramón went back to his cubicle nearby. Keith opened the file from s.purvis.

DATE: MON, 5 OCT 16:14:08-0700 (MST)
FROM: SAM PURVIS <S.PURVIS@NETCOM.COM>

To: "Keith Hellman" <kingfisher@gulfstream
.com>
Subject: Hi there
Message-ID:<Pine.BSD/
.3.91.950625171224.21538A-
100000@bud.virotec.com>
MIME-Version: 1.0
Content-Type: TEXT/PLAIN; charset=US-ASCII
Keith,
how are things out at your new job? We miss you
Penelope says to tell you Trey's crawdads just
aren't the same without you along.
Here are the expenses I show as incurred by you
on the Marshall project over the past several
months:
Mar-$746.36
Apr-$426.07
May-$772.08
Jun-$29.21
Jul-$589.18
Aug-$844.35
Sep-$704.01
Oct-$99.04
Please verify the totals right away, as we need
to get the bill out to the client tomorrow.

                                                        -Sam
P.S. Drop us a line. Everyone's asking about you.

"How's it going?" Ramón asked from behind him.
Keith jumped in his seat. He turned.

"Up and running. Think I'll call it a day, though."
He queued the message to print and logged off. The
nearby laser printer hummed; Keith folded the page in
quarters and put it in his pocket.

Ramón was heading out the door. Keith stopped
him.

"Uh—do you know where the facility's environmental compliance records are kept?"

"I'd guess over in Science, where Franz's office was. Unless they've moved them out. I don't know. Check with Dick Munzer. He handles most of the administrative stuff for Dr. Reynolds."

Barnes and Gorey's E-mail was the first order of business. Keith went to his bunk.

The mystery roomie wasn't there. All of Keith's luggage was still piled on the unoccupied upper bunk, except his dive gear, which he'd stowed in a locker in Mariculture.

Keith thumped the mattress. At this point nails would be as good as goose down. He pulled down and unpacked his duffel bag, set aside the *American Heritage Dictionary* Gorey and Barnes had given him, and put his clothing and toiletries away in the drawers. The empty bags fit—barely—in the bottom of the closet. Then he pulled out the piece of paper he'd printed earlier, and, seating himself on his roomie's bunk, got out his pen and the dictionary.

A book code was quite simple, and unbreakable if you didn't know which book. Gorey had said you could use any book, as long as both parties exchanging encrypted code had identical editions.

The encoding numbers were paired: the first number told what page the code word was on; the second told which word on the page it was. Or, in the case of a dictionary, which entry. So 746.36 should be the thirty-sixth entry on page 746. And so forth.

Keith flipped pages, counted entries, and wrote. Fifteen minutes later he had it.

MAR-$746.36   URGENT
APR-$426.07   MEETING
MAY-$772.08   WEDNESDAY

Jun-$29.21	A.M.
Jul-$589.18	RETURN
Aug-$844.35	MELBOURNE
Sep-$704.01	THEN
Oct-$99.04	CALL

He read it several times, a scowl growing on his face. He wondered what was going down, and—more to the point—how the hell he was supposed to get back to Melbourne without arousing anyone's suspicions.

He had till tomorrow to think up an excuse. Otherwise it'd have to be a call to Pendleton, and risk blowing his cover.

All of which got him to thinking about possible terrorist suspects. He checked off on the personnel roster the names of the people he'd met so far, all the way from Emma and Gloria and Flo to Jess, Nikki, Angus, Sean, Ramón, and so on. By the time he'd finished his list was almost two dozen long. Then he wrote down his impressions of each.

He started to doodle, his mind wandering. He was no specialist in terrorism, but—aside from the lab fiasco, which smacked more of laziness or stupidity than sabotage—no one yet had done anything out of the ordinary or suspicious to his eyes.

He wondered if the insider could be someone landside. That lawyer, Phil Evans. Or the CFO, perhaps. Or a disgruntled employee—one of Emma's landside engineers. Even a janitor or secretary could do great harm, if they wanted.

With a sigh, Keith stuck the paper back into his pocket and stood with a grunt. He just didn't have enough to go on—and, with a full-time job in addition to two separate investigations, too damn much to do.

*   *   *

First he went to Engineering and used his new computer to E-mail "Sam Purvis" a brief message confirming receipt of the mail. On impulse he looked up Emma's E-mail address and sent her a note:

ET—THINKING OF YOU.—KH

. Then he logged off and headed over to Science.

When Keith stepped into the main deck from the outside walkway he found himself surrounded by activity. People hurried to and fro carrying trays, bottles, equipment, and other paraphernalia, stuck their heads out of the labs, and called to each other. He asked someone where Reynolds was, and the man pointed at a lab.

Inside, Thomas Reynolds sat on a stool at a lab bench, writing notes in a bound notebook. A short, stout, middle-aged man with a boyish face and brown hair and eyes stood at a gas chromatograph, syringe in hand. Two young men were seated on the floor, loading equipment into cabinets. The room smelled of vinegar and petroleum.

"Dr. Reynolds."

Reynolds looked up. "Ah, our new environmental compliance person. Hellman, is it?"

Keith nodded. "Keith Hellman."

"I must say, you've given us a real headache," Reynolds said, showing very white teeth.

"Oh?"

"We're still unwrapping from your storm preparations. Nobody has gotten any real work done today."

Keith narrowed his eyes and flexed his hands. The man at the mass spectrometer and the two on the floor glanced at Keith, then Reynolds.

"It's very interesting you should say so. In fact, I'd very much like to have a meeting with you and your entire staff about appropriate emergency response pro-

tocols. We saw some serious violations of protocol.
Your man Munzer has some explaining to do.''

The man at the mass spec twitched and stared. Munzer?

Reynolds shook his head. ''Perhaps in a week or
two. We're very busy right now.''

Keith felt a wave of cold spread through his body.
He stared at Reynolds and said, ''A week or two is
out of the question. I'd like a meeting tomorrow morning.''

Reynolds turned in his seat and stared back at Keith.
Then he stood up.

''We'll continue this discussion in my office. Come
with me.''

Reynolds headed for the door, but Keith said, ''No
need. I have authority to call a debriefing whenever
the emergency response protocols are activated. That's
protocol ten-point-three-point-one in the Storm Response Manual, for your reference. So.'' He clapped
his hands together. ''I'll see you and your staff in the
main conference room upstairs, shall we say, eight-
thirty A.M.? Get it out of the way?''

Reynolds stood there staring at him as if he wanted
to strangle him, and waved the others out. They exited.
Then Reynolds walked back, sat back down on his
stool, and looked Keith over.

''You don't seem to understand. We *really* don't
have time for this. It'll have to wait. Is that straight-
forward enough for you to understand?''

''Oh, I understand you well enough,'' Keith said
mildly. ''But Pendleton has given me the responsibility for environmental, health, and safety issues for this
facility. The protocols give me authority to call a
meeting when I see fit. And putting off the debriefing
for a week or more is unacceptable.''

''As I said, holding it tomorrow is unacceptable.''
He spread his hands, giving Keith a smile.

"Let me be more clear. We hold the meeting tomorrow in accordance with the protocols, or I submit a written report to Pendleton detailing how one of your people left the module in disastrous shape, and you later refused to cooperate with a standard postemergency debriefing."

Reynolds didn't say anything for a second and his gaze was calculating. Then he gave Keith a rueful smile. The mood change was so sudden as to be obviously artificial. What was alarming was how convincing he was.

"You're right. You *are* entitled to call a meeting. But—let me put this another way."

He paused. Keith said, "Yes?"

"We're under considerable pressure to make up for the time we lost during the storm. Gulf Stream—well, I suppose it's no secret. The company is in serious financial difficulty, and it's my staff's work that is keeping this facility afloat . . ." He smiled. "If you'll excuse the expression. Taking up precious hours in rehashing what's already past and trying to apportion blame—"

"Hold it. First of all, if it hadn't been for our last-minute preparations you'd have a lot bigger problem on your hands than unwrapping some bottles and spending an hour or two in a meeting. You might not have had a functioning laboratory to come back to." He shook his head. "We can't afford to let that sort of thing happen again. The problem might be with the protocols, or it might be the training. We can't know until we analyze it—we have to know what went wrong, to keep it from happening again. And second, in a week or two people's memories won't be fresh. The value of a debriefing diminishes sharply with time."

He paused, eyeing Reynolds's poker face, and added, "It won't be a witch hunt. I'm not out for blood. If Munzer made an honest mistake, I won't hold it against him. Obviously if I find evidence of negligence I'll have to take disciplinary steps, but nine times out of ten when this sort of thing happens it's a case of someone making a dumb mistake or misunderstanding directions.''

"It was an oversight, I'm sure. A simple mistake.''

"In that case you have nothing to worry about.''

"Munzer's a good man, but''—the barest of hesitations; Reynolds rubbed his lower lip—"not the brightest technician on my staff, you see. He's a hard worker, though, and good at what he does, within certain limits. I'd hate for there to be repercussions . . .''

"I can't make any promises. All I can say is that I'm not looking for a scapegoat. I'm looking to identify the problem and fix it.''

"If you feel a debriefing is that important—''

"It is.''

Reynolds spread his hands wide. "—then of course we'll cooperate. Eight-thirty, you say? Tomorrow?''

Keith nodded once.

"Very good. I'll make sure everyone's there for it. Will there be anything else?'' His voice held just a hint of challenge. Keith ignored it.

"Yes. I need to know where the environmental compliance records are kept.''

Reynolds's expression soured. He eyed Keith with obvious annoyance. "Very well. Dick!''

The heavyset man stuck his head in the door.

"Keith Hellman, Dick Munzer.'' Keith nodded at the other man. "Dick, show Hellman where Franz's old records are.''

The look Reynolds gave Munzer seemed meaningful; Keith may have imagined it. Munzer gave Keith a nervous glance and opened the door wider to let him pass. "This way.''

They went outside.

The modules faced southeast. Keith went over to the rail and filled his lungs with raw, fishy air, looking southward at open water.

The sea beyond the breakwater buoys was becalmed. *La Pescadora* was docked at the base of Mariculture. The last rays of sunset spread across the western horizon like a Japanese fan, yellow and pink against the cloudless indigo sky; the wind had died down. Stars sparkled against the darkness. A silver haze on the southeastern horizon promised moonrise soon.

Keith took another deep breath, suddenly feeling every ache. It had been a long, hard day. Hell, a long, hard week.

He wished he were out on a sailboat somewhere, sprawled out on the cabin roof with an iced tea in hand, watching the stars come out, looking forward to some laughs and a game or two of canasta with his diving buddies before climbing into his bunk. He thought of the dusty boxes of paper below, waiting for him, and grimaced.

Munzer had started down the stairs. Keith descended around the curve of the module several yards behind the other man, hearing the slap of water against the beanpole, the splash of surface feeders in the dark water. Lights had come on along the catwalks and modules, reminding Keith of a circus midway. Gentle swells amid the modules made the reflected light into dancing loops and pools. People hurried across the outer walkways and the catwalks, carrying boxes and equipment. Repairing, redeploying. Sounds from Mariculture and Engineering carried across the water: hammering, pounding, the shriek and whine of metal against metal.

Munzer took him back inside, to a storage room on the utility deck. He opened the door and flipped a switch. Keith stifled a groan as the fluorescents flickered on. The room was jammed with file storage boxes stacked six high. Along one wall were shelves filled with stationery and office supplies.

Munzer gestured at the boxes. "There you are."

"These are all environmental records?"

"No, only some of them. You'll have to check each box. They're usually labeled on the end with the person's name and sometimes the contents."

"Usually? Sometimes?" He shook his head, and began rolling up his sleeves.

Munzer watched him for a second. "You want some help with the boxes?"

Keith frowned. This man was responsible for a near-disaster, and Keith might have to recommend punitive measures. He didn't want to be beholden to him. He shook his head. "I'll manage. I could do with a pad of paper and a pen, though." He gestured at the office supplies. "May I help myself?"

"Sure." Munzer turned away, then turned back and looked at Keith and drew a deep breath. He ran fingers through his thinning hair.

"Everybody's talking about how I screwed up the storm preparations." He stopped. Keith folded his arms and waited. Munzer took a deep breath. When he started talking, it was in a rather breathless monotone. "I know you won't believe me, but Reynolds called and told me to leave off. I was in charge of the module. So I told the rest of the team to go on. They argued with me. I told them I could finish by myself. And I lied to Flo about it. It wasn't their fault. It was mine. But . . ." He sighed. "I didn't know it was going to get so bad." A pause. "I knew it wasn't right. I should have done something. Should have told somebody." A tremor crept into his voice. "He told me if I bucked him I'd lose my job."

The edges of Keith's lips pulled down. "When did he tell you to leave off?"

"The day before the storm hit. I can't prove it, though."

"Why would he not want the module protected?"

"He didn't believe the hurricane would hit. He didn't want to lose time redeploying all the equipment and reshelving chemicals." Munzer's laugh was tinged with hysteria. "He called it a bloody nuisance, said Tooke and Jonas loved playing Emergency Response Nazi Bitches, and they weren't going to interfere with his labs' productivity."

"Pendleton needs to hear about this."

Munzer gave Keith a look equal parts entreaty and despair, and shook his head. "No way."

"Why not?"

"It's no use. Nobody's going to take my word over his. Even if they believed me—which they won't; why should they?—they can't afford to piss him off. I'm dead meat."

Munzer's shoulders slumped. He turned to go.

"I just wanted you to know the truth," he said without turning around, and closed the door behind him.

Keith stood there looking at the closed door. Maybe Munzer was lying to protect himself. Keith didn't think so.

The more Keith thought about it, the more little bubbles of rage surfaced and popped inside. He remembered his conversation with Emma.

Reynolds. Money. Connections. Taking him down meant taking Gulf Stream I down. But he wanted to; oh, he wanted to make the man pay.

Keep your perspective, Keith, he thought. Your job is to uncover environmental misdoings and help the FBI in their terrorist investigation. Neglecting storm response protocols, however stupid and short-sighted, wasn't his problem, wasn't his real job. He started slinging boxes.

He thought of Emma and all the sacrifices she must

have made to keep this facility going. It must burn her raw to have to deal with a man like Reynolds.

Hmmm. Maybe *Reynolds* was the inside terrorist. And if not, maybe Keith could frame him.

Laughing, he shifted boxes, locating seven marked *Environmental, Health & Safety* or something similar, and four labeled *Franz Uhlmann* or *F. Uhlmann.* He also found eight others that weren't labeled at all, or whose labels were unclear.

He stacked them separately from the rest and, before opening them, set up a chart to make notes on their contents. He used a separate page for each box. As he put the headers on he became aware that his bladder was painfully full.

That decided it. He set the pen and pad down. It was time for a break. Maybe some dinner and a couple of hours' rest before he continued.

Keith headed over to Residential, made a trip to the head, and then went over to the mess. A man and a woman wearing aprons, both college-aged or thereabouts, were loading a commercial dishwasher. A woman with messy blond hair, wearing an open-mouthed, surprised expression, sat at the far end of one table; on closer inspection Keith realized it was a life-sized inflatable doll dressed in a lab coat.

A man in his late forties or early fifties sat at the table chopping vegetables. He was short and dark-skinned, perhaps part Melanesian or American Indian, with long hair in a neat ponytail at his neck and prominent cheekbones. He looked up.

"Working late?" Keith asked.

"Isn't everyone?" He stood, wiped hands on his apron, and extended one. "Charles Lawson, chief cook and bottle washer."

"Keith Hellman." Keith shook his hand.

"Ah . . . ?" His tone rose as high as his eyebrows. One kiss and Keith had become a local celebrity. It was a good thing his investigation didn't depend on keeping a low profile. "Our new environmental person. Welcome to Gulf Stream. The graveyard shift lunch won't be ready for another three hours, but we have leftovers from the daytime dinner shift, if you don't mind them cold."

"I'll take what I can get."

"Water, condiments, and silverware are over there," Lawson said, pointing. While Keith rummaged through the bins at the stainless steel counter for a fork and knife, and filled a glass with ice water from the dispenser, Lawson got Saran-wrapped aluminum pans full of food out of the refrigerator and banged around serving up food.

He set the plate in front of Keith. The portions were generous.

"Who's that?" Keith asked, jerking a thumb at the life-sized doll. Lawson gave him a grin.

"Dr. Feelgood, the facility shrink. Got any problems, tell them to her. She's a good listener."

Keith chuckled. He wolfed down barbecued spare ribs, mashed potatoes, and creamed spinach. With a burp, he wiped his mouth and then dropped his napkin onto his plate.

"Thanks for the grub. I didn't realize how hungry I was."

"You want seconds?"

"I'm full." Keith dropped the recyclables in the blue container, threw the trash in the grey bin, and dropped the dirty dishes in the sink. "Thanks again. It was good."

Lawson waved him away. "Whatever. Just don't call me Cookie."

His roommate was in bed when he got to the room, a snoring lump under covers. Keith stripped down to T-shirt and briefs, climbed into bed, and crawled under his own covers. He yawned mightily, scratched, and set his watch alarm. A shower would definitely be in order at some point, but not now; he was exhausted. Maybe he'd sleep for three or four hours before going back to Science to sort through files.

He propped arms under his head with a sigh. Sleep, a drowsy, down-filled quilt, came softly down to rest on him. As it did he found himself thinking of Emma.

Chapter 24

EMMA: **Monday, 5 October, 7:40 P.M. EDT**
Waterfront, Melbourne Beach, Florida

"You sure have been moody all day," Gloria said, and heaved a stone out to sea. The stone skipped across the ocean's shining, slate-colored surface once, twice, three times, and then sank with a melodic *gloop*. She sent another one sailing after it, hopping on one foot like a shot-putter.

They had just eaten at Emma's place. White wine and fresh scallops lingered on her palate; traces of sunlight lingered on the horizon.

Emma rolled up her pants legs, took off her sandals, and walked into the surf. Water lukewarm and soothing lapped against her ankles; sand and shell fragments scoured her soles. Though the cool front had moved on through, the air was still a tad cooler than usual— maybe seventy degrees, now that the sun had set— and laden with mist. Crickets, frogs, and katydids sang hypnotic counterpoint in the tufts of salt grass that sprouted on the dunes.

This pressure had been building in Emma's chest all day. But there'd been no time at the office for per-

sonal revelations, and over dinner her tongue had been
thoroughly bound. Or perhaps, she thought now, all
dried up from disuse.

Why did telling Gloria have such potency? As if it
wouldn't be real, somehow, until she did.

"I have something to tell you," she said.

Gloria lobbed another stone, and shook fists at the
sky with a whoop. "Six skips! The crowd goes wild.
What?"

Emma held the pause a long time, walking along,
until Gloria gave her a punch in the arm. "Spill it."

She took the plunge. "I've fallen for Keith."

"Ah." Gloria gave her a quick, ironic look and
grabbed her piles of curly hair, which she tied in a
knot at her neck. Then she stooped to look for more
stones to throw. Emma frowned and stopped walking.

"Aren't you even a little surprised?"

"I had a bet with myself over how long it'd take
you to tell me." Gloria loosed another stone. "I think
you underestimate your newsworthiness, my dear.
Half the company is talking about the one you planted
on him last night at the port. Or was it two? Accounts
differ."

Emma's heart pounded hard, captive falcon, against
her ribs. She squatted and picked up a shell, washed
it in the surf, and turned it over, studying it: a small
crown conch shell. Not a particularly interesting spec-
imen. She chucked it into the sea and wiped her hands
on her cotton pants.

"I had no idea it would be such a big deal," she
said after a moment.

Gloria merely made a noise. Her obvious, piquant
delight made Emma smile, embarrassed. She climbed
above the tidal line and sat in the sand, digging her
toes in. Gloria joined her, smoothing her skirt and lying back, head pillowed on her linked hands. They
listened to the insects and the lapping surf.

She'd gotten his E-mail tidbit. It had pleased her absurdly. She hadn't been able to bring herself to answer.

"I never thought I'd feel like this again," Emma said. "I guess . . . I had this idea that everyone has one true love, and if it goes bad, too bad for you. You might care about others, even love them, in a way, but it'll never be like that first time. You'll never have that feeling of transcendence."

She drew a deep breath, pulled her shoulders up, leaned her head back. It was so easy to call back the sensations: Keith's body leaning against hers; the heat of his skin through cloth-thin layers; his arms around her; his breath's scent and its feathery touch on her cheek.

That wasn't love. It was lust. Wasn't it? And if so, what was she afraid of? Their bodies together? Or something else?

She shook her head hard and hugged her knees.

"Let me check my magic crystal." Gloria pulled a round, smooth stone out of her pocket. It was a piece of polished quartz a little larger than an egg. She waved a hand over it. "Sim-sim-salabimm, abracadabra, hocus-pocus, lacto-bacillus heartburn. Ah, yes. Things are coming into focus. It says here you are afraid of this tall-but-not-too-dark stranger."

Emma laughed heartily. "Mmm. What else does it say?"

"It says you fear to put too much of yourself at risk with any man."

"Smart rock."

"Go on."

"I keep wondering what the big deal is. People get into relationships all the time."

"So what *is* the big deal?"

Emma was silent a long time. "I keep remembering Gabriel. I loved him so much, and it was so wonderful at first, and turned out so awful. He ended up hating me, Gloria. Cursing me. I still kick myself for being so stupid. I did some really stupid, mean things in that relationship. And some other horribly painful things happened.'' She shook her head, dragging her fingers across her scalp.

"Once burned . . .'' Gloria said softly.

"Exactly. And I keep remembering all those horrible fights between my parents, before they divorced. It seemed like it was all my mom's fault, which of course is bullshit, but you know I said some really hurtful things. And then she had to go and die before I could make it up to her.''

"My magic crystal instructs me to point out that you were awfully young at the time.''

"So? I was still a shit.''

"It probably felt like a betrayal when she divorced your dad.''

"It did. I was so angry. So hurt. And when she got cancer and died, it was like she'd abandoned me all over again. Dad kept saying everyone had to die and I should get on with my life, but the pain just seemed to go on and on . . .'' She closed her eyes. "God, how I hated hurting so much. I don't want to hurt like that again. I don't want to love him and have him go away, or do nasty things to keep me at a distance, or ignore me. Or die on me.''

The muscles in her throat had balled up tight. Gloria looked at her for a long moment, and then squeezed her shoulder with a sigh.

"My magic rock is out of juju. Worthless piece of shit.'' Gloria tucked the rock back into her pocket. "I wouldn't trust what it tells you, anyway; it keeps giving *me* all sorts of bad advice about relationships.''

Emma looked at her, surprised. "You have *lots* of experience with relationships.''

Gloria grunted. "Yeah. Lots of experience at getting

into them. Not much luck at keeping them.''

"I didn't know you wanted to.''

''I don't. There's always something I don't like about them, or I get bored after a while. Or *they* do, and I don't want to be the one left behind.''

''Preemptive strike, eh?''

"Yeah . . . I don't know . . . I think maybe my expectations are too high. I keep finding flaws. I have this picture in my head of what I want, and nobody measures up. My magic crystal would probably tell me that my critical attitude is just another way of avoiding intimacy. Good thing I don't pay attention to it.'' Gloria sighed with great gusto. ''It's a great feeling, though, isn't it? Despite all the hassles. There's nothing quite like falling in love.''

Emma thought of Keith again, and warmth moved through her. She smiled. ''Yeah. I suppose it is a nice feeling.'' Then she sobered. ''There is something a bit odd, though.''

"About relationships? Sex?''

"About Keith.'' She gathered handsful of sand and let the grains bleed through her fingers. ''Or, no, not exactly, but . . .''

''Speak, oh swami.''

So Emma told her about the note.

"Maybe someone's playing a head game with you.''

"Yeah, but who? And why?''

"I don't know . . . maybe our good friend Thomas is trying to ruin your love life.''

"Why should he bother?''

''He's a vindictive bastard, that's why. Or—I know.'' Gloria laughed, and grasped Emma's arm. ''He secretly has the hots for you, and can't stand it if someone else gets you.''

Emma made a gagging noise and clutched her mouth. ''Oh, please.''

She lay back. The stars were coming out. The hunter Orion, two sets of three closely spaced stars at right angles inside a trapezoid, spanned the sky overhead. "I can't think of anyone with a reason to lie to me about Keith."

"It *is* odd. You're right." Gloria was silent a moment. "I think it's a prank. Who would benefit from sending you a mysterious note? It seems calculated to disrupt your relationship with him before it really gets started. Which sounds like unrequited love."

"Or it's someone who knows something about him, but can't reveal that they know." Emma dug fingers into the pebbly sand. "Search me. Anyhow, Shelly's doing a background check. I feel a little bit guilty checking up on him like this, but . . ." She let the sentence trail away.

"You're obligated to. You can't leave something like that without following up."

"Yeah. I expected Shelly to call back this afternoon," Emma said, "but she didn't and I got wrapped up with other matters."

Gloria snapped her fingers. "Oh—that reminds me. Venkatraman with Atlantic Mercantile Bank in Boston called you back while you were tied up this afternoon. Maybe he's got a lead."

"Ha. Maybe. Come on." Emma stood and brushed sand from her rump. She itched. The gnats were beginning to bite. "I've got to check my E-mail and see if I got anything from Gulf Stream."

Chapter 25

GABRIEL: **Tuesday, 6 October, 9:56 A.M. EDT**
Aboard *The Cherokee Princess,* **approximately four**
nautical miles southwest of Melbourne Beach, Florida

By midmorning Tuesday, Gabriel, Mark, and Boadica sat on blue vinyl cushions at the table, sipping tea in *The Cherokee Princess*'s cabin and studying the blueprints spread out on the table. Jax's footsteps thumped across the deck overhead, and he came down inside. His mood was better this morning, as was everyone's. It was good that they'd gotten out of that cramped hotel room and out onto the river.

The Cherokee Princess was a pretty boat with fresh, shiny, sunflower-yellow and white paint, a flying bridge, deck chairs, and a roomy cabin with a propane stove and refrigerator. She was, Jax had proudly announced, a thirty-foot cabin cruiser with twin inboard diesel engines, a top speed of twenty knots, and a range of five hundred miles—more than enough distance to get them out to Gulf Stream I and then to the Bahamas. Gabriel knew squat about boats, but this seemed like a nice one. An expensive one. The weekly rental fee and deposit must surely have taken a big bite out of their cash.

They'd anchored outside the navigation channel, about two hundred yards away from the shore. Though the cabin door was open, no breeze circulated inside. The air—still, warm, and humid—carried the strong, fishy smell of low tide, weed, and exposed mud. The floor dropped away and pushed upward in a brisk rolling motion that made Gabriel a tad queasy every time a boat went by in the channel.

"Okay, so let's talk about Gulf Stream," Boadica said. "What have you guys got?"

Gabriel exchanged a look with Mark. They had a plan for planting the charges, and it was a good one.

"Gulf Stream I has a delicate balance," Gabriel began, "between ballast and buoyancy. Destroy that balance and you destroy Gulf Stream."

Chapter 26

EMMA: **Tuesday, 6 October, 8:08 A.M. EDT**
Reflections, Melbourne, Florida

Venkat Venkatraman at Atlantic Mercantile called her first thing. Venkat was the banker in Boston who had originally helped structure the Gulf Stream–General Motors–Pacific Gas & Electric deal. Though she had not been directly involved, he had called her once or twice for help with technical details while they were preparing the deal documents.

"How was your vacation?" she asked.

"Wonderful. Two weeks of sun and sand, and no telephones."

"Sounds sublime."

"Now, I'm returning your calls. What can I do for you?"

"Hang on a second; I want Gloria and Angelo to be in on this." She paged Gloria and asked her to get Angelo and come into her office. Then she cut back to Venkat.

"You've probably already heard, but—"

"But the deal fell through. I did hear. This is terrible news. Have you talked to anyone over at GM? Or at PG and E?"

"I haven't," Emma said, "but Pendleton has. He got a copy of a public opinion analysis being circulated in GM management called *The Hindenberg Effect*—"

"I get the idea." A sigh. "I'm really surprised. They sank millions into their proof-of-concept vehicle, and it was a big success at the winter auto show in Detroit . . ."

Angelo walked in, followed by Gloria. Emma gestured for them to sit and put Venkat on the speaker phone. "Well you *know* I think they're wrong. I think fuel cell technology *is* viable. PG and E is still in if we can find an automaker to play ball with us. We need to locate a company—if not one of the Big Three, then at the very least an auto company with some decent capital behind it—that believes it, too. Or at least is willing to be convinced. And I need it soon. Like, yesterday."

Another sigh. "I'll see what I can do. Perhaps I'll even give my contact over at GM another call. Have any bridges been burned?"

Emma shared a glance with Gloria and Angelo and hoped Pendleton hadn't been up to something she didn't know about.

"We haven't sued them, if that's what you mean. But I got the impression from Pendleton that the deal was dead, dead, dead."

"Hmmm. I'll give you an update tomorrow."

"Before seven-thirty, please. I want to know before a big meeting we're having here."

"That may not be possible. I'll try."

"I *really* appreciate this, Venkat. Thanks." She

hung up. "Angelo, have you had any luck identifying any other markets?"

He pursed his lips. "I've been following up on one interesting possibility I spoke to you about a few months ago, but it's not likely to pan out in the short term."

"The aircraft industry?"

"Bingo. With pending federal carbon reduction measures likely to drive the cost of fossil fuel up, a group of airlines and aircraft engine manufacturers are looking seriously at jet engines using hydrogen and oxygen as fuel. The proposed SSTO aircraft also proposes to use hydrogen as fuel."

"SSTO?"

"Single Stage to Orbit. You know, the low-Earth-orbit spacecraft that's been in the news lately. Anyhow, in the long run I think the aircraft industry is where our main markets are. They don't have the problems with fuel storage capacity that cars do. But commercial applications are still a few years away so it won't help us with our immediate problem."

"What about NASA?"

"I spoke to our contact there, and they don't foresee an increase in their need. Trouble is, we're roughly at par with the chemical industry's pricing, they have existing contracts in place, and we can't afford to lower our price any further or we'll lose money hand over fist."

"Yeah. Well . . ." Emma didn't know what to say. "Keep looking, I guess."

Gloria leaned forward, a serious expression on her face. "What can I do to help?"

"Your primary focus remains acting as my liaison with the facility . . . but just be sure that, if for any reason I'm out when Venkat calls, you take the call, get all the particulars, and then track me down wherever I am."

"Right."

"And we're on a very short timetable here. The company could be out of business in a few weeks, if we don't come up with some answers."

Angelo and Gloria exchanged a look.

"Yeah," she said. "It's that serious."

After they left she called Shelly. "What's the word on Keith?"

Shelly's tone was strained. "Honey, I hate to tell you . . ."

"What?"

"Well." Shelly sighed. "All I can say is, *something* is amiss. The head of their Human Resources was out yesterday morning, so I left a message with the receptionist. And I chatted with her a bit, just to mention Keith's name and see what I could find out more informally."

"Yes?"

"Doll, she swears there never was a Keith Hellman at Groman Environmental. She was quite adamant. Told me she'd been there since the firm was started ten years ago, and she knew every Tom, Dick, or Oswald that had ever worked there."

"Shit." Emma put a fist on her stomach, which had started to churn, and looked out at their picnic table again, now awash in midmorning sunlight.

"Now, here's the strange part. Their head of HR called me back this morning, and went on about how Keith Hellman had been one of their top marine biologists for years. And when I mentioned what the receptionist had said, he hemmed and hawed and made out as how she was new and didn't know what she was talking about . . ."

"What do you make of all that?"

"Well, excuse me for saying so, honey, but I never heard such a load of bull pies in all my days. I don't know why, but that man was lying. Keith Hellman never worked at Groman. I haven't a jot of proof other than the receptionist's word, but that's what my intuition tells me."

"Is there any way you can verify?"

Shelly sounded thoughtful. "I could see if I could chase down some other employees, or former employees, from Groman, and quiz them. But other than that . . . I don't know . . ."

"Do what you can."

Emma hung up the phone. She looked out the window some more. Then she went into the bathroom, splashed water on her face, ran fingers through her hair.

Her image, dripping with water, was staring at her when she looked up. It wore an irritated expression. Never, *ever* get involved with your employees, it said; don't shit where you eat. Don't you know anything?

Yeah, yeah, she thought, grabbing a paper towel; you have all the answers *now*.

It was after lunch when she thought of Valentine Pilcher.

Val Pilcher was a civil engineer, a principal of Mandrake Engineering, the Miami firm that had done Gulf Stream I's environmental impact statement. He was fifty-some years old, and both highly regarded and well connected in his field.

Once she'd explained what she was after, he said, "I may be able to help you out. We've worked with them on a number of projects, and one of my managers used to work for them, a few years back. Janice would almost certainly know whether a Keith Hellman has ever worked at Groman, and I can cross-check that with some of my other people."

"Do me a favor, though, and keep a low profile on this," Emma said. "I don't want to create a ruckus over what may be a simple misunderstanding."

"I understand. When do you need something?"

"The sooner the better."

"I'll get back to you before the end of the day."

"Perfect."

She glanced up as she dropped the phone into its cradle; Pendleton stood at the door of her office as though he'd materialized from thin air.

He *never* came to her office.

Her hand went to her chest and she gasped. "Sorry; I wasn't expecting you. What can I do for you?"

He rubbed the back of his neck, gave her a smile. Behind him she glimpsed Gloria, hovering, craning her neck making faces of exaggerated surprise.

"I just got word," he said. "EPA wants to inspect our records. The inspectors will be here in the morning. Hellman is coming in by helicopter with Thomas and Flo. They're due in around six P.M."

Hellman. Her pulse rate picked up. "An inspection the day of our big strategy meeting. Great timing."

"Yes." He gave Emma a distracted grimace that might pass in some circles for a smile. "I suppose there's never a convenient time for an inspection."

"Is it just landside, or do they want to go out to the facility, also?"

"At this point, purely landside. A check of our records to make sure they're all in order."

"Well." Emma released a slow breath. "Phil's paralegal Treena keeps the landside records, and she's good, so I imagine they are in decent shape. Gloria and I will stay late to help Phil and Treena and Keith get things into shape, if needed."

"Good. See you at tomorrow's meeting . . ." He gave her a two-finger wave and turned to go. Emma grabbed the note and stood.

"Um—Mr. Pendleton."

Pendleton turned back, hand on the door jamb. "Yes?"

"I was going to wait till I had more information to come to you," Emma said, handing over the note, "but you should probably know about this."

He read it with no change of expression. Then he looked up at her and lifted the note. "Where did you get this?"

"It showed up on my chair yesterday morning. I'm investigating it. Unfortunately, it appears there may be substance to it—"

"Nonsense." Scowling, he crumpled it up and stuffed it into his pocket. "Purest rubbish."

"But someone at his former company says—"

"I said it was rubbish, and I meant it." His tone was sharper than Emma had ever heard it. "Drop it."

Once he was gone Gloria came in on cat feet, eyes huge. She closed the door and leaned against it.

"How much did you hear?"

"Every weird syllable." She sucked in her breath and shook a hand. "Who pissed in *his* Post Toasties?"

Emma frowned, her eyes narrowing slowly as the shock dissipated. "Stranger and stranger."

So when Val called back late that afternoon and told her that according to his people, Keith Hellman and Groman Environmental had never had anything to do with each other, Emma was anything but surprised.

Needless to say, she didn't take this bit of news to Pendleton.

Gloria brought Emma a diskette with the latest set of plant power-up run results at about five-forty, and Emma told her what she'd learned from Pilcher. Gloria winced.

"Look at it this way. At least you found out *now*."

Emma glowered at Gloria, cheeks propped up by her knuckles.

"I'm not being much help, am I?"

"No, no." Emma tried to rub the frown off her

brow with her thumbs. "You're right. Just wish I knew what to do about it."

"Want to borrow my magic crystal?"

Emma laughed and shook her head. Gloria hovered by the door, lingering.

"What is it?" Emma asked. "Something *else* about Keith?"

Gloria winced. "No, but it's not good. Maybe I should tell you later . . ."

"Gloria!"

"All right. You should know. I just overheard Reynolds on the speaker phone bragging to Dennis that he's got a line on a ten-million-dollar grant from the NSF *if* we can make more space available at the facility. He mentioned the hydrogen plant."

"What did Dennis say?"

Gloria looked embarrassed. "Dennis shut the door about then. I was tempted to listen at the keyhole, but *really*! I have to maintain some dignity."

Emma smiled, but she felt a sudden chill inside.

At about a quarter to seven Flo called her. Emma heard a child's voice in the background.

"Have dinner plans?"

"Well . . ." Emma hesitated. "We have an EPA inspection tomorrow and I promised Phil and Treena that I'd help them out. But I might be able to drop by for a bit. How was the flight back?"

Flo made a noise. "You mean other than the fact that I spent the entire time wondering whether Reynolds and Keith were going to kill each other?"

"Charming. What's going on?"

"Keith has decided to take Reynolds on." Flo chuckled. "The man's got nerve; I'll say that for him."

"What's he done?"

"He's been collecting information about the storm

prep debacle in the Science module, and Reynolds isn't liking it one bit. You know how snide he gets when he decides to make an enemy of someone. We had it all the way back in the helicopter.''

"Yecch.''

"You said it. Lordy. And to make matters worse, York had a rush delivery in Port Canaveral and couldn't drop us in Melbourne first, so we had an extra forty-five minutes of Reynolds in the company van, with Ronnie getting cranky, to boot.''

Emma asked, ''What did you have in mind for dinner?''

"Ronnie and I are having Keith over.'' Emma grimaced. "I'm making barbecued pork and Boston baked beans and Caesar salad,'' Flo went on. "We'd love for you to join us and make it a foursome.''

She wasn't ready to confront Keith, and didn't want to pretend nothing was wrong. "Listen, Flo—on second thought, I'd better not take the time. Thanks anyway.''

She hung up the phone. Her voice had sounded so phony. Flo must think she was nuts.

Chapter 27

GABRIEL: **Tuesday, 6 October, 1:22 P.M. EDT**
The Cherokee Princess, **approximately forty-five nautical miles east-southeast of Melbourne**

Jax glanced at the loran, then put his eyes to the hooded radar scope. "We should be able to see it by now. Bearing twenty degrees.''

Gabriel, binoculars at his eyes, scanned the horizon

to the northeast. Nothing but deep blue sea and traces of cloud. Then Mark shouted, pointing more to the north.

"Gulf Stream I, ho!"

Boadica climbed out onto the deck next to him. "Where? Where? Ahhhhhh. Got it."

Gabriel leaned over the rail, scanning in the direction Mark and Boadica were pointing. Nothing.

"At eleven o'clock, maybe five miles out. You don't need your binocs."

Gabriel lowered the binoculars, scanned—and had it. Amid orange flecks, four white domes stuck up out of the water like mushrooms, the puffball kind he used to kick in the neighbors' lawns as a kid. He sucked air through his teeth. "Yes. Ye-e-s."

Jax took them in closer, bouncing across four-foot crests that sprayed cool wet salt in their faces. Other boats dotted the horizon, including a number fairly close to the facility.

"They're fishing downstream of the power plant," Gabriel said.

Mark nodded, and quaffed a Budweiser. "The plankton blooms from the plant effluent attract surface feeders. Bound to be good fishing there."

Boadica sat down in a deck chair and put her feet up on the rail. The wind whipped her white hair. She looked pleased. "Gives us a good excuse to come in nice and close, doesn't it?"

They watched the facility a while, watched the people crossing the catwalks and working on the roofs. They tracked the boats, tried to read their names, and made more notes.

"You know," Jax said thoughtfully, "we have everything we need, right here on the boat with us."

Gabriel shook his head. "That place is crawling with personnel."

"So?"

Gabriel sighed with exaggerated patience. "What, you want to waltz in there when the place is full of people who might challenge us?"

"I knew you were going to say that. You're just looking for excuses not to hit the place, aren't you? Just like I told Bo. Why don't you just admit you don't have the balls, and get out of the way?"

"What the hell arc you talking about?"

Mark grabbed Jax's arm. "Chill out, buddy."

Jax turned away, swearing under his breath.

"What's with you, Jax?" Gabriel demanded.

"Let me," Boadica said, and followed Jax into the cabin. Gabriel dropped into his chair, nursing his beer.

"Am I losing my mind," Gabriel asked Mark, "or did we agree when we first formed our group that Wild Justice was going to avoid hurting people?"

"Yeah. Don't sweat it, Gabe. It'll be okay. He's just edgy"—he lowered his voice—"and horny."

Boadica came back out and sat down. "He'll calm down. He just needs some time to cool off."

Gabriel eyed her. What happened between you two in Miami? he wondered.

"My big concern right now," she went on, "is that if the feds *do* know we're in the area, they must also know, or suspect, what our target is. They may have laid traps for us out there." She gestured at Gulf Stream I with her chin. "We need to know a lot more before we strike."

Gabriel knocked off the rest of his beer, wiping his mouth with his hand.

"We need Tooke."

"Right."

"What about all that heat you spotted the other day?" Mark asked. "They might still be out there. We don't want Gabriel to be IDed."

Boadica leaned forward and gave them her little smile. "I've been thinking about that very thing, and I've got a plan."

Chapter 28

Jennifer took the hot dogs, fountain drinks, and change from the store manager behind the counter, pocketed the receipt, and handed Keith a hot dog. She held out a kraut-laden plastic spoon. "Sauerkraut?"

Keith shook his head, took the frankfurter, and picked up a yellow plastic squeeze bottle. "Just mustard. You?"

She held her dog out and he gave it a couple of lines of mustard. Food and drink in hand, they went outside.

Keith took a big bite. The skin popped, and hot, salty, tangy juices burst against his tongue and palate.

Jennifer dabbed mustard from the corner of her mouth. "Beats the heck out of airplane food. Even if plaque *is* lining my arteries as we speak."

They sat down on the wooden steps outside the store. Campers, tents, and motor homes lined the small park. A gentle breeze stirred the warm air. Across the road, an enormous cruise ship painted white and blue sat in the dock, with crew members in white uniforms moving about on deck. Shorebirds circled and called out overhead.

A family with three small children and an Irish setter piled out of a nearby minivan and crowded past Keith and Jennifer, amid shouts and giggles and scoldings. The woman herded the kids inside the store while the man tied the dog's leash to a post near Keith.

The dog sat eyeing them. His tail brushed dust across the boards, and he whined hopefully.

"Thanks for meeting me," Keith said, trying to ignore the dog.

"No extra charge. Did your traveling companions ask any questions?"

"Nah." Reynolds couldn't have cared less how Keith got back to Melbourne, and Flo was too busy chasing an energetic toddler around the dock to quiz him when he had turned down the ride back in the company minivan.

Jennifer shooed at a wasp that hovered around their drink cups. The dog whined again. Keith and Jennifer looked at him, then each other. Keith tossed him a bite of hot dog. The dog's lips barely moved, and the bit of food was gone.

"What have you got?" Jen asked.

"Not a hell of a lot. The only thing I've found so far of any concern are about three or four weeks' worth of sporadically odd lab data on the wastewater treatment plant effluent. I fear that someone may have gotten lazy in Reynolds's organization and falsified some analyses. I can't see a way to prove it, though. The paperwork is all in order, and the holding times for most of the samples with suspect analyses are past, and they've been discarded."

"Hmm. And nothing about Pinkle in Uhlmann's files?"

"Nothing. I spent most of last night digging through Uhlmann's old files and couldn't find anything on him."

"Too bad. Still, things may take an interesting turn tomorrow."

"What's going down with this big meeting, anyhow? The Internet message was cryptic."

Jennifer started to answer, but the store door slammed open and the kids clamored down the steps

between Jennifer and Keith, followed by the woman.
The man untied the dog, who nosed Keith's hand and
tried to take the rest of his hot dog, and then they all
climbed back into the van.

Jen took a bite of her hot dog and a swallow of
Coke, and stood, pulling keys from her jeans pocket.

"Let's get going," she said. "I'll tell you on the
way."

Once they were under way, weaving through the
NASA going-home traffic heading south on A1A, Jennifer told Keith, "Sometime this last weekend, Gabriel
Cervantes dropped out of sight. His car is parked on
the street near his duplex, but he hasn't touched it
since Friday. He's not at his apartment and he's
missed several regular meetings. His friends say that
they haven't seen him."

"So if he's not there, he could be here. Any sightings?"

Jennifer shook her head. "I spoke with Barnes this
afternoon. He and Gorey have several operatives
combing the city and the beach fronts, but nothing has
turned up so far."

"And this 'EPA inspection' . . . your idea?"

A smile. "Yep. I wanted to give you a legitimate
excuse to return. Unfortunately, it's gotten rather complicated. Florida has jurisdiction over Gulf Stream's
consent agreements, so of course I had to arrange for
the inspection through them. Which means they'll be
sending their own inspector to be the lead. And guess
who they're sending."

Keith looked at her. His eyes widened. "You're
kidding."

"I'm serious. No doubt Pinkle's heard about Gulf
Stream's new environmental person and is curious."

"Christ."

Jennifer laughed. "And who knows—maybe we'll
get lucky and he'll try to extort money from you."

Keith's only response was a wry glance. "Hey, it could happen. Looks like that's how it happened the last time—or at least, how it started."

"How do you know?"

"The lead you suggested the other day paid off. I've spoken to Franz Uhlmann. He *was* around during the original consent order negotiations between Gulf Stream and the DEP; in fact, at least initially he was Pinkle's primary Gulf Stream contact. And he says that twice during that time Pinkle made intimations to him that the process could be expedited if Gulf Stream was willing to 'play ball.' That, in fact, they might never get their landside permits unless they did."

"Oho. So what happened? Was there extortion? Was he involved?"

Jennifer pursed her lips. "It was a long time ago and he said he doesn't remember a lot of the details, but that he just played dumb and Pinkle pretty much dropped it."

"You think he's on the up-and-up?"

"Yeah. I do. If he were dirty he wouldn't have been so open. I'm not convinced that means Gulf Stream is clean, though."

Keith finished off his hot dog and washed it down with the rest of his lemonade. "You know, Jen, I've been thinking about this and it just doesn't make sense. Gulf Stream doesn't need permits to operate. They're outside U.S. waters. If Pinkle was trying to extort money from them, why not just tell him to take a hike and operate without consent agreements?"

"Two reasons." Jennifer looked over her shoulder and signaled, moving into the left lane to pass a pair of cyclists. "First, Pendleton has some major investments in the phosphate mining industry, over near Tampa. Pinkle couldn't force Gulf Stream to pay, per se, but he could hold Pendleton's other investments hostage."

Keith lifted his eyebrows. "You think Pendleton was involved in a payoff, then."

"I don't know. But we have to consider it."

"But then why would he let the FBI bring me in? Wouldn't that be too risky?"

"Not if he feels secure that no trail of evidence connects him with the payoff. And after all, my case against Gulf Stream—and Pinkle, for that matter—is all circumstantial."

"You know, you never said what your original source was on Pinkle."

She returned his look with a smile. "Let's just say it's a reliable source, but we can't use it in court."

An informant, then. Perhaps someone still employed by the Florida DEP, and under Pinkle's power. "You said you had two reasons Gulf Stream would play ball with Pinkle."

"Have you taken a close look at Gulf Stream's last two annual reports? A good sixty-eight percent of their income last year came from scientific grants and studies. And some of their key clients for those scientific studies are major environmental advocacy groups like NRDC and the Center for Marine Research. Another major source of revenues is the National Science Foundation, which has stringent environmental grant criteria.

"So, Gulf Stream may not be required *by law* to get permits, but they're under some powerful pressure to go beyond the bare legal minimum in terms of their environmental protection measures."

"I get your point." Keith slouched, staring out the window at the sandy, vine-covered hills. "It really stinks, doesn't it, that they should get tangled up in a scandal over a series of permits they're not even required to get?"

"Yeah, but the voluntary nature of their agreements with DEP doesn't alter the fact that it's criminal to pay a government official to grant them concessions."

Keith glanced over at her. She gave him a meaningful look. He rubbed his eyes with a sigh.

"Jen," he said, "the truth is, I'm compromised. I can't continue to pursue an investigation against Gulf Stream."

"What are you talking about?"

"I've gotten involved with the place. With the people. I want Gulf Stream to succeed as a commercial venture. I don't want to find out that they're dirty." He gave her a look, pinching his lip. If he told her the rest, there'd be no going back.

She had to know.

He said, "I've gotten involved with Emma Tooke."

"You what?"

"You heard me."

She slapped the steering wheel, "Jesus, Keith! She's the FBI's prime suspect!"

"I know, and it's a hose job. There's no way she'd be involved in a terrorist attempt."

"Christ." She pulled over to the side of the road and turned in her seat. "I can't believe you'd lead with your dick like this! Damn it, Keith! How could you?"

"Just a goddamned minute. You have no right to talk to me like that."

She pressed fingers to her lips, regarding him. "You're right. I'm sorry." She sighed. "But how could you jeopardize our investigation this way? You're throwing away the best opportunity I've ever had to catch Pinkle playing dirty."

"I'm sorry, Jen."

She shook her head and pulled back onto the road, lips drawn thin as wire.

A few minutes later, he asked, "So what happens next?"

"You tell me."

He shook his head, watching the scenery blur past. Then he sighed.

"I guess I'll turn in my resignation. With Emma, I mean," he added at her sharp look. "And Pendleton. You can get a replacement for me. Maybe Mickey Hodges."

She didn't respond. Her eyes were on the road ahead.

"Well?"

"I need time to think," she said. "And so do you. Let's talk about it in the morning."

They didn't talk for the rest of the drive. She dropped him off with a brief good-bye and drove away.

Keith trudged leaden-footed up to his apartment from the street. He dumped his suitcases on the bed and sat down, and picked up the phone to dial. It rang four times and a woman's voice said, "Ramada Inn. How may I direct your call?"

"Room 237, please."

There were several clicks; the phone rang twice more.

"Yeah?" It was Gorey.

"Hellman here. I just got into town."

"Good. Where are you?"

"At my place. Jennifer briefed me on what's going down."

Keith heard another voice in the background. "Yeah, it's him," Gorey said, and then asked, "Can you come over?"

"When, now?"

"As soon as possible."

"I'll be there in half an hour."

He hung up and called Flo. "This is Keith."

"Hi! The barbecue's just about ready. Come on over."

"I'm not going to be able to join you tonight after all. Something has come up."

"Oh." She sounded disappointed. "I guess it'll be Veronica and me, then."

"Emma's not coming?"

"No, she was tied up at work. Well, we can make it some other time."

Chapter 29

EMMA: Tuesday, 6 October, 8:18 P.M. EDT
Outside Reflections on the River

Emma pushed the door open. The night air that hit her in the face felt like low-pressure steam. Ron the guard was just walking up the path; she held the door for him.

"Thank you, ma'am. G'night."

"I'll be back. Just getting takeout." She let the door go, then had a thought and grabbed the door's edge. "Have you eaten?"

He pulled a paperback out of his back pocket and an iced tea out of a brown paper bag. "Yes, ma'am. Thank you, just the same." He put his cap on and adjusted the brim, sat down in his chair, and opened his book.

Emma headed across the parking lot, digging around in her purse for the car keys. Her blouse and skirt clung. Nights shouldn't be so steamy, not in October. After almost three years she wasn't used to the weather.

She found her keys among the clutter at the bottom of her handbag and pulled them out as she reached her

Honda Del Sol. She was unlocking the door when a white Toyota turned into the parking lot. The driver rolled down the window and held up a map.

"Excuse me—I wonder if you could give me directions to..." His sentence tapered off and he looked at her, and Emma recognized him. For a moment she hadn't thought it could be him—he'd cut off all his hair; it, and his eyes, were lighter than she remembered. His face had changed a lot, and not much at all.

"Oh my God. Gabriel?"

"Emma." He stared. "It's been forever! This is unbelievable. What are you doing here?"

"I live here. You?"

"Vacationing. Fishing with some buddies."

"How have you been?" they asked each other, and smiled.

"This is amazing," Emma said. "I was just thinking about you the other day."

"Listen, this is rather sudden, but have you got plans for the evening? It'd be great to catch up with each other."

She grabbed lip with teeth, looking over her shoulder, up at the south end of the third floor where lights were on. Gloria, Treena, and Phil were up there, digging through the regulatory files.

"I have to work late—I was just making a quick run for takeout. Maybe tomorrow?"

He shook his head, brow creased. "We'll be out on the water for several days starting tomorrow, and then I head back west. Can you make it sit-down instead of takeout? Tonight's our only chance..."

It'd been a long day and she was needing a break; it was why she'd volunteered to go get the food to begin with. And how often did chances like this come along?

"Wait right here, would you? I need to tell my co-workers."

In the anteroom, Ron asked about the stranger waiting in the parking lot. Emma looked back. Gabe slouched in the seat, staring into the distance, one arm on the wheel, hand dangling, and the other elbow propped on the windowsill. It was exactly how he'd used to look when he picked her up at the dorm for a date.

"Old friend," she said.

"I meant to tell you; I got plenty of rest today, ma'am," Ron said, as the elevator door started to close.

She gave him a fond look and a sober nod. "Keep up the good work."

Upstairs, she couldn't locate Gloria, but Phil and Treena were where she'd left them, in the conference room: Phil sorting paper into piles, and Treena typing manila file labels at the ancient Selectric typewriter. Treena was sixty years old or so, slender and elegant, with a demeanor of solemn serenity. Phil had brought her to the firm with him; they'd worked together for years and years.

Emma said, "The most unbelievable thing has happened. I've run into a friend I haven't seen in fifteen years."

"You did?" Phil said. "Jolly!"

"Yeah. Downstairs in the parking lot, believe it or not. I'm going to take an hour or so to catch up on old times. I'll work as late as I have to tonight to make up the time. Don't worry."

"That should be fine," Treena said.

Phil dropped papers onto a pile. "I'll go ahead and send my driver after food for Treena and Gloria and me." He gestured at the rows of file cabinets outside the conference room. "We've got five drawers to go; I'm sure we'll still be here when you get back."

Emma flashed them a smile. Unaccountably, her mouth went dry and her heart started to beat harder. "I won't be too terribly long. Where's Gloria?"

"In my office, sorting through a couple of files," Phil said.

She found Gloria sitting at Phil's desk. Emma perched herself on the edge of the desk and told Gloria what was happening. Gloria leaned on her elbows and smiled, archly.

"Wow, with you and men it's feast or famine, isn't it?"

"Very funny."

Emma stood. The motion knocked a letter opener into the white paper recycling bin. As she was retrieving it, she caught a glimpse of something familiar and pulled it out. It was a torn piece of the crumpled note—the anonymous tip-off about Keith.

She pulled the note's four pieces out and flattened them, and met Gloria's widened gaze.

"What the hell . . . ?"

"Pendleton must have given it to Phil," Gloria said.

"Obviously. But why?"

Gloria gave her a helpless shrug.

"What the hell." Emma folded the pieces carefully and put them in her billfold.

Downstairs, she said to Gabriel, "I know just the place. It's not far from here."

"Great. Hop in."

"Why don't I drive?"

There was a pause. "Actually, I'd rather drive."

"Come on, Gabe; I know the town and you don't."

"But it's just as easy for you to navigate and tell me where to turn, isn't it?"

She ground her teeth. Some things never changed. "Tell you what. We'll both drive. You follow me."

It was stupid. Nanny Lee's was less than half a mile away.

She folded herself into her car, cursing herself—and Gabriel—for stubborn idiots.

Nanny Lee's was not too crowded. Gabriel wanted to sit outside, so the maître d' seated them at a table beneath a gnarled, old, moss-bearded live oak. The waitress handed them menus and took their drink orders. Emma stuck with iced tea; Gabriel had a tequila with lime.

She studied Gabriel while he read his menu. The years had been good to him; he had stayed in shape, and his face had matured in an attractive way. He was, what, now?—thirty-six? thirty-seven?—she did mental calculus. Thirty-six, on September twelfth. He smiled at her, but something in his manner was reserved. Not that she was surprised; she felt a little wary herself.

"What are you doing with yourself, these days? Where do you live?"

"You mean you didn't read about me in last week's *Newsweek*?"

"Actually, I did." She hesitated and looked at him.

"Fame is so fleeting." He laughed ruefully. Then he lifted fingers in a Boy Scout salute. It reminded her of Keith. "I didn't do it, ma'am. Honest. It was a frame-up."

She released a breath she hadn't known she was holding. "I didn't figure you had. What happened?"

"I guess I've pissed off too many powerful people over the years." He shrugged. "It worked out okay. The other two bombings happened at times and in places that I couldn't have been, and once it was obvious it couldn't have been me, they left me alone."

Emma shook her head. "I've thought about you a lot over the years, you know." He touched her hand with a smile and she smiled back. "About us, too, but that's not what I meant." She paused.

"Go on."

"I'm about to be brutally honest. Get ready."

He grabbed the table edge. "Do it."

She smiled and shook her head, then sobered. "You were a major jerk an awful lot of the time, Gabriel. You antagonized people. You never let anything go. You put your principles before everything. Before people, even. I hated that."

He sat back, looking thoughtful, rubbing a thumb across his upper lip. "Guilty as charged."

"Yeah." She paused. "But you know, on looking back, I wish I had a little more of that quality myself."

"Putting your principles first, you mean?"

She nodded, then frowned. "Well, not my principles, exactly . . . but my vision. My dreams."

He gave her a fond look. "Emma Tooke. Always the pragmatist. Actually, I always cherished that trait in you. You kept me rooted to reality. Do you still collect shells?" he asked suddenly.

"Oh, yes." She winced. "Well, not really. My friends collect them for me, mostly. I need to get back to that, someday. When I have time."

"You have to make time for your dreams, *querida*."

She sighed. "I know. I just don't know how. Work seems to consume me. It takes over my life. Every time."

There was a long, awkward pause.

"Anyhow," he said, "in answer to your question, I moved to New Mexico about ten years ago. I'm still heavily involved in environmental activism, as you might have guessed, and I'm also a writer."

"Really?" She leaned forward on her elbows. "What do you write?"

"Regional nature and travel articles, mostly." He lifted a hand in a shrug. "It doesn't pay that well, so I pay the bills by doing architectural drawings and drafting work. I know what you do, of course; Tina wrote me a letter when you got the Gulf Stream job.''

''You're still in touch with Tina Gerrold?'' He nodded. The waitress came and took their food orders. When she'd gone, Emma said, ''I haven't heard from Tina in ages! How is she?''

''Divorced, again. Bossy as ever.''

Emma laughed. ''Still trying to fix you up with one of her friends, eh?''

''All of them.''

''You think she'd get tired of playing matchmaker.''

''Ha. Maybe someday. Half an hour after she's in her grave.''

''Or maybe she'll eventually figure out your taste in women,'' Emma said, then winced. Tina had been the one to put the two of them together. Another awkward silence ensued.

With a look of—compassion? regret?—Gabriel laid a hand on hers. The touch stirred up too many conflicting feelings. She squeezed his hand, then slipped hers loose from his grasp.

''Tell me about your vacation. You said you're here to do some fishing. What kind?''

He sat back. ''Actually, this is sort of a working vacation for me. A local environmental group has paid my way out here to help them monitor local fishermen's tuna catches—to make sure they're using dolphin-safe methods. We're pretending to be sport fishers, but it's just a front.

''We were out all day today, but we didn't spot very many trawlers, so we're going out into deeper water tomorrow, for a multiday excursion. Where do they all hang out? Can you recommend any good spots?''

''I don't really know the best places to fish. I do know there's plenty of good fishing out near Gulf Stream. We get commercial and sport fishers out there all the time." She paused. "If you do make it out that way, drop by. I expect I'll be back there by the end of the week. I can give you a tour of the facility." She smiled. "I'd love to be able to show the place off to you. It's got a lot of environmentally friendly features you'd be interested in."

He seemed startled, and remained silent long enough for Emma to wonder whether she had offended him.

"Is that allowed?" he asked finally.

"Well . . . we don't open the place up to the general public on any systematic basis, but boats occasionally drop in. And besides"—she gave him a grin—"I'm the boss. I can pull rank."

"Ah. That'd be great." His brow was furrowed, though, and he sounded less than enthused.

"Don't feel obliged. It won't hurt my feelings." She paused, remembering old arguments, old pain. "I know you're not out here to ogle my stupid machines."

He shook his head and took a deep breath.

"No, no, *querida*. It's not that. I was just . . . my mind was somewhere else. I'd love to see Gulf Stream, if we make it out that way."

"Wonderful."

He leaned forward, and smiled. "So, tell me about Gulf Stream. How many people work there? What do you produce?"

They spent the entire dinner talking about Gulf Stream; he had many questions and it was certainly her favorite subject. When the waitress brought the check Emma paused long enough to look at her watch, and yelped. It was ten o'clock.

"I really have to get back. We have a surprise meeting with the Florida DEP tomorrow and a bunch of us have to burn the midnight oil to get ready."

He wiped his mouth and dropped his napkin on his

plate. "Well, gee. Thanks for taking the time to meet with me, especially considering your deadline. I've enjoyed spending this time with you."

"Likewise. But I've spent the whole dinner talking about myself and I haven't got a clue what you've been up to."

He laid a hundred-dollar bill on the check with a wistful smile. "Up to no good, I'm afraid."

She laughed, and held out two twenties, but he pushed them away.

"You don't have to treat me."

"I want to. Please. I owe you."

"For what?"

He paused, rubbing at his upper lip again, with a slight frown between his eyebrows. "For making you do all the talking."

On the way to her car he rested his hand on her back, and at the car he opened the door and kissed her on the cheek. It was nice to be cherished in that way. She had forgotten how good he was at that, and how much she had loved it. She gave him a hug.

He handed her in and leaned over the open door.

"It was good to see you again, Gabe. Thanks for dinner."

"Por nada, querida."

It was their old routine and Emma found herself reflexively leaning toward him for a kiss. She stopped herself, alarmed. Keith's face imposed itself in her mind's eye. That was even more alarming.

"Good night." They said it simultaneously. She pulled the door shut, started the car, and drove back to the office slowly, frowning, deep in thought.

Chapter 30

A tall, slim, dark-haired woman in a red skirt, black belt, and white blouse crossed the street down the hill as Keith was heading up toward Route 1. He did a double take.

Yes, it was Emma. There weren't many women so breathtakingly tall. She had just gotten out of her car and was crossing the street toward a man he didn't recognize, a short-haired man in a black T-shirt, jeans, and sandals, perhaps a couple of inches shorter than she. Keith approached.

The man looked familiar, but Keith couldn't place him. He wasn't one of the Gulf Stream employees that Keith had met. The man turned slightly and his profile—the way his aquiline nose butted up against his brow—struck Keith. He mentally painted a mustache on the man. It was Gabriel Cervantes.

Keith froze in the middle of the street and watched them walk up the steps to the pink-trimmed mansion. Behind him a car honked; he moved to the side of the street, and stood near the cannon mounted on Nancy Lee's lawn, frowning up at the windows. Lace curtains framed tables with lighted candles; couples sat at several of them.

Were they right, then, about her?

No way. He couldn't believe it.

He went up the steps. A young man holding laminated pink menus met him in the alcove. "Will you be dining alone tonight? . . . This way, please.''

Keith looked around as the maître d' escorted him into the restaurant's labyrinthine interior. It was a magnificent old house, trimmed with dark wood, lined with windows. There were four or five intimate dining areas, as well as a bar with a mirror behind it. Antique dolls and carvings and other knickknacks were displayed in lighted cases. Several couples and groups were eating, but Emma and Cervantes were nowhere in sight. Next to an old player piano was a wooden staircase. He pointed.

"Is there another dining area upstairs?"

"Yes, but we have it closed down. Saves on electricity. The bathrooms and telephone are up there, though, if you need them. How's this?'' The young man pulled a chair out from a small table.

The table was next to a window. Keith looked out and saw that a dining area had been set up on the patio next to the house. Lanterns hung from the oaks. Moths, bright flecks, danced against the velvet-black backdrop of evening, beyond the lamps' soft glow. Emma and Cervantes were sitting at a table beneath a tree, not too far away.

"This'll be fine," he said, sitting, and took the menu.

After ordering—he didn't even remember a moment later what—Keith watched them. They were laughing. Gabriel reached out and laid a hand on hers. After an instant she pulled hers away. Keith grabbed that reluctance and held on to it tightly. He wished for a microphone.

During the storm, when they were trying to cut the catwalk loose, he recalled how she'd looked, lashed to the utility pipes, pelted by rain and hundred-mile-an-hour winds, hands ensnared in the lifelines. Remembered how when they'd been examining the power plant, her low voice had come through his headphones, vowing to protect her power plant.

They were using her. He was sure of it.

His fists balled; he stood.

Jennifer's accusation—*leading with your dick*—came to mind as he headed for the patio. How could he be sure, really, that his feelings weren't clouding his judgment? He could end up blowing the whole investigation.

And he didn't know how she felt about Cervantes. She'd admitted to still having feelings for him. Suppose she asked Keith to leave? In a way, that would be harder to take than that she might be in collusion with the terrorists.

I'll risk it, he thought, and opened the door to the patio.

A neatly groomed young man in shorts and a polo shirt stood up in front of him.

"Can you tell me the time?"

Keith glanced at his watch. "About twenty till nine."

He started past, but the man continued to block his way. His posture and gaze were oddly intent, Keith frowned. "Do you mind?"

"I wonder if I could have a word with you, Mr. Hellman," the man said in a low voice. Keith looked from him to his dinner companion, another man in his early twenties.

The first man escorted Keith back inside the restaurant and pulled out a badge. Keith looked it over. FBI. Special Agent Mahler.

"I'd appreciate it if you didn't interrupt," Mahler said. "We're attempting to monitor their conversation. You might scare them off."

Keith stared at him, annoyed. He took another look out the window at Emma and Cervantes. Cervantes said something and she laughed, throwing her head back. A sharp pain lanced his chest.

"You're probably right," he said.

"Cancel my order," he told the waiter on his way out.

"What the hell do you think you're doing?" Barnes asked him, as the hotel room door closed. "You had no authority to tail Tooke."

Keith sat down in the chair by the window. "I see Agent Mahler has checked in."

"You're damn straight he did." Barnes jabbed a finger hard, nearly touching Keith's solar plexus. "I told you once and I'll tell you again. This is the FBI's investigation. You were way out of line. One more incident like this and you're off the case. I don't care what it takes."

Keith eyed Barnes with great dislike. He wondered what Barnes would say if he told him that he had resolved on the way over to announce his resignation from the case. "You know, your Wyatt Earp attitude is really getting on my nerves. Give it a rest."

Gorey interposed himself. "Easy, Will. Let's hear him out."

Barnes glowered past Gorey, arms akimbo. "Well?"

"Well, what?"

"What were you doing tailing Tooke and Cervantes?"

Keith's tone was mild. "I spotted them entering the restaurant together and I followed them. I live right across the street from the restaurant, you know. And how was I supposed to know you already had them under surveillance? I didn't even know you had extra agents at your disposal."

"We do now," Gorey said. "Our bureau chief increased our budget and authorized several additional agents when we learned Cervantes had disappeared from his usual haunts—"

Barnes had been pacing like a caged cat; now he gave Gorey a look of annoyance and interrupted. "You could have ruined everything, Hellman. What were you trying to accomplish?"

"I don't get your beef. When Mahler revealed his presence to me I left the situation in his hands. I'd love to know exactly what you think I did wrong."

"Mahler said you were approaching their table."

"I was. And why not? I'm an employee of hers. I just finished teaching her how to dive. It would've been stranger if I was in the restaurant and *didn't* stop by to say hello.

"And consider this. If she's an innocent, and Cervantes was plying her for information on Gulf Stream, he would have no reason to change his approach."

"And if she's *not* an innocent? You would have squelched their conversation."

"Or perhaps they would have asked me a question or said something that would have revealed what they were after. Mahler and his cohort weren't exactly right at the next table; I'll give you odds they're only catching a word here and there. Unless you have her bugged?"

Barnes and Gorey exchanged a look.

"We don't," Gorey said. "Not yet."

Barnes shrugged. "All right, all right. But next time check in. Don't go off on your own."

Keith gave a shrug and a grudging nod. He was willing to let the point rest. "So what's your plan? Are you going to bring Cervantes in?"

Barnes started to pace. "On what grounds? We've got nothing on him, other than an anonymous tip that he was responsible for the New Mexico factory bombing. No witnesses we could take to the stand, and not a jot of proof." He shook his head. "He'd be out in

twenty-four hours, taking with him the knowledge that
we're onto him.''

"We just don't know enough," Gorey interjected.
"We don't want to flush him out till we know a lot
more—like who his accomplices are. And whether
Tooke is in with him. I know," he said as Keith
opened his mouth. "You don't believe she's in on this,
but she's been reported as saying—in public that
she'd sink Gulf Stream herself before she'd let Thomas Reynolds have his way."

Keith snorted. "If you knew Reynolds, you'd feel
the same."

Barnes glowered at him. Gorey went on, "And it's
all over the papers how big a financial stew they're
in. Rumor has it that a big fight is brewing among
Pendleton's staff and that Reynolds is bringing a lot
of pressure to bear."

"She was indulging in hyperbole. Blowing off
steam. That's all."

Gorey gave him a wry look. "I'm not convinced."

"And no way he's working this job without a demolitions man," Barnes said. "That factory job was
expert. He doesn't have those kinds of skills."

Gorey sighed, shaking his head. "We've been over
this ground before, Will. We don't really know who
else is involved in this job or what they have planned.
I want to keep an open mind."

"You keep as open a mind as you want, my friend.
I think we're dealing with a group of three or four
former Earth Firsters, friends of Cervantes. Figured
they wouldn't get enough publicity spiking trees.
Probably one was in the military for a while, picking
up demolitions skills . . .''

"Maybe," Gorey said, "and maybe Sidney'll get
off his butt and finish his computer search by tonight
like he said, and will E-mail us some dossiers in the
morning. Till then''—he turned back to Keith—

"we're watching. Let him lead us to his coconspirators. Then we'll pounce."

"You could bluff him out," Keith said. "Make him think you have him dead-to-rights on the New Mexico bombing and if he doesn't turn on his coconspirators you'll prosecute . . ."

"They tried that with him in New Mexico and it didn't work. This way has risks, but . . ." He shook his head.

While Gorey was speaking, the cellular phone, in a stand by the bed, rang. Barnes picked it up and listened, then hung up, tucked the phone into his back pocket, and grabbed his suit jacket, gun holster, and keys. Gorey did likewise.

"We'll discuss this later. Let's go."

"What's going down?" Gorey asked as they ran across the parking lot.

"They've just asked for the check. They came in two cars. Mahler and Heimricht need backup."

Their timing couldn't have been better; they turned left onto New Haven Avenue as Mahler's voice on the car phone's speaker informed them, "They're exiting the restaurant."

Keith, in the backseat of the sedan, leaned forward and looked past Barnes out the windshield. Emma and Cervantes were walking down the front walk toward the street. Cervantes's hand was on Emma's back. Keith sat back into the shadows of the car as they passed.

"We'll take Cervantes," Barnes said. "Mahler, you stay on Tooke."

"Ten-four."

Barnes drove to the bottom of the hill, near Front Park. Keith twisted around to keep an eye on Cervantes and Emma out the back window. It was a short distance and he could see them clearly in the streetlights. They stood at Emma's car talking, while Mahler and his partner came down onto the street and got into their car, a brown Ford Taurus parked next to the restaurant. Cervantes gave Emma a kiss on the cheek, and she gave him a hug, and started to get into her car. Then Barnes turned the corner and Keith lost visual contact.

"Report," Gorey told Mahler, as Barnes wheeled the car in a quick U-turn. Mahler's voice issued from the speaker.

"We're on Tooke. She's stopped at New Haven and Route 1. Cervantes is—he's leaving his car where it is; he's heading into the parking lot of Melbourne Harbor Suites—"

"Shit." Barnes floored the pedal and they turned, tires grabbing pavement, back onto New Haven. Up the hill, Emma's Honda turned right onto Route 1, followed by Mahler's brown Taurus. Keith caught a glimpse of Cervantes at the far end of the parking lot, near the pool.

"Turn around," Keith said.

"What?"

"Turn around. He's heading for the marina. That's the only place he can get to. You can't follow in the car—the parking lot dead-ends. There's a nature spot under the Route 1 overpass he might be heading for."

Barnes turned again. Tires squealed and the centripetal force shoved Keith against the arm rest. Once on New Haven, Barnes braked hard and crept along the street; Gorey got his binoculars out.

Barnes asked, "Anything?"

"Nothing."

"How can you see?" Keith asked, gesturing at the binoculars. Gorey held them up.

"They're light-amplifying. Looks like midday out there." Then he put them back to his eyes and scanned the marina. Keith eyed the parking lot and the little strip of park near the street. No sign of Cervantes.

"Let's split up," Gorey said. "Hellman and I will head up toward the nature spot and search the area west of Route 1 on foot. You take Front Street and the marina. I'll take the cell phone and check in with you on the car phone in ten minutes."

Barnes nodded, pulling over. Gorey and Barnes checked first their watches and then their guns, then reholstered them. Gorey took the handheld cellular phone and stuck it into his jacket pocket. Keith jumped out of the car and onto the wood planks of the marina's walkway. He and Gorey ran toward the manatee viewing spot, looking around.

They paused under the overpass. Traffic overhead pounded the bridge, setting up baritone echoes across the water. The lighted, wooden walkway extended for several hundred feet alongside Crane Creek, bounded on this end by Route 1 and on the far end by the educational pavilion. Beyond that, a set of old, graffiti-stained railroad tracks arched over the estuary. The dark waters were still and fathomless but insects sang and reptiles croaked; rodents' eyes glimmered, fluorescent beads, amid the struts of the overpass.

Keith and Gorey paused in the shadows. Keith crouched at the creek, squinting. He could see no place nearby to hide, and in these still waters a swimmer's movements would be easy to spot. Then Gorey pointed, lowering his binoculars. "There he is."

Keith followed Gorey's gesture and spotted Cervantes at the educational pavilion. He was standing at the table with the historical models of Melbourne, partly obscured by the structure.

They couldn't approach unnoticed. Here they were concealed from the streetlights, but once they entered the manatee viewing walk they would be in plain sight of the pavilion, and this late only three or four people were on the walkway.

Gorey and Keith approached slowly, strolling past an older couple that stood at the rail looking out at the water. Cervantes straightened and looked toward them.

"Let's not scare him," Gorey said in a low voice. "Follow my lead." He walked over to the low guardrail. Keith followed and leaned on the railing.

A teenage boy crossed the street toward the walkway. The couple passed Keith and Gorey, arm in arm, laughing. They were heading toward the pavilion. The boy followed them, hands in pockets, slouching, though he and the couple did not appear to be together.

An obese woman sitting nearby on a bench stood and moved toward the railing beside Keith. The teenager stopped about halfway between Keith and Gorey and the pavilion, and stooped to pick up something—a stone, perhaps. He pitched it out into the creek. In the quiet waters, it made a noisy splash.

"Looky there," the woman said. "I see a manatee."

As if she could tell a manatee from a sea monster under those waters at night. Other than ripples, there was nothing to see. Keith glanced at Gorey, who gestured with his head and started toward the pavilion. They walked slowly, postures casual, uttering pleasantries about the view.

The older couple entered the pavilion and began reading the posters, their backs to Cervantes. The boy pitched another rock into the water. The couple approached Cervantes at the table, who looked up at Keith and Gorey and started across the street beside the railroad tracks, half walking, half running.

"Shit. He's onto us." Gorey broke into a run. Keith started running, too, a few yards behind. The teenager turned as Gorey neared and moved close behind him, his arm raised, holding something. He jerked it back in a swift sideways motion.

Gorey stopped abruptly, took a step back. His hands

went up. He turned and fell at the same time. The boy ran up the street, a different street than Cervantes had.

The older man and woman turned around just as Keith got to Gorey. Hands at his throat, Gorey gave Keith a stunned look; bright red blood was gouting from between his fingers. His eyes were glazing.

Keith yelled a curse and grabbed him. Blood spurted into Keith's face, blinding him, suffocating him. He coughed and swiped at his face, stuck fingers in the slash wound at Gorey's throat, seeking to plug the artery. It was too late. The flow of blood was slowing to a sluggish trickle. Gorey was dead.

"Oh my God," the woman said and, looking down at herself, her voice rose in cadence to a shriek; the front of her dress was spattered with blood. The man grabbed her by the arm, and they both stared down at Keith and Gorey.

Gorey's blood was on Keith's face, in his hair, all over his shirt, his jeans, his shoes and hands. He knelt in a great, black pool of it, and the stuff that covered him was going sticky and cold.

A great wave of nausea washed over Keith. He spat to rid his mouth of the iron taste of Gorey's blood, closed Gorey's eyes.

The obese woman had come up and looked down. "I never seen no one kilt before. It's just like the movies."

Keith felt a scream rising in him. "Call nine-one-one." No one moved. He launched himself to his feet. The obese woman stepped back with a look of alarm. Keith grabbed the man by the shirt, shoving him. "Call nine-one-one! *Go!*"

Then, with a yell of revulsion and rage, he burst into motion up the street, after the boy who'd killed Gorey.

He ran, and ran, and ran, falling into a rhythm, his breath harsh and noisy in his ears, under the railroad and up the street past the cleaner, into the residential neighborhood where he'd seen the boy head.

It was darker here. Tree branches moved, susurrous against the star-laden sky. Dogs barked. Frogs and crickets chirped. He stopped, panting, sweating, and scanned the street. His eyes were adjusting to the dimness, but there was nothing to see. It was a quiet street: a few porch lights were on, a car or two lined the street. He looked around and beneath them. Nothing.

It hit him that he was chasing an armed killer with no weapon of his own. He thought of Gorey's gun and his night-vision binoculars.

And he'd left the cellular phone in Gorey's pocket. Keith could have called 911 himself. Those bystanders were probably still staring vacantly down at Gorey. Or wandering around looking for a pay phone. But if he went back now he'd lose the kid for sure. And there was no help for Gorey, anyhow. He slowed and listened.

The barks of the dog in the yard just ahead of him were diminishing, but another dog was taking up the chorus, up the street to his right. He crossed the street, following the barks. As he passed the first dog it began barking again, frenzied yelps that rose to a howl. He smells the blood, Keith realized.

Ahead, a figure silhouetted against a distant porch light crossed a lawn and dashed behind a house. Keith sprinted around the near side of the same house, swung wide around its back corner, leapt the low chain-link fence. The terrier in the neighboring yard went wild, hurling itself against the fence at Keith and howling.

Keith spotted the kid making for the back fence. He was gangly, not too tall, in the throes of puberty. Keith launched himself, knocking the boy off the fence.

The boy's baseball cap flew off as he scrambled away from Keith's grasp—a mane of white-blond hair exploded in Keith's face—he glimpsed the boy's face. Several details fell into place—the face and hair, the posture, gait, shape of the figure. It was no boy. It was a grown woman.

She shoved him back against the fence. They squared off. She circled, arms out, wearing an odd Mona Lisa smile that gave him the creeps. In one hand was a long black object that tapered to a point. Then she moved and something flashed in the dimness, pale and liquid; Keith threw himself back against the fence again as a whisper brushed his face.

She followed him and he feinted away, as if to run, then threw himself at her, low, under the knife. She jabbed past him as he drove his shoulder into her gut. They fell, the woman on top, Keith grabbing for her knife arm and she twisting the knife to stab him.

He missed her wrist, but her stab was wild, thrown off as she hit the ground with a thud and a grunt. She stabbed again, but this time Keith captured her wrist and pried hard at her arm. She was fast—and fucking *strong*. They rolled once, twice, on the grass. He bent her arm back with all the force he had. She let out a groan that turned to a cry, and the knife tumbled from her grasp. Keith snatched it.

A light came on. Someone shouted, "What's going on out there?"

Keith and the woman, arms and legs locked in an embrace, looked toward the light. Someone screamed.

"Call the police!" he yelled, going onto one knee with his hand entangled in her T-shirt. He rose onto his feet, leveraging himself to haul her up, and suddenly he was flying; she had used his momentum to launch him over her head.

He struck earth face-first and wrenched his shoulder, rolled onto his back with a groan. A foot came at his face and blinding pain exploded in his jaw.

Chapter 31

After bidding good night to Emma, Gabriel went to the nature viewing spot at Crane Creek. It was a warm night and a beautiful creek, but he hardly noticed. He headed straight for the pavilion and bent over the table, pretending to study it. Though his pace had been leisurely, his heart was hammering.

Boadica was to watch him leave the restaurant with Emma and follow him here at a distance, to see whether he had picked up a tail.

His thoughts at that moment were mostly on Emma. *You put your principles before people. You were a major jerk.* The way he was using her made him feel like shit.

But his glance fell on one of the posters nearby: a manatee, gentle giant, lay in the water, dying, its back sliced to ribbons by a speedboat. Fewer than two thousand left. And who was doing anything about it? Anything that would make one bit of difference to the manatees. Some things *are* more important than others, he thought, and his resolve strengthened. He looked back the way he had come.

Five people were on the walkway: an old black man and his woman stood looking out at the water; a fat young white woman wearing too much makeup and a Hawaiian muumuu sat on a bench; two Anglos about his age were coming his way.

The hair on his neck bristled. Cops. He needed no

signal from Boadica to confirm it. They went to the rail. Gabriel steeled himself, waiting for Boadica.

Then he spotted her, in teenage-boy drag, crossing the street. Gabriel walked over to a poster and pretended to read it. Out of the corner of his eye he saw her arm go up: a stone landed in the water. He was being tailed. He waited.

The two men started his way. A second stone landed in the water. *They're onto you—run!* That was all he needed. He burst into a sprint up the hill.

When he looked back a couple of blocks later, no one followed. He slowed to a brisk walk at the top of the hill and made his way through the streets of the historic district. After ducking through an alley, he passed the library and church and down a residential street, and finally reached the graveyard where they had agreed to rendezvous.

Among the graves and live oaks he slowed even further, holding his side against the stitch he'd gotten, and at the caretaker's shack he sat down to wait.

The air, damp and mossy-smelling, was noisy with nocturnal animal sounds, rustlings in the grass, hoots, croaks, screeings. To the east of the graveyard the three-quarters moon hovered above the low skyline, casting soft shadows among the headstones and crosses. He leaned back on his hands, breathing deeply and slowly.

So many humans. The earth is littered with our dead, he thought. Locked away in their sealed concrete boxes, trying—and failing—to cheat the cycle of life.

When he died, he wanted to be laid out in a forest somewhere, left for the animals to feed on. If not a stray carnivore, then insects and bacteria and fungus could have him, with his blessing.

A car turned onto the graveyard's dirt road. It had a rack on its roof. Cops.

Gabriel scrambled to his feet and ducked behind the building. Tires ground against gravel, slowly nearing. Headlights, or a searchlight, shone past the edge of the building, near where he crouched. He moved farther back and lay down in the tall grasses there. The sound of tires against gravel stopped and the light moved back and forth across the grass. He held his breath. Something white burst into motion and bounded away: a rabbit.

Then tires crunched against rock again and the headlights scanned across the graves as the car turned around. Gabriel peered around the building and let out his breath; the car was turning back onto the street. It crept along, its searchlight moving across the undeveloped land to the east of the graveyard.

When Boadica showed up a few minutes later, she was limping. He walked out to meet her.

"Are you all right?"

She didn't answer. He reached for her and she leaned into him for a moment, breathing heavily. She smelled sour. Then she pushed him away.

"Let's get out of here. Cops are everywhere."

"What happened?"

She shook her head and didn't answer.

"Come on. I need to make a phone call first," she said, and pulled him toward the street. Jax was bringing the boat up the river; they were supposed to hold station about forty feet out, opposite the Holiday Inn. Gabriel and Boadica would swim out to it.

"There's a pay phone at Route 1," he said. "I spotted it the other day."

They stayed out of sight of the street as best they could, moving from bush to parked car to building in short dashes, hiding when cars passed. At the pay phone, she asked him for a quarter, and dropped it in the slot. Then she waved him away. And still you don't trust me, he thought.

He crouched beside a Dumpster at a closed auto parts dealership while she made the call. Each car's passing was agony. She wasn't on too long. A word here or there drifted over to him—something about driving to Miami.

Then she joined him.

"What was that about?"

She shrugged. "Just arranging for a little diversion. When no cars are coming in either direction, we'll stroll across," she said, "arm in arm, like lovers."

"Let's do it," he said. Then he got a good look at her. This was the first moment there were both light and time to notice: she was filthy—streaked with blood, scratched, and bruised. A slow, terrible rage built in him. He took her arm

"Who did this to you?"

Maybe it was the smile she gave him, or the oddly ecstatic look in her eyes; he released his grasp.

"I appreciate your concern, but there's no need for you to worry." She looked both ways. "It's clear. Come on."

He put his arm around her and she nestled into him, and they strolled. It took forever to get across. A car came up Route 1 and stopped at the red light; another came down NASA Boulevard and turned left behind them. Gabriel didn't look. Then they were across, and the cars were past.

They made their way down the bank to the river.

PART THREE

FIRE

Chapter 32

Keith smelled adhesive tape and medicine, and heard sounds. About the time he realized the sounds were voices, he also recognized Barnes's voice.

". . . FBI investigation . . . undercover . . ."

A second, unfamiliar voice with a heavy Southern drawl spoke, more loudly. "Whoa. He's one of yours? That certainly puts a different spin on things."

Keith opened his eyes. He was lying on a pad-covered metal table of some kind. A big light in a reflector base overhead shone in his eyes. The air was cool. His head, face, and jaw hurt like hell.

Lifting hands to his face, he felt around gingerly. His jaw on the left side was swollen and very sore. A tender spot on his right cheek had a square, crinkly Band-Aid on it. His arms and legs also ached as if he'd been overexerting himself. With his tongue he probed his mouth; a molar felt loose near the sore spot in the jaw, but not too loose. He'd probably keep it. Otherwise everything seemed intact.

Keith sat up, and the room did a sickening loop-the-loop. He doubled over and retched, then clenched his teeth and clutched the edges of the table with his eyes closed until the spinning slowed to a languorous pitch-and-roll. Then he looked around.

Along two sides, the little room had a multipaneled tan curtain on an overhead rail, and along another wall, a cabinet with a chrome countertop, a deep sink, and

white cabinets above and below. The countertop
sported packets and rolls of gauze and other hospital
supplies, and a red plastic container with a medical
waste warning sign on it.

Next to his examining table stood a wheeled, elevated tray of strangely shaped scissors, black thread,
and some high-tech gadgets whose purpose he was
uncertain of. There was also a pile of wadded-up
gauze with brown and yellow stains and two metal
bowls: one full of dirty, red-tainted water, and one
half-filled with a dark orange substance. The dark
orange substance was the medicine he'd smelled: Be-
tadine.

He threw off the olive-green sheet draped across his
lap. Someone had removed his jeans, T-shirt, socks,
and shoes; he was wearing only his briefs. He spotted
a green hospital gown in a chair next to the wall, half-
obscured by the curtain.

Keith got down from the table and slipped the robe
on, tying it. Then he pushed the curtain aside and
stepped out.

Barnes stood with his back to Keith, speaking to a
man in a pair of navy slacks, red tie, and short-sleeved
white shirt. Two uniformed policemen stood at the
double doors marked *Exit*. A man in a lab coat and a
woman in a nurse's uniform stood talking next to another curtained cubicle.

". . . probably just a mild concussion," the man in
the lab coat was saying, "but—" Then he saw Keith
and hurried over. The others turned. He took Keith's
arm. "You should lie back down."

Keith brushed the man's hand away. "I'm fine."

"You have a concussion. We have no idea how
serious it is. The possibility exists that you could hem-
orrhage."

They were all looking at him, now: the cops, the

doctor and nurse, Barnes. He wondered if they thought *he* had done it.

"All I need is a good night's sleep," Keith said.

"You've been unconscious for almost half an hour," the doctor said. He turned to the man in the short-sleeved white shirt. "We want to keep him under observation overnight, just to be on the safe side. There is risk of a coma."

"Don't look at me," the man in the short-sleeved shirt said, spreading his arms. "He's not a suspect anymore, I suppose. It's his investigation." He gestured at Barnes. Keith looked at Barnes, trying to get some sense of what was going on in his head.

Barnes had every hair in place. His tie was snug at the neck. His face was so expressionless that if he had tried to grimace, hairline fractures would have spread across it.

To the doctor Keith said, "I appreciate your concern, but I really can't stay here."

Barnes nodded slightly, but he seemed distracted. Keith thought of Gorey dead on the walkway, his blood pooling on the boards.

"We can't afford for his cover to be blown," Barnes said. "There are two news crews and at least a couple of newspaper reporters out in the waiting room. They've already gotten to some of the witnesses. They will probably link the two incidents and try to get a story out of . . . this man. We need to keep him out of the public eye."

The man in the short-sleeved shirt looked disgruntled. "What'll we tell the press, then? They're all over me for a story."

Barnes shrugged. "You don't have to tell them anything."

"They aren't going to like it."

"Nobody said they had to. What, you tell them everything you do?"

"No. But this is big news." Short-sleeves shrugged.
"We can keep a lid on it for a while. A day or two,
maybe three. But this whole thing is going to blow up
in our faces soon, whether we like it or not."

"Fine; we'll deal with it when the time comes."

The doctor listened to this exchange between
Barnes and the local official with a deepening frown.
"You'll need to sign a release if you're going to leave
tonight. We can't be held responsible if there are complications . . ."

"Where are my clothes?" Keith asked.

"They've been wrapped for you," the nurse said.
She looked uncomfortable. "They're a mess; you
won't want to wear them. We can give you some surgical scrubs to wear home tonight."

"That'll do fine. Thank you."

They brought Keith a liability release form. He
signed it "John Doe." Then an orderly led them via
nonpublic corridors to a back exit. Keith had to walk
slowly to keep from losing his balance, but the fresh
night air made him feel better.

He followed Barnes through the parking lot to the
agent's car. Barnes opened the door for him and he
sat down gingerly, with a sigh. He kept his eyes closed
while Barnes, wordless, drove him back to the Melbourne Harbor Suites.

In the parking lot, Barnes turned off the car. He
said, finally, "I want to know exactly what happened."

"Yeah. Come on up."

The agent followed him up the outdoor stairs to his
apartment, carrying his clothes. Keith opened the door,
took the package, and gestured at the couch.

"Sit down. I need some coffee. You?"

Barnes nodded. He paced while Keith went into the
kitchenette.

Keith unwrapped the bloodied clothes, doused them

with blue liquid detergent, and dropped them in the miniature washer in the pantry. As he set the controls he had a flashback—his ex-wife, exasperated: "*Cold* water for bloodstains, Keith!"

He put ice into a plastic bag and wrapped a wet washcloth around it, then pressed it against his swollen jaw. One-handed, he washed the coffeepot and filter, filled the reservoir with water, put fresh coffee grounds in the drip filter, turned the coffeemaker on, and watched the dark fluid dribble into the glass container.

This was all, to some extent, a delaying tactic. Keith was dreading this interview.

"How do you take yours?"

"Black. Two lumps."

Keith brought two mugs out, handed one to Barnes, and sat down, taking the ice pack from beneath his arm and pressing it to his jaw again as he leaned back into the cushions. Barnes held the coffee cup as if he didn't know what it was for, looking at Keith with that frozen expression on his face. Keith looked away—it made things a bit easier, not having to look at him.

"It was a woman. Platinum-blond hair, five foot six, maybe?" Barnes made a noise. Keith glanced over; Barnes's eyebrows were up, but he didn't say a word. Keith continued. "Big-boned but wiry. Very strong and fast. Martial artist, I think. She was disguised as an adolescent male and had a knife with a blade, oh, about this long." Keith held up his hands about six or eight inches apart. "I think she must have had it strapped to her belly, or down her shorts or something."

Barnes's eyes had narrowed. "How good a look did you get at her? Could you identify her?"

"A good, hard look. Not then but later, when I caught up with her. I'd recognize her if I saw her."

It occurred to him then that she reminded him of someone. Someone he used to know . . .

Barnes nodded, thoughtfully. "I'll send you to a police artist tomorrow to do a sketch. Go on."

Keith took a breath. "Cervantes was at the pavilion and she was at the rail between us and him. We were approaching slowly, just strolling, when Cervantes spotted us and ran. Gorey pursued. I wasn't far behind, maybe a few yards. She stepped up behind him—"

Keith rubbed at his face, nauseated again.

"Jesus fucking Christ," he said, and his voice cracked. "If I'd just been a little faster I might have stopped her. I didn't even know he'd been cut till his blood sprayed me."

Barnes shook his head. Beneath his careful, neat demeanor, he looked haggard. He didn't say anything for a moment.

"Don't blame yourself, Hellman." He smiled, grimly. "Leave that to me."

"Then you *do* think I'm to blame."

Barnes sat down in the chair next to the couch. He took a slug of coffee. "Hell, yes. I blame you for not stopping it, and for letting the murderer escape. I blame me for letting Gene go off without me. You're not trained in apprehending armed criminals. I am." Keith wanted to argue. *There was no way I could have known, no way to stop her; and I nearly had her.* He fought the impulse.

"And I blame Gene," Barnes went on, "for underestimating these motherfuckers—for not watching his back." He shook his head sharply. His eyes were rimmed with red and a muscle in his jaw twitched. "I want Cervantes's ass. And I want the woman. They're going to fry in hell."

He drank the rest of the coffee, slammed the cup down on the coffee table, and stood, dropping a card onto the table. "I have a lot to do. If you think of any other details I should know, my cellular phone and car phone numbers are on that card. Call me. I'm going to call Pendleton tonight and get the meeting time moved up. We need to move fast. Someone will call you with the time and place as soon as we know.''

After Barnes had left, Keith went to the bathroom and looked at his jaw in the mirror. The left side was truly Technicolor, swollen as though he'd had a wisdom tooth pulled, a mottled purple-green with orange and yellow fanning around the edges. That half of his face was swollen up like a hamster hoarding walnuts. And the Band-Aid on his right cheek—he peeled it back, took a peek, then pressed it back down—covered a short cut with four or five tiny stitches. It was hardly a serious cut; he was surprised they'd bothered with stitches. Maybe they didn't want a scar to spoil his good looks. Ha.

He removed the surgical scrubs and took a long, hot shower. They had cleaned him well in the hospital; the only dried blood he found was a bit crusted at the opening of the ear canals and a tiny stiff patch of hair at one temple. Still, there wouldn't be enough hot water in the entire city to make him feel clean.

After putting on some clean jeans and a cotton shirt, he went back out to the living room. His coffee was still untouched. Keith sat down, picked up the mug, took a swallow of cooling coffee. He ached all over. He thought of Emma, and wanted to curl up in her arms. Instead he called Jen.

''Yes?'' Her voice was groggy.

''Sorry to wake you.''

''What's going on?''

''Did you hear about Gorey?''

''Hear what?'' He heard rustling, and a click, a light being turned on. ''What about him?''

''He's dead. The terrorists killed him. About an hour or so ago. I was there when it happened.''

A long pause. A whispered *"Christ."*

"I've got a mild concussion. I need help staying awake for a few hours."

"I'll be right over."

He paced. It was hard to stay awake, anyhow; the room spun and his eyes kept going cross-eyed with fatigue. Or perhaps it was the shock of seeing a man murdered. *I never seen no one kilt before.* His mind wanted to sleep, shut down, go away—anything to forget the look on Gorey's face.

Twenty-six minutes after his phone call the doorbell rang. When he opened the door Jennifer Murdley stepped inside and, without a word, hugged him. A huge, hard lump formed in his throat. He hugged her back, hard. Tears squeezed out of his eyes.

Jen headed over to the couch and sat down.

"You want to talk about it?"

He stood at the door, silent. The view out the window was Route 1, lit by street lamps and the occasional headlights rushing past; beyond was the nature viewing spot where Gorey had died, marked off now with police tape.

Looking out the window, he said, "Gorey's death has clarified things for me, Jen. I'm a federal marshal. If Gulf Stream's management is dirty, they should be brought to justice." He came over to the couch, sat down, and looked at Jen, on whose face a smile was breaking. Her own eyes had filled with tears.

He said, "I'm in it all the way."

Chapter 33

They finished checking the files and organizing the compliance records shortly before midnight. In the parking lot, Emma bid good night to Gloria, Phil, and Treena, and drove over the causeway, homeward through dark streets, amid a light fog that smeared the world beyond her headlights as though someone had dropped gauze over the windshield.

At home she showered and put on her nightshirt. She wasn't tired, so she poured herself a cognac and got out her shoe boxes of unlabeled shells. For maybe an hour she worked on them, categorizing each, creating calligraphic labels in India ink on card stock of fine, handmade paper, and then picking spots for them amid the other shells on her display shelves.

You have to make time for your dreams, querida.

After that she put the shoe boxes away and got up into the back of the closet to dig out her old photos. They were boxed, too; she'd never bothered to put them in albums. Sipping her Courvoisier in her easy chair for a while, she sifted through snapshots from college, and looked at the young, laughing faces.

How had so many years slid past? Those people who had meant everything to her then, they were all strangers now. She'd kept in touch with none of them. Only Tina, who was dogged about that sort of thing, still dropped her a card or called now and again.

Emma found a picture of herself with Gabriel. They

were seated on a fallen log together, wrestling for the canteen.

She remembered the shot. It was on the camping trip where she and Gabriel had not had birth control handy, and had decided to chance it. It was a couple months after her mother had died. Things were already rocky between them. Three weeks later she started throwing up, and an over-the-counter pregnancy test kit confirmed her fears.

In her mind her engineering career had dwindled to nonexistence; her future filled up with babies and diapers and midnight feedings. Terror dazed her.

Gabriel became evasive when she told him. When she pushed him he started avoiding her calls. Finally she decided to get an abortion. Then Gabriel called; Tina had told him about Emma's intent. In a grim and angry tone, he offered to marry her.

You have to drop out of college, he'd said. You'll have to stay home and take care of the baby.

She wasn't willing to give up her career for a child. It's got to be share and share alike, she'd told him, and he'd said, if you weren't willing to take responsibility for the child, you shouldn't have fucked me without birth control.

It takes two to make a baby, she'd said, and I won't give up my career.

All right, he'd said, forget it. Do what you wish. The baby's death is on your head.

It was a hateful, manipulative thing to say. He hadn't meant it, really; they had always fought dirty, and made up tearfully afterward. Maybe he'd been counting on that. But his remark, on top of everything else, had been too much. It was leave him or kill him.

Afterward she had spent months in a stunned haze, had spent so many nights crying herself to sleep that she'd given herself swimmer's ear from the buckets of tears that had rolled into her ears.

She wasn't ready for a baby. Certainly not alone. But she hadn't wanted to lose Gabe.

The child would be, what, now, she wondered, putting the pictures away—fifteen? Christ. Where had the years gone?

She wondered what he?—she?—would have been like. Wondered what it would have been like to raise that child.

Even if Gabriel had agreed to her terms, though, the marriage wouldn't have lasted six months past the baby's birth. They'd been too mean to each other, and even if they hadn't, their values were so vastly different. And Emma had friends who were single parents. No way. Single mothers got the shaft.

On impulse, she called her father. It should be okay, she thought, as the phone rang; it was before eleven in San Diego, and he was a night owl.

A woman's voice said, ''Hello?''

''Barbara?''

''Yes?'' Said warily; after almost seven years, she still didn't recognize Emma's voice.

''This is Emma. Is Dad there?''

''Oh, hi. Uh . . . I'm afraid he's not here; one of his patients had a myocardial infarction this evening . . . I'll tell him you called, though.''

''Thanks.''

Emma replaced the phone in its nook.

He wouldn't call back. She didn't know whether it was because Barbara didn't tell him—he had a sizable estate and, as she'd told Emma once, in her velvety way, she had her own three children to think of—or whether it was because he was always too busy. Or maybe he just didn't give a fuck about his only child, she thought angrily. Why did she bother?

By the time she'd finished her Courvoisier and gotten to bed, the clock said it was about 2:00 A.M. Through the remainder of the night, her sleep was interrupted by troubling dreams she couldn't remember on waking.

Chapter 34

GABRIEL: **Wednesday, 7 October, 12:30 A.M. EDT**
The Cherokee Princess, **in the Atlantic a few nautical miles east of Melbourne Beach**

"The best time to hit them is over the weekend," Gabriel told Mark and Boadica. Gabriel and Boadica were wrapped in beach towels Mark had provided when he and Jax had fished them out of the water. She still had that look in her eyes, both intense and distant.

"We're well set up for it," Gabriel said. "Emma even invited us to drop by. We'll have no difficulty getting access."

Mark hooted and Boadica smiled. Gabriel's face grew warm . . . and not with pleasure.

"The facility houses maybe seventy people during the week," he went on, "but they have extra staff on board to make storm repairs right now. The good news is, most personnel go ashore every Friday night for the weekend except for a skeleton crew of eight to ten, and maybe a dozen or so scientists who can't leave their experiments. Right now due to storm damage and financial troubles they're more heavily staffed during the weekend than usual, but even so, two to three dozen's still more manageable than eighty or ninety.

And it gets all the kids off; they go ashore with their parents every weekend.''

Mark looked surprised. "There are kids?" The idea seemed to sober him.

"Yeah. Maybe a dozen. Ages two to fourteen."

"Fuck." Mark grimaced.

Gabriel tossed off his towel and leaned forward. "Look. It's not that complicated. We'll kill the next couple of days fishing. On Friday night you and Jax will do a night dive, sneak in, and plant the charges. Bright and early Saturday morning we make our appearance, take over their communications center, and force an evacuation. Then we refuel, make our announcement to the press from the communications center, and scram for Bermuda. No one's going to get hurt."

"You're awfully cocky for someone who's been a total deadweight lately," Jax said, coming down the stairs.

"Goddamn it." Gabriel slammed a hand on the table and came to his feet. "You've been a son of a bitch ever since you got back from Miami."

Jax bunched his fists. "Oh, yeah?"

"Yeah. And I've had enough. Either straighten up your act or get out."

"And why should you be in charge, I want to know? Mark and I are the ones with the technical know-how and Bo has the funds and the information network. It took you forever to get to Tooke; otherwise you've just been sitting around being a blowhard. You're *dead weight*, pal." Jax poked at his chest. *"Dead. Weight."*

Gabriel knocked his hand aside and made a fist. Jax hesitated, scowling.

"Tell him, Bo," he said, over Gabriel's shoulder. "Tell him I'm the one who should be in charge."

"Jax, you're way out of line. Sit down." Boadica

spoke sharply. "Stop waving your dick around. You're acting like a buffoon."

Jax stared angrily at her, but her gaze was steady and chill. Glowering, he dropped onto the bench next to Mark, who was looking from one to the other of them in obvious distress. Gabriel followed suit, taking a few deep breaths to calm himself. This fighting was stupid.

Boadica threw off her own towel and stood, walking over to look out the portal. After a moment she spoke. "Gabriel. Did you get the sense that any extra security has been installed at the facility?"

"No. If anyone would know, it'd be Emma, and she was completely open, not holding anything back. The feds' investigation must be undercover."

"Any chance she was tricking you?" Mark asked.

Gabriel shook his head. "Nah. I'd know. She never was much of a liar."

Boadica nodded thoughtfully. "I like Gabriel's idea," she went on after another pause. "It's clean and simple. But I propose one change. We hit them tomorrow. Not Saturday."

Mark said, *"What?"* and Jax nodded, looking pleased.

"I'm getting sick of waiting," Jax said. "The longer we wait the more likely something will go wrong."

"It's a mistake," Gabriel replied. "What about all the extra people? The children? It complicates things. It increases the risk someone'll get hurt."

"What's the hurry, Bo?" Mark asked.

"A lot of heat will be coming down, hard and heavy. We need to move fast. I've arranged a diversion, but it won't hold them long."

"Why the heat? Because they spotted me with Emma?"

"That, yes. And I killed a cop."

She met their shocked silence with that smile of hers. He glanced at her T-shirt. The blood had been rinsed off by the river.

"I thought it was yours." He meant the blood. Boadica's glance followed his and she understood; she shrugged, her affect flat. With a disgusted groan he laid his head down on his hands.

"Well, now they'll know we're serious," Jax remarked.

Inside Gabriel, something blew: an aneurysm of horrified revulsion. They were talking but he didn't hear their words. He stood, numbly, and walked up the steps, out of the cabin, and up on deck.

The breeze that blew in his face was cool and moist, and smelled as fresh as air gets. Stars blazed against the night sky, little hindered by light pollution from the coast. The bridge was a study in faint green geometries against black. To the southwest, sheet lightning illuminated great, dark thunderheads; whitecaps, moonlit, glowed in the black water. A storm was rolling in.

What have I unleashed? he thought.

His jeans were still damp; he shivered; goose bumps rose along his back, arms, and legs. He crossed the swelling deck to the rail. On the horizon flickered an irregular string of tiny lights: Melbourne Beach, perhaps. He wondered how far it was, and whether he could swim it.

Things were so tight between us, before she came along, he thought. She's tearing the group apart. Stupid bitch.

But he had to be fair. It wasn't her fault Jax—and come on, Cervantes, it's you, too—were suffering from testosterone poisoning.

Still, she'd killed a cop. She'd taken them to a place he'd never intended them to go.

We're outlaws for good and forever, now, he

thought. Monkey-wrenching was one thing; among the American public there were those who had enough anger at polluters they could tolerate the destruction of polluting machinery. But now Wild Justice would be branded as a group of thugs and murderers. With that single act, she'd cut them off from the very people he'd been trying to reach.

What do I do? he thought. Oust her? I'll lose Jax, too, then, and Mark is Jax's best buddy from way back; I'll probably lose him, too. So ousting her would mean aborting the mission. It seemed the only choice. But then they'd just go on without him.

He heard them arguing below, in lowered voices. Gabriel climbed up onto the foredeck, crawled around to the bow of the boat, and sat down, arms resting on his knees, to stare up at the small white moon. The wind was wet on his face.

"He'd pulled a gun," Boadica said from behind him. Some time had passed since he'd come out, though he was unsure how much. She climbed over and sat down. "He was aiming it at your back."

Gabriel turned. She met his stare without flinching.

"I couldn't let him hurt you," she said. Hunching her shoulders, she hugged her knees. The jeans she had changed into had holes in the knees, and the knees had scrapes and bruises on them. "So sue me."

"I don't like it when people get hurt."

He thought she'd chide or mock him, but she didn't speak. Not for a long time. Finally she sighed.

"This is a war we're fighting, Gabe. In war, people get hurt."

He turned and looked at her. He remembered their discussion up in the Manzanos that first afternoon.

"Is any one life more important than the survival of our planet?" she asked. "Are any of our lives more important than that?"

"I told you where I stand on killing."

"I couldn't let them hurt you. I can't apologize for that. Gabe . . ." She leaned toward him and put a hand behind his head to draw him to her for a kiss.

The idea of kissing someone who had so recently murdered another human being revolted him. He entwined his fingers in hers and pulled her hand from his neck.

"I'm grateful to you for saving my life," he said. "But please go away."

From the sharpness with which she jerked her hand loose from his grasp he figured she must be angry or hurt, but just then he didn't care. She went.

He thought for a long time, rubbing at his bald lip. I can't unkill the cop, he decided finally, but if I'm with them, maybe I can keep anybody else from getting hurt. I unleashed this wave; I have a responsibility to ride it out.

Chapter 35

KEITH: Wednesday, 7 October, 6:59 A.M. EDT
Melbourne Harbor Suites, Melbourne

Keith awoke to a knock on the door and the sound of water striking the bedroom window. A hard rain was falling. The digital clock clicked to 7:00 as he rolled over to look at it. He dragged himself out of bed and opened the door; Jen handed him a cup of coffee.

"Barnes just called."

"I didn't hear the phone."

"I caught it on the first ring. The meeting with the Streamers has been moved up to seven-thirty A.M. because of last night's development. We need to get going.''

"How does my face look?" he asked. She gave him a look.

"Don't ask."

Jen headed into the living room to straighten the sheets and remake the fold-out couch; he went to the bathroom to change.

She was right. He looked rather dreadful. His jaw was still swollen and the discoloration had spread over the lower left side of his face. And after only four and a half hours' sleep, his eyes looked gaunt and hollow. His head still hurt; he took three ibuprofen.

But with some more rest and a day or so for the swelling to go down, he'd be fine. He peeled the Band-Aid off his cheek. The little stitches poked up like whiskers. Speaking of which . . . Keith rubbed a hand over his face. He needed a shave, but with the bruise and the stitches, no way.

After washing up and throwing on khaki slacks and a light cotton shirt, he went out to the front room. Jen stood by the door with car keys and his umbrella; they made a dash through the downpour to her car.

The drive was slow going because visibility was so poor. They crawled along the street, swiping at the windows with Kleenex and staring at the blur of red taillights ahead of them. The rain roared against the roof, windows, hood, and trunk, punctuated by frequent flashes of light and rumblings of thunder. It was as though he were back in the middle of the hurricane.

At the Ramada Inn, the door of the meeting room was slightly ajar. Keith knocked and they entered promptly, dripping water, at seven-thirty by his watch.

Barnes was seated at the conference table. Pendleton and Evans were not there.

"Any new developments?" Keith asked, sitting down. Jen pulled out a chair next to his.

Barnes's lips were drawn tight and his face was wan. His sparse hair was perhaps a bit less tidy than usual and he wore the same suit and tie he'd been wearing the night before. Otherwise, Keith would hardly have guessed he had been up all night. "I'm expecting an update any minute, but so far they haven't been located. We think we've got two more IDs, though."

He tossed a couple of enlarged photos and some artists' sketches onto the table. Keith picked them up and scrutinized them, with Jen looking over his shoulder.

The photos were both mug shots, head and shoulders from the front and sides, with numbers and names printed across the bottom. One looked like a lumberjack on speed: full black beard, receding hairline, a big, toothy grin, and close-set eyes. The name printed across the bottom of the shot was Jackson Amis. The other had a long, oval-shaped face with not much of a chin, and lighter hair. He looked rather sad, somehow. Name: H. Mark Flyer.

The artists' sketches made the two men look quite a bit older, but there were strong resemblances.

Keith gave Barnes a querying look.

"They're ex–Navy SEALs. Demolitions. They served in Operation Desert Storm together in 1990. Amis received a dishonorable discharge for assaulting an officer, and has been arrested once or twice for other violent behavior—bar fights, mostly. He spent most of the intervening years in Ohio, but last year moved out to Colorado. Flyer served out his term and moved to Montana, where he has a couple of marks on his rap sheet for drinking-related problems: DWI, drunk-and-disorderly.

"They got back together in Colorado, working as firefighters for the National Forest Service. They quit together and moved down to Santa Fe, where they were involved with an effort to stop development in the Sangre de Cristos.

"Over the past three months they've been seen at various parties with Gabriel Cervantes."

"So you have your demolitions men," Jen said. "What about the woman?"

"We don't know. The staff at the hotel couldn't identify her from any of our photos." He turned to Keith. "As I mentioned last night, I'd like for you to take some time with our police artist after our meeting with Pendleton; you've probably gotten the best look anyone has."

Keith nodded. He doubted he could ever forget her face.

"What search measures are you taking?" Jen asked.

"We have roadblocks on all the major highways, and ground and sea search teams combing the area. The storm has been interfering with our search. We found their location until yesterday morning, though—"

Barnes broke off as one of the agents tailing Emma the night before, Mahler, entered.

"Breakthrough. They've been spotted."

Barnes leaned forward, fists clenched. *"Where?"*

"Miami. A break-in was reported at a construction yard at four-thirty this morning. The car's license plate is the one Cervantes was driving last night, and one of the crooks matches his description."

"You mean no one posted a watch on the car?" Keith demanded.

At the look on Barnes's face Keith regretted his outburst. Any mistake, any oversight, must burn him like acid. "We did, about twenty minutes after they got Gene. As soon as we had a minute to think. The car was already gone. They must have circled back almost immediately.

"What was stolen from the construction company?" Barnes asked Mahler.

"Apparently they were after munitions. The company keeps several cases of TNT on hand for its demolition work." Mahler grinned. "They didn't get anything; the security guard caught them trying to jimmy the lock to the storage shed and set the dogs loose on them."

"Anything else?"

"Not yet."

Barnes looked out at the storm. The calm facade had sloughed off. His knuckles, still clenched, were white; his voice was taut; his expression was downright predatory.

"Shut down operations here. Get the unit down to Miami pronto. I'll be down to join you as soon as we're done here."

"Right."

"And stay off the two-ways; we don't want a bunch of ambulance chasers to pick up the broadcasts."

"Right."

He was silent another moment, as the mask slid back onto his face. His shoulders dropped and he took a breath. "And leave Jamie in town here with the photo books; I want Hellman to get a good look at the photos, and I want to get a sketch of the woman from his description."

Chapter 36

The phone rang for the fourth time. Please, *please* be there, Venkat, she prayed. And please have something for me.

"This is Venkat Venkatraman." *Damn, damn, damn.* "I'm currently away from my desk. Please leave a message at the sound of the tone."

"Venkat, this is Emma again. Where are you? My meeting is in eight minutes. Help! Call me. If you get this after seven-thirty, call Gloria or Angelo and get them to call me out of the meeting."

She hung up the phone and tapped fingers on the desk for the next three minutes, as the rain pounded against the window. Lightning and thunder did a syncopated *flash-boom, flash-BOOM.*

She sighed and stood. He wasn't going to call. It was time to take her medicine.

Emma got to the conference room to find Flo and Reynolds already there. She walked in slowly, taking deep breaths, marshaling her thoughts. She *had* to be persuasive. Had to buy more time.

Ha. More like had better be prepared to be shot down in flames.

Dennis came in behind her. She made small talk with him, asking about his weekend golf game, as they helped themselves to the beverages, coffee, tea, and juice, set out along the credenza beneath the window.

She wanted him, if not on her side, at least not ill-disposed toward her.

Pendleton entered the room with Phil.

"We're going to have to postpone the meeting," he said, "till at least the beginning of next week. An urgent matter has arisen that I have to deal with right away."

Emma turned, surprised. Pendleton and Phil were both poker-faced. Emma looked around; the others seemed as baffled as she was.

Pendleton told them, "I'll have Kyle contact you all to reschedule," and left, with Phil behind him.

Flo leaned over, whispering, "Saved . . ."

Emma shook her head with a frown and glanced over her shoulder. Dennis and Reynolds were leaving. "There's something passing strange about all this . . ."

Flo shrugged. "Maybe it's some new development about the firm's finances."

"Then why is Dennis in the dark? Oh, well." Emma stood. "We can sure use the time."

Coffee and orange juice in hand, she exited the room—and nearly ran into Gloria, who was coming from the elevator at full tilt. "I was just coming to tell you . . . what happened to the meeting?"

"It's been canceled."

"Venkat called—he says it's critical he speak to you right away."

They snared Angelo on their way to Emma's office.

"He's on line two," Gloria said, "if he's still there."

The light was still flickering. Emma touched the speaker button.

"Venkat?"

"Emma?"

"With Gloria and Angelo. Gloria says you have news."

His voice rose. "Yes! I've been on the phone with

Halbertson at Chrysler. Chrysler wants to discuss a possible three-party arrangement with PG and E and Gulf Stream.''

Emma, Gloria, and Angelo all stared at the speaker. ''Are you serious?''

''Positively. We have to get to Bradley Pendleton right away. Their CEO wants to speak to him directly.''

''Slow down. We talked to them over a year ago and they weren't interested. What's changed?''

''The state of California has just released a hundred-fifty-million-dollar request for proposals for the creation of a fleet of ten thousand alternate-fuel vehicles, and changes to the fuel distribution infrastructure for them.''

Emma gasped. ''You're kidding.''

''I'm serious. They are subsidizing what you wanted to do in the first place. And state regulators have already told us privately that they are likely to be inclined toward having Gulf Stream involved, because your means of hydrogen production is perceived as 'greener' than a lot of your competitors.'''

''My God—this is a perfect opportunity!''

''It is. GM will be competing for it, too—maybe with its fuel cell design, maybe with its flywheel one— but we have PG and E on our side. That gives us a big advantage.''

Emma tugged at her lip. ''You're right. We have to get to Pendleton. Listen, Venkat, sit tight for a little while, okay?''

''Don't waste any time; I don't want one of the chemical companies to get wind of this and cut you out of the picture with Chrysler—''

''I'll hurry.''

Chapter 37

"A sketch of what woman?"

They all turned. It was Pendleton who had spoken; he and Evans stood at the entry to the conference room. His glance took in Keith and his eyes widened. Barnes stood.

"Mr. Pendleton, Mr. Evans. Come in."

They shook hands with Barnes, Keith, and Flo, then draped their dripping raincoats over the back of a spare seat by the door, set down their briefcases, and seated themselves at two adjacent chairs across from Keith and Barnes. Mahler, at a nod from Barnes, stepped out and closed the door.

"Agent Gorey was killed last night by one of the terrorists," Barnes said. "Hellman here was injured attempting to apprehend the killer."

Pendleton muttered, "My God."

"Have you caught him yet?" Evans asked.

"The killer was a woman, and no, we have not. Though we have located what we believe to be their most recent hideout— the Holiday Inn just down the road. They checked out yesterday morning. We have reason to believe they're now in Miami, trying to get their hands on explosives."

"Go on," Pendleton said. His expression was grave.

"There appear to be four of them. We have descriptions from the hotel staff."

"Slow down." Evans held up his hands. "Why don't you tell us exactly what's been going on?"

Barnes sat back and templed his fingers. "A man named Gabriel Cervantes, who we have known about for some time and believe to be the terrorists' ringleader, had dinner last night with Emma Tooke."

Pendleton and Evans exchanged a glance, both visibly shaken.

"She was at work all evening," Pendleton said. Evans shook his head, frowning.

"She told us she ran into an old friend in the parking lot. She was gone for a couple of hours, between eight and ten. It did seem quite a coincidence, even at the time."

"We've had a tail on Tooke for some time. We have long suspected and are now certain she is the inside contact our informant told us about."

Keith added, "I believe that she's an innocent and they are using her." Barnes made a noise, but Keith continued, "I've observed her closely out at the facility and I don't believe she would knowingly be involved in an attempt to harm Gulf Stream I."

"I have to agree," Pendleton said. "I've worked with her for years. She's very devoted to the facility."

"Cervantes was an old flame," Barnes said. "She could be doing it for love." Evans and Jen both gave Keith a speculative look. He felt a twinge of annoyance. "She may figure there is little to lose; frankly, it's common knowledge your company isn't doing well financially." At that, Evans and Pendleton exchanged a glance.

"Or there may be an element of revenge," Barnes continued. "We understand that there is deep animosity between her and your lead scientist, Reynolds—and that you may be about to approve facility modifications that would shrink her purview and increase Reynolds's . . ."

Evans said, "I don't know where you get your information, Agent Barnes, but I wonder about the legality of the method—"

Barnes's tone was flat. "I assure you it was all through legal means." He waved a hand, as if brushing at a fly. "The important thing is that she is the terrorists' lead, and has probably already given them whatever information they're seeking. While they appear not to have the explosives they need, we have to consider that Gulf Stream I is, or soon will be, in grave danger."

"What do you propose, then?" Pendleton asked.

"We'll arrange for stepped-up Coast Guard activity in the vicinity of Gulf Stream I, for one. And I want extra security out at the facility right away. A team of agents."

Pendleton and Evans exchanged a glance, and Evans minutely gestured with his head toward the door. Pendleton lifted a finger and turned to Barnes.

"How many agents? For how long? Hydrogen production is at a low but storm repair work is under way, and our mariculture and scientific divisions are nearing full capacity again. We can't afford work slowdowns."

"I would like to get eight men out there, and have all unnecessary personnel—"

"Especially the children," Keith said. Barnes nodded.

"—especially children, off the facility."

Barnes broke off as a flat buzz issued from Pendleton's briefcase. Pendleton bent down, pulled out a cellular phone, and opened it up. His brow puckered, then cleared, as he listened.

"Yes. Ah. Yes. Tell her I'll be back at the office in less than an hour and will speak to her first thing." He tucked the phone back into his case. "Excuse the interruption. Please continue, Mr. Barnes."

"I was saying, increased security is critical. I understand your concern about affecting production. Our agents will be as circumspect as possible. As to how long we'll need a presence there . . ." He shrugged. "It depends on how long it takes us to apprehend the terrorists. Let's revisit that question once we have a better idea of where we stand."

"Are we talking days, weeks? What?"

Barnes shrugged. "I don't know. But the terrorists can't hide for long, and they can't approach Gulf Stream I without being spotted."

"What about Emma?"

Barnes looked thoughtful. "What do you anticipate her schedule to be over the next day or so?"

Evans said, "She said she was heading out to the facility this afternoon after the EPA inspection."

At the mention of the inspection Keith glanced at Jen, who was watching the exchange, deadpan, fingers linked around her crossed knees.

Barnes was silent for a moment, rubbing a thumb across his chin. "For the moment, let her go about her usual schedule. Even if the terrorists have somehow found another source of explosives between four A.M. and now, and are already at sea—extremely unlikely under the circumstances—this storm would have to be interfering with their plans, too.

"As soon as weather permits, we'll station our men out there and evacuate unnecessary personnel, and bring Tooke in for questioning at that time."

Evans was giving Pendleton an intent look. Pendleton gave him a tiny nod and said to Barnes, "Excuse me while I have a word with counsel."

They retreated into the hallway. From where Keith was sitting, while he could hear only inflections, through the gap in the door he could see Evans talking and gesturing emphatically. Pendleton listened, nodding, then replied. Evans spoke again. Then Pendleton again, briefly. Then they came back in and sat down.

"Agent Barnes," Pendleton said, "please treat what I'm about to tell you as strictly confidential. Your sources were correct; the company is on the brink of bankruptcy. A large, obvious FBI presence and major evacuations are bound to have a serious impact on our operations. It could push us over the brink." Barnes opened his mouth, but Pendleton lifted a finger. "On the other hand, I'm aware that if terrorists attack Gulf Stream I, the damage could make bankruptcy seem trivial. And these terrorists have already blown up a plant and killed an FBI agent, so clearly there is a risk.

"However. Gulf Stream I is a good deal more remote than the New Mexico plant, in clear waters, and strangers are quickly spotted. And we are not just a one- or two-shift manufacturing plant; we're a community: a round-the-clock team of highly intelligent, dedicated people. Lastly, as you yourself pointed out, as of a few hours ago they did not have all the supplies they need to strike at the facility. So the size of the risk is difficult for me to estimate, but my guess is that it is not as high as our worst fears might make it.

"With all that in mind, along with the Coast Guard in the area, I would propose a smaller-scale evacuation, perhaps just the children, and a more discreet FBI presence for the time being—perhaps two men in addition to Keith."

Barnes frowned. "That's awfully lean."

"Gulf Stream has limited capacity, especially right now," Evans said. "We already have additional contractor personnel there to assist with repairs. Another eight raises the head count by a good ten percent, when we're already strained. We can't afford that large a presence."

Barnes considered it for a moment. "We could live with four, including Keith. If we get *any* indication the terrorists are heading for the facility, I'll want a substantially larger presence—at least double that."

Pendleton nodded. "Agreed."

"Let's get Keith out there right away. We can have the rest of our men out there by this evening."

Keith looked at Barnes with a twinge of pleased surprise—not only at the phrase "the *rest* of our men," but at the confidence in Keith his urgency evinced. But Jen's brow had furrowed.

"That's a problem," she said. Everyone looked at her. "We have the multimedia permit inspection coming up in an hour. If it were just us, we could 'reschedule' "—she put quotes around the word with her fingers—"but the DEP is now the lead on this inspection. Their representative could make some serious trouble for Gulf Stream if your environmental manager, Keith, isn't there."

"Can't you smooth it over?" Barnes asked Jen.

"Not really. The state has its own independent environmental regulatory authority; we have oversight but no hands-on control over state programs unless we can make a strong case that they are neglecting one of their programs."

"How long would this inspection take?"

"How many permits does Gulf Stream I have?" Jen asked Keith.

"None," Evans said. "They're consent agreements."

"Whatever," Keith said. "Let's see . . . they have permits—or rather, *consent agreements*—for their hydrogen flare, emergency generators, and storage tanks, another set of hazardous materials storage agreements for the tanks. There is also a discharge agreement for the wastewater treatment unit, a hazardous waste storage agreement, and the lab is permitted to handle certain analytical tasks for the wastewater treatment plant. I'd say the inspection would take a couple hours, maybe three. It could be longer, depending on how detailed the DEP rep wants to get.''

"So perhaps you could be out there by two in the afternoon, if we could get a chopper out there,'' Barnes said.

"More like three or four P.M., I'd guess.''

"And we want you to spend some time with the police artist, as well. That would put you out there closer to five.'' Barnes glanced at Pendleton. "What is the weather out at Gulf Stream I?''

"As of a half hour ago, the same as it is here. A large tropical storm has lodged overhead. I believe the forecast is for more of the same, tapering off gradually by midafternoon.''

Evans said, "I think trying to accommodate this inspection is a really bad idea.''

Pendleton gave him a surprised look; Keith and Jen exchanged another glance.

"We don't know where the terrorists are or what they are doing, and we have people out at the facility who might be in danger. We need Keith out there as quickly as possible. The inspection can surely wait till next week.'' He lifted his eyebrows at Jennifer and Barnes. "I have a hard time believing that not one but two federal agencies are unable to persuade the Florida DEP to postpone its inspection by a week or so.''

Jen sat back, eyeing Evans. Keith knew what was going through her mind. The investigation would wrap in the next few days, one way or another, and Keith would be out of the picture; they wouldn't get another shot at Pinkle.

She smiled. "I'm confused, Counselor. Before, you said that you didn't agree there was an urgent need for protection out on Gulf Stream I, and now you're saying it's urgent for you to have it right away. It's a confusing message and makes one wonder whether you're trying to avoid an inspection—and if so, why.''

"There is a difference between questioning the *level* of protection needed, and saying we need *no* protection." Evans's lips drew back. "Believe me, we are quite grateful for the FBI's offer of protection. We merely seek to minimize disruptions to our business. As to the implicit accusation that we have something to hide . . ." He spread his arms wide. "We have always cooperated fully with your agency; Keith was given full access to all our records and work areas, from the beginning. And of course, you are welcome back any time, once this crisis is averted. I know Brad will support me when I say our doors are wide open.

"However, for now, we would feel a good deal more comfortable with Keith out at the facility as soon as possible. A seven- to eight-hour delay seems ill-advised, under the circumstances."

He glanced at Pendleton, who pursed his lips. "I must agree, Ms. Murdley. The inspection was merely an excuse to bring Keith back without raising suspicions, in any event. Why take chances?"

Jen's gaze went from Evans to Pendleton, and she sat back. "The trouble is, *I* can cancel, but I can't get them to stop their inspection. They've taken it over. I was merely to be present as an observer. Getting them to change their schedule would take intervention on the part of the FBI."

Everyone looked at Barnes. He shifted in his chair, scowling. "It's hardly my bailiwick, telling the DEP whether or not they can conduct an inspection of a facility under their jurisdiction . . ."

"Agent Barnes," Pendleton said, "I hope you can appreciate that an inspection right now draws on resources we need to cope with this crisis."

"And it seems to me you do have a responsibility," Evans added, "given that it was you who precipitated the inspection to begin with."

Barnes gave Jen a disgruntled look. She shrugged.

"I want to avoid press coverage," he said, "and I don't like the idea of word about our investigation spreading outside this room. Media coverage is exactly what those terrorists want." He sighed. "I suppose I can have my superior have a quiet word with the head of the DEP . . ."

Pendleton nodded. "Thank you, Agent Barnes. Here is my cellular phone number, in case you need to reach me. Call at any time." He handed Barnes a card. "Keith, if you would prefer, you may head directly out to the airport. I'll have my assistant arrange helicopter transport for you, as soon as weather permits."

He stood, picked up his raincoat, and left; Evans followed suit, looking pleased.

Keith turned to Barnes. "When should I expect reinforcements?"

"No later than nightfall. I'll send you an update this afternoon by E-mail."

"He's dirty," Jen said, as soon as they were alone together in the car. She started up the car and turned on the defogger; they had brought so much water in with them—on their clothes, in their hair—that the front windshield had instantly turned opaque with dew. Rain was coming down so hard windshield wipers were almost a waste of time.

Keith didn't have to ask whom she meant. He shook water from his hair and wiped his face.

"Yeah. The question is, is Pendleton?"

"I don't know." Then she rested her forehead on the steering wheel. "Damn. We were so close."

"You had no choice, Jen. Much as it galls me to say it, he was right. We can't push our bribery investigation at the expense of innocent lives. Stopping the terrorists has to be our first priority."

She shifted into reverse, and gave him a wry smile.

"Listen to yourself. I seem to recall you singing a very different tune last week."

God, he thought, was it really only last week? He'd thought the terrorist angle was a joke. He thought of Gorey and winced.

"Sorry," she said. He shook his head, and slumped in his seat.

"No need to apologize. Just . . . thinking." He fell silent.

The local FBI office was downtown, four small rooms sharing a floor with the district attorney's office. Jennifer dropped him off.

"I'll pick up a change of clothes for you back at your place, and then park in the lot across the street to wait," she said. He squinted at the lot she was pointing at. It was barely visible through the gusts of rain.

"See you in a bit," he said. "Come on in if you get bored."

Four people were in the FBI office: two men and two women. One of the women came forward and introduced herself as Jamie Wilkes.

"You must be Keith Hellman," she said. She had a mild New York accent. "Agent Barnes just called and said to expect you."

Young and plump, she wore jeans and a snug-fitting top, and had very short hair. Numerous small silver rings ran up the side of one ear and one ring pierced through an eyebrow.

"You don't look much like an FBI agent," he said.

She gave him a piquant smile. "I'm not, silly. I'm an artist. I work for them on contract."

She led him to a desk near the back. On the desk were stacks of three-inch-thick three-ring binders.

"Take your time. I'll be ready to do a drawing whenever you get done."

"Ugh," he said, eyeing the binders. With a sympathetic smile, she gestured toward the front, at a coffeepot on top of a miniature refrigerator. "Make free with the coffee. Or there's soda pop in the fridge. Drop fifty cents in the plastic foam cup for soda, or a quarter for coffee."

The binders contained mug shots of women. Thousands and thousands. He spent close to an hour poring through them; none of them was the woman who had killed Gorey.

But this odd sense of déjà vu was growing in him; he had had it ever since he had first seen her.

He knew her somehow, from somewhere, a long time ago.

He frowned, closed the book he was looking through, and shook his head. It was too outrageous a coincidence, that he would know the terrorist from his own activist past.

And yet . . . what was the old saying? *There are only ten thousand people in the world.* The environmental activist community was comparatively small and Keith had been gregarious and hardworking; he had gotten around.

Perhaps she had been a member of Greenpeace? The idea made his skin tingle as if he had stepped into an electrical field.

He *had* known her. Somehow, she'd been connected with Greenpeace. He had no proof, but his gut told him he was right.

He wanted to make a call. But first he needed the drawing. He shut the photo album with a snap.

"Let's sketch," he said to Jamie, who sat nearby.

"No luck with the photos?"

"Zip."

Jamie grabbed a pad and charcoal pencils. That surprised him; he had expected her to use computer software. Thirty minutes later, after several discards, they had it: the sketch of the woman. It was a good enough rendition to give Keith the chills.

He gave Jamie an appreciative look. "I begin to see why you don't need a computer." She gave him a self-deprecating smile. "May I borrow your phone?"

She looked amused. "Of course!"

Drawing clutched in hand, he dialed a number he hadn't dialed in over a year. A familiar voice mumbled, "Hello?"

His heart leapt; his chest tightened. "Tricia?"

"Keith?"

"Yeah." He cleared his throat. "Listen, it sounds as if I woke you. Maybe I should call back."

"No, no—it's okay. I should get up." He heard rustling, and a muffled voice. A man's voice.

"It's for me," she said. Then, "It's been a long time. Um, what's going on?"

Keith drew a deep breath. His ex-wife, with her eco-travel business, was extremely well connected in environmental circles. She knew just about everyone. He eyed the drawing again.

"Listen, if I fax you a drawing of someone, could you take a good look at it, show it around to some of your environmental buddies, and see if anyone recognizes her?"

"Sure . . . I suppose . . . no problem. What's going on?"

"Well, I can't really say at the moment, but it would be a big help to me. It's a drawing of someone I swear I knew back during our Greenpeace days, and I'm trying to find her again."

He suspected that she assumed there must be a romantic component to his interest—he had pursued a number of women after the divorce, in an effort to staunch the pain, and she had heard about a few of them.

"It's work related," he said, feeling stupid at his

embarrassment. "Strictly professional. And rather urgent."

"I'll see what I can do," she said, and gave him her fax number.

"Thanks."

"It's good to hear your voice. You should call more often. Really."

He hesitated, half wanting to go, half wanting not to.

"So how have *you* been?" he asked.

"I've found someone." Her voice held a smile. "It's serious."

"That's great. Congratulations."

"I'd like you to meet him sometime." She paused. "We're expecting a baby."

He was struck dumb.

"It's due in March. I've been meaning to call and tell you."

After a pause, "Are you still there?"

"Yes."

"It just happened, and, well, we decided, why not?" She laughed nervously.

"I'm happy for you." His tongue had turned to clay, but he got the words out. "Listen, call me as soon as you find out anything about the woman in the sketch. Okay?" He rattled off his Melbourne Harbor Suites number and had her read it back to him.

"Sure thing."

He hung up, and borrowed the office copier. Next he faxed the copy of the sketch to Tricia's office. He took the copy for himself and returned the original to Jamie, who promised to have it hand delivered to Barnes on his arrival in Miami.

"Luck," she said, with a cheerful little wave.

Outside, the rain had abated a bit. Jennifer was parked in the lot, as promised, reading a book. The door was unlocked. She put the book in the glove compartment and handed him a towel as he climbed in.

"How'd it go?"

The question, irrationally, pissed him off, but he managed to control himself. He closed the door, dried his face and hair, tossed the towel into the backseat, and didn't respond to Jen's question.

"You going to tell me what happened, or what?" she asked after a moment. He could feel her gaze on him. That annoyed him, too, but he made light of it.

"Um, what."

She frowned. "In case it's slipped your mind, I'm your boss, and I'm asking for a status report."

Keith glared. "My goddamn wife divorced me because she didn't want children and now she's about to have a baby with someone else. That's what happened."

"Ouch." Jen hesitated. "Sorry I snapped."

He sighed. "Ditto."

Jen pulled out into traffic.

"Sorry to hear about your ex," she said.

He shook his head. "Forget it."

He filled her in on the way to the airport, and at a red light showed her the copy of the sketch.

"Doesn't look much like a terrorist."

"What does a terrorist look like?"

She handed the drawing back. "Touché."

When they reached their destination Keith jumped out and, as he started to close the door, she said, "Be careful, Keith. Stay in touch."

"I'll E-mail you."

He dashed through the rain into York Aviation's office, where Freddy sat with his feet on his desk, eating a doughnut and drinking coffee from a plastic foam cup.

"Grab a doughnut and set a spell," Freddy said. "I just got the word from Gulf Stream HQ to get you out to the rig as soon as this gully-washer lets up." He dipped the doughnut in the coffee, bit into it, and mumbled, "Won't be too long. Winds are gusting up to forty-six or -seven now, but the gusts aren't coming as often or as strong as they were a while ago. They ease up a hair and we're out of here."

Keith grabbed a doughnut and a cup of coffee and went over to the window to munch, staring glumly out at the rain.

Chapter 38

EMMA: **Wednesday, 7 October, 8:12 A.M. EDT**
Reflections, Melbourne

Kyle, a slim young man with black hair, expressive black eyes in a rather patrician face, and fine, very pale skin, could adopt the most sympathetic demeanor of anyone Emma knew. But he was immune to her blandishments. Not too many people could say the same, when Emma was going full blast.

He said for the third time, when she repeated her request yet a different way, "I really wish I could help you; it sounds important. But he'll be back in less than two hours, and he specifically said he did not want to be disturbed unless it was a crisis—on the order of the facility sinking or burning down." He made an apologetic gesture. "Those were his very words."

"But, Kyle, this *is* a crisis! A crisis if we don't respond immediately, and it's got to be him."

"Perhaps you could call the interested parties, open the discussion, and tell them Mr. Pendleton is tied up but will get back to them shortly."

Emma wanted to scream. Instead she said with enforced calm, "I can't call the CEO of Chrysler. He'll never talk to me."

He looked thoughtful. "Is there another contact? One of his senior staff must be involved in the deal."

Emma stared at Kyle. Then she turned and paced to the door, counting inhalations. Flaming Kyle would not help.

Besides, he was right. Someone at her level would be involved. Venkat would know who was managing the deal on Chrysler's end; he had even mentioned someone's name. She forgot now who it was, but that might be the right person to call.

She had wanted to talk to Pendleton before taking action—negotiating deals wasn't her specialty—but she couldn't imagine he would object to a preliminary discussion. And even Chrysler's CEO, Robert Eaton, was probably willing to wait an hour or two to talk to another CEO.

But Jesus, she was terrified they'd lose this chance.

She turned and came back to Kyle's desk. "I'll see if I can reach someone. You're right, there probably is someone I can talk to. In the meantime, please, *please* promise me you'll call and let him know about this, so he knows to make it a priority when he gets out of his meeting."

Kyle nodded after a pause. "Very well. If it's as important as you say, I suppose it's the sort of thing he wants to know about. I'll get in touch with him and let him know you urgently need to speak to him."

Emma's knees weakened with relief. "Thank you."

Back in her office, someone had turned on her computer and called up a spreadsheet. A yellow sticky with a note in the center of the screen obscured part of the data.

> *E—*
> *YOU SHOULD HAVE A LOOK AT THIS.*
> *—G*

Gloria's handiwork. Emma removed the sticky and glanced at the spreadsheet as she sat and picked up the phone receiver to call Venkat. The data showed the latest power plant run results from Gulf Stream I.

Frowning, she dialed a different number instead.

"Ben Jonas, Engineering."

"Ben," Emma said, "I just got the latest power-up data."

"Yeah. I didn't expect to hear from you so early. I was going to call you when you got out of your big meeting."

"It was canceled. What's going on? You've only got an overall performance of forty-three percent on the cold water intake pumps. Three-B is only giving you *thirty-five* percent! I thought you said you'd be at eighty percent or better by this morning."

A heavy sigh. "I know. We started having difficulties early in the morning. The intake pressure began to fluctuate around three-thirty A.M. and has been dropping steadily since."

"Sounds like a blockage in the intake."

"I agree. We've switched over to diesel power and reversed the pumps to flush the lines, but it hasn't done any good, so far. We can blow out just fine but as soon as we start suction, the pressure starts dropping again. I think we're going to have to send Mac down in the *Guppy* to check it out." *Guppy* was the facility's one-man, rigid-hulled submersible. It was used mostly for research, but occasionally Engineering used it for deep inspections of the intake pipe and deeper sections of the beanpoles.

Emma hesitated only a moment. It was time to get

back. She'd been away too long. "I'll be there as soon as weather permits. Hold off on the deep dive until then. Be sure to keep Tetsuo apprised. He might want to take advantage of the dive to do some filming of deep dwellers."

"Sure thing, chief."

She smiled, faintly. "Don't call me chief."

Then she dialed Venkat and told him about the delay in reaching Pendleton.

"I think we'll be all right," Venkat said. "It's still early. Chrysler's an hour behind us and PG and E is three hours behind—as is CalEPA. As long as we get the right people together by ten-thirty our time, we'll be in a good position to open discussions with California."

"Are you going to do it over the phone?"

Venkat coughed. "Well—ah—when I heard about the deal I took the liberty of sending my colleague out on a flight to Los Angeles. She'll be at LAX before eleven A.M., their time."

"I'm not authorized to spend money on this yet, you know."

"Don't worry; we'll work out the agreement for our fee and expenses when Pendleton is on board. Meanwhile, I'm taking some materials Chrysler sent me on their fuel cell design, and cutting and pasting them into the package you put together last year with GM. We'll need a more formal bid package to respond to California's RFP, but this at least will give them something to look at when we talk to them. It puts us way ahead."

"Excellent. Let's go ahead and call your Chrysler contact."

Venkat tied in a second line and they tried the number Venkat had for Halbertson at Chrysler, but got the man's voice mail.

"This is Emma Tooke with Gulf Stream I," she

said, after the tone. "We're very interested in pursuing this venture with Chrysler and I'd like to talk to you as soon as possible. I expect that my CEO, Brad Pendleton, will also be calling Mr. Eaton as soon as he returns from a meeting. Please call me at your earliest convenience." She left her landside office number, her cellular phone number, and her direct line out at Gulf Stream.

Gloria stuck her head in as Emma was hanging up.

"I'm making a breakfast run to McDonald's. Can I get you something?"

"Yeah." Emma reached for her billfold and pulled out a ten. "I'll take a bacon-egg-and-cheese biscuit and a large OJ."

"Coming atcha."

"By the way, I'm heading back out to Gulf Stream as soon as I can get a helicopter, if Pendleton will authorize the expense, and I'd like you to come with me. Think you can get things wrapped here in the next half hour or so?"

Gloria thought for a moment. "Sure. Just let me know when and I'll be ready."

"Great. Oh, and let Flo know we're looking to hire a helicopter. She may want to hitch a ride."

"Right." Gloria closed the door.

Catching a glimpse of it, Emma pulled out the crumpled and torn anonymous note about Keith. What an annoyance. But it needed attention, and now was as good a time as any.

She picked up the phone and dialed Angelo on the intercom.

"Yeah?"

"It's Emma. Could you pick up my calls for me, for the next little bit?"

"Sure."

She got up and closed the door, spread the note out on her desk, and taped it back together with Scotch tape. *Keith Hellman is not what he seems.*

She thought, Let's assemble the facts. She opened the word processor on her computer and started typing.

Facts:

1. On Monday morning I get an unsigned note warning me about Keith.

2. I know the note wasn't there at 11 p.m. Sunday.

3. A security guard was posted at the door all night, although he may have fallen asleep at some point.

4. The note turns out to be true.

5. I inform Pendleton, who gets royally pissed, takes the note, and stomps off.

6. That night I find the note in Phil's wastebasket.

Her fingers paused above the keys. She was remembering the meeting in which she'd met Keith—the totally uncharacteristic way Pendleton had forced Keith on her, and his nervousness about it; Phil's veiled scowl. It struck her.

Pendleton *knew* Keith wasn't who he said. And so did Phil. Pendleton was furious because *Emma* wasn't supposed to have found out.

All kinds of unrelated observations struck her at the same time. Keith's attitude when he had first boarded Gulf Stream. His evasiveness when she'd asked him certain questions. Pendleton's asking Shelly not to check Keith's references. The unexpected, unexplained meeting Phil and Pendleton were attending right now, a meeting whose importance in Pendleton's mind superseded a critical strategy meeting he had insisted on.

Something really big, and really secret, was going down. Keith was a plant.

Did Pendleton set him up to spy on Gulf Stream? On Emma, specifically? Did it have something to do with her turf war with Reynolds? Nah, that was paranoid. It had to be something totally different. Perhaps Keith was a private investigator, looking into some possibility of fraud or theft.

Whatever Keith was up to, it was Pendleton's idea, she thought, remembering Phil's scowl; Phil didn't like it one bit.

With that, she was suddenly certain Phil had left the note on her chair. He'd wanted her to be an unwitting ally—to apply pressure to Pendleton to get rid of Keith. Or to upset Keith's position, somehow. He saw Keith as some kind of threat.

It was a leap; an outsider might have sneaked in from outside, or it could have been someone else in the office—though who? She'd been at work late Sunday night, and was back in seven hours later, when only a couple of people were in, including Phil—but no. She knew.

And, judging from where she'd found the note after Pendleton took it, Pendleton must have come to the same conclusion she just had, and confronted Phil about it.

She stood, picking up the note. There was a knock. Gloria entered carrying a brown McDonald's bag and deposited it on Emma's desk, along with a pile of change.

"Do you know whether Phil's back yet?"

"Yes, he and Pendleton arrived at the same time I did—just a moment ago."

The phone's ringing punctuated Gloria's sentence,

and the name on the display was Pendleton's. Emma grabbed the receiver.

"You wanted to speak to me?" Pendleton asked.

"Yes; do you have a moment?"

"If it's critical."

"It is. I'll be right there."

She hung up the phone and stuffed the note into her pocket. Gloria held out her bacon-egg-and-cheese biscuit, sheathed in its cheese-yellow wrapper and ready for a bite. Emma took it gratefully and took a big bite, and then another. Then she wrapped it back up and set it on the desk, and headed for Pendleton's office, chewing hard. She swallowed just in time for Kyle to wave her in.

Pendleton looked up. His demeanor was somber.

"Tell me what you need," he said.

Emma looked straight at him. Her racing heart had more to do with what she had just guessed about Keith than the deal.

"I have a market for the hydrogen. A big one."

That sparked some interest. "Oh?"

"Yes." She told him about California's solicitation of bids for alternative fuel vehicles and a distribution network. "And Chrysler is interested in talking to us."

"How real is this deal?"

"Chrysler's CEO, Robert Eaton, is expecting a call from you."

Pendleton leaned back in his chair, swiveled, and looked out the window.

"I've heard," she said, "about the NSF offer that Dr. Reynolds has landed. And I know that this alternative is only a maybe, right now. But it's a huge opportunity. It puts us at the forefront of the transformation of America's fuel economy." She pressed fingers to her lips. "Whatever my personal feelings about Thomas Reynolds are, the oceanographic research we do out at Gulf Stream is extremely important. I'm not denying that. But at the core of the firm's business is ecologically sound energy production. This opportunity is perfect.''

Pendleton had looked back, and seemed to be studying her. ''Government contracts can be more trouble than they're worth.'' Distress swelled in her heart, but he went on after a second, ''but I agree with you, this is worth pursuing.''

''I'll give Kyle the contact information,'' she said. She paused. ''We're having some difficulties with the power-up and it looks like we're going to have to send the submersible down. I need to get back there right away. I'll track this deal from there, and use Angelo for any information gathering or write-ups needed.''

''Fine. Oh.'' He snapped his fingers. ''If you want to head back, you should call York Aviation right away. Keith Hellman is waiting at their office. They'll be heading out by helicopter as soon as weather permits.''

Though startled, she managed to suppress any reaction.

''Thanks, Mr. Pendleton.''

He barely noticed her go.

So that was that. His lack of enthusiasm about the deal depressed her.

Maybe his caution was a good idea; they didn't know what might happen with this deal. But no, it was something else. He was distracted. Her thoughts turned again to Keith and the note.

The more she thought about it, the more she felt the direct approach with Phil would be best. But first, a phone call to make sure Freddy held the helicopter for her.

She borrowed Kyle's phone to call Gloria and get her to place a call to Freddy. Then she took the elevator down a floor and headed over to Phil's office. She saw as she approached that his office was empty.

"He's in the conference room with Dennis and the Florida environmental inspector," Treena said.

Emma slapped a hand over her mouth. *Shit.* She had completely forgotten the inspection!

Why was Dennis involved? And for that matter, what the hell was Keith doing, sitting over at York Aviation, waiting to catch a helicopter to Gulf Stream, with an EPA inspection imminent?

As she opened the conference room door, a stranger's voice was saying, "We-ell now, yes, I did get the message, and frankly, it is a crying shame. I was looking forward to having a gander at y'all's records, to see how things are coming along."

The man was short, maybe fifty years old, and bald as a cue ball. He wore thick-lensed glasses and a short-sleeved button-down shirt buttoned all the way up with no tie, and his booted feet were up on the table. Though rather scrawny everywhere else, he had a sub-stantial gut that listed to the side. Phil and Dennis sat opposite him.

When Emma entered, all three gave her a surprised look. The stranger stood hurriedly; Emma towered over him. She extended her hand.

"Wow," he said. "You're certainly a tall one, ain't you?"

Emma refrained from a remark about *his* height. "So I'm told. Emma Tooke."

He took her hand and pumped it. "Chuck Pinkle. DEP." She checked her hand once he'd released it. No slime. Amazing.

"Emma is our chief operations officer," Phil said.

"Well now, that's a hefty title for such a pretty lady," Pinkle said, sitting back down.

"I always thought it had a nice ring to it," Emma said.

"The inspection's been canceled," Phil told her. She nodded. It explained why Keith wasn't there.

"That's right," said Pinkle. "Since I was in the neighborhood, though, I thought I'd drop by to have a little chat. For old times' sake."

He chuckled. Dennis and Phil looked uncomfortable.

"There's no need for you to stay," Phil said. "We'll talk with Mr. Pinkle for a bit and then see him on his way."

Emma looked from one to the other of them. Something reeked.

She stood. "Well, I've got plenty to do. Phil, I'd like a word with you later."

"Sure. No problem."

"It was nice to meet you, honey," Pinkle said. Emma gave him a smile.

"You can call me Ms. Chief Operations Officer," she said, and left. Bad girl, she thought. But that was nothing. She had something even more wicked planned.

The conference room and the pantry on that floor shared a walk-through closet. While in the conference room she'd happened to notice that the closet door was slightly ajar.

The pantry was empty; one or two people in cubicles could have seen her if they'd looked her way, but no one seemed to be looking. She quietly opened the closet door and slipped inside, closed the door, and made her way amid the boxes and clutter to the back. A thread of light came through the crack between the door and the frame. She could hear very well. Dennis was talking.

". . . understand. You're trying to squeeze blood from a turnip. We're on the brink of bankruptcy."

"Well, that *is* a problem, ain't it? But I'd think you'd want to avoid the risk of fines and penalties for environmental crimes. I'm sure that would put you at even greater risk than the kind of money I'm talking

about. Not to mention all the embarrassing publicity.''
A pause. ''I'm a reasonable man. Why don't y'all see
what kind of offer you can scrape together, and I'll
see about keeping Gulf Stream I out of trouble.''

''Well, thanks very much for the offer,'' Phil replied, ''but we're not interested.''

''You better think it over, son. A series of consent
order violations could get y'all in hot water real fast.
I figure a close inspection could come up with violations and penalties to the tune of a good hundred thousand or more. All I'm asking is a modest fifteen
percent. Fifteen thousand dollars. Less than half what
you paid last time.'' *Last time?* Emma thought.
''Think of it as insurance,'' Pinkle said.

Phil said, ''I think we'll take our chances. Without
the extra insurance.''

''Oh?'' A heavy, dramatic sigh. ''You're making a
big mistake. But, oh, well, I guess some folks have to
find out the hard way.

''We'll be setting up an inspection for next week.
You give me a call if you change your mind in the
meantime. Otherwise . . .''

The word hung there for a moment. Then there were
scrapings and rustlings.

''Don't get up,'' Pinkle said. ''I'll see myself out.''
A door closed.

''Can you believe the nerve of that bastard?'' Dennis said, in a low voice.

''Relax. I've gone over the records in detail with
Treena. We're not in too bad a shape. Some minor
record-keeping glitches is all.''

''He could falsify his inspection report.''

''He could. But I believe we can arrange for the
EPA to send a representative, too—as an impartial
witness.''

''I suppose . . .''

''Trust me. Things will be fine.''

More rustlings and scrapings. Emma grabbed a bag
of coffee and stepped back out into the pantry, where
a young woman was pouring hot water into a cup with
a tea bag in it. Phil and Dennis walked past, looking
preoccupied. Emma nodded a hello to the woman, deposited the bag of coffee in the cabinet under the pantry, and left.

She went back to her office, shut the door, and
stared out at the storm. Her heart was pounding fiendishly and she had a hard time breathing.

The torrent outside seemed to have lessened. Freddy
was probably ready to go. But she couldn't leave without figuring out what the hell to do about this big,
stinking mess that had just fallen into her lap.

Fallen? . . . More like she'd grabbed it with both
hands and put it there. Sometimes, Emma, she thought,
you're too damn nosy for your own good.

So. Good old likable Phil, and Dennis, grouchy old
friend of her family for decades, had paid extortion
money to Pinkle. Somewhere upward of thirty thousand dollars.

It had to have been while they were negotiating the
consent agreements, two years ago. They hadn't had
any dealings with the Florida regulators before or
since. At least, none that she knew of.

She had to go to Pendleton with this.

It'd be an ugly stink. He'd question Phil and Dennis,
too, and they'd probably deny it. A close examination
of the financial records from around the time of the
consent agreements might turn up a discrepancy—or
not, if Phil had paid it out of his own pocket. He could
certainly afford to. Somehow, though, she doubted it.
That was probably why Dennis was involved to begin
with: Phil had needed him to hide the unauthorized
expense in the balance sheet.

But she didn't know whether Pendleton would have
the courage to audit the books—especially since, once

he found the discrepancy, he'd be obligated to report it. Such a scandal could bring down the company. It would be easier to force Emma to drop it, or, if she refused, make her a scapegoat.

I can't second-guess Pendleton, she thought. I have to give him the information and let him make his own decision.

Her big conch shell was sitting on the window ledge. She sat down on the ledge and picked up the shell, fingering its rough outer surfaces, its smooth inner ones. She leaned against the water-streaked glass.

She counted Phil a friend. She had always liked and admired him. He never made an issue of his wealth. He was hardworking, intelligent, and pleasant to deal with. And Dennis was, if not a friend, a man with whom she had old and close ties.

With a reluctant sigh, she set the shell down and headed back downstairs to Phil's office.

He motioned her in when he saw her approaching through the open door. She closed it and leaned on it. Her breath was short again, and her stomach had knotted up.

"What can I do for you?" he asked.

She stood there looking at him for a long moment.

"I guess," she said, and caught her breath, which was still short, "that I have a question and then something to tell you."

He templed his hands, smiling. "All right."

She pulled out the anonymous note.

"Why did you send me this note about Keith?"

His face went through a series of swift changes, ending up absolutely blank. He took the note and turned it over. "What's this?"

"That's what I want to know. I know Keith is a plant, and that you and Pendleton are the only two who know it. Why did you send me this note, Phil?

Why did you want me to know about Keith, against Pendleton's wishes?''

He looked at the note some more. Finally he shrugged. ''I wish I could help you, Emma. But it wasn't me who sent this note. I imagine it was a prank.''

A whisper of doubt crept into her mind. But no.

''I suppose it's the same line you fed Pendleton. But have it your way.'' His expression inched toward annoyance. She held out her hand for the note and he gave it to her—after an instant's hesitation.

''And the other matter?''

She drew a slow, deep breath. ''I overheard the conversation you and Dennis had with Pinkle, after I left. I know that you paid him extortion money once, and that he's pressuring you to do it again.''

His expression went through several more changes, this time sticking at outrage and alarm. ''Oh, for Chrissakes, Emma! Don't you know when to quit?''

''I know when not to. Goddamn it, how could you put the firm in this kind of jeopardy? You should know better than anyone, it's illegal to pay bribes!''

''Don't lecture me about legalities. You weren't there; you have no idea. He held all the cards. There was nothing we could do.'' He leaned back, smoothing his hair back with a deep breath. ''And if you hung around long enough you also heard we aren't going to play his nasty little game this time.''

''So why didn't you find a way to outmaneuver him last time?''

Phil frowned. ''Oh, grow up. It was a cost of doing business. Companies do it all the time. It usually gets dressed up a little more nicely, unless you're dealing with pond scum like Pinkle.'' He spread his hands, assayed a smile. ''In any event, believe me, it's well in the past and best forgotten.''

Emma was shaking her head as he spoke. ''Look.

I'm not here to argue legalities and ethics with you. I'm here to tell you that I want you to come with me to Pendleton and tell him, right now. If you don't, I'm going to him alone.''

Phil stood, gripping the edge of his desk. "Don't do this. Let it drop. You'll hurt the company."

The corners of Emma's lips turned down. She went to the door. "I've got news for you. I'm not the one who's hurt the company." She paused. "You coming?"

Phil sat back down.

"I'll deny everything," he said.

"Have it your way." She closed the door behind her.

Next she went to Dennis's office. He was on the phone. She waited outside the door for him to get off.

"*Damn it.* What are we going to do?" He listened for a long moment. "We have to talk her out of it. I never should have let you talk me into this," and he hung up the phone.

Emma stepped in.

He gaped at her. His face was dark red and his eyes were protruding.

"Well, I guess Phil's told you," she said.

"Now, don't get all into a tizzy about this," he said. "There's a very simple explanation."

Emma held up a hand. "As I told Phil, I'm not interested in a big discussion. Pendleton needs to be told. You can either come with me right now and tell him, or I'll go myself."

Dennis stood up and came over to her, attempted to put an arm around her. She moved away from him. He frowned.

"What's done is done. You're only going to create trouble if you stir things up."

"Like I told Phil, I wasn't the one who created this trouble. You going to come, or not?"

He merely sat back down and folded his arms, wearing a truculent expression. She left him there, and headed up to Pendleton's office. She half expected to find him, too, on the phone with Phil. That was her secret fear: that Pendleton already knew.

But they wouldn't have been so upset about her going to Pendleton if he'd already known.

She knocked on the door. Pendleton was just hanging up the phone, and he was beaming.

"You're still here, then," he said. "I just got off the phone with Eaton at Chrysler. The preliminary discussions are going very well. I believe we have an excellent shot at the bid."

"I'm glad to hear it." She hesitated. "Unfortunately I have some very bad news."

"Oh?"

"Yes." She came in and closed the door. He was looking at her intently. "Oh, boy," she muttered, and swiped at a lock of hair that had escaped her French braid. She sat down on the couch against one wall.

"Just dive in," he said. "I've heard lots of bad news in my day. We'll cope."

"Well, this is a doozy." She paused. "I just learned that Phil and Dennis paid off a Florida regulator to get the environmental consent agreements for Gulf Stream I."

His eyes and mouth gaped wide. "They did *what*?"

She described what she had overheard in the conference room. "I just spoke to them both, and told them I was going to be talking to you." She rubbed her brow, shrugged helplessly. "I'm really sorry, Mr. Pendleton."

He was looking out the window again. His expression was one of shock. "That's a doozy, as you say." He shook his head with a sigh.

"Phil told me they'd deny it to you. It may take an audit of the books to uncover the truth."

Pendleton sighed again, heavily, and picked up the phone. "Phil, could you get Dennis and come to my office right away?"

They filed in, Phil looking calm, Dennis, stiffly, like a man going before a firing squad.

"Sit down," Pendleton said, gesturing at the chairs on either side of the couch Emma sat on.

"What's this about?" Phil asked, sitting.

"Emma has just informed me that she overheard you two discussing an illicit payment that you made to a regulatory official. Would you care to explain?"

Phil lifted his eyebrows. "I wish I could. I don't know where she got the idea, but it couldn't have been from overhearing us. I know nothing about it." He turned to Emma. "What's going on here? Why are you inventing this story?"

"Oh, give me a break," Emma said.

Pendleton held up a finger in her direction. "Dennis?"

Dennis looked as if he were going to explode. He clutched hands in his lap, and sweat had beaded on his face.

"I d-don't know anything about it, either."

"Why are you so nervous?" Pendleton asked him.

Dennis looked at Phil. Phil glared at him.

"Well?" Pendleton asked.

Dennis sprang to his feet. "It wasn't my idea! It was his!" He pointed at Phil.

"Shut up!" Phil snapped.

Emma said, "You may as well come clean."

"Please have a seat," Pendleton told Dennis, who sank back into his chair, rather like a large balloon deflating.

After a pause, Phil sighed. "May I speak to you privately, Brad?"

"I think not."

"I was trying to protect you."

Pendleton looked pained. "Spare me the justifications and tell me what happened."

"He told us we didn't have a chance at getting a consent agreement with the state unless we came up with forty thousand dollars," Phil said. "We had nothing on him; it would have been our word against his if we'd gone to anyone."

Pendleton slammed a hand onto his desk. "I'm golfing buddies with the governor! All it would have taken to stop him was one phone call!"

Phil shook his head. "This was three summers ago, Brad, before the elections. We had no real recourse. You know how tight our timetable was! And it was such a trivial amount of money, given how much we'd spent already." He spread his hands. "It's a cost of doing business, these days. Set it aside, Brad. Forget about it. It'll never happen again. I guarantee it."

Pendleton looked at Phil for a long time without saying anything. Then he stood and opened the door.

"I need to think. We'll speak later."

Phil and Dennis got up and left without glancing Emma's way. She looked out the window. The rainfall was lessening now. Freddy's helicopter could take off any time. She stood.

She felt like a fink.

"Are you heading back to Gulf Stream I?"

"Yes." She gave him a look, wishing she had something to say that would make all this less of a disaster.

"Thanks for bringing this matter to my attention," Pendleton said.

Emma wondered how much he meant it.

She and Gloria hitched a ride with Flo to the airport. All her anxiety at seeing Keith evaporated when she opened the door of York Aviation's office and saw him in a chair by Freddy's desk.

"Oh my God, Keith! What happened?"

He rocked forward in his chair, lowering his feet to the floor. The half grin that chased a rather gloomy expression from his face lifted her own spirits. His hand went to his jaw, as if he had forgotten about the swelling and bruises there.

"It looks worse than it is. Really."

"Hey, Emma," Freddy said, standing. "Gloria, Flo. How y'all?"

"Could be worse, I guess," Emma said.

Flo added with a twist of a smile, "Sure. Could be raining."

Emma laughed. Freddy snatched his rain poncho from the peg on the wall. "I'll go warm up the bird. Give me a minute or two and then come on out to the pad."

Flo went over to pour herself a cup of tea, and Gloria went to the bathroom. Emma went over and perched on the desk next to Keith, inspecting the bruises. She reached out to touch it. "Jesus. Did you get into a brawl or something?"

He grimaced and took her hand. "Something. Easy. It's still tender."

It mildly alarmed her how glad she was to see him. She was also annoyed at the equivocation. Too many mysteries, too many lies. She sighed and pulled her hand free. Gloria came out of the bathroom as Flo turned around, stirring her tea. Both of them carefully avoided looking at Emma or Keith. Emma stood and glanced out the window.

"I think Freddy's about ready for us," she said.

To Emma's annoyance, Thomas Reynolds arrived at the last minute to share the flight. With him wearing one of the cabin headsets, she felt awkward talking to or even touching Keith.

It would be a long ride to Gulf Stream.

Chapter 39

GABRIEL: **Wednesday, 7 October, 11:00 A.M. EDT**
The Cherokee Princess, **about one nautical mile
south of Gulf Stream I**

The storm, finally, passed. Though seas were still choppy, the clouds had begun to lift, revealing patches of raw, rain-scrubbed sky. The breeze was warm and moist.

They were all out on deck. Mark and Jax were wiring the charges. Boadica sat on the aft deck, scanning the waters with binoculars, watching for boats. Gabriel had climbed up onto the foredeck. With his own binoculars he was keeping an eye on Gulf Stream I. Or where it should be, though the rig was slowly disappearing before his eyes. Over the past several minutes as the clouds had lifted, a mist had begun to swallow the facility.

It was a little creepy, how fog hugged the facility while clear air and clear water surrounded it. It was as though someone had cast a spell to shroud Gulf Stream I from its enemies. Or as if it were enchanted, now passing from Earth back into some other time and space. It seemed a bad omen.

Don't spook yourself, Cervantes, he thought. He eyed the nearer catwalks, barely visible now in the thickening fog, that hung between the modules; blotches of color moved back and forth along them. He wondered if any of the blotches was Emma.

A helicopter approached from the east as he watched and settled into the fog. The chopper didn't appear to be military. On its side were some markings and a sign he couldn't quite make out before the fog swallowed it.

"Hey, Gabe," Mark called. "Could you give me a hand?"

When he crawled back around and scrambled down onto the main deck, Mark was alone, wiring the charges into the radio-controlled detonators. Clattering noises issued from the cabin. Jax and Boadica were unloading more equipment from the storage cabinets downstairs. Gabriel caught a glimpse of what they were unloading. He didn't know from guns, but those suckers were *nasty*—compact automatic weapons with long ammo clips. They looked expensive. And deadly.

Guns. Hitting a facility not empty. One with kids on it. He shook his head, and briefly, closed his eyes. Ride the wave, Cervantes. Ride the wave.

Mark pointed at a pile of waterproof bags with his chin. In his hands he cradled one of the assembled explosive charges. "Hold those open while I ease these in, okay?"

"Sure."

"This is it, man," Mark said, easing the charge into the bag. His eyes were bright with excitement. He sealed the bag and set it aside, and picked up another charge. Gabriel held another bag for him. "These are going to make for one big boom." As he sealed each waterproof bag, he loaded it into his yellow mesh dive bag.

Gabriel wiped sweat off his hands, between bags. They finished the last one and when Mark took it out of his hands, Gabriel blew out a breath in relief.

Jax and Boadica came upstairs, guns slung over shoulders and boxes of ammunition stacked in their arms. Boadica tossed Gabriel and Mark each a large, watertight bag. They bagged up all of their guns, ammo, and spare explosives, and stacked them alongside the rail. Then Jax and Mark donned their suits.

"We're ready for the dive."

Gabriel nodded. "Very good."

"First we'll secure the spare munitions and the guns beneath the boat," Jax said. "Then we'll resurface and pick up our dive bags and charges. We need you two to hand us down both sets of bags."

Gabriel helped Mark don his buoyancy compensator jacket and tanks, and steadied him while he put on his fins. Boadica did the same for Jax.

Then Jax sat on the edge of the boat and rolled backward into the water with a splash. Boadica handed him down a string of bags. Mark followed; Gabriel handed him another string. The divers jackknifed beneath the water's surface. Gabriel scanned the horizon with his binoculars, and spotted a cutter on the edge of visibility that looked like it might be Coast Guard. It was heading roughly away from them.

"Coast Guard, I think," he said, pointing. Boadica's gaze followed his gesture and she nodded.

A sharp whistle drew them back to the aft deck. Jax and Mark clung to the outside of the boat, masks pulled down around their necks.

"Equipment secured beneath the boat," Jax said. "Hand down the rest."

Gabriel slung their dive bags over the side. He was particularly careful with the mesh bag filled with charges. Jax and Mark secured the bags, ropes, and tools to rings on their wet suits.

Boadica glanced at her watch. "Let's synchronize. I have twelve-fifty-three."

Jax adjusted his watch. "Check."

"Check," Mark echoed.

Gabriel set his own watch one minute forward, to match. "Check."

"We'll meet you one mile due north of Gulf Stream

I at three P.M. sharp,'' Gabriel said. "We'll get there as early as we can.''

Jax bared his teeth in a grin. "And if we get there before you or fuck up our compass directions, we're shit out of luck, because we don't dare light flares.''

"So don't fuck up,'' Boadica said.

Gabriel glanced at Mark, then, deliberately, at Jax. "Good luck.''

Jax and Mark put their snorkels in their mouths, touched their heads, and then swam downstream, into the waves.

Gabriel exchanged a long look with Boadica. He felt a little short of breath. "This is it.''

Boadica was silent, gripping the rail and staring after the others. She looked like a little girl. Despite himself, damn his *cojones,* he still wanted her.

Jax and Mark were moving fast with the powerful Gulf Stream current, despite the head wind. In moments they were well north of the boat and barely visible.

"I'll be below,'' Boadica said. "I need to do some work on myself. Warn me if the cutter gets closer.'' She headed down into the cabin.

Gabriel headed up to the bridge with his binoculars. He looked toward Gulf Stream I, now completely invisible in its fog blanket. Then he scanned the horizon.

And had a bad scare. The cutter was back, maybe two or three miles away, and nearing swiftly.

It was white and had a series of numbers just behind the bow, behind which a broad swath the red of a blood orange and a narrow blue swath angled back. On the red-orange swath was a symbol of a life ring with crossed anchors and a shield. COAST GUARD was written on its flank in big block letters, and on the deckhouse were the words CAPE STARR.

Gabriel dashed back down into the cabin. Boadica was wrapping her hair in a towel. Her eyes were now blue. Brown smears marked her forehead. Her bottles and jars of goo were spread out on the table, on a sheet.

"Coast Guard approaching," he said.

"Shit. How close?"

"Couple of miles, and closing fast."

"The guys?"

"Well away. I doubt they were spotted."

She bundled the makeup and dyes in the sheet and tossed them to Gabriel. "Weight it down and pitch it overboard. *Away* from the cutter."

He lashed the bundle with some cord and anchored it with more cord to a twelve-inch pipe wrench lying on the table. He dashed up the steps, dry-mouthed, heart racing and, with a mental apology to the fishes, tossed the bundle over the side. It floated briefly, releasing pockets of air, then sank.

He watched the water for over a minute to make sure nothing resurfaced. Nothing did, other than a few more bubbles. He breathed a sigh of relief. Even if they were watching and knew he'd tossed something—which didn't seem likely, given that he'd done it on the opposite side of the boat—they wouldn't know what.

When he checked again the Coast Guard cutter had come within a hundred feet. Crew members wearing baseball caps, life vests, and blue uniforms were out on deck; he spotted four. A fifth one, wearing a life vest, khakis, and baseball cap, came out of the cabin with a bullhorn. He put it up to his mouth.

"Boat on my bow! Stand fast and prepare to be boarded!"

Gabriel stood, hands on railing, as they put a Zodiac over the side. It skipped across the waves to *The Cherokee Princess* and drew up alongside. He watched them set onto the diver's platform and scale the stern ladder, wondering if they had pictures of him and

Boadica. Even in disguise, he felt vulnerable. It was hard to believe they wouldn't see right through it.

The one in khakis who had held the bullhorn earlier stepped over the gunwale, followed by two others in blue. He was clearly an officer; his cap had a chrome chevron, and an eagle and chevron were on his sleeve. He was quite young and had an officious look. The bullhorn had been replaced by a clipboard. The two with him, also wielding clipboards, looked more relaxed, even cheerful.

"Is this your boat, sir?" the officer asked, pen poised above his clipboard.

"Nope, it's a rental," Gabriel drawled. His voice came out steady.

"This is a safety inspection. Are you the captain? Is this a charter boat?"

"No, we don't have a captain. Just us. A private rental." His supposed Texan accent didn't seem to be giving them any pause.

"Any other passengers?"

"Yes, my girlfriend. She's below."

"Can you show us the rental contract, please?"

"I'll go get the papers. Y'all wait here."

He went down into the cabin. Boadica was nowhere to be seen. He could hear water running in the shower. He didn't know where the hell she had put the papers, and went about the cabin opening cabinets, feeling increasingly desperate. On the deck above, the guardsmen's sneakers and pants legs shifted back and forth. Finally he knocked on the bathroom door.

"Honey, the Coast Guard is here and wants to do an inspection. Where are the rental papers?" He prayed she was in there and not hiding somewhere else.

Her muffled voice replied, "They're in the toolbox. Up on the bridge."

He suppressed a sigh of relief and went up to the

flying bridge. Inside the toolbox, amid the screwdrivers, wrenches, and jars of parts, was a Zip-Loc bag full of papers. He pulled out the rental agreement and handed it to the officer, who scrutinized it, flipping pages.

"Are you Samuel Feinway?"

"That's correct."

"May I see some identification, please?"

Gabriel's heart rate shot up. He patted his pockets. "My wallet's downstairs."

Jax was the "real" Sam Feinway. Gabriel found Jax's wallet in his slacks, on the bed in the bow, and removed the driver's license—the only ID with Jax's picture on it. Then he dug through the cards as he ascended the stairs.

"My driver's license seems to be missing. I've got my credit cards and some other stuff." He handed them to the officer, who looked them over. "Will they do?"

With a terse nod, the officer handed the cards and rental papers back to him. "Please show us your life jackets."

"We have some up here and some below."

"Let's check these first, then," the officer said. "We'll go below in just a moment."

Gabriel opened up a compartment and the guardsmen removed and inspected the half dozen life vests inside.

"This one here has quite a bit of wear; you should replace it as soon as you get back to port."

"Yes, sir. I'll tell the charter company."

The officer made some notes. "We'd like to inspect your catch."

Gabriel led them to a compartment built into the aft deck, which served as their ice chest. In it were seven or eight fish of different sizes, on ice. He couldn't have told what they were to save his life; they'd bought them at a fish market the evening before.

One of the two in blue squatted and picked up a couple. "No prohibited species, sir," he reported to the officer. The officer made a note on his clipboard.

"We'd like to have a look at your fire extinguishers now," he said.

Gabriel pointed at the large one set next to the engine compartment. "There's that one," he said, "and a smaller one inside the cabin."

While one of the sailors inspected the big extinguisher, Gabriel led the other two back down into the cabin. He took them into the private compartment in the bow and pulled their other half dozen life vests, and a couple of packets of flares, from an underberth cabinet. The officer nodded, seeming pleased, when he saw the flares, and made more notes.

As they were stowing the life jackets, Boadica exited the shower, rubbing a towel in her hair. She was wearing a very short, cherry red satin wrap, with bare legs and a lot of cleavage showing. Her hair was now a rich brown, her eyes blue, a mole above her lip, her nose more aquiline. She was wearing makeup. Her facial alterations weren't especially dramatic, but then, the sailors weren't looking at her face.

"Gentlemen," she said.

The officer came to his feet and visibly struggled to maintain his official manner. "Ma'am. Excuse the intrusion. We'll be done with our inspection of your vessel in just a moment. If we may have a look at your fire extinguisher?" He gestured at it. Boadica was standing beside it.

"I'll be glad to show you whatever you'd like," she said, with a little smile that made Gabriel grit his teeth. She removed the fire extinguisher from its mounting on the bulkhead in such a way as to give them all a great, if brief, side view of her breast inside the wrap, and handed the extinguisher to the officer, who had turned the same shade of red as the extinguisher. He fumbled for it and almost dropped it.

"Here." He handed it to the sailor with him, who made a big deal of checking its inspection date and pressure, grinning at Boadica all the while. Boadica sat down at the table and crossed her legs, smiling at the sailors. Gabriel refrained from rolling his eyes.

"It's fine, sir," the man said, and handed it back to Gabriel. The officer made a note. He was studiously avoiding staring at Boadica's legs.

"That'll be all. Thank you for your cooperation."

Gabriel followed them back up and watched the three sailors board the Zodiac and return to the cutter. In moments the other boat was a good distance away. He rubbed at his hair with a long, drawn-out exhalation, and then went below.

Boadica was seated on the berth across from the table, cutting her nails.

"That was quite a peep show you gave them," he said.

She shrugged. "It served its purpose—it distracted them and threw them off guard. Probably unnecessary; they didn't seem overly suspicious, but . . . it's better to be safe than sorry."

The curve of her breast drew his eye; he watched her chest rise and fall.

She'd killed a man. He didn't trust her.

None of that mattered. He wanted her so badly he could hardly bear it.

She saw it in his face. That smile came back to her face. Untying her wrap, she let it drop to the floor.

"What are you doing?" he asked. Is this what she did to Jax in Miami? Seduced him and set him against me?

You're being paranoid, Cervantes.

"That should be obvious."

She strode up and locked her arms around his neck,

pulling his mouth down to hers. He resisted, briefly, then opened his mouth to her questing tongue. Then he nuzzled her neck, sliding his hands across her back. She gripped his hands and pulled them forward, over her breasts. With a groan, he massaged them. Her grip loosened; she arched her back.

Gabriel rubbed thumbs across the nipples. She inhaled sharply and the nipples grew hard. He slid his right hand down her abdomen and entangled his fingers in her pubic hair; with his left hand he cupped her buttock and pulled her to him and kissed her again. Boadica pushed his right hand farther, down to moist folds of velvety flesh.

He gasped.

"Come on," she said, and took him back to the big bed in the bow.

He dropped his jeans and briefs while she got something out of the bathroom. She crawled up onto the bed, holding up a condom. He slipped it on, then spread her knees, bent them up to her chest, and entered her, hard and fast.

His anger, his sense of betrayal, all of it surfaced, rising with his desire. I'm out of control, he thought, and tried to turn away, but she pulled him back, fed his anger, returned it. They hurt each other, biting, clawing, bruising each other's limbs, banging elbows against ribs and knees. Finally they came, first her, then him, half a second behind. He rolled off her and fell onto his back with an arm over his eyes, while she got up and got dressed. She went up on deck without a backward glance.

Jesus, Mary, and Joseph. That had to be the worst lovemaking he'd ever experienced. He wanted to cry.

Bruja, he thought. And then shook his head at himself. Emma was right. He was a total jerk.

Chapter 40

EMMA: Wednesday, 7 October, 10:39 A.M. EDT
York Aviation Helicopter York One, three thousand feet
above the Gulf Stream, en route to Gulf Stream I

The ride bounced them around and threw them against
their straps in irregular jolts. Rain blasted the windshield. Emma got motion sickness early on, and the
grey pressing close against the windows made her
claustrophobic.

Gloria, up front, looked a little green, too. Beside
her, Flo was reading a book, totally unscathed. Emma
hadn't yet looked back at Keith, though she was very
conscious of him in the seat behind her. He hadn't
spoken since they'd left Freddy's office.

After a while the rain began to subside and the buf-
feting lessened; she began to catch rare glimpses of
water below.

"Gulf Stream says storm's clearing!" Freddy announced. They were about forty-five minutes out of
Melbourne.

"ETA?" Emma asked.

"Fifteen, twenty minutes, maybe."

She glanced back at Keith then. He was alone in
the third row of seats. He appeared lost in thought,
staring out at the clouds and rain that whipped past.

A bit later they broke through into clear air. They
were a few miles west of Gulf Stream I, which was
visible only as a fog bank and some orange buoys.

Above, the cloud ceiling hung close enough to touch. The rain had stopped.

"Gulf Stream I, this is York One. Request permission to interrupt y'all's volleyball game . . ."

Lee's voice came through the headphones. "Give it a rest, Freddy. Permission granted to land."

"What do y'all have for a wind direction?"

"We have a breeze from the north at eight to ten knots, York One. Come on down."

They swung around the fog bank to enter it from the north. Fog was forming above the OTEC plant's cold water effluent, just downstream of the spillways, and the wind, opposing the Gulf Stream current, carried the fog south to blanket the modules. The reefs and their buoys were visible amid a pearlescent haze, and pillows of fog cushioned the spillways. The rest of the facility was completely engulfed.

Freddy put the helicopter down slowly into the grey mass, whipping tendrils from the top layers. Soon the fog was dense enough to obscure vision beyond a foot or two; Emma strained to see Mariculture's landing lights. They were upon the lights before she saw them, and touched down an instant later.

"Nice flying," Flo said.

"Naturally," said Freddy, flipping switches on the instrument panel above his head. "All ashore that's going ashore."

Emma took off her headphones, tossed them on the seat, and shoved the door open. Gloria, Flo, and Reynolds had already debarked. She and Keith grabbed their overnight bags and stepped out. Others, dim figures, mostly contractors she didn't know, moved in.

Emma followed her compatriots into grey nothingness, in the direction those embarking had come. By the time she reached the stairway the helicopter was completely invisible, though the twin roar of its blades and turbines nearly deafened her, and its wind pelted her as it lifted off.

She started down the disembodied stairs. Keith stopped and looked back at her. Gloria and Flo continued down and in a moment were swallowed by mist. Their footsteps faded; soon the only sound was the muffled slapping of waves against the module's beanpole. Keith and Emma couldn't have been more thoroughly alone.

"I was thinking . . ." He cleared his throat. "If the wave action isn't too bad, we could do your checkout dive sometime today, out at the reefs."

Emma shook her head, opened her mouth, then closed it. "I can't—we've got a deep dive coming up as soon as I get over to Mariculture. And I have a lot of work to catch up on besides."

He shrugged. "Sure. Maybe some other time."

She raised her eyebrows. "Maybe? You mean *definitely*. I want my c-card." She hesitated, thinking, I shouldn't do this, and then smiled. "How about this evening?"

He smiled back, but there was a shadow under his brow. "You're not ready for night diving yet. We'll try for tomorrow, seven A.M. sharp, at the Mariculture dock. Bring your gear. We'll get Jess or Nikki to be our dive tender."

She nodded, briskly. "It's a date."

The rather grim look lifted from his face. "Good. I have something to look forward to."

The pleased, gentle look he wore lingered in her mind.

She went down to the utility deck. No one from Engineering was there, and the minisub was still in its cradle: battery hatches open, lifting eyes not connected to the crane. Frowning, she borrowed a radio from one of Flo's fish wranglers, who was shifting bags of fro-

zen shrimp from the walk-in freezer at the front end
of the deck, and called Ben.

"Why's the sub not prepped for the dive?"

"Looks like we won't need it. We're in the power
plant," Ben said. "Why don't you join us? We have
something to show you."

The "something" was an enormous tentacle, separated from whatever it had once belonged to. It lay,
inert and pulpous, on the grating beneath Compressor
Three's dismantled intake port, in a pile of rotten sargasso weed, near a filter screen and numerous bolts,
nuts, O-rings, washers, and tools. Ben, Rob, Mac, and
a couple other engineers and technicians were looking
down at it.

Emma adjusted the mike of her headset.

"Yuck. What is it?"

"Tet is on his way over to answer that very question," Ben said.

Emma squatted and poked it. It was cool and rub-
bery to the touch. The tentacle must have measured
twelve feet long, and eighteen inches in diameter at
its thickest point. It was light grey with a dual row of
suckers running down the flat side. The thick end was
chewed up pretty badly.

"About half an hour ago," Ben said, "we registered a pressure surge in the line. All of a sudden we
had full capacity. The obstruction was gone. Ten
minutes later we had a pressure loss at Number Three.
I had Mac disassemble the screen, and"—he gestured—"that fell out."

"The one that got away," Emma said, eyeing it.
"Mostly."

"I'd hate to think what a creature that size would've
done to the minisub," Mac remarked.

One of the technicians laughed. "Probably had you
for lunch."

"Speaking of which," Rob said, "I wonder if it's

edible? Maybe we should let Charlie know.''

Emma grimaced. "Please, my stomach. We don't even know what it is.''

She went back up to her office to deal with the paper- and computer-based tasks that had piled up while she was gone. And lost herself in it; over an hour later she looked up, bleary-eyed, when Gloria suggested they walk over to the mess together for a lunch break.

Keith was just picking up his lunch tray to leave as Emma and Gloria sat down with theirs. "Are we still on for your checkout dive tomorrow?''

"Seven o'clock sharp,'' she said. She'd rather hoped he wouldn't mention it in front of Gloria.

"Let me know if you change your mind about this afternoon,'' he said. "Jess tells me visibility and sea conditions are decent for diving out at the reefs.''

Gloria gave her an inquisitive look, and a grin, which she ignored.

Everyone at lunch was talking about the Tentacle from Twenty Thousand Feet. Tetsuo had confirmed that the appendage belonged to an extraordinarily large squid, and Charlie was reputedly going to make a squid dish for supper. Opinion was split as to whether or not this was a good thing.

Two interns were messing around with Dr. Feelgood, making the doll gesture and flap its arms, talking dirty in falsetto. Emma winced as she sat down with her tray.

"I hate that damn thing,'' she said.

"Why don't you get rid of it?''

"I nearly have, a couple of times.'' Emma shook her head. "I think it'd cause too much resentment—especially after all that heat I took when I made all the guys put their girlie calendars out of sight.'' She shrugged. "Maybe I'll just sneak in some night and poke some big, unpatchable holes in the thing.''

Gloria laughed. As they ate, she filled Emma in on the computer situation, and they sketched out their schedules for the next couple of days.

"Will you have any free time this afternoon?" Emma asked.

"Well, like I said, we've been having problems with the Science server, but Ramón should be able to handle it. Why?"

"I've sorted through my work and gotten the critical stuff taken care of, but the rest needs a re-sort, and there's a lot of filing to be done. I'd love some help."

Gloria smiled over her tea mug. "I'd be happy to. In fact . . . maybe you could leave the paperwork to me, and go ahead and take advantage of the opportunity to do your checkout dive this afternoon."

Emma smacked the table with her palm. "Goddamn it, stop meddling! I've got too freaking much to do to go off on a pleasure dive with a—" She noticed that people were looking at her, and lowered her voice to little more than a whisper. "With a man who falsifies his résumé."

Gloria sighed. "Emma, I have been listening to you bitch about not having your diver's certification for three years now. You keep telling me you need it to do your job. And then you keep manufacturing reasons why you don't have time to get it—or have a relationship, or take a vacation, or have a life at all outside your stupid job!

"You just got through telling me you completed all the critical tasks. Did it ever occur to you that maybe the facility wouldn't stop functioning if you diverted your attention from it for a few hours?"

Emma stared at Gloria, fuming. She looked around. The others in the mess were pretending not to listen. Emma stood, picked up her tray, and tossed it, uneaten food and all, into the soapy water at the sink, earning a glare from the man scrubbing a pot in the suds.

"Thank you, Ann Landers," she said to Gloria, and left.

Emma went to her quarters on the next level down. The tiny room was in its usual state: a shambles.

That was not exactly behavior befitting the chief operations officer, Tooke, she thought.

With a sigh, she hung her radio belt on the hook behind the door, tossed all the dirty clothes off her bed onto the floor, and kicked the pile into the corner by the closet. This unearthed one of her pairs of khaki shorts, which had a two-week-old bloodstain on the seat.

Jesus, she thought. Gloria's right. You don't even take the time to change your tampon, for Christ's sake. She flopped down on the bed and bunched up her pillow, brooding. What did Gloria think she was afraid of, anyhow?

She sprang up, fists clenched. *That does it.* She grabbed her radio out of its holster.

"Hellman, come in."

"Keith here."

"This is Tooke. I'm ready for my checkout dive. Are you still available?"

"Right now?"

"Right now."

The barest pause. "Sure. I'd be glad to."

"I'll meet you at the Mariculture dock in ten minutes."

"Great. But make it fifteen. I need to track down Jess."

"Right. Out."

She released the button and took a couple of deep breaths to slow her heart. Then she got down on her knees and started digging through her clothes pile. Now if she could just find her swimsuit.

*   *   *

She shouldn't have done it, she really shouldn't have, but she was about to put her life in his hands.

Once she'd thrown on her swimsuit, a cotton shirt, and shorts, after dropping her dive bag off at Mariculture's dock deck, Emma headed over to her office in Engineering. She closed the door, picked up her phone, and punched in Pendleton's extension. Kyle's voice said, "Brad Pendleton's office."

"This is Emma out at Gulf Stream. Does Mr. Pendleton have a moment?"

"I'll see," he said.

There was a long pause. Then Pendleton came on. "Emma, hello. Is everything all right out there?"

"Yes, everything's fine. I just had to know . . ." Her voice broke. She couldn't believe she was doing this. She drew a breath. "I'll make this quick. Keith isn't who he says. I've confirmed it. I'm not asking who he really is. I'm sure you have your reasons for whatever it is you're doing. I just need to know, is he as experienced a diver as he says? Is he qualified to train a new diver?"

Pendleton didn't respond.

"Are you still there?" she finally asked.

"Yes." His voice was hoarse. He cleared his throat. "If he says he is qualified, you can believe him."

"Thanks."

She hung up and stared at her trembling hands, feeling as if they belonged to someone else.

Then, with a sigh, she went across the hall. Gloria was at her computer. Ramón stood next to her.

"Excuse me." They looked up at Emma. "Gloria, have you got a minute?"

"Ramón, will you excuse us?"

"Sure." He squeezed past Emma and headed down the corridor toward the bullpen. Emma stepped inside, closed the door, and sat down next to Gloria.

"I'm sorry," she said.

Gloria shrugged. "Forget it."

"No, you were right." Emma grabbed a stray strand of hair and tucked it behind her ear. "I've changed my mind. I'm doing my checkout dive this afternoon."

Gloria's eyes went wide. Her crow's feet appeared and the corners of her mouth turned up. She nodded. "You're doing the right thing."

"I don't know who Keith is or why he's here," Emma said slowly, "but he really pitched in during the storm and proved himself. Pendleton knows who he is and trusts him to be here. And, it'll sound stupid, but . . ." She worried at a loose cuticle. "Whyever he isn't on the up-and-up, my *gut* tells me, underneath it all he's okay."

"You should listen to your gut."

"You're lucky I don't need to fart right now."

"How considerate." Gloria gave her a gentle push. "Go do your dive. I'll take care of the filing and sorting as soon as I get Ramón set up. Maybe you'll even get a chance to meet Louie, after all this time —who knows?"

"Don't get my hopes up." She paused. "Thanks a lot, Gloria. You're a good friend." She came to her feet, pulled the door open. "Wish me luck."

"Good luck. But you won't need it. You'll do great." She held up her quartz egg. "The magic crystal says so."

Emma was just finishing her sunscreen application when the elevator came to a halt and the door opened; Keith and Jess stepped out. Keith handed her a quarter-inch wet suit.

"Aha, your new equipment," he said, gesturing at Emma's tank, BC, and regulator.

"Yeah." She grinned. "New toys."

Jess and Keith squatted next to her and looked them over.

"I see you got the dive computer I recommended," said Jess. "Later model, though."

"They don't make the other one anymore. This model replaces it in their product line."

Keith got his tank and BC ready while Emma struggled into her wet suit. Instantly she was too warm. Keith donned his suit in about a quarter of the time it had taken her. She put on her weight belt, loaded her BC's pockets with the flashlight and flares, and strapped the knife to her calf. Sweating, she followed Keith out, carrying her fins and her tank and BC, onto the dock.

Jess had climbed into the Zodiac. He was handing Keith a bang stick. Emma frowned.

"Do you think we'll have problems with sharks?"

Keith shrugged. "Probably not. Better safe than sorry, though."

Sharks were regularly spotted by Gulf Stream's divers; like other large pelagic fish, they were drawn by the dense sea life attracted by the power plant's nutrient outflow. Emma knew that ordinarily they weren't a problem. Visibility below the first ten feet was usually good, seventy to eighty feet, sometimes a hundred feet or more, and sharks usually only attacked humans in murky waters—biting what they couldn't see to find out if it was edible.

Still . . . she eyed the bang stick nervously.

"Should I have one, too?"

"Uh-uh. You'll have your hands full with the dive basics. I'll take care of antishark defense."

He handed her a coiled rope with D-clips on both ends and clipped his to a ring on his wet suit. She did likewise. They shared Emma's antifogging drops and rinsed their masks in the water that splashed up from below the dock, then steadied each other to don their tanks and fins.

"What's the dive plan?" Emma asked Keith.

"We'll go into the water here and stay on the surface, using our snorkels and letting the current take us out past Engineering and the spillways. Jess will track us in the Zodiac." Keith pointed northward. "You can't see it in this fog, but just upstream of the reefs is a dive platform at thirty feet, marked with an orange buoy. You'll be able to see the buoy once we get past the spillways.

"At that point, follow my lead," Keith said. "I'll signal you when we're getting close. We'll descend on the buoy line to the platform, moor ourselves, and do your checkout."

"Which is . . . ?"

"Everything we did in the pool. Decrease buoyancy and descend, stabilize buoyancy, fill your mask with water and clear it, take the mask off, then put it back on and clear it, share an octopus, buddy breathe, do an emergency ascent." He broke into a grin. "And anything else I can think of." Then he sobered. "Currents are strong out there. If you feel at any point that you're about to lose control, or need help in any way, you let me know right away. Jess will be keeping a close eye on our bubble trails from above, too."

Emma nodded.

"Let's review hand signals. Show me the signal to descend." She gave him a thumbs-down. "Ascend." Thumbs-up. "Level off." She moved her hand side to side with the palm down. "Danger over there." She held her fist out, arm extended, in the direction he'd indicated. "Low on air." She held her fist in front of her sternum. "Out of air." She ran a finger across her throat. "Ears not clearing." She pointed at her ears. "Which way to the nearest bar?" She laughed and mimicked tilting a beer mug into her mouth.

"What do you do if you're out of air and I'm out of sight? Not that that will happen, but let's be thorough."

"An emergency ascent."

"Which is . . . ?"

"Drop my weight belt and ascend in a spiral, one arm extended up, saying ahhhhh all the way."

"Good. Now, if you do get swept away by the current at any point, do a normal ascent and when you surface, if Jess isn't in sight, light one of your flares. I'll surface and come for you, and Jess will also be watching and will come get you. Tread water and don't fight the current. Always keep your eyes open for boats when we surface—those fishing boats out there don't always keep their distance."

"Tell me about it."

"You ready?" he asked.

He and Jess were both looking at her. She donned her mask with trembling hands, looking at the swirling waves beneath her feet. And froze.

Keith will be there to help me. Jess will be close by. I can do this.

But she didn't really believe it. The image of the great wave superimposed itself—*swept away, water in my sinuses, can't breathe!*—

Can't do this. Will. Can't. Must. I'll die!

Keith, standing beside her, cleared his throat. "Take your time."

She shook like a horse twitching off a fly. "Let's do it," she said, put the bit of the snorkel in her mouth, and stepped into a wave.

The swim out past the spillway was no big deal—she merely floated on the surface and let the current carry her. Keith swam just behind her and to her right; if she lifted her head over her shoulder, she could see him. For most of the way, though, she stared into the blue water, pulling air through her snorkel and watching fish swim slowly into sight, then turn away from them. Here, upstream of the power plant effluent, the nutrient layer was minimal and visibility was decent, perhaps forty feet. Before her, in a moment, she made out the Engineering power plant nestled at the water's surface. The beanpole extended far into the depths.

She'd designed it; she shouldn't be surprised by its size. Somehow, though, the way the enormous pole disappeared in the water's depths gave it some great magnitude—imbued it with a majesty it hadn't had on land, lying horizontal in the shipyard.

She lifted her head above water. They were barely kicking their fins, but the few visual references—the dimly glimpsed power plant, and then the buoy lines and spillways—dropped behind so quickly it seemed that they, not Emma and Keith, were moving through the water.

In the wet suit she was definitely too warm. But just downstream of the spillway effluent they ran into faster-moving currents and cells of cold water, which quickly overcame the warmer, ambient Gulf Stream temperatures, and she shivered, glad for the extra protection.

They reached the dive platform's buoy shortly and entwined their hands in the loops of rope provided for that purpose. It was then that the current's strength struck her. Emma's arm muscles stretched; she tightened her grip on the rope. Between the current and the up-and-down motion of the swells, it felt as if she were riding a massive bucking horse.

The fog was light here; with her head above the water she couldn't make out Engineering too well, but northward the reef's buoys were visible through the mist, and the sun was a pale yellow ball overhead.

Jess, holding station just downstream in his Zodiac, gave her a wave; she put her hand on top of her head to signal she was okay. She saw him hold up the handheld radio in its plastic waterproof case to report *divers down* to Control.

Keith was smiling at her. She was grinning so hard her cheek muscles were straining. The fear had been swept away by a desire so strong it made her eyes tear.

My God, it's really going to happen . . .

"Ready to descend?" Keith asked.

Exultation swept from her toes to her head in a heated rush. "Yes!"

"Here we go, then," he said, and gave her the thumbs-down. She returned it, bleeding air from her BC. She pushed herself downward with her free arm and cold water closed over her head with a gurgling sound.

It shouldn't have made a difference—she'd snorkled extensively—but the second she was deeper than her arm could reach she felt cut loose, isolated, in a totally alien world.

Chapter 41

KEITH: **Wednesday, 7 October, 1:40 P.M. EDT**
Gulf Stream I

Keith watched Emma carefully as they hand-over-handed down the rope. The images from Gorey's death—all the blood, the utter stillness of his form—were at the front of Keith's thoughts. He was determined not to have another death on his hands.

This dive, after the head blow he'd received last night, was probably a mistake. But other than tired, he felt fine now, and the rest of the counterterrorist team would be arriving in a few hours; either tonight or at the latest, tomorrow, the ruse would be over. He didn't even know if Emma would speak to him again, after that. This might be his only chance to dive with her and he wasn't going to lose it.

The initial ten feet were murky, a thick soup of phytoplankton thriving in the nutrient-rich outflow from the spillways. Then, almost as if someone had flipped a switch, the visibility increased dramatically. Emma froze on the rope, staring down as yawning blue depths opened beneath her.

Keith had been waiting for this moment. This was not a typical checkout dive—the bottom was over three thousand feet below and held life-forms ranging from great white sharks to the squid that had lost a tentacle in the power plant inflow. But the thing Keith most feared, the thing that was far more likely to kill Emma than any marine life-form, was that she'd panic.

He waved a hand below her head, in her field of vision. She jerked her head up, surprised. Her eyes were wide but her breathing rate was even. *Okay?* he signaled with his hand.

She blinked, then brought her own hand up. *Okay.*

Keith gave her a thumbs-down and Emma continued the hand-over-hand descent, pausing only once to clear her ears.

The diving platform, a three-meter-square plastic grating moored to one of the reef's main cables and made buoyant by Styrofoam pallets beneath, floated in a lucent, aquamarine world devoid of features. They stopped and clipped themselves to ring bolts.

Keith adjusted his buoyancy until he floated just above the platform. Then he motioned for Emma to do the same. It wasn't a fair test since the current and the tether were acting on her, but Emma managed it. He reached out and pulled her mask away from her face, letting it flood with water. She pressed the top of her mask in and cleared it by blowing air out of her nose.

They went through a few other drills as well: Emma breathing on Keith's spare regulator, his octopus; buddy-breathing, taking turns with a single regulator. Then they disconnected from the platform and Keith pointed at Emma and drew his hand across his throat, indicating that she was out of air. He reached up and pulled the regulator from her mouth and pointed at the surface.

Emma launched herself from the platform and kicked for the surface. Keith followed her closely to make sure she was exhaling all the way up. He held his right hand with the fingers stiffened, ready to poke her in the diaphragm if it looked like she wasn't exhaling. Holding her breath as the air expanded in her chest would rupture her lungs, something drilled in over and over, during training, but even experienced divers had come down with embolisms when they forgot to exhale, or when runaway buoyancy compensators lifted them suddenly to the surface.

Emma spiraled up, her arm held overhead, bubbles tumbling steadily from her mouth and nose. As they entered the soup of plankton near the surface, Keith watched overhead, looking for the Zodiac or any other surface vessel. He could hear the sound of the Zodiac's outboard motor, but the bright silver-and-blue surface was unobscured by any shadows. They broke water and Keith heard Emma's deep intake of breath.

"Okay, Tooke?" he said loudly.

"Okay," she said. Keith turned in place and spotted her as she swept her arm back down and captured her regulator.

Keith located Jess, seventy feet away in the boat, and signaled *okay* to him, and then signaled *dive* to Emma. "Let's get back down, before we're carried past the reef," he said. They dropped back into the depths.

When they dropped below the plankton curtain, they'd already crossed the front edge of the reef. Keith led Emma cross-current to one of the marker buoys and snagged the line. Emma missed, but grabbed onto Keith's ankle as she swept past. He extended his arm and pulled her back upcurrent to the rope. They pulled themselves down the line, to the long orange reef flotation tank running down this section of the reef, then down to the plastic netting that was the floor of the reef.

Each reef segment had baffles at its upcurrent edge to deflect the current. The resulting turbulence was not gentle, but one could stay in the vicinity without being swept away.

Artificial structures—tubes, spheres, and boxes made of calcium carbonate—provided niches for a host of smaller fish and invertebrates not usually found in pelagic conditions. Colonies of coralline species of red algae were spreading over the structure, competing with noncoralline red, green, and brown algae as well as barnacles. Larger pelagic fishes cruised nearby, attracted by the abundance of food.

As before, the sheer abundance of fish in and around the reef astounded Keith, overwhelming in its detail and scope. He had to make an effort to concentrate on Emma, to monitor her performance and safety.

He saw movement below the frame and pointed, through the netting, and Emma looked. A seven-foot blacktip shark swam upcurrent under the reef, moving through schools of unconcerned fish. Keith smiled as he saw Emma's breathing rate increase, tracked easily by her exhaled bubbles.

Emma made a fist, pointing at the shark, and then pointed at the bang stick hanging from Keith's BC. He shook his head, smiling. He led her around the corner and a group of yellow-and-black rock beauty angelfish turned in panic and fled their approach. A massive Warsaw grouper gave a lazy flip of its tail, turned on its side, and went under the reef through a gap in the netting to get away from their bubbling approach.

Keith took Emma's hand and kicked up, into the current, which promptly swept them down the reef. When they'd cleared the next baffle, they kicked down again, into the next section, a forest of rockweed.

The greenish-brown weed rippled and leaned in the current, reaching up at an angle. Hand-sized yellowtail damselfish grazed the algae, their black bodies contrasting sharply with their stumpy, rapidly beating, brilliant yellow tails. Other fish used the weed as cover, flitting in and out of the forest. A school of greater amberjacks, each one over four feet long, were working the edges of the growth.

Keith and Emma swept through the rippling forest, surprising fish and each other. As they approached the amberjacks, the sleek silver fish turned as one and streaked off into the deep blue, off to the side of the reef. Emma shook her head. Then she stiffened. Keith thought something was wrong, but she swam down and, hanging onto the reef's structure, pulled her knife from its sheath on her calf and dug something out of the carbonate structure. Keith gave her an inquisitive look. Beaming, she held up a shellfish. It was a small bivalve of some kind. He wondered if it'd been deliberately introduced or its larval form had drifted here and settled.

They cleared the rockweed and dropped down behind the next baffle to another reef. This one was made of old car tires bound to the net in offset stacks that maximized corners and crevices and cul-de-sacs. This reef seemed fully as popular as the calcium carbonate structures from the earlier grids, though algae and barnacles were not as dense.

Keith settled to the web netting, right against the baffle, and checked his gauges. They were at thirty-five feet. He motioned to Emma to let him see her console. Emma's air was down to a thousand psi. Keith's was down to fourteen hundred. He signaled *okay*?

Emma's grin around the mouthpiece told him her answer, even before she raised her hand.

He led her cross-current, behind the baffle, to this grid's flotation tank. There was a gap between the netting and the tank, to discourage any reef encroachment. Holding on to the edge of the net, Keith led Emma under the reef.

The current was strong beneath, accelerated by the hydrodynamic shape of the baffle, and Keith and Emma had to hold on with both hands to avoid being swept away. Shafts of light, shaped by openings in the reef netting, gave Keith the impression of a vast blue cathedral.

He signaled Emma and, when he had her attention, motioned for her to follow. Then he pushed down and let go of the crossbeam they'd been gripping. After a second's hesitation, she followed. In that time he'd been carried four yards downstream. She kicked hard to close the gap and Keith kicked against the current briefly, until she'd caught up.

The reef seemed to be sliding by overhead, the light from the surface winking at them through gaps. Keith kept an eye on his depth gauge and adjusted his buoyancy to remain at forty-five feet, far enough away from the reef to avoid hitting it.

Emma, her eyes on the depths below, started sinking slowly. Keith reached out and touched her shoulder with his fin. She looked at him and her eyes widened; then she kicked hard to rise back up to his level. Keith

pointed at his buoyancy compensator and she added
air a bit at a time until she, too, floated level beneath
the moving reef. Keith gave her the *level off* sign and
she returned an *okay* hand sign.

There were fish below. Three barracuda swam by,
the largest one almost six feet long. Keith waved his
arm and they turned away, going wide around the two
divers. In the distance Keith saw a dark shape swimming effortlessly upcurrent. He pointed it out to
Emma.

It was a manta ray, at the extreme limit of visibility,
on the other side of the reef. The ray was at least ten
feet long, with wings that stretched twenty feet from
tip to tip. The edges of its wings fluttered like silk in
wind; its mouth was open and it was plowing through
a swarm of tiny silver fish, so small that only en masse
were they visible where they lightened the water.

Emma put her hands together in silent applause.

The tail end of the reef slid by a few minutes later.
Keith checked and Emma was down to 550 psi. They
surfaced slowly, turning around, looking for boats, but
the only one they saw was the Zodiac, circling carefully around the rising divers' bubbles.

"Let's go again. Right *now*," Emma said, as they
clung to the side of the Zodiac.

Keith laughed.

Jess took their tanks and BCs, then let them kick
their way up onto the boat. As soon as they were
aboard, he radioed Control and Sean to report *divers
up,* then gunned the outboard and buzzed upcurrent,
toward Gulf Stream.

Emma took her mask off and shook her hair out.

"How was it?" Jess asked.

"Man oh man oh man! That was *great*! Look." She
held up the bivalve. "I found a shell!"

Keith grinned. Her delight was so uncomplicated,

so pure, it made him want to hug her. He laughed again.

"So, teach—did I pass?"

"Well . . ." he drawled.

"I'll push you over," she said, her expression suddenly fierce.

"You pass. I'll sign your temporary card when we get back."

The fierce expression dissolved into that uncomplicated delight again. Keith basked in the glow, warmer than the sun, and for the first time since it had happened, the memory of Gorey's death faded.

Chapter 42

Gabriel stood on the foredeck, watching the water upstream. They'd been holding station in the current, the diesels turning the screws at low RPM. He ran fingers through his hair. "Where the hell are they?"

Mark and Jax were late and their original plan hadn't counted on the fact that the area downstream from Gulf Stream swarmed with fishing boats of all sizes. It was all Boadica could do to hold station without colliding with another boat.

Boadica, on the flying bridge, didn't hear him. He didn't repeat himself. He was sitting at the bow, holding a fishing pole, but the line in the water didn't have any bait, just a weight, barely four feet under the surface.

Boadica increased the throttles and the boat surged forward suddenly. Gabriel had to grab at the railing to regain his balance. He pulled the fishing line up and dropped the pole on the deck.

"Get the rope over," she shouted down to Gabriel.

The rope was a hundred-foot length of five-eighths-inch nylon with a crescent wrench knotted to its end. Gabriel scrambled down the side rail to the stern and pushed the rope's weighted end over the side, feeding it out to keep it from tangling. It streamed out at an angle. When it was all out, he scooted up the ladder to the flying bridge.

"What's happening?"

Boadica pointed toward another fishing boat—a large cabin cruiser almost identical to their own. "The idiots are heading for the wrong boat."

The boat in question was pointed south, into the current, making just enough headway to hold station.

Gabriel couldn't see the divers. "Where are Mark and Jax?"

"You can't see them right now—one of them stuck his head out of the water a minute ago to take a bearing. Then I saw them kicking toward that boat before they sank out of sight."

She crossed in front of the other boat, close enough to earn a shouted curse from its captain, then throttled back, continuing cross-current. "Get back down and watch the rope. Let me know if they grab it. I want to get away from the rest of this mob. We don't want to be seen taking them aboard."

Gabriel climbed back down and pulled a foot of rope back aboard, testing the tension. For a moment there was just the drag from the rope and the wrench. Gabriel was afraid that they'd missed them. Then the rope jerked out of his hands, pulling tight against the stern cleat.

"At least one of them has it!" he shouted.

Boadica throttled back even more, but kept going cross-current at about three knots. Gabriel continued to monitor the rope, hoping they were strong enough to hold on after their two and a half hours in the water, but it stayed tight. Five minutes later, when the nearest boat was at least three hundred yards away, Boadica turned the boat in a tight circle and pointed it back toward the other fishing boats.

Mark and Jax surfaced on the starboard side and Boadica said urgently, "The stern! Get back to the stern where you can't be seen!" They ducked back under and came up behind the boat, clinging to the swimmer's platform.

They looked exhausted.

Boadica and Gabriel made short work of snaking their tanks over the gunwales. Then the two ducked back under the boat and pulled up the bundle of equipment they'd secured to the rudder post. Boadica took this while Gabriel helped the two climb over the side. They went immediately below and stripped off their wet suits, shedding puddles in the cabin.

"The charges are all set," said Mark, when they returned. "We had a close call when we were doing one of the modules. Two divers entered the water not ten feet from us, but they floated out to the reef on the surface, so they didn't see us."

"I thought I'd shit my pants," said Jax. "We were up under the dock at the waterline—and these two go in, plus a guy jumps down into a Zodiac and starts it up. We pulled down to ten feet and exhaled in-*cred*ibly slowly to avoid obvious bubbles. Fortunately, they were gone almost immediately."

Boadica snarled, "That's *two* close calls. You guys nearly went to the wrong boat."

"We would've figured it out," Jax said.

"*After* someone saw you!"

Gabriel interceded. "It's okay. Relax. We're on schedule and we're undetected."

Boadica closed her eyes and shook her head.

Gabriel asked, "How was the placement of the charges?"

Mark said, "Good. On the power plant, we were able to improve on the plan. Because of the fog we were able to set the charges up top. That should break the stem right off and at the same time flood the main compartment of the power plant. It'll go down like a stone."

"Good. What about the hydrogen storage barge?"

"It's all set. We've got charges fore and aft, each lined up on a liquid hydrogen tank."

Gabriel exhaled with a nod. "All right. You two check out the weapons and our demo charge. See if they took on any seawater. Then get some rest."

He headed down into the cabin. He wanted to check the video equipment and go over their announcement one last time.

Boadica entered and knelt by the gear, stowing the tanks in an under-berth locker. "The script's fine. Leave it alone."

Gabriel, bent over the laptop's screen, said, "I'm just reading it over one more time."

It *was* a good script. Succinct, and powerful. Julian Miles, the environmental news reporter he'd chosen to release the announcement and the videotape to, would have the nation's best scoop on the event. Then Gabriel stood to get the videocamera case and unpack it.

Boadica was pulling a bundle out of the berth that Gabriel hadn't seen before—an extra set of twin tanks strapped together with mask, fins, regulator, BC, and weight belt. She stowed the empty tanks in the back of the locker and put the unused tanks at the front.

Boadica saw Gabriel looking at the tanks and said,

"Spare set. We couldn't afford equipment failures."
She slid the locker door shut and stood. "I'm going
up top. You'd better get some rest, too. We board Gulf
Stream I at five-thirty."

Chapter 43

EMMA: Wednesday, 7 October, 3:30 P.M. EDT
Gulf Stream I

Go ahead, she chided herself. *Ask him*. She was on
the dock at Mariculture, waiting for Keith to hand up
their tanks from the Zodiac.

A swell lifted the boat and Keith timed it, lifting
Emma's tank and BC with the swell, halving his work.
Emma snagged the tank valve and laid the tank and
BC down next to the beanpole, then turned back just
in time to accept Keith's tank at the top of the next
swell.

"I have a favor to ask," she finally said.

Keith, hand on the ladder, looked up at her, eyebrows raised.

"I've always had to rely on secondhand reports—
from divers, video cameras, stuff like that. I've never
been able to inspect the exterior of my power plant
firsthand. Could we do a second dive—a short one, at
Engineering?"

Keith looked at Jess.

Jess shrugged. "I've got the time. You'll need
DPVs."

Keith looked back at Emma. "The plant is operational. What about the warm water intakes? I wouldn't
want to dive near them."

"I'll have Two, Five, and Six shut down. Those are the generators on the side that took the damage. We'll stay on that side. Intake is only on the surface, anyway. It shouldn't affect us below fifteen feet."

Keith's expression was thoughtful. "Let's look at our bottom time, computer *and* tables, and if we've got the margin, we'll do it."

At Emma's smile, his face brightened briefly. Again, Emma wondered what had happened to Keith back in Melbourne; he'd been morose all day. And he didn't seem to be the type to get into a barroom brawl.

Jess tied the Zodiac to the dock on the bow line and let the current carry it away from the dock. "I'll be over in Science when you're ready."

Emma and Keith stripped off their wet suit tops and took their tanks up the elevator to the compressor station on the utility deck. Keith put them in the tank recharging bath, a tub of refrigerated water, and hooked up the compressor hoses.

Sean stuck his head out of his tiny rat hole of an office and, when he saw Keith and Emma, waved.

"About time, Tooke!" he called, grinning.

The bank of reservoir bottles—tanks taller than Emma—filled both tanks quickly up to their rated three thousand psi, without even triggering the compressor.

Then they went back down to the dock level and sat down outside to go over the dive tables. Keith had her figure the nitrogen time for both of them, giving her his max depth and down time.

She reported, "We could do it now and stay up to an hour at less than fifty feet."

"Okay—we'll wait a half hour and do it. I'll go check out a pair of DPVs from Sean if you'll go get me a Coke. Got the cotton mouth pretty bad."

Emma licked her own lips, surprised at how thirsty she was. "Two Cokes. Coming up. Diet or leaded?"

Keith pinched his waist through the neoprene of the wet-suit pants. "Leaded. I'll burn it off in the water."

They met back on the dock a few moments later and sat on the grating, backs against the bulkhead, on the shaded side of the shaft. The breeze had shifted to the west and the fog was lifting—merely a glassy haze now, it clung to the modules and softened their edges.

Emma looked out at the catwalks that reached like outstretched arms to the other modules, and up at the module overhang that shaded them from the sun; she listened to the slapping of the waves and the bird calls that echoed across the water. She drank the last bit of her diet cola and said, "I nearly backed out at first, when we were about to do our entry."

Keith nodded, still looking at the water. "Thought I saw something then. You seemed to have overcome it, though."

She twitched her shoulders. "I don't know if I would have, if you'd pushed me. You took the pressure off when you said to take my time."

Keith tilted his head to look at her. "What was it about?"

"I nearly drowned, in the hurricane."

His eyes widened. "What happened?"

She brought her knees up. "When the great wave hit I was out on the stairs. The wave came down on top of me. By pure chance it threw me against the stair rail, halfway around the module and a story higher up. I managed to grab it. Otherwise, I'd be fish bait." She shuddered and laid her chin on her knee.

"Jesus," he said. An arm went around her, and then another. She hugged back and her cheek pressed against his pectoral. Being wrapped in a Keith hug felt good.

He patted her back. His chin rested on her shoulder. She couldn't see his face, but his back muscles tensed and he said, "I saw a man killed last night. I couldn't do anything to help him. It haunts me.'' He paused. "I thank God you found that railing and hung on."

She straightened and studied him. *Saw a man killed? Who* are *you?*

Silently, with his eyes, with a slight shake of his head, he was begging her not to ask.

She rested her cheek on his chest again. Give me this moment, she thought. I'll face hard truth later, whatever the truth about Keith is. Give me this time.

Following Keith's example, Emma trimmed her weight belt and left off the wet-suit hood and pants. The water felt ridiculously warm after the colder water downstream.

It took Emma several minutes to get used to the DPV. Keith kept to the surface under the fog, in the open area between the modules, until Emma was comfortable with the controls. Then they drifted downstream to the plant.

She started at the surface, where the catwalk had ripped at the edge of the plant, and inspected the welds. She knew they'd been ultrasonically checked, but it was nice to look with her own eyes, especially when the welds were underwater. Then they descended slowly to the bottom edge of the plant, at thirty feet, holding position against the current with the DPVs.

The water rushing past her made her feel like she was flying through the water, especially when she looked away from the OTEC plant. She had an urge to turn the DPV cross-current and just *go*, fly through the water, forever, as free and fast as a dolphin or a shark.

She turned her attention to Keith's legs, the way the hairs floated in the current across hard muscle lines, and decided there were other reasons to remain a temporary visitor to this world.

The plant exterior, she was pleased to see, was doing very well. There was some algae and barnacle for-
mation, but the 410 stainless the plant was made from
was resisting corrosion well. There was just the hint
of discoloration in areas. She knocked a few barnacles
free with her knife and smiled when they scraped free
without trouble.

She eyed the dark shadowy area under the plant
wistfully. It would be nice to go beneath the plant all
the way to the beanpole and inspect the annular locks.
She pointed that way and Keith shook his head, pointing at the overhang. She understood. For a new diver,
overhangs were a no-no.

On their way to the surface, floating just behind
Keith, she *almost* goosed him. Only the secret, the
thing that Keith was hiding, kept her from doing it.

But, *man*, she wanted to.

After showering, and cleaning and stowing her dive
equipment, she went back to Engineering. Gloria was
on her knees in Emma's office, surrounded by piles of
paper. Emma threaded her way carefully to her seat
and flopped into her chair, beaming at Gloria's inquisitive look. She answered the unspoken question,
lifting her hands in a shrug and then dropping them.

"Words fail me."

"Oh, really?"

"Yes, really." She frowned, good-naturedly, at
Gloria's titillated grin. "No, not Keith; the dive."

Television, books, photos—they so dimly reflected
the reality that they almost did it a disservice. How
could she make anyone, anyone who hadn't experienced it, know what it was like to look at the surface
of the ocean, now, and suddenly see it not as a barrier,
a featureless surface, but as an interface—passage to
a world of great marvels? She felt like Alice must

have; she had passed through a looking glass, briefly, had romped in an alien sphere.

She held up to the light the bivalve she'd found on the reef. It was a little petricola shell of sōmc kind, that had burrowed into the reef's carbonate structure. She had no idea how it had gotten there: hitchhiked on a passing boat, perhaps. It was a common shell, and—except for its special meaning to her—not especially collectible. She thought about her Oregon triton, and remembered the summer with her grandparents in the San Juan Islands off Washington State.

Back then, she'd discovered that the world held vast secrets. Reality held magic. She had wanted to unearth those secrets, find that magic. To understand it all. She had made a vow then to cling to her integrity and her vision—not embrace a culture of surfaces and appearances, the way her mother had; not embrace a culture of status and wealth-seeking, as her father had. And in one sense, perhaps, she had remained true to that vision, but in another way she'd made both her parents' mistakes.

After their divorce and her mother's death—and after the abortion and the breakup with Gabriel—she had neglected a part of herself, turned away from that wise and frightened adolescent. She had held on to her love of the ocean in her choice of careers, but chose engineering more because it was a good career path, a way to gain security—money and status—than because it had absorbed her intellect; she had busied herself with the surfaces not of society but of her profession. And she'd tried numerous relationships after Gabriel but had avoided real intimacy, kept herself so isolated from her partners emotionally that no bond could form.

The other day she'd criticized Gabriel for putting his activism before people, but who was she to talk? She'd put her career ahead of people. Ahead of everything. She hadn't looked within enough, hadn't opened herself to experience enough. Hadn't opened herself to *people* enough.

I can change that, she thought. I may not have pursued the ideal career, but I've shaped it now into something I like; I don't have to chuck it all. I just need to add some other things into the mix.

Sometimes, though, she thought with a sigh, that sort of change was easier decided than done.

Gloria was watching her. Finally she shrugged, and set the shell down. "It was the most wonderful thing that's ever happened to me. That's all."

Gloria smiled. "I take it you passed your checkout dive."

Emma pulled her temporary PADI c-card out and showed it to Gloria. "It's official."

Gloria took it and examined it. "Who'd'a thunk it? After all this time." She handed it back with a big, happy smile. "Nice work, chief. I'm proud of you."

The phone rang. Emma snatched up the receiver. "Tooke here."

"Emma, this is Brad Pendleton."

"Oh! Hello, Mr. Pendleton; what can I do for you?"

Gloria motioned toward the door with a querying look; Emma nodded. Gloria let herself out.

Pendleton's voice was leaden and slow. "I'm calling to let you know that I've suspended Phil and Dennis and ordered an independent auditor to examine our books."

Emma grimaced, not sure whether guilt or relief was her primary emotion. "Oh."

"I plan to notify all the company officers and the other partners tonight," he went on, "and tomorrow morning make a call to the regulators about the illegal payment. I'll also be notifying our existing clients. As well as Chrysler, CalEPA, and PG and E."

Emma pushed her damp hair back, which she had left loose. Her mouth was dry; she licked her lips.

"Do you think . . . it'll bring us down?"

"I don't know. The deal with Chrysler, PG and E, and California may collapse, and we may lose many—if not most—of our existing grants and hydrogen and mariculture contracts over this." Pendleton sighed. "Some may stick with us, I hope. After dealing with the regulators, mending relationships with clients will be my first priority."

"Mr. Pendleton—" Emma hesitated, biting a cuticle. "Brad. I know how hard this must be for you. I feel responsible."

"No." His tone was sharp. "No, Emma. You did what you had to do." His voice broke off. After a moment he spoke again. "I was a hippie during the sixties; did you know?"

Emma's eyes went wide. Pendleton as a hippie? She shook her head, cleared her throat. "No, I didn't."

"I grew my hair down to my waist and spent my college years barefoot in jeans, smoking dope, protesting war, preaching love and peace and harmony with nature."

"That's a little hard to imagine."

"Is it?" He chuckled, with a hint of the warmth she was more accustomed to. "I suppose I've picked up protective coloring over the years. I imagine it's become more than that, by now."

His words reminded her of her own, earlier reflections. Since he seemed inclined toward self-revelation, Emma gave rein to her curiosity. "How did you end up where you are now?"

"Inheritance, in large part. I always thought I'd give away the family fortune when it came into my hands, but shortly after I finished law school, when my parents died and I inherited, I discovered a knack for finance and commerce. So I decided to put the money to use.''

"Gulf Stream."

"Ultimately, yes, though it took a long time to decide what I wanted to do. . . . I was partly inspired by what Biosphere II *tried* to do, back when.''

"You *have* made a difference. People know now it can be done.''

"Hmmm. I'm not so sure. But I've never kidded myself that Gulf Stream I is anything but an incredibly risky gamble. The economics were marginal, at best. When I invested most of my fortune in Gulf Stream I, I knew there was a decent chance I'd lose it all." A deep sigh. "I just thought I'd lose it to bad market conditions or short-sighted investors. Not because my trusted colleagues would do something so staggeringly stupid as to pay off a regulator.''

Emma didn't know what to say. She looked out the window. She could see the breakwater buoys bobbing in the waves, and sea birds floating on the water.

"But in any event, what happened certainly wasn't your fault, Emma, and you did right to come to me. If you hadn't, sometime down the line this whole mess might very well have been discovered by the authorities. By voluntarily reporting, we gain a certain amount of credence. It may not help, in the end, if a bloodthirsty prosecutor decides to use us to make his career, or if our clients and potential clients refuse to do business with us, but . . . as I see it, the facts are clear-cut. I've consulted outside counsel, and there are no legal grey areas here. The law was broken. We have to report.''

Emma swallowed, hard. "Thanks for calling to let me know. May I tell Flo?''

"I'd prefer to tell her, and Thomas, myself. I'll be

coming out this evening at seven-thirty and would like to hold a staff meeting with the three of you. I have other announcements to make, as well.''

"May I let the staff know that you're coming out, then? They'll want to gussy things up a bit.''

"I suppose that would be all right.''

"Very good. I'll see you tonight.''

She hung up the phone. A lump had formed in her throat.

There was a knock on the door.

"Enter!''

Ben stuck his head in. "Hey, chief, we've got someone on the radio who says he's a friend of yours.''

Emma stood, wiping away rogue tears. Ben, tactfully, didn't ask.

"On the radio?'' she repeated.

"Yeah—they're in the area on a pleasure boat and they want to dock. Name's Gabriel Cervantes.''

"Oh!'' She started, and glanced at her watch. It was five-thirty. The timing was awful.

"Tell him—'' we don't have time, she started to say, and then stopped, glancing at the shell, still wet, that sat on her desk. *Make time for your dreams. Make time for people.*

She sighed. Things were hardly more hectic right now than they usually were, and how could she turn him away, after inviting him? And for that matter, if the place went out of business in a few weeks, what difference would a few moments of her time away from the helm make?

"Yes, please do go ahead and authorize them to board. I'll give them the two-penny tour. Meanwhile, Ben''—he had turned to go, and now paused—"Pendleton is coming out tonight to have a look around and make some announcements. He'll be here in about two hours. Could you pass the word around?''

Ben's eyebrows shot up. "Two hours? Holy shit."

"I know it's not much time," she said.

"The place is pretty discombobulated, with all the repairs. But we'll mobilize the troops and do what we can."

"That's all I can ask," Emma said. "He'll understand." She didn't say what she was really thinking: that Pendleton would probably hardly notice, under the circumstances.

Chapter 44

KEITH: **Wednesday, 7 October, 4:12 P.M. EDT**
Gulf Stream I

Before rinsing his dive equipment, Keith went to the Engineering bullpen. The place was packed, and everyone was busy—bent over computer screens, or arguing over drawings on the drafting table at the back by the portal. The noise level was high. He knew none of the dozen men and women there, though a couple greeted him.

A young man was at his computer. He cleared his throat. "I'll be needing to use my computer now."

The man looked up, startled. "Oh, is this yours? Someone told me this was a spare I could use." He gathered his papers. "Sorry."

"Don't sweat it."

Keith slid into the still-warm seat as the young man slid out. He rebooted his computer and checked his mail. There was a message in his in-box from s.purvis@netcom.com at 2:43 P.M.:

KEITH

THOUGHT WE'D GOT ALL THE EXPENSE STUFF VERIFIED
BUT MILDRED FOUND SOME MORE NOTES IN THE MID-
GLOBAL ACCOUNT FOR JULY. DO THESE LOOK RIGHT TO
YOU?

RENTAL CAR	706.27
FAX	13.05
PHONE	38.27
HOTEL (SEATTLE)	783.15
FEDERAL EXPRESS	56.12
PHOTOCOPYING	26.03
SAMPLE DRILL BORES	507.02
MEALS (SEATTLE)	462.30
AIRFARE (SEATTLE)	705.39
LAB WORK	711.43
AIRFARE (DC)	616.06
HOTEL (DC)	58.13

IF YOU COULD LOOK THEM OVER, I'D APPRECIATE IT.
BEST,
SAM

He printed out the message, then picked up the
phone and punched in his Melbourne Harbor Suites
number to check for messages. Tricia had called less
than a half hour before, according to the automated
time stamp.

"Give me a call," her voice said. "I have an update
for you on the mystery woman."

Keith punched in her business number and asked to
speak to her. The receptionist put him on hold. After
a moment Tricia came on.

"Keith, I think I have something for you," she said.
"Do you remember Rachael Whitehorse?"

Keith pressed a finger in his ear to shut out the
conversations in the surrounding cubicles. "Of
course." She'd been Greenpeace's press liaison, back

when he had been a staff member.

"Well, I faxed her a copy of your drawing and she just called me back a little while ago. She's convinced this is a picture of one of her press contacts from way back. There's something odd about the whole thing, too . . . but I'll let Rachael fill you in. Have you got a pen handy?"

"Fire away," he said, and jotted down the number she reeled off. It was a Washington, D.C., number.

"Thanks a million, Tricia. I owe you one. Is she in right now?"

"She should be—I spoke to her about an hour and a half ago, and she said she'd be in the office all afternoon."

"Thanks. Um . . . how are you feeling?"

"A little queasy. Sleepy. Otherwise, fine."

"Be sure to get plenty of rest," he said, and rolled his eyes. Old habits died hard. It was more than that, though. She'd meant a lot to him, and still did. It struck him that he wanted her as a friend.

"Thanks, Keith." A pause. "Come by sometime, next time you're in Houston. I'd like to introduce you to Ralph."

"Will do. Perhaps I can introduce you to someone, too."

"Oh?" She sounded intrigued, and pleased. "That's good to hear."

"I'll call you," he said, and hung up, wearing a mild smile. Nice change, feeling good about Tricia again.

He dialed the number she had given him. A woman's voice said, "Congresswoman Aldridge, press information office; may I help you?"

"I'm calling for Rachael Whitehorse."

"This is she."

"Rachael, this is Keith Hellman."

"Keith! How are you? I just got off the phone a

while ago with Tricia—'' A bell started tinkling in the background as she spoke. ''Can you hold?''

''Sure.''

There was a click, and Brahms's Symphony Number Four in E Minor played into his ear. After about three minutes Rachael came back on. ''Sorry. Occupational hazard.''

''It's all right. I know Tricia sent you the drawing —''

She cut in at the sound of another phone ringing. ''Hang on.'' Another Brahms-filled delay ensued, this one only a few seconds in duration. ''Sorry. It's a busy day. Anyhow, yes, Trish faxed me that drawing. The picture looks an awful lot like someone I knew back when we were in Okinawa. I'll remember the name in a minute; it was part of the weirdness. Dark. That's it. Jean, JoAnne? No, it was Jean. Jean Dark.''

''Who was she?''

''Remember how we got stranded in Naha during the typhoon?''

''Yeah.''

''Well, this woman showed up right after the storm, while we were waiting for clearance to leave port. She claimed she was a reporter with *Buzzworm* and had flown out to do a story on us.''

'' 'Claimed'?''

''Exactly. The incident sticks in my mind, because of her name, and because I remember thinking it was a little odd that my usual contact from *Buzzworm* hadn't contacted me to tell me she was coming. Of course, with the time difference and the international factors, we weren't exactly easy to reach, so I didn't think much of that part of it at the time.''

''What was weird about her name?''

Her phone tinkled again. ''Hang on.'' Another delay, this one several minutes long. The Brahms had been replaced by a baroque composition: Handel's

Water Music. She cut back in in the midst of the trumpets. "Where was I?"

"You said something was odd about her name—"

"Oh, yeah. I was a big Mark Twain fan when I was growing up. He wrote this account of Joan of Arc's life that made her out to be a big heroine. So I got on this Joan of Arc kick. Only her real name was Jeanne D'Arc. Jean Dark. Get it?"

"Got it." He frowned, and scratched himself a note.

"I asked this woman if there was any relation, just making a joke, and she, well—" Rachael coughed. "Got a little strange. Said as a matter of fact, she'd been Joan of Arc. I laughed because I thought she was joking, but she gave me this really scary, cold stare, and I dropped it."

"Wow."

"Yeah. Anyhow, I blew it off—I mean a lot of people are a little strange, you know? She held a series of interviews with several staff members. I think she even had a short interview with you; do you remember it?"

He gasped. "Oh my God." He did. White hair, ash-dark eyes. Questions, questions, questions.

"She spoke to a couple of the others as well, but during our reception that evening, the same night of the explosion at the cannery, she canceled the rest of the interviews. That was the last I saw of her. No article ever came out of it."

"What did you make of it?"

"I didn't know what to make of it. But my *Buzz-worm* contact did finally confirm that she had pitched an article to him some weeks before we met. She'd told him she would be traveling to Okinawa on other business and could set up some interviews—though they didn't exactly authorize it, as she'd represented. They didn't have a contract with her or anything. She

never followed up with him afterward, either. A real
flake.''

"Hmmm." He scratched more notes.

"Where has she resurfaced?" she asked, and then
said, "Hang on—" as a phone rang again in the background.

"Do you have anything else?" he asked hurriedly.

"Not really."

"Then I'd better sign off. Thanks."

"My pleasure," she told him, and the line went
dead.

He doodled, and thought. His memories of the interview were vague at best, try as he might to remember some useful detail. Just the face. He'd found her
attractive; that was why he recalled the face. Then he
remembered: he had asked her out, that night of the
explosion. She'd politely declined.

So. In 1978 she had been snooping around their
ship, this woman who thought she'd been Joan of Arc,
and she had been on the ship the evening of the explosion. They'd had no real security; she could easily
have planted explosives in their first mate's cabin. But
the dockworker who had tried to frame their first mate
had said an American *man* had paid him off.

Keith thought about her disguise, when he'd caught
her after she'd killed Gorey. She was certainly capable
of looking like a man. Or she might have had an accomplice.

But it didn't make sense. Why would she have acted
on an *anti*environmental plot in Okinawa, and be in
on a *pro*environmental one now?

Keith laid the pencil down and sat back, rubbing his
brow. Something was missing. Finally, with a sigh, he
logged off his computer.

He spotted the young man who had been using it
before, now standing with some others at a nearby

cubicle. "You can use my desk now, if you want," Keith told him, and left.

Back at his quarters, his mystery roommate wasn't there—again—but had been there since Keith had last been in the room earlier in the day; a robe was slung across the dresser and some rumpled clothes now lay on the lower bunk. Keith pulled out his dictionary, a pen, and the message from Barnes, and got to work.

616.06	(SEARCH)
58.13	(NEGATIVE)
706.27	(THREE)
13.05	(AGENT)
38.21	(ARRIVE)
783.15	(WITH)
56.12	(BARN)
26.03	(AND)
507.02	(PENDANT)
462.30	(NINETEEN)
705.39	(THIRTY)
711.43	(TODAY)

Nineteen-thirty: 7:30 P.M. Barn and Pendant must mean Barnes and Pendleton, arriving with the counterterrorist team to make an announcement to the senior staff. And search negative must mean the terrorists had slipped away. He thought about Gorey and felt his fingernails bite into the palms of his hands.

He glanced at his watch. It was almost five o'clock. He decided to shower, clean his equipment, and then catch a little sleep before they arrived. With the forthcoming meetings, evacuations, and interrogation of Emma (he winced), it would doubtless be a long night.

Chapter 45

Gabriel and three others—two men and a woman—
were climbing onto the dock as Emma neared Mariculture on the catwalk. They wore baggy windbreakers
and pants, which the breeze snatched at. The woman
carried a nylon bag slung across her shoulder Flo
stood on the dock, shaking the visitors' hands as they
debarked a white-and-yellow yacht.

As she reached the annular walkway at the beanpole
Emma called out and waved down through the grating.
They all looked up.

"I'll be right there!"

"No," Flo said, "go in and wait at the elevator.
We'll pick you up on our way up."

Emma stepped into the antechamber. A moment
later, the cage door opened and she stepped into the
elevator, smiling broadly, arms extended to give Gabriel a hug. He accepted the embrace but seemed stiff,
and his glance flitted toward his female companion.
She and Gabriel must have something going. Emma
nodded at her with a welcoming smile and extended
a hand.

"Emma Tooke. Gulf Stream's chief operations officer."

"Nice to meet you." The woman took Emma's
hand. Her grip was firm and she gave Emma a warm
smile. Her hand was cold, full of bones and tendons.
"Boadica Jones."

Emma shook hands with the other two: a stocky, sunburned, rather surly-looking sort—Sam Feinway— and a man fairly tall, though not as tall as Emma, and thin, with a narrow face that seemed a little sad— Randy Pyle.

"Welcome to Gulf Stream I," she said, as Flo punched the button to take them up to the utility deck. "Flo, may I give them a tour of your playground?"

"Of course." They reached the utility deck, and one of Flo's people stuck her head in the antechamber and called to her. "Excuse me," Flo said. "Enjoy your tour." With a brisk nod she stepped out and walked away.

"Come on," said Emma, pressing *Main* on the elevator controls. "I'll give you a quick tour of our Mariculture unit here, and then we'll make the circuit through each of the modules and end up back here. The tour will have to be rather rushed, I'm afraid— our CEO is flying in tonight and we're trying to get ready."

Gabriel and his companions exchanged looks. "That's quite all right," he said. "We understand."

The elevator came to a stop. "Right this way, then." She led them toward the tapered end of the deck. "These over here"—she gestured toward the two stories of long, narrow PVC vats that filled the main deck—"are the shellfish farms. Lobsters on the mezzanine, shrimp below."

Gabriel had come up beside her. He pointed at the dimly lit mezzanine. "What's the blue and green lighting for?"

"Well, lobsters in particular don't like much light. We use dim blue-green light to simulate underwater conditions for the animals. It improves breeding and growth. The lights are also on a day-night cycle for the same reason. Shrimp aren't as picky about light, so the lighting's a little better on the deck level." She ducked under a pipe. "Watch your heads. This way."

They reached a shrimp runway. The white PVC vat was about chest-high, three feet wide, and perhaps forty feet long, with baffles every few feet. Murky water coursed down its length, and inside, the algae-coated floor and walls were alive with shrimp of all sizes: a moving, rust-colored blanket of insectoid limbs and bodies. Emma stuck a hand into the icy water.

"Go ahead. Stick your hands in," she said. Gabriel went first; the woman, Boadica, and the other two men followed suit. Gabriel whistled and shook water off his hand. "Cold."

"This water is piped directly from the OTEC plant's cold water outflow. It's nutrient rich and approximately fifty degrees Fahrenheit, prime temperature for these exotic prawns, and it also provides food for them, which means we don't have to feed them as much."

Emma grabbed a juvenile shrimp and lifted it to let them see; russet-colored, it curled its fanned tail, waved its antennae, and stared at her with shining, black-marble eyes. She put it back in the water.

"How do you harvest them?" Randy asked. "By hand?"

"No, we use sieves that slide in between the baffles. The sieves catch only shrimp larger than thirty centimeters. It's a quick and easy method, and we avoid removing shrimp that are too small and haven't had a chance to reproduce. We harvest about five hundred pounds of shrimp a week, ship it to port aboard our trawler, *La Pescadora,* and air-freight it to restaurants all over the U.S."

She took them to a stairway and up to the mezzanine, and walked them along a row of lobster vats. Dimly, they could see the lobsters crawling around in the baffled vats.

"Pretty much the same as the prawn vats, just bigger critters," she said. "They maintain a freeboard of twelve inches here to keep the lobsters from escaping."

Then she led them through to a room where two men were using pitchforks to load seaweed into a large metal hopper. Rollers at the bottom of the hopper squeezed the brownish-red weed flat onto a metal conveyor belt that marched continuously into a long series of drying ovens.

"This is *Porphyra,* a red alga, one of the varieties we grow on the reef, in the outflow from our power plant. We're drying it for direct consumption, as nori. People use it in soups and sushi. We also sell various kinds of unprocessed seaweed to plants that make guar gum and guareen, fillers and stabilizers used for food products and pharmaceuticals."

"You must use a lot of electricity in those ovens," Gabriel said.

Emma laughed. "Quite a bit, but I need *more* uses for our power, not fewer. We're using less than sixty-five percent of our capacity. For instance—" She led them next door to an antechamber where another door, white and insulated, was mounted against a metal wall. She pulled the handle back. Icy cold air spilled out, forming condensate fog that swirled around their legs. Inside, metal shelves held boxes and plastic bags. "We freeze our harvested fish, prawns, and lobsters. This freezer is twice as big as my apartment back in Melbourne Beach and we have four more of them on this module—and another one in Residential. I'd take you in but none of us are really dressed for it." She shut the door. "We've got a lot of projects in the planning stages to use up some of the excess power."

From there, she took them to the beanpole antechamber and summoned the elevator. "The top two decks of Mariculture are offices, plus some labs and experimental pilot projects, so given our time constraints I'm not going to bother with those. Let's head on over to Engineering. I'll show you our OTEC plant and the hydrogen and wastewater plants.''

Boadica whispered something to Sam and Randy while Gabriel turned to Emma. ''We're especially interested in your control center. I understand you have some state-of-the-art computerized process controls. Groundbreaking stuff.'' The others nodded emphatically.

Emma nodded. ''Why don't we stop there first, then?''

''That would be perfect,'' Boadica said.

Ben and Rob were at the console, conferring. System displays for the reef, power plant, and hydrogen plant were on-screen. Mac was picking up a printout from the printer along the wall, and Nikki was filling out paperwork in the office behind the inner door of the room. Emma ushered the four visitors in and gestured at the banks of equipment and electronics. ''This is our control center.''

She'd barely gotten the words out when someone shoved her aside and the inner door slammed shut. Guns were suddenly in the air, everywhere, waving about, and Gabriel and his friends were yanking Ben and Rob away from the console.

Emma said, ''Stop! *What are you doing?*'' and made a grab for Gabriel's arm—missed, stumbled— and found herself staring into a gun barrel hole.

''Don't fucking move.''

She went rock-still. Boadica, whose gun was in Emma's face, grabbed Emma by the arm, and half pushed, half dragged her over to the console, barrel jabbing her in the kidney.

''Gabriel,'' Boadica said, ''disable external communications. Hurry.'' Gabriel passed Emma and went into the switch room. She heard the metal cabinets clang open. Tearing, banging, and electrical spitting noises ensued. "Jax, secure the rest of them. Mark, the doors." Then Boadica turned to Emma and gestured at the windows. "Close the storm shutters. *Now.*"

Arguing would be stupid. Emma brought up the proper screen and typed a command into the console. Grey shutters slid down over the window, obscuring the view.

Their guns bristled around the room, terrifyingly large; she was conscious of all their locations and angles of trajectory. But by now she had gained an artificial calm. Her mind seemed tethered to her body, and the chaotic signals of its terror, by only a long, thin strand.

While she closed the shutters one of the other two men herded Mac, Rob, and Ben into the tiny office with Nikki in it, next to the control room door, and the third man locked first the inner door and then the outer door. The man herding Emma's staff told the four of them to put their hands on their heads and sit on the floor.

I can't believe this is happening, Emma thought.

"Do what they say," she said, as the others looked at her. "No heroics."

She caught Ben's glance through the office window as he knelt down. His gaze flicked to the cabinet where the radios were kept, and he lifted his eyebrows. She gave him a tiny nod. The larger of the two other men, whom she knew as Sam but Boadica had called Jax, stood at the door entrance, his gun trained on the people in the office.

"We are taking over your facility," Gabriel said. "Cooperate with us and no one will be hurt."

A bubble of rage rose up through the fear. "You *fucker,*" she whispered. Her voice rose and she started toward him. The man who had called himself Randy interposed himself, blocking her access to Gabriel—over his shoulder she leveled a finger. "You lied! You used me!"

He stared at her, poker-faced. "Well, yes. I did. It was necessary."

"Necessary?"

She turned her back and lowered her head, pressing fists against her temples, sick with rage and fear. I'll get you for this, she thought, trembling. I'll get you.

Pull it together, Tooke. Your people need you. She lowered her arms, drawing a deep breath, and turned back around. "What do you want with us?"

"We'll get to that. Mark, take the demo charge up to the hydrogen storage tanks."

Demo charge? Near the hydrogen tanks?

"Wait!" she said, urgently. They trained their guns on her again. Emma swallowed hard. "You can't plant an explosive charge near the hydrogen tanks. You'll take the whole module down. And if Engineering goes down, so do all the others."

"Bullshit," said the one she'd known as Randy, whom Gabriel had called Mark. "Why would an explosion on *top* of the module take the whole thing down? She's lying."

"No. Listen. If one of the tanks goes, the shock wave will shove the module downward suddenly, causing a large, quick decrease in buoyancy that could overwhelm the buoyancy controllers." She took a breath. "Why take the risk? Your demonstration would be just as effective, and a lot less risky, if you plant your demo charge on top of one of the other modules. Mariculture, perhaps." The one with no valuable equipment or gardens. "Just as many people will see it, and it'll be far away from the hydrogen."

Boadica gave Emma a quizzical little smile. "But

we *want* it close to the hydrogen. We want a big boom."

Gabriel spoke up. "Not if it'll sink the module prematurely." Emma stared at him. *Prematurely?* "A smaller explosion will serve our purpose just as well. And perhaps there are locations up top here that are safer than others." He turned to Emma. "Are there?"

Emma eyed Gabriel and considered whether she should lie. She decided not to. "There are two nitrogen tanks up there, off to one side. They're green and labeled. They'd be the safest spot for a *small* explosive charge. *If* you're careful about planting the charge well away from any white tanks or pipes, or the piping manifold."

Gabriel told the others, "It's not as big a boom as our original plan called for, but it'll still work, and there's less risk."

Mark shrugged. "I say she's lying, but what the hell. I guess we can live with a smaller boom."

Boadica gave Emma a long, thoughtful stare. Then she handed the nylon bag she carried to Mark. "All right. Do it."

Mark left through the outer door. At that moment someone tried the inner door's handle, jiggled it, and knocked. Gloria's voice said, "Rob? Ben? What gives, you guys?"

Shit.

Boadica grabbed a handful of Emma's shirt in back, pressed her gun into Emma's kidney, and propelled her to the inner door. "Open it."

Sweat crawled down Emma's torso. She cracked the door open. Gloria tried to push the door farther open, but Emma jammed it with her foot.

"Uh-uh. We're having some problems in the hydrogen plant and I have Control isolated right now. For safety reasons. Come back later."

"This is a joke, right?" Then Gloria took a closer look at Emma's face. "What's wrong?"

The metal door of the control room office cabinet rattled, and Emma heard a scuffle. Tight in Boadica's grip, she caught a glimpse past the door of Ben getting a gun butt in the mouth. He went down with a groan. Jax struck him at least twice more.

"What's going on in there?" Gloria repeated during this, pushing at the door. "Emma, are you guys all right?"

Emma shook her head, helplessly. Boadica, hidden behind the door, pulled Emma back and opened it and, when Gloria had entered, closed it again and locked it.

"Into the office," she said, gesturing with her gun. "On the floor with the others."

Gloria stared at Boadica, then at Emma. Her face drained of color.

"Do it," Emma said. Her facial muscles were made of stone, but she felt like crying. Nikki and Mac were tending to Ben, who was huddled on the floor by the cabinet. Emma couldn't see Ben too well, but she saw blood on Nikki's and Mac's hands, and on the floor. Jax handed a radio to Boadica. "He was trying to use this. That cabinet's full of them."

Emma stared at Gabriel, back at the console. At least he had the grace to look chagrined.

"Get them all out here," Boadica said. Jax began grabbing and shoving. As the prisoners stumbled out, she gestured. "On your stomachs. Kiss the floor. Hands on your heads." She hung on to Emma by the back of her shirt as the others lay down on the floor of the control room.

Emma had calmed a little. They hadn't fired their guns yet, and Emma had a feeling they didn't want to if they could avoid it. It'd bring the whole facility population down on them.

"What do you hope to accomplish with all this?" she asked. "Do you honestly think you can keep the entire facility at bay, forever?"

"If they value your lives," Boadica said.

A complicated knock sounded at the outer door; Gabriel went over and opened it. Mark slipped inside, short of breath.

"Charge planted," he reported.

"Any difficulties?"

"None. A couple people saw me but they didn't ask any questions."

Of course not; the place was crawling with contractors no one knew, doing things to equipment that the regular staff didn't always know about in advance. Emma rubbed at her face.

"Here's what's going to happen," Gabriel told Emma. "We are going to set off the demo charge. Then you're going to get on the loudspeaker and announce that an emergency condition exists in the hydrogen plant. You will order all personnel to evacuate immediately."

Emma looked at Gabriel. She folded her arms. "Not until you tell me what the hell is going on here. Who are you people? *What do you want with us?*"

With a growl, Boadica grabbed Emma at the nape of the neck and ground the gun's barrel into her breast. Boadica's face was inches from Emma's; her breath smelled of mint, and her blue eye color was from contact lenses. She hissed, "Don't get cute with us or I'll see your fucking guts splattered all over the walls."

Emma gritted her teeth against the pain; tears sprang to her eyes. Gabriel grabbed Boadica's gun arm and pulled her back. "Lighten up!"

Boadica loosened her grip on Emma, though she didn't lower the gun. Gabriel told Emma, "We're Wild Justice, and we're staging an environmental demonstration at your facility."

Wild Justice? It sounded like a preadolescent garage band. Emma refrained from saying so. "But our work benefits the environment! Our very existence promotes sustainable development. Why are you picking on us?"

" 'Sustainable development'? Don't make me laugh," Boadica said. "Sustainable development is a lie. A phrase coined by big business to allow them to continue plundering nature, while the populace is placated with clever words and sophisticated explanations."

Emma shook her head. "You're sick, you know that? Totally insane."

"You don't have to agree with us, as long as you do what we tell you," Boadica said.

Emma glared at Gabriel. He gave her a pained look and then turned. "Jax, detonate the charge."

Jax shoved a lever on a small, black-and-grey, hand-held device. A loud boom rattled windows and equipment, and the floor trembled. On the radio speaker set into the console, a babel of alarmed voices demanded to know what was going on.

"Okay." Gabriel handed the confiscated radio to Mark. "Get back up top and keep an eye on what goes on out there. Monitor radio broadcasts. We'll be monitoring in here as well, but I want you to make sure they're doing what they say they're doing. If you see anything unusual, get back down here and report immediately."

"We could just use a different frequency," Mark said.

"No. I don't want to risk detection. Now go. Jax and Boadica, stay on the hostages. But *stay chill.*" He directed a hard gaze at both of them.

He sat down and put on a headset, and after a moment of studying the screen, with a few false starts, managed to bring up the communications control software. "Okay, it's time to evacuate." He held up a mike. "Emma, if you would be so kind."

A wave of pure hatred rose up in her. "Drop dead, Cervantes."

He pinched the bridge of his nose with a sigh, as Boadica came forward. With a snarl, she thrust the mike at Emma and pressed the gun muzzle against her cheekbone. "Evacuate your people. Or die."

Her expression was cool, lethal. A gunshot might be taken simply for another explosion, and then they'd make Ben or one of the others order the evacuation.

Gabriel pushed his chair back. "Bo, you're going too far."

She spared him barely a glance. "I know what I'm doing. If you don't want anybody hurt, you'd better let me handle this." She pushed the mike at Emma again. "Gabriel doesn't want to hurt anybody," she said, her teeth bared. "I'm not so squeamish. Evacuate, or die. Now."

Emma believed her. She took the mike and started to reach for the keyboard in front of her; at Boadica's threatening gesture, she said, "I have to activate the evac sirens."

"All right. Do it."

Emma called up the alarm systems screen and entered a command. Sirens wailed over the loudspeakers outside, two short blasts and one long one, repeated three times. Then she keyed the mike.

"Attention, all personnel," she said. Outside, the loudspeakers carried her voice, out-of-phase, across the water. "This is Tooke. An explosion has occurred in the hydrogen storage area. Dangerous levels of hydrogen exist in the Engineering module. All personnel are ordered to evacuate *immediately*. This is not a drill. Repeat, this is not a drill. All personnel, report to your lifeboat station immediately."

She released the button. The sirens blasted again;

they'd continue with their thrice-repeated, two-short-and-one-long evac sequence, every fifteen seconds, until the alarm was shut off.

Boadica took the mike from her.

"Wait—the divers." Emma reached for the mike, but Boadica held it away. "If I don't follow up, they're going to be suspicious."

Boadica eyed her. "All right. But if you try anything cute, you're dead." Putting the gun in her face again, Boadica handed her the mike and Gabriel switched the console control over to radio.

"All personnel," Emma said, "clear the air, clear the air." She repeated it till radio silence greeted her. "Sean, this is Emma. Come in."

"Sean here."

"Order all divers up and into their Zodiacs. I want everyone to clear away from Gulf Stream immediately. At least two hundred yards. Got that?"

"Got it. *Divers up* already in progress."

Flo broke into the transmission. "Emma, this is Flo. Are you all right? What's going on? Is Ben with you?"

"Ben's with me. We've got a real crisis, Flo. I've got Control isolated for security reasons. We're going to purge the plant. Will you handle the evacuations and make sure everyone gets off okay? And fast."

Flo's tone was businesslike. "Will do. What about your guests? Their boat is still out at the slip. Are they with you?"

Emma eyed Boadica and Gabriel. Think fast, Tooke. "I sent them back to their boat; they'll be getting underway soon. I'll monitor them. Don't worry about them; just get the Streamers off. Use all available craft. Check back with me as soon as the evacuation is complete. I'm off-line till then."

Boadica took the mike away again. "Now, on the floor with the others."

Emma lay down next to Ben. Reynolds was calling her over the radio, demanding to know what was going on, saying he'd be damned if he was going to let another interruption disrupt his people's work. Well, that was Flo's problem now.

Ben's right eye was swollen shut and blood still trickled from his mouth. *Sorry,* she mouthed. He shook his head and gave her a wink with his left eye.

And then they waited.

Chapter 46

KEITH: **Wednesday, 7 October, 6:08 P.M. EDT**
Gulf Stream I

The sound of sirens blaring dragged Keith out of sleep. He scrambled around for clothes and his wits, as Emma's announcement echoed outside the window and through the hallways.

As he stepped into the hall, a man was exiting down a side corridor; the door closed as Keith approached. He hurried out onto the exterior walkway and looked around.

Three stories below, people were waiting to board Residential's lifeboat. *La Pescadora* was pulling up to dock at Mariculture, and at another of Mariculture's docking slips was a yellow-and-white, thirty-foot pleasure boat named *The Cherokee Princess*. Keith frowned. Strange. He headed around the walkway to see the other modules. Across the water, lifeboat evacuations were also in progress at Engineering and Science. Oddly, Control's shutters were closed.

His frown deepened. Control room shutters drawn and a pleasure boat at dock—?

He dashed up the stairs, yanked the door open, and stepped into the conference room. It was empty, though cups of steaming liquid and scattered notes lay on the table. He picked up the conference phone and tried for an outside line. Dead, dead, dead. He slammed it down.

No doubt lingered. The terrorists were here. Emma had made the announcement—the terrorists had her and God knew how many others holed up in Control.

He left the conference room and started down the corridor, throwing doors open. The third one he came to was an office, with a computer and phone. He booted up the computer, paced while it went through its utilities and memory checks, and then called up Eudora and entered his user name and password.

No time for codes; security be damned. He'd just have to hope the terrorists weren't monitoring E-mail. And that they hadn't disabled the computer system's phone lines.

He sent mail to both Jennifer and s.purvis@netcom .com:

SOS. TERRORISTS ARE ON GULF STREAM I AND HAVE TAKEN HOSTAGES.
SEND IMMEDIATE AID. SOS.

He transmitted the message, and then switched the phone line to intercom and dialed Control. The flat double-buzz sounded numerous times with no answer. He let it ring until finally, a very long time later, Emma responded. From the echo, she was on the speaker rather than a handset.

"Tooke here. What is it?"

"This is Keith," he said. "Is there anything I can do to help?"

"No. We'll handle it. Just get to your lifeboat right away." Her tone was steady and flat of affect. For the barest instant he wondered about her—but tossed away the doubt with a mental twitch. No way. She was just trying to keep things from going all to hell.

"I'm about to board," he lied. "I just wanted to check in. I guess this means we'll have to postpone your checkout dive yet again, eh?"

"But—" she said, and then fell silent. *Get it, Tooke. I'm telling you I know you're a prisoner. I'm here to help you.*

A note of emotion crept into her voice, a wavery chuckle with an edge to it. "I guess so. Guess I'll never get that damn c-card."

He hung up and made for the interior, beanpole stairway at a flat run, and leapt down them three at a go, jostling two or three people aside in the process. At the catwalk level he went out and around, onto the catwalk toward Mariculture, keeping his eyes on the shuttered windows of Control as his footfalls clattered noisily across the grate.

As he neared Mariculture, he saw *La Pescadora* had docked; its gangplank now extended into the catwalk deck. People were boarding at a brisk pace. Below him, at dock level, small groups were also waiting to board *La Granjera, La Auxiliadora,* and the module's lifeboat. He ran into the antechamber and up the beanpole's inner stairs to the catwalk level, and pushed his way through the crowd to the front of the boarding line, earning several annoyed looks. Michael was checking names off a list as people stepped onto the plank.

"Where's Flo?" Keith demanded, then spotted her, standing out on the afterdeck with a radio at her mouth as she stared down at a clipboard. He scrambled down the gangplank while he grabbed his wallet from his pocket, and put his hand over Flo's radio, interrupting her in midsentence. She looked up at him with a scowl and pushed his hand away.

"Do you mind?"

"I need to talk to you. *Now.*" He put his wallet down open-faced on her clipboard, displaying the U.S. marshal badge. Her eyes widened. He pocketed his ID; she handed the radio and clipboard to one of her people and followed him back down the gangplank, through the crowd, and to the deserted dive center area at the front of the utility deck.

"What's going on here?" she asked, hands on hips. "Since when are you a cop?"

"There's no time for me to explain now. Just listen. I'm here undercover, and I believe that terrorists have seized your control room and taken hostages. Including Emma."

"*What?* Are you sure?"

"Pretty sure."

Her face went grey. "Ben's in there."

"Do you know who else?"

She took a deep breath, struggling to master herself, and shook her head. "No. I'll have a pretty good guess when we finish checking the rosters, though." She gave him a serious look, her expression grave and drawn but her demeanor calm. "What do we do?"

"First, I need you to ask around. I'm presuming that yellow boat out at the slip is the terrorists'." She appeared startled. "Send a runner around," he said, "to find out if anyone knows how they got on board—how many of them there are, how they were dressed. *Any* details they can remember."

"We don't need a runner. I can answer your questions. There are four. Three men and a woman. One of them knew Emma. They were wearing windbreakers."

"Oversized? Could they have concealed weapons in them?"

She shrugged. "I suppose. I wasn't looking that closely. One or more of them might have been carrying bags."

Keith took a deep breath. "All right, then. These terrorists specialize in explosives. We need everyone off the facility—but I don't want a panic. So keep this to yourself for now. Let the evacuation proceed, but the minute you're all clear, get an SOS out right away. And add my name to the roster of evacuees. Do the lifeboats have radios?"

"Yes. EPIRBs. And *Pesky, Granny,* and *Ox* all have state-of-the-art radio equipment, as well. We can get a signal out right away. Why wait?"

"They're surely monitoring those frequencies. I want everyone safely off before they're alerted that their cover is blown. Wait till you're off the facility, and then use the radios in addition to your EPIRBs. The Coast Guard is supposed to be patrolling these waters more closely than usual—you might get lucky and get a very rapid response. Give them a full account of what's going on. How much longer do you think the evacuation will take?"

She glanced at her watch. "Ten minutes, maybe less. Reynolds has been dragging his feet, but we're almost there." She paused. "What are you going to do? Surely you're not going after them alone, are you?"

He glanced at his watch. It was 6:14 P.M. "I won't be alone for long—help is on the way. I'm going to stall them until that help arrives. Are there any other boats, or ways to evacuate, other than the lifeboats?"

"Half a dozen Zodiacs, maybe, from the divers coming in," she said.

"Have those Zodiacs moved away from the facility as well."

Her brow creased. "But that'll mean—" Then her eyes and mouth opened. "Oh."

He smiled, humorless. "Exactly. Let's see how willing they are to blow themselves up along with the facility."

"They'll still have their boat."

"Not when I'm done with it." He started to turn, then snapped his fingers. "Oh, yeah. I'll need a set of binoculars."

"Check in my office, in the upper left-hand drawer. Top deck, next to the conference room." The room from which he'd sent the E-mail.

She looked grim and determined, but her face was still pallid. He gave her shoulder a squeeze. "Ben'll be okay. I'll be on them like a burr—and an FBI counterterrorist unit is on its way."

She gave his hand a squeeze. Then she strode off, back toward the ship.

Keith went up to the top deck, again using the inner stairs, and grabbed Flo's binoculars. He walked down the corridor to a room that would face Engineering in the current facility configuration, entered, and scrutinized the module from the window. On the roof of Engineering, a man leaned against the rail. Keith lifted the binocs; he didn't know him and he'd never seen him on the facility. He looked like one of Barnes's sketches of the two ex-SEALs. The man wore a windbreaker and was holding binoculars to his own eyes, aimed at the docks of first one module, then another, then scanning the catwalks.

So they had posted a watch. That would make things a little trickier.

Keith made his way back down to the utility deck. It was deserted. *La Pescadora* had already debarked; it was partially visible through the open hatch, moving swiftly away. Good.

At the dive center he grabbed a full tank and snagged his dive equipment from his locker. He set up the tank and BC on the deck, tucked his flashlight and

two flares into a goody bag, which he clipped to his
BC, and hung the mask, snorkel, and fins on the tank
valve. He grabbed several large wrenches, pliers, and
wire cutters from the maintenance table, stuck those
in assorted pockets, and, after jerking his skins on,
strapped on the weight belt and knife.

His search for a fully-charged diver propulsion vehicle wasn't so fruitful. At the DPV battery-recharging
station, he found no DPVs lined up beneath the Fully
Charged sign. Most were dumped on the floor near the
battery charging outlets, under the Needs a Charge
sign. Several DPVs were hooked up to rechargers, but
none of the charging units' "fully charged" lights
were on.

Diver activity had been extremely heavy over the
past few days, and it looked as though when the emergency horn went off the divers had just brought the
units in and left them to be charged later.

He'd just have to take his chances with one of the
charging ones. He grabbed the one closest to the Fully
Charged station, in hopes that they were orderly about
how they hooked the DPVs up to the chargers.

At the deck opening he knelt and looked down to
see the Mariculture lifeboat pulling away. He glanced
at his watch. It was 6:23 P.M.

Hefting his BC up, he shrugged it onto his shoulders, then grabbed his gear and went down the inner
stairway to the dock. From there, he slipped out the
door and around to the side obscured from Engineering's view. The other three of the facility's four lifeboats were heading away from the facility, pulled
downcurrent by the Gulf Stream, with the two work
boats shadowing them.

Any minute Flo would begin transmission of her
emergency message, and the terrorists would hear it;
he'd better hurry. Holding the diver propulsion vehicle
close to his chest, he jumped into the water.

Chapter 47

Gabriel pressed a hand to the earphone, listened, and then raised a finger. "Another call coming in for Emma. Bring her over."

Boadica, who'd been leaning against the console with her gun pointed in the general direction of the hostages, stood and came over. "Who is it this time?"

"The one called Flo. Calling with an evac report."

Jax pulled Emma up. Gabriel handed her the mike and switched the radio to speaker.

Her expression was wooden, but the look she gave Gabriel held reproach. He looked away. *I'm sorry, querida.*

"This is Tooke," she said into the mike.

The other woman's voice issued from the speaker. "Evacuation is complete. We've got everyone aboard either the lifeboats, *Pesky, Granny,* or *Ox.* All personnel are accounted for, except for you, Ben, Gloria, Rob, Nikki, and Mac."

"We're all here."

"Then we're away. The current will carry the lifeboats downstream and we'll dog them in the other boats. All craft will moor themselves or hold station at the breakwaters beyond the reef, and wait there for your all clear."

"Good." She slumped and her voice broke. Then she straightened. "Thanks, Flo. You'd better get going."

"How do things look over there? Any improvement in conditions?"

"Not yet, I'm afraid," she said, eyeing Gabriel. "I'll let you know as soon as there's any improvement."

Boadica took the mike from her and handed it back to Gabriel, who switched the broadcast back over to his headset.

"How long do you think we should give it before *we* evacuate?" Gabriel asked.

Boadica glanced at her watch. "Another five minutes, maybe."

Boadica opened the window shutters and looked at the boats streaming away to the north, downstream. Then she turned and grabbed Emma by the neck, thrusting her at the window. "What's that Zodiac doing at the hydrogen barge?"

Gabriel winced as Emma thrust her hands up against the glass to keep her face from bouncing off the window. "They're decoupling it."

"Speak English!"

"They're disconnecting the hydrogen pipeline and electrical connections preparatory to unmooring it."

"Who told them to do that?"

Emma stared. "It's standard procedure," she said. "In the event of an explosion danger. If it were to explode, it's relatively close to the reef."

She's lying, Gabriel thought, then shook his head at himself, standing to get a better view out the window. I'm being paranoid. He rubbed at his upper lip and watched as the distant figures released the mooring cable and it dropped over the bow of the barge to splash in the water. The barge began moving away from the mooring buoy immediately, pulled by the current.

Gabriel said, "If they stay abo—" then cut himself off in midsentence, when the two figures on the barge climbed back down the port boarding ladder and cast off in the Zodiac. "Well, never mind."

Emma closed her eyes and exhaled.

Boadica pulled her back from the window and said, "Back on the floor."

A moment later Gabriel stiffened and pressed the headphone against his ear, listening. His lips thinned, and he switched what he was hearing to speaker. Flo's voice issued from the console.

"—day, mayday. Gulf Stream 1 is under attack by terrorists. Location twenty-eight degrees thirty-one minutes north, seventy-nine degrees west. They are armed and have taken hostages and we believe they plan to blow up the facility. Mayday, mayday."

"Shit." Boadica went over and yanked the outer door open. "Mark! Get down here—NOW!"

She turned to Jax and Gabriel. "Change of plans. The Coast Guard will be on us in no time—we'll need hostages." She gestured at the six prisoners lying on the floor. "They're coming with us. Jax, get them on their feet."

Gabriel turned, his jaw setting. "No way."

"Get real," Jax said, but fell silent when Boadica gestured sharply at him.

"Have you got an alternative?" she demanded. Gabriel stared at her for a long moment. Then he shook his head. He turned back to the console with a muttered curse and continued listening to the broadcast. Keep people from getting hurt. What a joke.

He had just enough time to hear a Coast Guard cutter respond to the broadcast when Mark burst into the room. Boadica grabbed at Gabriel's arm—"Scramble!"—and they were on the run, herding their prisoners out into the corridor. They crowded into the elevator in the module's center and Boadica pushed a button on the control panel.

The elevator inched downward, and the inner walls

of the beanpole crawled up: one floor . . . another . . . another. Gabriel felt as though his heart would burst. When the cage door opened at the catwalk level, they hurried the prisoners out to the catwalk and across it to the module where their boat was docked. The metal grating rattled under the frenzied pounding of their feet; a jagged chorus of breaths rasped counterpoint.

After another agonizing—though shorter—trip in the elevator, they reached the bottom-most level and hurried out onto the dock. Gabriel scrambled over their boat's gunwale. Jax and Mark began to usher the prisoners on-deck while Boadica climbed up onto the flying bridge to start the engine.

A moment later she jumped down, fury stamped on her face.

"What is it?" Gabriel asked.

She went to the aft deck and threw open the battery compartment. A cloud of smoke rose around her. Looking down, she swore, long and low.

Gabriel came and looked over her shoulder. Two banks of batteries stood amid acrid, eye-burning smoke. Across the negative and positive battery terminals was a three-quarter-inch box wrench. She slammed the compartment door shut, hard enough, almost, to break it.

"What?" Jax demanded.

"Some dick-head has fucked with our batteries. He was just here. Thirty seconds earlier and we would have had him." Her knuckles whitened around her gun and she eyed the prisoners. Terror gripped Gabriel. Was she going to kill them right then? He fingered his own gun. If I have to, by God, he thought, I'll shoot her myself.

"Boadica," Gabriel said sharply, "cast off. Jax and Mark, take the prisoners below. We'll ride the current downstream and detonate the charges once we're a safe distance away."

She glared at him. Gabriel moved between her and the prisoners and stared her down. Muscles jumping in her jaw, she lowered her weapon and drew a deep breath. "Okay," she said. "Okay."

"We'd better tie them up," Jax said, and at the same time Mark said, "It'll be a while before we can detonate, then."

Gabriel frowned. "What about the Coast Guard? Without power we'll be sitting ducks."

Mark looked gloomy. "It's worse than that. Without batteries we have no radar. We won't even see them coming."

Boadica shrugged. "So we'll post watch. And as for being sitting ducks—they may try to intimidate us, but they won't touch us." She gestured with her chin at the prisoners. "We've got an insurance policy, remember? And they know it."

She climbed up onto the aft deck. Out of the corner of his eye, as he turned to head up to the foredeck, Gabriel caught sudden motion. He turned.

Jax and Mark were preoccupied with the prisoners and didn't see the auburn-haired man leap up from the cabin and launch himself across the deck. But Gabriel had a clear shot at him.

The man grabbed Emma, whose hands were now secured behind her with nylon rope, and swept her over the side. Jax leaned over the side and emptied a full clip of ammunition into the water, cursing with each round: "You goddamned. Motherfucking. Shit-eating. Butt-wipe. *Son of a BITCH!*"

For a second, once he'd emptied it, Gabriel thought Jax was going to throw the gun overboard, too. Instead, he turned and struck the nearest prisoner—the young woman with short blond hair—with the butt of his gun. She collapsed on the deck with a cry, arms raised over her head.

Rage turned Gabriel's vision red. He grabbed Jax's

wrist as the bastard raised his gun to strike her a second time. "Back off, *pendejo,* or I'll tear out your heart and stuff it down your throat."

Jax took a swing with his gun butt—Gabriel ducked under the blow and kidney-punched Jax, who staggered back against the railing with a grunt. A single gun shot hit the wood rail next to Jax, who froze with a terrified expression and lifted his hands in a placating motion; at almost the same instant something struck Gabriel in the back of the head. He staggered under a sea of stars and turned, rubbing his head.

Boadica stood there. She looked ready to kill again. And her gun was aimed at him and Jax.

"We don't have time for this. I'll see you both dead first. Understand?" Pause. *"Understand?"*

"All right," Jax said, "easy," and Gabriel nodded, hands raised.

She was right, of course. But he had the feeling that he was either going to kill her before this was over, or she was going to kill him.

"I understand," he said.

She lowered her gun and shook her head, muscles in her jaw twitching. Jax ejected the empty ammo clip from his gun, took a full one from his vest pocket, and shoved it into the gun's handle.

Boadica said to Jax, "What were you shooting at?"

"Someone was hiding in the cabin," he replied, and Mark interjected, "Probably that asshole who took out our batteries."

Jax nodded. "Yeah, probably. He just made a run for it a minute ago. Ran into Tooke and knocked her overboard."

Gabriel opened his mouth, then closed it. He'd seen it all. The man had had a dive suit, a mask and snorkel, and a knife. And he had *swept* Emma overboard. It hadn't been an accident, but a rescue. They were probably under the dock right now.

Boadica leapt onto the aft deck to scan around the boat. "No sign of blood in the water. Was Tooke tied?" Gabriel nodded. "She may be dead, then. Or maybe not. But *he's* still out there." She turned, glaring. "Don't just stand there! Gabriel, station yourself astern and scan downstream. Mark, check out the dock. He might be hiding underneath. And keep your eye on the catwalks, too. If you see anything move, shoot it."

"I'll finish tying up the hostages," Jax said as Mark leapt over the gunwale onto the dock.

Gabriel stared at the prisoners. The five of them stood in a cluster, their eyes glassy, their postures stiff with terror. He looked down at his gun. It was all he could do to keep from walking over and tossing the weapon overboard.

Shaking his head, he slung his gun over his shoulder and climbed up onto the foredeck.

Chapter 48

EMMA: Wednesday, 7 October, 6:26 p.m. EDT
Aboard *The Cherokee Princess*, docked at Gulf Stream I

The one called Jax tied her hands behind her so tightly that pain shot from her hands to her shoulders, and then shoved her toward the boat's cabin. As she stumbled, something struck her from the side and knocked her off the boat into the water.

She flailed, trying to kick her way back to the surface, but a weight was pulling her down. A face behind a mask blurred in front of her—Keith's face?

He was signaling her. Thumbs-down. *Descend.*

He had a hold of one of her arms and was pulling her under the boat, kicking hard against the current. Despite his efforts they were dragged along the boat's flank. Bouts of bubbles streaked past them from the surface. She didn't know what they were for an instant. Then she realized. Bullets.

Ignoring her bursting lungs, she kicked down, too, aiding Keith's efforts.

They passed beneath the boat's bow, fighting the current, and in a moment the water's ceiling grew dark. Keith tugged her upward. As Emma broke surface she inhaled sharply, leaning back against Keith's grip, wheezing in her thirst for air.

They were under Mariculture's dock, braced against one of the dock's Styrofoam float billets. As swells moved through there was barely room for them to keep their faces above water, beneath the boards. The current bumped her hard against the float billet.

Keith's breath was warm in her ear; his words were barely audible. "I'm cutting you loose. Hold still."

She tried to tread water as Keith sawed at the nylon. It seemed to take forever. She got a snootful of salt water as a swell struck her, and gagged, trying to time her coughs with the waves slapping the float.

Meanwhile, the terrorists were having some kind of fight, shouting and scuffling. There was a gunshot— she jerked, and Keith nicked her with his knife. Emma bit down hard on her lip. She was terrified one of the other hostages had been killed.

Then the bonds loosened. She pulled her hands free and dug her fingers into the float. It was awkward, hard to hold on to—big and square. Again he put his lips against her ear.

"Wait here."

Keith sank beneath the surface. Emma clung to the foam block, slipping with each swell and then scrambling for her grip.

Footsteps thumped against the dock, nearing, then paused. She froze, expecting a face and a gun to appear at the dock's edge, but they started up again, and their vibrations traveled through her hands to her arms. The steps came overhead, and the cracks in the boards grew shadowed. There was a shuffling—he was kneeling next to the edge. *Shit.* She saw movement at the crevice between water and wood, and shoved herself underwater.

The current carried her downstream to the next billet. She kicked up, grappling with the billet as she surfaced, and lay sideways against it until it killed her forward momentum.

Wait for Keith, she told herself, doggedly. Breathe. Rest between swells. Wait.

About the time she grew convinced Keith had drowned he resurfaced, removed the mask and snorkel he'd been wearing, and handed it to her. Then he slipped on another set—his own; she recognized it from earlier in the day.

He had gotten a BC from somewhere, which was equipped with a tank, and she saw a DPV just beneath the water. He handed her his octopus regulator and gestured for her to grab on to his tank in back. Emma gripped the mouthpiece with her teeth, put on and adjusted the mask, and then grabbed hold of the tank valve. He held his arm up over his shoulder and made a thumbs-down; she reached in front of him to return the signal. They sank beneath the surface.

Without weights, the first ten feet were tough. Her buoyant body tried hard to pull away from Keith and resurface; she had no fins with which to force herself downward. She hung on as the DPV pulled them down, and as they gained some depth the tugging subsided. Her ears popped; she risked freeing one hand to clear her sinuses. The saltwater burns in her nasal cavities and throat made it difficult for the sinuses to clear.

Keith took them down to thirty feet, angling upcurrent past the terrorists' yacht toward the Mariculture beanpole. Soon the dark opening of the beanpole's uppermost buoyancy chamber loomed ahead.

Keith guided them into the chamber, and they surfaced in the black, rippling pool. The only light came from underwater: a green glow at the chamber's entrance. Then light splashed against the ceiling as Keith turned on his flashlight. Emma blinked. He looked over his shoulder toward her, and his silhouetted profile appeared against the backdrop of the lighted wall.

"You okay?"

She nodded, blew salt water from her nose, and wiped her face with the back of her hand. "Yeah. Thanks." Their voices and the water's lapping echoed weirdly in the pressurized chamber. She fought the urge to whisper.

The chamber was about half-filled with air; they had maybe ten feet of head space. Emma released her grip on his tank valve, handing him the octopus, then swam over to the diver handholds that lined the side of the chamber. Her cotton shirt and hair clung to her shoulders, dripping, as she toed the submerged handholds and lifted her shoulders out of the water. Beneath the water, her shirt and shorts felt like seaweed, brushing against her torso and limbs. Her water-laden deck shoes felt like lead weights; she was tempted to kick them off but decided against it. And her panties were crawling up her crack.

At least the water wasn't too cold.

Keith swam over and took a handhold beside her, pulling his mask onto his neck. Emma wrung out her wet hair and twisted it to keep it back. She licked at the salt that trickled down alongside her nose. "Man. I feel like someone put me through a wringer."

"Someone did."

She gave him a fleeting smile, then said, "We need to get back out there. They've planted explosives on the facility somewhere."

Keith shook his head. "They might spot us, or see our bubble trail. We'd better wait till we know they've given up looking for us. They're not going to blow the place while they're moored to the dock. Nor for a while after that—at three or four knots, it'll be a while before they're far enough away to safely detonate explosives. We should have some time to take care of the bombs between their departure and detonation."

"How will we know when they're no longer moored?"

"I'll check every couple of minutes." He glanced at his watch. "Six-twenty-eight. I'll check at six-thirty."

Emma looked at her own, new, waterproof dive watch. It read six-twenty-six. She changed her time to match his, flashing a sheepish grin at Keith. "Hey, they always do it in the movies."

"Not a bad idea. Meanwhile," Keith said, "let's strategize."

Emma frowned, pensive. "I don't know what we're going to do even if we find the explosives. I know jack about defusing bombs. You?"

"Not a thing."

Then she pursed her lips, as a thought occurred to her. "But you know . . . maybe we *can* remove the bombs and drop them. The current will carry them away from the beanpoles."

Keith was nodding as she spoke. "Good. That's good. Where are Gulf Stream's most vulnerable points?"

She thought for a moment. "Depends on what they're trying to do. The hydrogen plant or the storage tanks would be obvious targets . . . or they could have planted charges to wipe out the infrastructure in Science or Mariculture. Not as big a bang for the buck, but equally devastating since they're the facility's money-earners right now.'' She paused again. ''The OTEC plant, maybe. If they put a charge there it'd take the whole facility down—they'd only need one big charge to blow a hole in its side. I'm pretty sure they mined the hydrogen storage barge, but Flo had her people release it, so it's floating downstream. I just hope nobody tries to take it in tow. They might also have put charges on the reefs. Though it's not a very environmentally conscious thing to do. But neither is bombing Gulf Stream, seems like.''

Keith gave her an odd look. ''It's funny you should mention that. I've known a few monkey-wrenchers. It's the highly destructive industries—the ones that deplete nonrenewable resources and the major polluters— that they really hate. Gulf Stream doesn't fit the profile. It's basically a clean technology. It's odd they picked it as a target.''

''Hmmm. That woman, Boadica, said that sustainable development was a lie—that it gives people a false sense of security. I think they believe that *any* big technology is bad.'' She thought for a moment. ''Gabriel certainly used to believe that. He used to tell me how technology was evil and addictive, that we used it to numb ourselves out and separate ourselves from reality. He hated the fact that I was an engineer.''

Keith nodded thoughtfully. ''The *Deep Ecology* mindset. Even so, it doesn't explain why they picked Gulf Stream over, say, an oil or timber company.''

''I could make a rationale for it. I mean, I think it's nuts, but—if they believe that *all* industry is bad, they might get more angry at an industry that pretends to be a Good Guy than an industry that is up front about its Badness.''

Keith made a noise she didn't know how to interpret. "Or maybe these jokers aren't real environmental radicals."

Emma started to reply, but Keith glanced at his watch and said, "Hang on." He put his mask on and sank soundlessly. A moment later he was back. He shook his head at her querying look. "Still there."

"About what you said before, that they aren't real environmentalists." She shook her head. "Look, I know Gabriel. He could be a real asshole. He was opinionated and rigid and he brought out the worst in me. But he really cared. One time, I remember, I was with him on a hike, and he broke down and cried when he saw what real estate developers had done to a formerly undeveloped mountainside in the Sierras."

Keith gave her lifted eyebrows. "He's changed, Emma. He's not the man you knew."

She scowled, shaking her head. "You don't know him like I do." At his expression she said, "Okay, like I *did*. No one changes that much."

He gave her a speculative look and shrugged.

"It doesn't matter now," she said, waving a hand impatiently. "Let's get back to bombs. Thing is, I was with them the whole time they were on board, so I don't know how they could have planted charges." She covered her mouth with a gasp. "Except the thinner man, the one called Mark. That woman, Boadica, made it sound like he was just supposed to keep watch, but he could have been out there planting more charges—"

"Uh-uh. I saw him off and on, every few minutes, for the whole time. He stayed up on the roof, watching the evacuations."

Emma looked out at the water. Like Jell-O, the dark green water with the lime green blob beneath it wiggled back and forth in the chamber. She shoved her hair back again. Concentrate, Tooke.

"They didn't have any real chance to plant charges

on the modules—they couldn't have sneaked on before their official arrival and risk being seen and challenged. So they had to have planted charges another way—'' She turned to Keith, eyes widening as it hit her. "Underwater. Weak points. The beanpoles. They've planted bombs on the beanpoles.''

Keith's eyes glittered in the cast-off reflection from his flashlight. "And it would be in the first thirty feet of depth. To approach and leave the facility unseen they'd have been in the water too long to be able to do a deep dive.'' He glanced at his watch. "Hang on.''

He sank underwater again. In a few seconds he was back. "They've cut loose from their moorings. It'll be a bit before they're far enough away to detonate—depending on how close they want to cut it. Let's call it a mile—so seventeen minutes. Fifteen, to be conservative.'' He pushed a button on his watch. "I've set a timer.''

"Let's do it.'' She reached for his octopus.

He had a frown. "It's best if I go alone.''

"No way.''

"Hear me out. We're two divers on one tank. That will cut our dive time way back. We can't afford to be seen surfacing to get tanks and then reentering the water. The terrorists might spot us and blow things early. You have no fins and you're an inexperienced diver. Our chances of success are better if I take you up and then go it alone.''

"And what am I supposed to do—sit down with my knitting needles? Forget it. We're in this together.'' He started to speak, but Emma interrupted. "Look. I'll be dead anyway, if you can't get to all the bombs in time. I know the facility better than anyone. And what if you're injured and get swept away by the current?

"I can hold the flashlight. I can be an extra set of eyes and hands. In that current you'll need them. And you said yourself I'm a quick learner. With the two of us we stand a better chance of succeeding. We should work together.''

'With a sigh he dropped his shoulders. ''We could die, you know.''

''Not if we hurry.'' She held out a hand for the octopus. He caught her gaze and held it, for just an instant.

''I'm in love with you, Emma Tooke. Just for future reference.'' He held out the octopus. ''Ready?''

She took it and smiled at his suddenly shadowed form as he turned off the flashlight and put it in her hand. She put her hand on his face and, leaning forward in the dark, found his lips, which responded quickly. Warmth, softness, salt. They parted and breathed each other's breath. A barest glint in his eyes was all she could see of him.

''Ready,'' she said. The darkness made it easier to add, ''I'm in love with you, too.''

He entwined his fingers in hers. She put the silicone bit in her mouth and slid her mask on. Together they sank underwater.

They exited the chamber and circled up the beanpole, Emma scanning the barnacle-covered surface while Keith steered the DPV. The water was cloudy. Fish darted out of their way. They passed submersible lights and some permanent equipment set into the pole, but no bombs. Once they passed a device in a taped-shut plastic container, tied to the pole with rope; Keith paused and pointed, but Emma made an *okay* sign and waved him on. That one was a detector used by Reynolds's group to measure salinity, temperature, and nutrient density as part of their tomographic analysis of the Gulf Stream's eddies.

But as they neared the water's ceiling, she tapped Keith and pointed a fist at the beanpole. Just above their heads, two strands of three-sixteenths-inch cord

encircled the beanpole, about a foot apart. Suspended
between the two lines, strung through on top and bottom by large, metal-rimmed eyelets, was a large, clear
plastic bag, some of its surfaces turned silver by sharp
angles of defraction. It could be something the science
staff had installed while she was in Melbourne, but . . .
as far as she knew, it shouldn't be there.

Keith gave her an *okay* over his shoulder and
steered them toward it. Emma reached over and tugged
at the bag to see better what was inside. The device
was a whitish blob with wires and a little box half-
buried in it.

Emma's arms, gut, and legs cramped in fear. Being
this close to a bomb was worse than facing the hollow
end of a gun. Keith bent over and pulled his knife
from its sheath on his calf, and handed it to Emma.
Then he motioned that he would hold them level, and
she should cut the device free.

She had read that plastic explosive was stable unless
heated suddenly or given an electric charge or sharp
shock. Or detonated.

Courage, Tooke.

She handed Keith the flashlight and, using him as a
launch, kicked forward and up. The current grabbed
at her, trying to sweep her around the barnacle-
encrusted beanpole.

Emma scraped her fingernails across the barnacles
and stabbed with the knife blade, seeking purchase.
The octopus regulator line was long in comparison to
an ordinary regulator line, but not that long; she was
at the end of its length when Keith grabbed her wrist
and pulled her back. He grabbed on to the waistband
of her shorts and held her steady.

She worked her fingers under the knot beside the
bomb, worked the knife beneath the rope and then
sawed hard, outward, at the cord. The knife's tip
caught on barnacles and scraped against the bean-

pole's concrete-composite surface—then, finally, the line severed. Swiftly, she entwined her hands in the line.

Moving down, she cut through the second line the same way. Then she gathered both lines in her hand and pulled them away from the pole. The end she wasn't holding on to, the end with the bomb on it, fell away around the far edge of the beanpole. The lines dug into her hand. She wrapped the lines three times around her palm and hung on tight.

She didn't want to drop the lines until she'd verified the bomb had fallen off; they might entangle in the support structure or anchor lines at seventy feet, or get caught around one of the other beanpoles. So she bent around and took hold of Keith's tank again, clinging to the lines with her other hand, and gave him a signal to move forward; they headed upstream a short way. The beanpole, with its drag-reducing fin, was almost thirty-seven feet around, and all thirty-seven feet of the lines pulled at Emma's arm.

She rolled onto her side and looked; the device had slid off and was receding into the depths, carried far from the beanpole by the current. Two other devices, identical to the first, were being pulled along between the lines also. One was just now falling off; the other had a short way to go.

She tapped Keith and he looked over his shoulder. His eyes widened. The last bomb fell off the dual line as they watched. Then Keith geared up the DPV and made a tight turn with the current. Emma released the cord.

It was only then she realized how quickly her heart was racing. She tried to slow her air intake. They had little enough to spare.

They came around Mariculture's beanpole again, into a cloud of horse-eye amberjacks. Emma started to gesture in the direction of Engineering, but Keith was already angling that way.

The sun must be setting; visibility was dropping. In the moment since they'd dropped the bombs the aquamarine waters had darkened to a deep teal and the seventy-foot support beams were no longer visible below. Keith turned on the flashlight and handed it to Emma over his shoulder. She aimed it over his shoulder, wondering why he didn't turn on the DPV headlamp. Darkness would make their task all the harder.

The DPV and the current combined to all but hurl them through the fish school toward the structure—the OTEC plant and beanpole appeared and swelled rapidly in size. Emma squinted at the structure and thought about the submersible lights set into the plant and the beanpole—if only she could get to Control. But there wasn't time—and underwater lights might alert the terrorists.

As they neared the plant, Emma considered possibilities. No charges were visible. The plant itself would be an excellent target, due to its buoyancy configuration, but the enormous circumference of the plant made setting charges anywhere along its length difficult, and the powerful suction of the intake vents made setting charges within ten feet of the surface virtually impossible. A much better spot would be in the annulus between the plant and the pole—either from above, or from underneath.

Keith was angling downward. She gave him a thumbs-up over his shoulder—and felt his hesitation in the tension of his shoulders and back. Then, with a nod, he angled upward.

As they approached the intake its suction caught them, and Emma lost her grip on Keith's tank. The octopus was ripped from her mouth and she landed, back first, on the suction screens. Pinned like a bug. With a grunt, she flipped herself over and dragged herself up the screen, inch by inch, to the surface, and heaved a great breath of air. Keith surfaced beside her, hand on her back. They were beneath the lip of the raised deck, obscured from the terrorists' view by the bulk of the plant.

"You okay?"

She nodded, panting. "You go down and check the annulus between the plant and pole, from underneath. I'm going to crawl across the deck and check it from above."

Keith frowned. "Waste of time. Why risk being seen? Could they really have scrambled across the deck to plant a bomb in full, view of everybody?"

"Remember the fog. It was pea soup for hours."

He snapped his fingers. "Right. But you've got the only knife. If there are charges below I won't be able to cut them loose."

"I'll hurry, then, and meet you back here in a minute. Wait for me."

"Stay down."

"Of course. Back in a flash."

Keith gave her an *okay* sign. She grabbed the lip of the plant, dragged the lower half of her body up away from the intake, and, as a wave lifted her, shoved upward as Keith boosted her rump. She rolled onto the deck.

Lying prone, she scanned. The terrorists' boat was a few hundred yards downstream. At that distance she'd still be visible. Two terrorists' heads and upper torsos were in view. She scrambled through the waves that washed across the deck, putting the power plant's entry hatch between herself and the boat, and splashed again on hands and knees through the water till she reached the cover of the beanpole. Then she stood.

The sun was setting: a flattened, bloodred blob lacerated by yellow clouds, it hovered above the horizon, beneath the chin of Residential's catwalk deck. A handful of stars were air-brushed against the sky. Her shadow stretched long and tenuous across the deck—into view of the terrorists. She dropped to a crouch. Then the mercury catwalk lights came on, and sodium lights mounted on the dock level lit up the OTEC plant's deck.

The bright lights threw several Emma shadows into the terrorists' view. She dodged toward the pole's center, under the dock, praying the terrorists hadn't seen her shadows . . . and that they would realize the lights were an automatic sequence. Kneeling in the shallow water, she shone the flashlight into the annulus between plant and pole.

The gap between plant and beanpole measured eight inches. And there it was, at arm's length, right above the waterline: a milk-colored cord. She shone the flashlight first to the right, then the left—and spotted a bagged charge. There was only one line, not two as in Mariculture.

With a smile of fierce satisfaction, Emma moved over to the bomb, lay down, and reached into the annulus with both arms.

Her smile faded. The line was tightly bound—she could get her fingers underneath the line beside the bomb, but her grip wasn't sure. And she didn't dare drop either end of the line, or the bomb—bombs?—would fall into the water and lodge against the first set of O-rings that locked the plant in place against the pole. Certain death.

She looked back. Keith had resurfaced and was peering over the edge directly behind her. She crouched and splashed back to him, making sure the pole was always between her and the yacht—and that her shadows also remained behind the pole.

"I need your help."

"There are bombs?"

She nodded. "At least one, just above the waterline.

It'll take the two of us to lift the bomb line up. Down below?''

"Nothing." As he spoke, he stripped off his weight belt, bang stick, and DPV. She took them, and also his tanks and BC, and laid them on the deck. He hoisted himself up, slipped off his fins, and hung them on his tank valve.

At the pole they positioned themselves on either side of the bomb. Emma tucked the flashlight into the waistline of her shorts, then reached in and slipped the knife under the cord. She curled the index and middle fingers of her left hand around the cord, and then slid her fingers as far to the left, away from the bomb and cut point, as possible. She pinched hard with her thumb. The line dug into her fingers, cutting off circulation.

Sweat beaded on her lip and her breath grew short. Keith had gripped the bomb in his right hand and slipped his fingers under the line to the left.

"Ready?" she asked.

"Do it."

She began sawing at the line. Damned cord—so hard to cut. Swearing, sweating, she sawed harder. It snapped. She held on hard with the three-finger hold, tossed the knife onto the deck, and brought her right hand over to help—bumping Keith's shoulder on the way. In that instant the nonbomb end of the line slipped almost out of her grasp—but not quite.

She and Keith stood, separating, working the line up over the annulus's lip. As he stepped back from the pole, Keith slid the bomb farther down the line and bound it several times around with the cord. He knotted the bundle and then laid it down on the deck, and gave Emma the signal to reel the other end in. She began coiling line, swiftly, elbow to palm.

The line dragged, caught, and, as the end of it came around her side of the beanpole, two additional bombs bumped across the deck, up hard against the bundled bomb Keith had tied at the far end of the line.

She held the string of bombs up—they dripped and wiggled like caught fish. Keith held out his hand, and she gave them to him. He slung the coiled cord over his shoulder.

"We'd better not risk a shock to the detonators," he said. "Let's release them underwater."

"Right." Emma stooped and picked up the knife. At that instant the alarm on Keith's watch went off. He shut it off and exchanged a look with Emma. Her heart sank.

Water is an incompressible fluid and the energy from an explosion carries a long way. If one of the bombs went off while they were in the water, it'd kill them even if they were nowhere near the bombs.

She looked around at the structures, four pale monuments, tombstonelike against the darkening sky—more still and empty than they had ever been since that moment (was it really over a year ago now?) after the construction crews had departed, just before the first boatload of permanent Gulf Stream I staff had arrived and she had stood awaiting them, amid bird cries and the shush-shush of swells brushing past the poles.

They had to try.

"Come on," she said, and they ran back to the deck's edge. She helped Keith into his BC and handed him the DPV. He clipped the bang stick to his BC, adjusted his mask, and put the regulator bit into his mouth. He was looking at his dive computer. She caught a glimpse: only five hundred psi left.

Another look passed between them. Keith plucked the knife from her hand and the flashlight from her shorts, saying, "Sorry."

She asked, "What are you apolo—" and then he gave her a shove that landed her on her buttocks with a splash. Barely a ripple marked his entry into the water.

Outrage propelled Emma to her feet; she narrowly avoided shouting a curse after him. Then her sinuses stung and her vision blurred. The fucker was going to get himself killed. Gulf Stream was *her* baby. Going down with it was *her* job.

The ladder to the dock was in view of the terrorists, on the other side of the pole; dock level was about seven feet above the plant's deck. Climbable, for her. She jumped up, grabbed the railing support, and pulled herself up onto the grating. Then she moved around toward the door, flattened herself against the wall, and peered downstream. The yacht was even farther away now. She decided to just do it, and slipped around the pole and through the door.

No boom. They must not have seen her.

The elevator lifted her with aggravating slowness to the top deck, where she entered Control and sat down at the console. She slammed a fist on the counter. Keith, damn you.

Then she shook her head, a sharp motion. If our positions had been reversed you'd have done the same thing, Tooke. With five hundred pounds of air, the only chance we have is with one experienced diver on that tank. No time for argument—every second is precious. And I would have argued, and he knew it.

But she was terrified. Terrified he'd be blown up when the modules went.

If, Tooke. If. He may make it in time.

She propped her forehead on her elbows, laid gentle fingers over her eyes, and took a deep breath. She took all the fear and rage—her fear for Keith's fate and for her own, anger at Gabriel's betrayal, fear for her friends imprisoned by the terrorists and for Gulf Stream itself—and released them, like ashes, like dust . . . let them all wash away. Then she opened her eyes.

If Keith didn't make it, she was the only one who stood between Gulf Stream I and the briny deep. She had to focus.

Whatever happened, the facility needed as much buoyancy as possible. Sophisticated buoyancy control wasn't needed, and could put the facility at risk — she'd been telling the truth when she'd told the terrorists that an explosion might overwhelm the control system.

She entered the requested security codes and called up the buoyancy control software. The screen before her filled with a schematic of the facility, buoyancy tanks highlighted, all showing different levels of air. She shut off the controllers. And sprang out of her chair, heart racing, when the alarms blared.

A little tense, Tooke?

Rueful, she pulled her chair back under her and quieted the alarms. Then she began blowing water ballast out of all tanks. Not too quickly; the terrorists would notice — but as quickly as she dared.

She glanced at her watch: 6:52. Eighteen minutes since the terrorists cut loose. They'd be a mile downstream. Plenty of distance. With a sigh, sick at her stomach, she stood. Nothing left to do but wait, watch the water, and pray.

She went out to the walkway and leaned on the railing. A cool breeze from the southeast created ripples atop the swells, which broke the reflections from the modules' lights into shards of glass amid liquid obsidian. He'd go to Science first, she figured. She looked for bubbles — and spotted them, a whitish, foamy mass, about twelve feet downstream of the structure.

In the past two minutes, since she'd started pressuring up the tanks, the facility had risen a good seven feet. Not that noticeable, but . . . she prayed she wasn't putting Keith in greater danger.

Emma decided to risk a look northward to see what was happening there. She headed around the walkway till she neared the edge closest to where she had last seen the terrorists, and edged farther along.

Orange flares blazed, marking the bobbing life rafts tethered to the downstream edge of the reef. The three facility craft held station in the vicinity. At the breakwater downstream of the reef was the terrorists' yacht, now lit by floodlights from a Coast Guard cutter off its stern—though the cutter was keeping its distance. Perhaps the cutter would keep them distracted and they wouldn't notice what was happening here.

She moved back around the walkway to look for evidence of Keith again.

The bubbles were gone.

And he burst to the surface at Science's beanpole ladder; she could hear his gasps.

"Keith—" she called softly. He turned in her direction and made the *okay* sign with arm and head, and then cut a hand across his throat. Out of air. He slid the DPV and bang stick onto the dock and climbed up, pointed to the DPV, and drew his finger across his throat again. Out of charge. Shit. With at least one set of bombs left.

Then he stripped off his weight belt and his BC and tank, and dumped them. He pulled his mask down around his neck, tucked fins under his arm, gave her another *okay* sign, and then ducked inside the beanpole antechamber.

What was he up to? She didn't know of any extra air tanks in Science. She wanted to go to him, but didn't dare head across the catwalks. They were well-lit, and the terrorists would be watching.

A moment later she spotted him—dashing out onto the catwalk between Science and Residential.

"Oh, my God," she whispered. She ran along the walkway a short distance, watching as he ran along the catwalk. He still had his fins, mask, and snorkel. He must plan a free dive from Residential's dock to get the last set of charges.

She clenched hands around the rail, every muscle in her body rigid, watching him, willing him on before he was seen. The catwalk seemed impossibly long. *Move your ass,* Hellman!

Halfway there, now—two-thirds—three-quarters— at the walkway—now he yanked the door open, and disappeared inside, pulling the door closed behind—

And the water beneath Residential's dock lit up, turned milky white, and erupted in a hemispherical dome that rushed at Emma. The sound of the explosion was muffled by the water, but it rang the Residential beanpole like a giant bell: a clear, guttural tone deeper than a foghorn's call.

She dropped to the deck as the water, a cloud of droplets traveling at several hundred miles an hour, slammed into the side of Engineering. The deck shielded her from the worst of it, but glass shattered above her. Her ears popped.

Emma crawled across the deck to the railing, staying low, in time to see water rushing back into the pit created by the explosion. Just as the waters met the pole she saw that it had fractured in two. The module and upper portion of the beanpole—a thirty-foot-long section—had been shoved a little up and sideways by the blast, and was now dropping straight down. The jagged end of the lower beanpole rose above the foamy turbulence, its buoyancy tanks no longer having to support fifty thousand pounds of module and upper beanpole.

The spear of the lower beanpole tore through the dock deck's steel grating as if it were tissue, then tore through the catwalk deck, just missing the catwalk to Mariculture. Then the beanpole slammed into the bottom of the descending module.

As the beanpole smashed upward through the decks, windows blew out in succession; glass, papers, cushions, and other light debris ejected outward as collapsing decks compressed air too rapidly for it to escape through existing openings. A body burst out one of the top deck's windows amid a spray of glass and flew splay-limbed through the air. Emma gasped, then realized it was only Dr. Feelgood. Poor Charlie's garden took the last hit, greenery flying like tossed salad as the beanpole erupted from the roof, where it stopped with about five feet of jagged concrete sticking into the air.

The bottom of the module is caught on the seventy-foot cross-beams, Emma thought; those beams must've torn completely through the dock and catwalk walkways.

By now Residential's utility deck was completely underwater and the walkway of the main deck was awash. The catwalks angled down into the water—they must still be attached, or caught on something. The facility's anchoring lines must also still be attached—if the main anchor line between Residential and the anchor buoy had broken, Gulf Stream would be heading up the coast toward the North Atlantic right now, and if the stabilizing line between Residential and Engineering had given way, Gulf Stream's diamond shape would be collapsing lengthwise, with Mariculture and Science drifting together. Emma eyed the water level and tried to picture the structure.

The level of the waves put the catwalk antechamber, the last place Emma had seen Keith, more than twenty feet underwater.

Chapter 49

The door closing became the ultimate noise—a minute click that swelled to a sound so loud it filled Keith up and slammed him to the floor.

Only then did he realize what had happened.

The structure was vibrating, a deep thrum. The floor dropped like an elevator and he tried to stand, fell to his knees as the floor jerked, and grinding, ripping sounds screamed through the walls. The floor dropped again. His ears popped, hard. From the stairway above came crashing, ripping. From below came the high-pitched squeals of tearing metal.

The fluorescent lights went out and the emergency lights came on, spotlights that threw hard shadows, making the scene more unreal.

More metal ripped outside the immediate chamber. The wall cracked near the floor with a sound like a gunshot and a jet of water sprayed into the chamber, catching him in the face with surprising force.

He flinched.

I'm underwater, he realized. And not just a little bit.

For an instant he pictured the structure plunging to the ocean floor four thousand feet down, and his heart beat harder, but then he realized the utility deck above must still open on air—no water was rushing in from the hatch above.

Snatching at his fins and mask, he tried to stand, but the floor wasn't cooperating—it dropped again and, with a crashing sound from above, jerked to a stop. This time when he went down his right hand folded back and he felt something give way. Oddly, there was no real pain. He pulled himself back to knees and good arm.

Water started pouring down the stairway.

Shit.

One look at the flood pouring down the stairwell and through the cage doors on the elevator shaft convinced him he couldn't force his way past the flow.

He threw himself at the door to the outer walkway and tried it, but it wouldn't budge. The pressure differential was too great. He looked past the torrent pouring down the stairwell to the dock level below. Water was pooling on the floor of the dock's antechamber, both from the flow coming down from above and from another plate-sized hole low in the wall.

He tried to get some sense of motion. Was the entire structure settling steadily into the depths, or had it stabilized at some survivable depth?

The water volume pouring down had increased to columns the size of the openings. He could no longer see past the torrent to the chamber below, and though water was still draining out of this level, it was coming in faster than ever. The water rose to his knees.

Keith put his mask on one-handed, clamping his fins between his legs.

The dock chamber below finished flooding and suddenly the water level was rising in inches per second. He struggled to put his fins on one-handed. By the time he finished, the door to the outside was nearly underwater.

With three quick, deep breaths he ducked under, just as the water rose to the battery box on the emergency lighting unit, and it blew in a shower of sparks. The chamber went pitch dark, but his hand found the edge of the door. He groped down to the latch. The handle turned easily, but the door still wouldn't move.

Keith wondered if wreckage from the catwalk platform, or even the dock, was holding it shut. His ears popped—the water overhead was getting deeper. He used his good hand and his other arm to hold on to a conduit next to the door; he braced his feet against the door itself and pushed as hard as he could.

Nothing. It must be fouled by wreckage.

He pulled himself down the conduit to the floor, felt his way along to the stairwell to the dock deck, and kicked down into the dock antechamber, yawning to equalize pressure in his ears. It was pitch black except for faint yellowish light coming through the plate-sized hole in the wall—which had been about four feet to the right of the door.

Swimming to the wall, he groped till his fingers caught the edge of the door. As on the floor above, he found the latch, braced himself with one hand around a pipe conduit and both feet against the door, and shoved for all he was worth.

The door opened a crack—water rushed inward past him, equalizing pressures—and then gave way. Dim, yellow-green light trickled into the chamber. He saw that the dock platform was gone and, twisting around as he kicked through the door, saw that the catwalk deck above was missing, too. Past the catwalk level, a snarl of gratings was jammed against the bottom of the module—a large section of which seemed to be underwater.

How deep am I?

His depth gauge was on the console of his tank, now back at Science, but he could see the surface beyond the dark silhouette of Residential. In the distance, catwalk and module lights above the water's surface wavered, mixing to create the weird, yellow-green glow. He kicked hard, going forward to clear the wreckage

before rising, cradling his injured wrist. *Now* it hurt.
And his body was screaming for air.

He'd been under more than a minute now. Probably
closer to two. His best free dive time was two minutes
and fifteen seconds, but these were hardly optimal conditions. And he must be close to thirty feet below the
surface. With the wreckage and the submerged bottom
of the module blocking his path to the surface.

Fortunately the current pushed him steadily in the
direction he wanted to go. He started up as soon as he
was clear. It was agony; his lungs felt close to bursting. Twenty feet, fifteen . . . a little farther; come on,
just a little farther. Then his vision went black.

And water slapped him in the face. He convulsed
and had a fit of coughs. An arm stretching over his
shoulder and across his chest held him on his back,
face just out of the water.

Emma said, "Easy, I've got you. Just relax." Her
voice was muffled, as if he had cotton or wax in his
ears.

He stopped flailing and went limp, still coughing.
Emma had him in a cross-chest carry. He stared at the
starry sky and cradled his right hand, which hurt like
the devil.

The back of his head bumped a hard, metallic edge
as suction pulled his lower legs onto an angled grating.
He realized they'd reached the OTEC plant.

"Hang on," Emma said. He rolled over and
grabbed the edge of the deck as she scrambled out of
the water. She hooked her arm around his thigh at the
crotch—he could feel her upper arm against his tes-
ticles; under other circumstances, he'd have been delighted—and together, with the aid of the waves that
surged up over the OTEC plant's lip, they got him up
onto the deck.

He crawled up onto his haunches, panting. She

crouched, smiling at him. Her hair hung in ropes around her face.

"You look a mess," she said. Her voice was still muffled. His eardrums must still be affected by the noise of the explosion. "Are you okay?"

He nodded, wiping his mouth. "Yeah," he croaked. His own voice came out sounding muffled, too.

Actually, he felt like warmed-over shit. His right hand was either broken or severely sprained—the hand was completely useless. And his whole body ached, as if he'd been worked over by baseball bats.

"Help me stand," he said. Once upright he insisted on walking by himself over to the ladder up to the dock deck. He only weaved a little.

"You go first," Emma said. He did so—and it was awkward; he was trembling. His muscles felt like jelly. She kept her hand on his back to steady him, and he managed to get up to the deck level.

Keith propped himself on the railing as Emma climbed up the ladder and looked around the edge of the pole at the dark wreckage of the Residential module. The main deck was now mostly underwater.

"It's sinking," he said, pointing, as Emma joined him. Her gaze followed his to the ruined module.

A horrified look came onto her face. "Oh my God. It'll take the rest of Gulf Stream with it."

Chapter 50

GABRIEL: Wednesday, 7 October, 6:50 P.M. EDT
The Cherokee Princess, about seven-eighths of a nautical
mile north of Gulf Stream I

"We used a *lot* of C-4," Mark had said. "Shrapnel will go everywhere."

So they planned to tie off at the farthest downstream breakwater buoy and detonate the charges.

Gabriel, astern, lifted the binoculars to his eyes yet again to scan the facilities, then turned to scan for the breakwater. The orange buoys were perhaps an eighth of a mile or so downstream; it'd be probably another few minutes. Not much longer.

Everyone had settled down, and Gabriel was calmer. Just get the job done, he thought, and then I'll force them to free the hostages. A prison sentence beats committing murder. I'll use the gun if I have to.

He got up and peered through the viewfinder of the tripod-mounted video camera, adjusting the angle so the entire facility was in the shot. Plenty of charge remained, and the camera's low-light capability made the facility quite visible even in twilight. Swells were about four feet and the boat was pitching quite a bit; he experimented with the zoom, trying to keep the facility in the shot despite the pitch.

Then Gulf Stream's external lights started to come on. Gabriel started—but realized it must be an automated process, activated as the sun set. There'd been no signs of life at Gulf Stream for the past twenty minutes; he prayed Emma and the man who had carried her over the side were now well away from the facility.

Boadica was below, guarding the hostages. Jax sat just behind him, down on the main deck, amid a scattering of tools, working on the battery leads. Except for the banging and clattering, and an occasional swear word, he was silent. Gabriel guessed repairs weren't going well.

A moment later Mark, up on the foredeck, announced that they'd reached the breakwater. Gabriel hurried forward to help him. Mark snagged the anchor line beneath a buoy with a boat hook. Together they pulled the entire buoy aboard and Mark tied it off at a cleat at the bow. The boat swung around to face upstream.

Gulf Stream's life rafts, filled with evacuees, were moored to other breakwater buoys, not all that far away—maybe an eighth of a mile or so. Farther away, three boats with the Gulf Stream I insignia—a hundred twenty-foot commercial trawler and two thirty-five or forty-foot work boats—held station a short distance downstream of the breakwater line.

Gabriel and Mark both looked back at Gulf Stream.

"Time to blow that sucker," Mark said.

Jax stood. "And about damn time. Better let Boadica know."

Gabriel glanced at his watch. It was 6:53. "I need to make sure the camera is set up for the shot. Give me two more minutes."

"Hurry it up," Jax said.

While Mark put his binoculars to his eyes again, watching for the Coast Guard, Gabriel jumped down from the foredeck, stepped over Jax's tools, and climbed back up to the aft deck to adjust the camera shot. Then Mark shouted.

"Heads up! Coast Guard cutter, closing from the east-southeast!"

Boadica took the steps up from belowdeck two at a time. Brilliant light flooded them, moving across the deck as she stepped out; Gabriel blinked and turned, shielding his eyes. The silhouette of a large boat—a ninety-footer, perhaps—lay behind the bright light. Boadica said, "Jax, bring me the bullhorn and one of the prisoners. Hustle!"

Jax leapt to his feet, wiping his hands, and headed into the cabin.

"Boat on my bow! This is the Coast Guard! Stand fast and prepare to be boarded!"

It was the same cutter that had boarded them earlier in the day, and Gabriel recognized the voice as that of the same young officer who had performed the inspection of their boat.

Boadica caught the bullhorn Jax tossed her. He shoved the tall young man, the Anglo with blond hair, up the steps. Jax made a big show of holding the man in the cutter's floodlight with the gun pointed at his temple. The young man was stiff-backed, but tears were streaming down his face and he was making choked sobbing noises. Gabriel rubbed his lip with his thumb and sighed, shaking his head.

Boadica held the horn out to Gabriel. "You're our spokesman."

He stared at her. He had to choke off a laugh— *you've got to be kidding*. She half lifted her own gun with a warning look.

"The hostages were your idea," he said. "*You* deal with it."

And, quite deliberately, he turned away and lifted his binocs to watch the facility. The hair stood out on his neck; he doubted she'd have compunctions about putting a bullet into the back of his head, if she were angry enough.

So be it.

After an intense pause—he could feel the heat of her fury on his back—Boadica said, "Mark."

A moment later he heard Mark's voice on the loud-speaker. "Stay back! We have five hostages and will kill them if boarded. Starting with this one," and he gestured at the blond man Jax held.

A long pause ensued.

"What do we do?" Mark whispered finally.

Boadica said, "Wait it out. It's their move."

More time passed.

The voice on the bullhorn this time was a different one, deeper and more authoritative. "You are under arrest. Surrender your prisoners and throw down your weapons. *Now*."

Gabriel heard Mark and Boadica speaking in low tones. Then Mark said through the bullhorn, "Not until we have some guarantees. We want to speak to someone in authority."

"I'm Lieutenant Arneson, the ranking officer of this cutter. I have authority. Name your demands."

Mark scoffed, and Jax hooted, loudly enough to carry across the water. "Give us someone with *real* authority and we'll talk. Get us the governor. You have"—an exchange of whispers—"half an hour."

Gabriel, watching the facility, saw movement on the catwalk, quite visible under the mercury globes strung along the walk. He lifted his binoculars. A man was heading for the southernmost module at a dead run. Gabriel stiffened.

He felt a presence behind him and turned; Boadica stood there. "You're our spokesman. Our leader, remember? What the *fuck* are you trying to prove?" Then she read his expression and frowned. "What is it?"

She looked toward Gulf Stream, and her expression

changed to alarm. She spun. "Jax, detonate the charges. *Now!*"

"No!" Gabriel lurched to his feet. *"There are people there!"*

He lunged toward Jax, but Boadica tripped him and he fell forward onto the main deck—an eighteen-inch drop that jarred his wrists all the way up to the shoulder sockets. Tools went skittering across the deck. Stepping away from Gabriel as he sprawled, Jax pulled the detonator box from his pants pocket and pressed the button.

Gabriel climbed to his feet as the sound of the explosion reached them. It was not as loud as he had expected. He looked back at the facility in time to see a spray of water settle over it. One of the modules had risen slightly into the air; it was falling now, into a crashing wave.

One module. Only one. Three were intact.

"What the fuck—?" Mark yelled.

Then a second shock wave, from the north, hit them and Gabriel felt heat on his neck, like sunshine. He turned. Where the hydrogen storage barge had been, floating away a mile downstream, was an expanding ball of flame several hundred feet in diameter. As he watched, a white cloud of steam rose in a classic mushroom cloud, propelled by the heat below.

Even Boadica stared for a moment, awestruck. Then she shook herself. "Gabriel, get below! Jax, you too— bring the prisoner. Mark, stand watch. Keep your head down. They may have snipers."

Jax shoved the Anglo prisoner back belowdeck. Gabriel limped over to the steps and followed them down, rubbing his wrists. He sat down at the table, his semiautomatic cradled in his arms.

The hostages, hands tied, were in shadow, all crowded onto the double bed up in the bow. Jax boosted the young Anglo back up onto the bed. Someone was moaning. One of the prisoners, the black man, said, "You'd better get some air in here or you're going to be ankle-deep in vomit. We've got some pretty seasick people up here."

Jax made a derisive noise, but Boadica said, "Go ahead."

So Jax reached up and cracked open the forward hatch above the bed. A moment later Gabriel felt a breeze on his face. The moans diminished.

"They got to most of the charges." Jax came back into the main cabin and slammed a fist into the wall. "After we risked our asses."

Boadica was staring at Gabriel, rigid, skin and lips marble white. Her hand was on her weapon, knuckles also white. "Explain."

He stared back. "Explain what?"

"You refused to deal with the Coast Guard. You didn't shout a warning when you saw someone on the facility. They had people running around on the cat-walks while you just sat there! How much else did you see, and not warn us?"

Jax gaped at Gabriel. The shock on his face mutated to anger.

Gabriel looked from one to the other. That's it, he thought. He stood and pointed his weapon at them.

"Enough. *Enough!* This is going to stop right now."

"I'm afraid not," she said.

"Oh, yes. You can blow up all the goddamned plants you want to, Bo, and I'll be right there beside you handing you charges. They're *things*. I don't give a damn about *things*. But I'm not in this to kill innocent people."

Jax groaned and rolled his eyes. "What are we supposed to do? Turn the hostages loose and tell the feds we're sorry?"

"Exactly," Gabriel said.

"You dumb *fuck*. Chickenshit!"

"Jax, shut up," Boadica said, and came at Gabriel, slowly, motioning him toward her with her hands. "Come on, then. Stop us. You're going to have to shoot us to stop us. Shoot Jax and me. Come on."

Gabriel took aim at her. She smiled that little smile he was coming to loathe. His hands trembled. *Fuck.* Of course he couldn't.

She snatched the weapon away and handed it to Jax. Her voice held so much rage it came out a coarsened whisper. "You'll do exactly what I tell you to do."

Gabriel sighed heavily. "I don't think so, Bo."

She pointed her gun at his head, that cool, quizzical smile rising on her lips. "Then you're dead."

Gabriel dove as she fired and, with a shout, Jax grabbed the barrel of the gun. Sound pummeled Gabriel's ear and air brushed his cheek. With a scream he scrambled back toward the prisoners.

There was nowhere to run.

Boadica was coming toward him, aiming. He was a sitting duck. And five innocent people were behind him, in her line of fire.

"Are you crazy?" Jax yelled, so loud Gabriel could hear him over the ringing in his ears, and wrestled the gun barrel down. "You can't! It's *Gabe*, for Christ's sake! Stop it!"

Mark jerked the cabin door open. "What the hell is going on down there?"

"Nothing," Boadica snarled. "Get back to your station!"

Mark hesitated, staring, then closed the door again.

Jax grabbed Boadica in a half nelson. She fought him, silently, her eyes dilated, teeth clenched, the muscles in her back and arms standing out, as developed as a weight lifter's; for a second Gabriel wondered if she was going to shoot *him*. But Jax had enough strength to contain her until his words had an impact.

Slowly she released her breath and dropped her shoulders—stopped fighting. Carefully, watching her, Jax let her go. She shoved the gun into the waistband of her pants. Boadica's gaze returned to Gabriel. Over her shoulder, to Jax, she said, "Looks like you get your wish. You're in charge."

"What do we do about Gabe?"

She gave Gabriel a disgusted look. "We can't trust him. Tie him up and put him with the others. I don't want to have to look at him again."

Chapter 51

Emma stared at the shattered, slowly sinking module. Then slapped her forehead. Of course. The buoyancy control lines that ran though the pole's wall, to and from the module's controller, had to have been severed. And now that she was listening for it she could hear the hisses and spitting as wet air was released from the jagged end of the lower beanpole that jutted up from Residential's roof.

Emma turned to Keith. He looked dreadful: hunched over, new scratches on top of the old bruise on his jaw, eyes sunken and haggard, wrist clutched to his chest. She hated to leave him, but . . .

"Can you make it up to Control on your own?"

"Yeah." He straightened with a deep breath. "Think you can fix it?"

She looked back at Residential. "I'm going to try. Radio Flo, would you? *Pesky*'s spare buoyancy can buy us more time. Tell her to position the trawler up-stream of Residential right away, and snag the anchor line. The main anchor buoy is going to be threatened soon, and we can't afford to lose that.''

''Right. We can also get a lot of divers with spare tanks down to the buoyancy chambers to refill them. Buys us yet more time.''

''Excellent idea.'' She touched his shoulder—partly for his comfort, partly for hers. ''Hurry.''

Then she dashed into the antechamber, snatched up her mask, snorkel, and fins, and headed up the two flights of stairs to the utility deck.

As she climbed she called up a mental diagram of the facility design. It had been a long time since she'd designed the facility structure, but . . . the air lines were stainless steel; in fact, if she remembered correctly, they'd used half-inch or five-eighths-inch tubing.

In the maintenance shop were plenty of tapered dowels in approximately the right sizes, both wooden and rubber. She grabbed a bag and dumped as many dowels as she could find into it. She also grabbed a three-pound mallet, a pair of pliers, fifty feet of high-visibility yellow nylon rope, a submersible flashlight, some wrenches, and a life jacket. Then she ran back down to the catwalk level and made for Residential, via Science.

The darkened catwalk entered the water about thirty-five feet from Residential. She stopped where the steel grating met the water, set the bag down a few feet from the swells' reach, and pulled out the rope.

After tying the open-top bag up tightly—both to keep water from ballooning it out and to keep its tools secure—she tied the other end of the rope around her ankle and laid the coils of remaining rope near the bag. Then she put on her life jacket, fins, and mask, and duck-walked into the water down the submerged

catwalk. When the water was up to her thighs she sank
in and swam along, pulling herself against the current
using the mesh. At the point where the water reached
the railing she dovetailed over it, kicking off, and
headed straight into the current, swimming for all she
was worth.

She kept her eye on the submerged catwalk below
for as long as she could see it. It was the longest
twenty feet she had ever swum. Finally, the grating of
the mid deck's walkway, now awash, loomed ahead.
With a final, desperate burst of energy she scissor-
kicked forward, grabbed for the walkway's upper railing. And got it.

She pulled herself along the rail, getting slapped in
the face by swells, until she reached the outer stairway,
and climbed up the steps. After sitting down to remove
her fins and mask she untied the line from her ankle.
Back on the catwalk, the bag was now at the water's
edge. It scooted along the grating as she reeled the
line in and dropped into the water. There was a lot of
drag.

Then she picked up her fins, mask, and snorkel,
hauled the bag up onto her shoulder, rope and all, and
ran up the outer stairs past the broken windows, amid
glass shards, chunks of concrete, and other wreckage,
to the roof.

The module roof was on a tilt, maybe ten degrees
or so. It was so dark she couldn't see much beyond
weak shadows cast by the lights from the other modules and catwalks. She flipped on the flashlight and,
as she surveyed the ruin, burst into tears. Picking her
way through the destroyed vegetation, the shattered
planters and pots, she shook her fist at the yacht and
said, "Gabriel Cervantes, you bastard, if I ever see
you again, you're dog meat."

Once at the beanpole, she walked around it, shining
the flashlight on top till she located the severed lines.

They were easy to find—she simply followed the loud hissing noise. Then she set down her fins and mask and bag. Drying her eyes, she examined the lines.

There were seventy-five of them, most sticking up from the concrete in a tangle that resembled an explosion of noodles. The openings of many of these were bent, either partly or mostly pinched off. Another half dozen were severed cleanly, their openings virtually circular and flush with the concrete.

Emma dug out the mallet and tapered dowels. She found a dowel the right size, shoved it into one of the openings past the rushing air. Then she lifted her arm and brought the mallet down hard.

Chapter 52

GABRIEL: **Wednesday, 7 October, 7:03 P.M. EDT**
The Cherokee Princess, **about one nautical mile
north of Gulf Stream I**

Jax made Gabriel kneel on the floor and pulled duct tape from a drawer in the mess, shaking his head.

"Sorry it came to this," he said, as he jerked loops of duct tape around Gabriel's wrists. "But I always knew you were going to weasel out on us."

"Jax, you're making a big mistake," Gabriel said.

"Shut the fuck up." He hefted him up onto the bed among the five hostages.

Knees and buttocks shifted, trying to make room, but still Gabriel ended up half-sprawled across the short, dark-haired Anglo man's calves, lying back against the lap of the blond woman Jax had struck earlier, with the black man's elbow in his side.

"*Madre de Dios.*" He struggled into a sitting position and leaned his aching head on his knee.

The black man nudged him. "Hey."

Gabriel lifted his head. He could barely see the man. Jax was in the mess making coffee; he squinted into the shadowed bow at them. The black man stopped talking, and Jax went on with what he was doing. "We heard you up there trying to defend us. We want to escape. Are you with us?"

Gabriel eyed him thoughtfully. "You bet your ass, friend. But, no offense, I think we are at a slight disadvantage."

"I've got a penknife," the man said, almost too low for Gabriel to make out over the ringing in his ears. Gabriel leaned toward him to hear better. "Rambo up there didn't find it when he searched me."

He looked down and saw a dull glint of metal in the man's hand. The blade was pitifully small. "We've tried, but with our hands tied we can't get through the ropes. The blade's too dull. But it should work on duct tape. Can you turn your back to me?"

"I think so." Gabriel wormed his way around till he was mostly facing the blond man. The knife rasped across the tape; Gabriel pulled as hard as he could, wincing at the tearing sounds.

During this time, Jax sat down at the table facing them with a cup, then stood up and paced, sat, stood, and paced some more. Occasionally he looked out the portal; occasionally he glanced at the hostages.

Gabriel, unfortunately, was the easiest to see, since he sat at the center front of the bed. The bulkheads mostly concealed the black man and the blond Anglo, shadow partly concealed the redhead, and the two in the corners at the front were well concealed by both shadow and bulkheads.

The tape gave way and, when Jax's back was turned, Gabriel pulled his hands free. He bunched up the tape and stuck it to the wall, then quickly put his hands behind himself again.

"Give me the knife," he whispered. The black man dropped the tiny blade into his right hand. To the red-head he said, "Can you turn around?"

"I'll try." She squirmed around as the others contorted themselves to give her room. The dark-haired Anglo with the tattoos moaned.

"Jeez, I feel sick. It's too cramped in here. I need a cigarette."

"For God's sake, Mac," the blond young man whispered. "Don't even *talk* about tobacco, or *I'll* toss. Take some deep breaths and try to relax." After a minute he said, "Those blasts—poor ol' Louie. Sure hope he survived."

The other man made a noise. "*I'm* more worried about *us*."

Gabriel leaned back into the black man, letting what light there was shine past him to illuminate the red-head's hands. He took a good, hard look at the bonds. The cord was three-sixteenths-inch white nylon, the same rope Jax and Mark had used with the charges. Small diameter, and stiff; it must hurt like hell. It cut deep into her wrists—the skin was red above and white below, where circulation had been cut off. The knots were multiplex and complicated, and the boat's pitching was pretty bad here.

This was going to take some doing.

He swung his legs down off the bed to give himself some more room and, reaching behind himself, took hold of her wrists. Jax looked up and frowned; Gabriel froze.

"Don't get cute. Get back up there."

"Have a heart. It's crowded in here."

"I want your legs all the way up on the bed."

"Have it your way, dick-head."

He shouldn't have. But Jax didn't seem particularly

upset; he just shrugged and, as Gabriel tucked his legs up under him, turned and looked out the portal again.

Gabriel began to work at the woman's bonds, going by feel and using the penknife as a wedge in the knots. He had no idea how long he was at it.

Eventually her hands came free. Gabriel whispered, "Take the knife."

"Give me a minute. My hands are numb."

"Say when."

In a moment she whispered, "When."

He dropped the knife into her hands and she started to work on the dark-haired Anglo, who was moaning again. Gabriel prayed the man wouldn't lose it, or they all would, and ruin their chances.

Able to work without being seen, once her hands had recovered, the woman made quicker progress than Gabriel had. Shortly the dark-haired man made a satisfied little noise, brought his hands forward, and shook them out, while the redhead turned to the British woman beside her. A moment later the dark-haired Anglo started on the blond man's bonds.

Gabriel eyed the partly open bow hatch, thinking.

The door opened and Boadica came in. She didn't spare a glance in his direction, though, merely spoke briefly with Jax. Jax went up top, and Boadica bent down, doing something in the underberth compartment aft of the table, the one that held the spare dive equipment. Gabriel figured he wouldn't get another chance.

The young British woman was now working on the black man's bonds, and the blond man was now free.

"Listen, quick," Gabriel whispered. "Life jackets and flares—compartment under the bed. Grab them and get out through the hatch."

So saying, he started to slide off the berth, but quickly tucked his legs back up as Boadica straightened. They all froze while she set the spare set of dive equipment on the floor by the stairs and opened the tank valve. Then she reached back into the compartment and removed a radio he hadn't known was there.

"Gryphon, this is White Harpy, come back." She repeated the message at least three times. Then the radio spat static and a reply came.

"This is Gryphon. Go ahead, White Harpy."

"I'm ready for the pickup," she said, squatting next to the compartment. "Come on in. I'll be there in about fifteen or twenty minutes. The arranged signal."

"Fifteen to twenty. Roger. See you then."

She put the radio in a waterproof bag and tucked it into a pouch at her belt, then removed something else from the compartment and came forward with it. Gabriel gasped as he got a good look at it. "*Shit*. She's planting a bomb."

Around him were gasps of dismay. Meanwhile, Boadica knelt on the floor of the cabin, repeatedly pushed a button on the detonator control panel, and then flipped a switch. She set the bomb down as she removed the bilge hatch and he caught a glimpse of the time on the display: fifty-eight seconds and counting. She lowered the bomb into the bilge, reaching in till her entire head and shoulders were belowdeck.

Gabriel slid off the bed. The black man was free now, too, standing and reaching for the bow hatch. Moving down the short hall toward Boadica, Gabriel undogged the French doors and pulled them to behind him, obscuring the forecompartment from her view. He grabbed the fire extinguisher from the wall and as he neared her, pulled the pin. She came up from the bilge hatch and saw him—her eyes widened and she drew her gun.

The extinguisher was an ABC dry chemical extinguisher. He blasted her in the face with ammonium phosphate. She fell back with a scream, free hand at her face, and her gun went off; the shot struck the bulkhead over the stove.

Gabriel kicked her in the chest, thinking, Forgive me, Mother. She fell back on her buttocks and scooted back, still blinking and coughing. Gabriel advanced, and she rose to her side, kicking out—the blow didn't fully connect with his knee, but it hurt enough to slow him down.

The door to the main deck flew open and Jax rushed down the steps, followed by Mark. Both had guns drawn, aimed at him.

"Freeze!"

I'm dead, Gabriel thought. He raised his hands, still holding the extinguisher. Behind him were soft scufflings from beyond the French door. Hurry, guys. Hurry.

"I'll freeze, all right, but we're all fucked. She was about to bug out," he said, gesturing at the spare set of dive equipment sitting next to the stairs. "She's planted a bomb in the bilge, and it goes off in twenty seconds—maybe less."

Jax and Mark stared at Boadica, still blinking and wiping at her eyes, then at the dive equipment. Jax yelled and charged her, grabbing her around the neck and knocking her weapon from her hand.

"You *bitch*!" He shoved her to the floor next to the bilge hatch. "Disarm it! *Now!*"

Gabriel moved forward out of their way. Jax threw open the bilge hatch. Mark had his weapon aimed at Gabriel, but all his attention was on Jax, who was forcing Boadica into the bilge. She wasn't fighting him, either.

It was too late—there couldn't be but a few seconds left. Sorry, Mark, he thought; sorry, Jax. Without lifting the extinguisher, Gabriel tilted the nozzle up at Mark's upper body and squeezed the lever. Mark gasped and stumbled back out of the way, clawing at his eyes as the exhaust struck his face. Gabriel swung the fire extinguisher up, connecting with Mark's elbow—Mark's whole body twisted at the impact and the gun fell from his hand.

Gabriel dropped the fire extinguisher, grabbed the dive tanks by the yoke, and headed for the stairs.

Chapter 53

EMMA: Wednesday, 7 October, 7:22 P.M. EDT
Gulf Stream I

As Emma's mallet struck the dowel a flash lit the night sky—blue-white, brilliant as a camera flash. She jerked, looking up as a loud ka-boom! ricocheted across the water.

It wasn't Gulf Stream. It was the terrorists' yacht. A balloon of glowing amber rose hundreds of feet into the sky amid a shower of water, illuminating the sea's surface for miles. In its light Emma could see all the men standing on the Coast Guard cutter's deck, and the Gulf Stream staff sitting in their Zodiacs, moored to the breakwater buoys. As the fire went out and darkness fell, debris, lighted by the Coast Guard cutter's spots, began raining across the water amid the floating pieces of burning detritus that had once been the yacht.

Emma's limbs went weak. She swayed and caught herself, hand over mouth. Gloria, Ben, Rob, Nikki, and Mac were on that yacht. *She'd* been on that yacht. If it weren't for Keith she still would be.

Numbly, she locked her knees and drew herself upright. Gulf Stream needed her. Think about the rest later.

Emma had plenty of dowels, so it was merely a matter of plugging holes, and then of pounding, bending, and pinching the unpluggable leaks shut with mallet and pliers. She worked fast. Gradually, the hissing sound diminished. She was at it a long time. At one point she heard a helicopter, and looked up to see its lights as it circled the facility, shining its spot. It took her a long time to realize that it must be Freddy arriving with Pendleton.

When she'd done as much as she could Emma straightened, working her arms. She'd pay for this night, in quartfuls of Icy Hot ointment. And in other ways.

Residential was still losing air, but much more slowly now. The stars were out in their full glory: the Milky Way lay, a brilliant trail of jewels, across the black, cloudless heavens. The breeze was cool. Water lapped against the module walls, a soft slapping sound.

To the southwest, *Pesky* held station near the anchor buoy; the helicopter was coming in to land at Mariculture. *Granny* and *Ox* were docked at the marina, and Emma saw three pairs of divers, all with spare tanks, near Residential: one pair on the catwalk nearing the point of submersion; one pair suiting up and checking out their equipment; and the last wading together into the water where the Mariculture-Residential catwalk lay submerged. Another diver surfaced along the catwalk as she watched.

She avoided looking any farther to the north.

Emma made her way to the stairway at the roof's edge. The water had risen above the mid deck as she'd worked. The swells lapping against the wall were only about seven feet down from the roof. She walked down the steps till she reached the water and sank in.

The water was warm. It felt like an embrace. She had no strength in her limbs.

Just let the water take me, she thought. Carry me far away. But she swam hard, cross-current. In a moment she reached the Science-Residential catwalk, a few feet north of where it entered the water. People there helped her climb over the railing and out of the water.

People . . . ? It was Keith. He helped her out of the life jacket and fins, and held her so tightly by the arms that it hurt.

"Let's get back to Control," she said, trying to pass him. But he held on to her.

"Emma, listen. The Coast Guard spotted some people jumping off the boat right before it went—we don't know who yet, but there may be survivors—"

Emma stared at him. The walls inside crumbled in the face of this unexpected hope. She went rigid and her fists balled. Something, a growl or shout, formed in her chest. She expelled the sound; her shoulders hunched; she pressed fists to her mouth.

"It's my fault, Keith—they'd never have gotten aboard if it weren't for me—"

"Stop it," he said. "It's not your fault." But she couldn't stop. So he pulled her close and held her in a fierce hug. She couldn't tell where the salt water ended and the tears began.

Chapter 54

They crossed the catwalks at a trudge, hand in hand, to Engineering, and took the elevator up to the top level. When Emma opened the door to Control, the engineers, technicians, and messengers there surged toward her with exclamations and questions.

With a last, regretful glance at Keith, Emma slipped her hand from his, straightened, and shrugged on her corporate honcho cloak. Stepping over to the console she became all business, asking questions, listening, organizing actions.

Keith backed up to a wall by the inner door. The noise and activity overwhelmed him. He was still unsteady on his feet and everything sounded muffled. He needed to lie down, but both his bunk and the medical center were in Residential. And his hand hurt like hell.

Lee Attewell came in the door, right hand and arm taped up with gauze and adhesive tape. He took one look at Keith and shook his head.

"You shouldn't be here. There's a first-aid station down on the utility deck with plenty of empty cots. Why don't you head on down?"

Keith glanced at Emma. It'd take a crowbar, or an airlift, to get to her right now and let her know where he was going. Lee's gaze tracked his.

"I'll let her know where you went," Lee said. "You go on, son."

Keith nodded weary thanks, and left. He stopped in the head, then went to the locker room and struggled out of his wet-suit top, ending up standing on part of it to pull it off his good arm. Getting a borrowed pair of coveralls on was also a problem, but he managed. He continued on to Utility.

Equipment and stored materials had been shoved out of the way at the tail end of the deck and three rows of cots and blankets lay out amid the forklifts, carboys, bags, and pallets. Perhaps a dozen people lay or sat around: a couple being attended to, others waiting or resting. Most of the injuries appeared to be relatively minor. Two people—Michael and a woman—were attending to them.

Keith sank onto an empty cot with a wince, lay back, and laid an arm across his eyes. With all the activity—not the triage; there seemed to be a bit of a lull at the moment; it was more due to the technicians and engineers who hurried about, moving equipment, hauling things beyond the periphery of the first-aid staging area, shouting at each other—the environment wasn't very restful. But lying down in here beat standing around up in Control.

He eavesdropped idly on snatches of conversations. From the sound of things, most of the other people in triage had been injured by debris from the destruction of the terrorists' yacht or the hydrogen barge. It also sounded as though most staff expected to be up all night trying to stabilize Gulf Stream's condition.

If dedication is any sort of currency, he thought, Gulf Stream is rich beyond measure.

A woman's voice said, "Hello, there," as a cool hand slipped behind his neck. He uncovered his eyes. The woman he'd seen tending to other patients knelt beside him, reaching with her left hand into a big plastic tackle box on the floor while fingering his neck with her right. She was in her fifties, perhaps, and wore a stethoscope and a radio at her belt. Her manner was brisk, quick, and pleasant.

"I'm Ann Sigda, the facility physician." She slipped a soft cervical collar out of the tackle box, lifted his head, and put the collar on him, Velcroing it shut. "How are you feeling? How's your breathing?"

"Fine, I guess."

"We're going to strip you for an exam." She put a hand on his chest when he tried to sit up. "No, no, lie still. Let us do the work. Michael, give me a hand." Together, she and Michael got his coveralls and swimsuit off, and covered him with a sheet. She took his left wrist, checking the pulse. Meanwhile she asked, "What happened to you?"

"I was in Residential when it blew."

Her eyes widened. "Pulse eighty-two, respiration twenty-eight," she said to Michael, who recorded it on a clipboard. "Where were you? How did you get out?" She started feeling around his chest.

"I was in the Residential beanpole. Catwalk antechamber. I swam out when the structure went underwater."

"Any idea how deep you went?" She got out the stethoscope, and paused for his answer.

"No more than thirty feet." He hesitated. "I did black out in the water. Emma pulled me out. Probably shallow water blackout—I had to hold my breath for a long time."

She pulled the top of the sheet down and listened to his chest. "Did you cough when you came to?"

"Like a son of a bitch."

"Hmmm. Well, your chest sounds clear, but you may have taken some water into your lungs."

Pulling the sheet farther down to reveal his bare abdomen, she moved the stethoscope to his belly and listened in several spots, and then poked at his guts, all over. Looking down, he saw a big patch of abraded skin down one side of his midriff, and a long, shallow gouge near his solar plexus. Now that he noticed them, they stung. He didn't remember either happening.

"Did you vomit?"

"No."

She slipped her hands under him, below the ribs, and poked around some more, pressed on his hip bones, and then on his pelvic arch and his bladder.

"Have you peed? Do you think you can take a leak?"

"I already have."

She pulled the top of the sheet up and then moved the lower edge up to expose his crotch and upper thighs, and scratched his inner thigh lightly with a fingernail. Then she pulled the lower edge of the sheet back over his legs and moved up to his shoulders. She checked his collarbone and his shoulder joints, and moved down his right arm, wiggling the elbow and wrist joints, feeling the bones and muscles of the arm.

"I sprained my hand, or something," he said.

"Okay, let's check it out." She put her hands inside his. "Squeeze my hands."

He squeezed, but he could tell that his right hand barely pressed her skin. She felt the bones of his hand.

"You've got quite a knot here," she said, and squeezed the outer edge of his hand. Something inside went clickety-click. It *hurt*. He yelped. She nodded.

"Looks like you've got a spiral fracture of your fifth metacarpal. The bone connected to your pinkie. Michael, get me something to splint it with."

"Back in a flash," Michael said. By the time she'd finished checking the other arm and his legs and feet, Michael had returned with a length of cardboard and some tape. They rolled Keith's right hand and forearm up in the cardboard and secured it with string, then, using a roll of bandage, rigged a short sling, pulling his hand almost up to his chin. "Try to keep it raised. That'll keep the swelling down."

Then she picked up the radio at her belt. It had been chattering and squawking all during his exam, part of the background noise, but he hadn't heard her name called until she responded.

"This is Sigda; go ahead."

Lee's voice said, "Coast Guard called. The hostages have all been recovered and they're bringing them to you for triage."

"ETA?"

"Another five minutes or so."

"Their condition?"

"Not a lot of detail. The Coast Guard medic will be with them." A brief pause. "Hannah says that the York chopper is ready to take your ambulatory patients to Holmes Regional whenever you're ready. The medevac chopper you ordered is also on its way." Pause. "ETA about an hour."

"Thanks, Lee."

"Oh, is Keith Hellman there? Emma's looking for him. Pendleton and some federal official types want a debriefing."

Keith sat up at that, threw off the sheet, and reached for the coveralls. That made Ann Sigda frown and point a stern finger at him. "Lie back down. I'm not done." Keith paused, then lay back down with a sigh.

"He's right here," she said into the radio. "I'd rather get him on the York chopper. He's not cleared yet."

A pause, and Emma came on. "It's critical he be present. He can go on the medevac chopper, can't he?"

She sighed. "I suppose. I'll finish up here and send him on up."

"Oh, and they want to talk to whichever of the hostages are up to questioning, too. Can you hold up the York chopper till after they're done, or are you going to need a third one?"

"Come on, Emma, these people have been through hell. Our first priority should be their health and well-being. Can't you tell the feds to hold on to their britches?"

A cough. "Well, they're being very insistent. But if you think any of our guys is too banged up or out of it to be questioned, just don't clear them from tri-age. I'll back you up."

"All right. Thanks. And no, I don't want to hold up the York chopper. Get another one out here for the last of the ambulatory ones. Bringing back the York chopper is fine, or one like it. Doesn't have to be an ambulance unit."

"Ten-four."

"Sigda out."

She tucked the radio back into its holster and, while poking around Keith's scalp, asked him his name and address, what day it was, and who the president was. She looked at his eyes, and then pulled an otoscope out of her tackle box and looked in his ears.

"I feel like my ears are full of water," he said.

"They are," she said, grinning. Then she shook her head. "You have a minor barometric injury, nothing serious. It'll clear up on its own."

After checking the reflexes in his elbows and knees, she went on, "I know you walked in, but I want to check your neck and back more thoroughly. Bear with us. Michael—"

She and Michael used the blanket he was lying on to roll him over as a unit. Michael braced his shoulder, while she felt all the way down his back from the base of his skull to the crack of his buttocks.

Then they rolled him onto his back.

He sat up and looked about for his coveralls while Ann Sigda gave Michael a list of blood work and X rays he would need.

"Can I take this collar off?" Keith asked.

"I don't know about your neck yet—leave the collar on. Now, listen." Her tone was sharp. "I'm letting you go for now, but you had better be on that medevac chopper when it gets here—you're going to need X rays and lab work within the next two hours."

"I don't feel all that bad."

She shook her head. "You've taken a twenty-five-foot fall; your torso is scraped up and contused. You've been submerged and you might have a case of near-drowning syndrome, with an electrolyte imbalance and pulmonary damage. And there's also the potential you have an epidural hematoma from a blow to the head."

"I wasn't hit on the head."

"Not that you recall. You may not be remembering all the details of the trauma. And right now you could be in the lucid phase between the initial unconsciousness and an impending coma due to an expanding blood clot between the brain and the skull. Hey, you—" She collared a passerby, who turned out to be Jess, and who broke into a big smile when he saw Keith.

"I need you to stay with this man wherever he goes," she said. "If he collapses or starts acting strange you radio me immediately. You got that?"

"Got it," Jess said.

"All right. I've got to go. Promise you'll be on that chopper?"

Keith lifted his hands in a placating gesture. "Okay, Doc, you win."

"Good." She gave him a smile, and then she and Michael moved on to one of the newcomers. Keith began putting on his coveralls. Jess sat down on the cot next to him.

"The scuttlebutt is that they're due back any minute."

Keith didn't have to ask who *they* were. "Yeah. Listen, can I borrow your radio?"

Jess handed it to him.

"Keith to Emma."

She answered almost immediately. "Emma here."

"Where's the debriefing?"

"The Engineering conference room. But first I'm heading down to triage. The hostages have arrived at Mariculture and they're debarking right now."

"See you in a minute, then. Out." He handed Jess his radio.

People had been entering the utility deck from the antechamber and the outer walkway over the past few minutes; among them was Flo. She exited the beanpole antechamber, looking around, her daughter Ve-

ronica holding her hand. Keith called out to Flo and
she came over.

Veronica tugged on Flo's pants. "Mommy, where's
Daddy?"

Flo stroked her head. "He'll be here soon, darling."
Then, looking at Keith, "Are you okay?"

"Yeah. Just a few scratches and a banged-up
hand."

To his surprise, Veronica climbed up into his lap.
He gave her a hug and she put her thumb in her mouth.
Then she scrambled down. "Mommy, I need to go
find Daddy. I'll be right back."

"No, Daddy's not here yet. You stay with me."

Veronica complained and pulled against Flo's grip
on her wrist, but quieted when Flo scooped her up and
put her on her hip.

"Have you heard anything?" Jess asked.

Flo shook her head. "I got to talk to Ben on the
radio a few minutes ago. They're all a little shocky, I
guess."

A hush spreading across the deck drew their attention. Wrapped in blankets, limping, wet, and bedrag-
gled, five figures exited the antechamber: Nikki, Rob,
Gloria, Mac, and last, Ben.

Veronica shrieked, "Daddy!" and ran across the
deck with her arms open wide. The people beginning
to gather made way for the little girl; Ben knelt and
grabbed her in a fierce hug. Flo, right behind, crying
now, made it a threesome.

The crowd of waiting Streamers surrounded the former hostages, pummeled them on their backs, cried,
and hugged them. Then, out of the corner of his eye,
Keith saw a tall, dark-haired figure come into view
around the corner of a storage aisle that led to the outer
walkway. It was Emma. The Streamers parted to let
her through.

"Break it up," she shouted. "Break it up! People,

this is an emergency medical station, not a reunion!''

People pulled back enough to let the five through to the waiting cots, then hung around talking and gawking.

A man in Coast Guard denims with a stethoscope hanging across the back of his neck asked the room at large, "Is the doctor here?"

Ann raised her hand and started to walk toward him, but he moved toward her with three quick steps and steered her to the side, right behind Keith's cot.

"What's the scoop?" she asked.

"I'd appreciate it if you check the older woman right away." He jerked his head to the cot next to Keith's. Both Keith and Ann looked —it was Gloria, sitting slowly down, one hand on her side. "She seemed fine at first, but she's fading. She's tachycardic—about one-ten. Her blood pressure is okay, but she complained about some stomach pain as we climbed to the dock."

"Hmmm." Ann turned to the room at large. "Michael? Give me a hand here. We're going to start with Gloria."

Keith wanted to stay and see what was wrong with Gloria, but Pendleton and Barnes were waiting. Wincing, he stood slowly. Jess stood nearby, hovering and looking worriedly toward Nikki. Keith patted Jess on the back when he started to follow.

"You don't need to hang around with me, Jess. I'll have Emma and a couple others keeping a close eye on me."

"You sure?"

"Positive."

Jess looked relieved. "Thanks." He pushed his way through the crowd.

Keith limped over to a nearby exit to the outer walkway. Outside, he leaned on the rail. On Mariculture's roof, beneath its floodlights, sat Freddy's York Aviation helicopter.

He heard a door open and turned; it was Emma. Her face was stiff. "We'd better go. Pendleton is waiting for a debriefing."

Keith touched her face with a reassuring smile. Emma put her hand over his, and the expression on her face softened. "Gulf Stream owes you a big debt, you know. Again."

Keith smiled back. "I'll send you a bill."

"You keep somehow being right where I need you, right when I need you."

He thought of her rescuing him after the explosion and grunted. "Likewise."

"Come on. We've got a date with Pendleton, and some guy named Barnes, whoever that is."

Keith opened the door and held it for her. "He's FBI. Counterterrorist unit."

Passing him at the door, she paused and gave him a look that went from surprised to speculative.

"Ah," she said finally.

Chapter 55

EMMA: **Wednesday, 7 October, 8:08 P.M. EDT**
Gulf Stream I

Pendleton stood as she entered. Seated at the conference table were two others. Nearest the door was a middle-aged man with a receding hairline and a rock-stern face that made him look rather military; across from him sat a short, stout woman also in her mid- to late forties, perhaps, with silvery hair cropped in a short bob, and laugh lines splayed alongside penetrating eyes.

"Jennifer!" Keith exclaimed, wearing a big grin as he crossed over to the silver-haired woman. "I didn't know you were here."

They hugged.

"I got your E-mail in time to catch the flight," she said. "What happened to your arm?"

Meanwhile Pendleton approached Emma. "What is the status on the hostages?"

"They just made it to triage." Emma pushed her hair back with a sigh. "There are still some people who need to be checked, including the hostages, but at this point we have six people, including Keith, with injuries that will require medevac. Mostly burns, cuts, and fractures—nothing too serious so far, except an eye injury that might result in loss of vision. Another eleven people have very minor injuries that have already been taken care of—and most of them have chosen to go back on duty."

"Is the facility still at risk?"

"There is risk, but I consider things pretty well under control for the moment. We have Residential's buoyancy fairly well stabilized. A crew is setting up right now to tie the leaking air lines into a temporary control manifold. My primary concern is hidden structural damage that might cause failures and create a new crisis. I've got our ROV and several emergency dive teams down checking all structures and connections. I'll know more in a few hours."

"What about the staff? Where will they be quartered?"

"Over half are on duty; the rest we're bedding down wherever we can find space. As soon as *Pesky* is freed up—Flo thinks it'll be before midnight—I'm sending all children and personnel not directly involved in inspections and repairs back to Melbourne.

We should be able to begin bringing the most critical activities back on-line by Friday, Saturday at the latest, as long as there is no serious structural damage.''

Pendleton appeared thoughtful. "How likely is it that we escaped damage to the structures?"

Emma shrugged, regretful. "No idea yet. I'd like to give you a best guess, but I just don't have the data to make a realistic assessment. As soon as I do, I'll update you."

"All right. Oh, forgive me. Please, sit." Pendleton sat and gestured at the chair next to his; she sank into it gratefully. "Long-term, how salvageable is Residential?"

She hunched her shoulders. "Not, I'm afraid."

The words struck him almost like a physical blow. Emma flinched mentally, but continued. "We can recover some of the equipment and materials inside, depending on how extensive the damage is, but the module is a complete write-off and the beanpole took a tremendous shock. Frankly, it's surprising me that it's floating as well as it is."

Pendleton gave his head a rueful shake without saying a word. He looked very tired and grey.

"It's not necessarily all that bad," she said. "I've been thinking it over, and I've got some ideas. Remember, I designed Gulf Stream for ready expansion—well, it works in reverse, too. Eliminating Residential from the infrastructure won't be expensive. We'll have to decentralize some of its former functions—convert some of the offices and storage areas in the other modules to sleeping cabins, shrink our staff, get rid of some of our smaller and less profitable projects. But we still have three quite functional modules and all our more expensive, specialized equipment is intact."

"It's not that," he said. "Our insurance covers this. We just can't afford the downtime that repairs this extensive will entail."

Emma was suddenly conscious of the others, listening. She thought about Phil and Dennis and the payoff to Chuck Pinkle, and saw that grim awareness reflected in his own expression.

He has no hope left, she thought. For him this is the final blow. Pain pinched at her heart.

"We'll have to see," was all he said. "Now, let me introduce you to Wilson Barnes, FBI, and Jennifer Murdley, EPA." Emma shook their hands. "Hellman, here . . . well, as you yourself have already surmised, he's not merely an environmental scientist. He's with the EPA and has been working undercover, together with the FBI, in an attempt to protect Gulf Stream from the terrorists who attacked us."

Though he didn't emphasize the words, the phrase *in an attempt* hung in the air. Emma looked at Keith. He seemed to be trying to tell her something without words, without gestures. An apology? An explanation?

Emma spread her palms on the table, sick at her stomach. "I feel responsible for what happened, Mr. Pendleton." Keith made a noise, but she continued. "You should know, one of the terrorists was an old friend of mine and I authorized them to come aboard—"

"I'm aware of all that," Pendleton interrupted. "No one blames you." This said with a glance at Barnes.

"What do you mean? You knew Gabriel Cervantes was involved?"

Barnes said nothing, watching her, so Pendleton answered awkwardly, "He was a prime suspect. He was involved in the murder of an FBI agent yesterday in Melbourne after he had dinner with you."

Emma gaped at the FBI agent. He returned her gaze with a look as cool as a fish's.

"Tell us what happened," Barnes said.

Numbly, she did, with Keith filling in gaps and adding commentary and elaboration. Barnes interrupted frequently with questions, as, occasionally, did Jennifer Murdley and Pendleton.

When she'd finished, Barnes asked, "Anything else?"

She thought for a moment then looked up, shaking her head. "Nope. That's everything I can think of."

Barnes started to say something, but the sound of a helicopter's turbines revving to speed and then taking off came through the walls. Emma picked up her radio. "Tooke here. I thought the helicopter was going to wait for Keith?"

Lee's voice came back. "Uh, Emma—Ann said—"

There was a burst of static and noise as another radio began transmitting. Lee's voice dropped out and another voice said, "Ann here. Gloria required emergency evacuation."

"What?" Emma frowned deeply. "She was fine when I left triage!"

Ann's voice was gentle. "She seemed that way, but her heart rate never went down and her abdomen became rigid and distended. She's bleeding internally—I'm afraid it's her liver."

"Is it serious? I mean, of course it's serious. Will she be okay?"

Ann paused and Emma went cold inside. The pause told her what Ann's next words confirmed. "I won't lie to you. We could lose her."

"Oh, God. Shouldn't you be with her?"

"There's nothing I could do for her and there are people here who need care. I sent Michael with our only oxygen set in case her systems crash. If the medical office wasn't thirty feet underwater I would've been tempted to operate here—but without that equipment . . . well, she's got to get to a trauma center with a decent surgery. Freddy's going straight to Holmes in Melbourne. They're very good."

Emma stared at the radio.

"You still there, Emma?" Ann's voice asked.

"Uh, yes. Sorry, Ann. I'm sure you did the best thing given the circumstances. I'm just worried."

"Understood. Got to get back to my patients."

They signed off.

Pendleton said, "Holmes is an excellent facility, Emma. They've worked miracles."

Emma looked down at the table. "If she doesn't die before she gets there."

Pendleton's pained shrug was eloquent.

Keith reached over and touched her hand. "Don't bury her before you have to."

Emma closed her eyes and nodded.

Barnes cleared his throat. "You must have a lot to see to. If we have any other questions we'll call you back." An unspoken *dismissed* hung in the air.

Pendleton stood and shook her hand again. "Thanks, Emma. As soon as we're done with the debriefings I'll check with you for another status report."

"Very good," Emma said. With a glance at Keith, who gave her a reassuring nod, she stood, made her good-byes, and left.

She thought about the last she'd seen of Gloria— down in triage, the briefest exchange of glances, a quick smile over others' heads. She remembered the gun barrel pressing into her back and Gloria standing at the door to Control, knowing by the look on Emma's face that something was wrong.

Very much on her mind was that look on Barnes's face when Pendleton had said no one blamed her.

Chapter 56

As Emma closed the door, Barnes turned to Pendleton and said, "Could we get one of the former hostages up here?"

Pendleton picked up the phone, "Any particular one?"

"Doesn't matter."

While Pendleton talked on the phone, Barnes told Keith, "We still have search teams out there. One of the sailors aboard the *Cape Starr* saw someone go over the stern of the terrorists' yacht, only seconds before it blew." At Keith's blank look he explained, "All the hostages went off the *bow,* so it had to be one of the terrorists, trying to escape."

Keith's eyes widened. "Oh, really?"

"Mmm. Chances are remote that whoever it was survived the blast, but maybe we'll turn up a body."

That reminded Keith of the female terrorist. "I'd sure as hell like to know who the woman was," he said, and filled them in on the *Buzzworm*/Okinawa lead that he had turned up just before the terrorists' attack.

Barnes didn't look happy. "That's a very cold lead, Hellman. I can't do much with it. Hell, you're talking about an almost twelve-year-old memory. Of someone who might not even have been the same person."

Keith sighed. He was sure the two—Jean Dark and this woman—were one and the same. But Barnes was

right. The old Okinawa lead gave them no hooks.
Nothing to go on.

"Oh, and Coast Guard radar picked up a sea plane
in the vicinity," he told Keith, "at a quarter after
seven. It circled the area for a while and then landed,
two miles due north of Gulf Stream, at around seven-
thirty. It didn't respond to their radio hailings. Our
counterterrorist choppers were close enough by then
to give pursuit, but the plane took off and got away."

"Any idea who it was? Maybe it was drug traffic,
something unrelated."

Barnes shook his head. "Maybe. But to land on the
water, so close to Gulf Stream, during a hostage situation—it seems too coincidental. I believe it must be
connected somehow."

"You think it might have been their getaway
plane?"

"Maybe." Barnes made a noise. "The strange thing
about this whole operation is where they got all their
money, who their connections were. I have the sense
that some powerful forces have been moving in the
background on this one, and Cervantes just didn't have
those kinds of contacts, according to our dossier on
him."

"Maybe someone powerful found *him*."

They turned to look at Pendleton, who was sitting
back in his chair, fingers templed. Barnes gave Pendleton a speculative look.

"As in, maybe he was a player in someone else's
game. Hmmm. Maybe. But we have no leads; I have
no idea how to begin to find them, whoever they are."

Someone knocked on the door. Pendleton said,
"Enter!"

Ben came in. He had a split lip, and an ice pack
pressed to his right eye, which was swollen shut. They
all stood and shook Ben's hand, Keith with his left.

Pendleton gestured at a seat, and Ben took it.

"We're all relieved that you made it through this ordeal."

Ben sighed noisily. "Amen to that."

"How do you feel?" Keith asked.

"I've felt better." Then Ben shrugged. "I'm fine, though. Didn't get seriously hurt, just a knock in the face early on and a little sloshed around from the shock wave."

Pendleton made introductions and asked Ben to tell them what happened.

Ben related what had happened in the control room.

"Did Emma Tooke's behavior seem odd to you in any way?" Barnes asked. Jennifer looked over at Keith, who rolled his eyes surreptitiously.

Ben seemed puzzled. "Odd? How so?"

"Did she encourage the rest of you to cooperate with them, or do anything that might lead you to think she was in league with them?"

"Emma? In league with the terrorists?" Ben laughed, with a confused glance at Pendleton. "This is a joke, right?"

"Just answer the question, please. Did she encourage you to cooperate? Did she help the terrorists accomplish their ends in any way whatsoever?"

Ben gazed at Barnes with obvious incredulity. "They had *guns* in our faces, Agent Barnes. Yes, she told us to cooperate, and yes, she did what they said. Under extreme duress."

Barnes's expression was unreadable. "Go on."

Wearing a disgruntled and baffled expression, Ben continued describing the event. Barnes prompted him with occasional questions when he paused, but let him go on uninterrupted, till he described how Cervantes was made a prisoner, too. Then Barnes held up a hand.

"Whoa. Stop. You mean Cervantes—the Hispanic man—actually *intervened* for you?"

"That's right," Ben said. "And it really made the

others mad. The woman started to shoot him but the big one they called Jax stopped her. They tied him up and put him with us.''

"How did you get free, then?"

"They tied him up with duct tape instead of cord, so I was able to free his hands using my penknife.'' Ben pulled the tiny knife out of his pocket and held it up. "He freed Gloria, then created a diversion while we all untied each other and climbed out the bow hatch. If he hadn't we'd all be toast.'' He shrugged and said simply, looking at Pendleton, "The way I see it, he gave his life for us. Any grudge I had against him . . .'' He paused, clearly searching for words, then shrugged. "Well, he atoned for his sins, is all I can say. I hope he's the one they say made it overboard before it blew.''

Barnes exchanged a look with Keith and Jennifer, frowning. Keith shrugged. He was as perplexed as Barnes was.

Jennifer remarked, "Very strange.''

Ben's mention that she had summoned someone by radio to pick her up before setting the bomb was not lost on any of them, either. Fifteen or twenty minutes was how long someone who jumped off that boat would need to ride the current to a point two miles downstream of Gulf Stream I.

Once Ben had finished, Barnes dismissed him and picked up the phone to have another of the former hostages brought in. At the door Ben paused. "Agent Barnes . . .''

"Yes?"

"If you're looking for a case against Emma Tooke, you're not just barking up the wrong tree, you know; you're in the wrong damn forest.''

Barnes said sharply, "That'll be all.''

One by one, the other former hostages, except Gloria, came in—first Nikki, then Rob, then Mac. Each gave their versions of what had happened. Barnes dogged them, hard, on Emma's behavior. All denied any possibility that she could have been in league with the terrorists, and their stories corroborated each others' on all key points.

Once they were alone, Pendleton leaned forward, hands on the table. "Agent Barnes, you've been looking awfully hard for evidence to implicate Emma Tooke as an accomplice. It's become quite clear that Emma wasn't involved in this attack in any culpable way. Her story agreed with all the others'—including your own agent's." He gestured at Keith. "She was clearly a hostage as well, and doing what she had to, to protect the people in her charge. Once free she did everything she could—to the point of risking her life— to save Gulf Stream I from destruction."

Barnes sat back and gazed at Pendleton for a moment that stretched painfully. He wants to make someone suffer, Keith realized, for Gorey's death.

"He's right, Will," Keith said. More softly; leaning close, he added, "This won't bring Gene back. She's an innocent. Let it go."

Barnes sighed and rubbed at his eyes. When he looked at Keith the hard expression on his face had been replaced by exhaustion, and a profound sadness. "Yeah. All right. I'm convinced."

The meeting broke up. Keith touched Jennifer's arm as she stood. "May we speak privately?"

"Of course."

He led the way down the corridor to a door that led outside. They exited near the tail section of the module and came out facing east. Nearby, a bench sat against the wall, opposite a row of planters at the railing filled with marigolds and clover. Keith gestured at the bench and they both sat.

Beyond the rail stretched a cool, breezy night. The Gulf Stream's swells were long and low, and topped

with ripples created by the breeze. They were playing
laser-tag games with the facility lights, making the water's surface look like a vast, billowing sheet of silver
lamé. Far to the east, moonrise: huge, all but full, the
orb balanced on the distant horizon like a balloon
about to loft itself among the stars. Its features were
blurred by haze and it glowed as red and smooth as
an uncut ruby, casting a warm, crimson path toward
them over the ocean's surface.

Keith sighed and leaned his head against the wall
with his splinted, injured hand resting against his
chest. Every muscle in his entire body throbbed. I *really* need a vacation, he thought. But first things first.

"Jen," he said, "I'm going to resign from the
agency."

She didn't say anything for a moment, merely
looked at him. "What are you going to do?" she asked
finally.

"Apply for a position as Gulf Stream's head of environmental operations. If they'll have me."

She made a dismayed noise. "Oh, for heaven's
sake, Keith."

"What?"

"Gulf Stream won't even be around in a month.
You're making a big mistake."

"I don't think so. Even so, my decision stands."
He sighed. "Jen, I belong here. These people need
someone like me. And I want to do what I can to keep
this venture alive."

"Is this about Gulf Stream, or Emma Tooke?"

"Both." A little smile. "Same difference."

Jen's lips had thinned. "Well, then, there's something you should know. Brad Pendleton and I spoke
earlier. He's made an unofficial report to me that Gulf
Stream paid forty thousand dollars to Charles Pinkle
of the Florida Department of Environmental Protection
about two and a half years ago, to obtain their oper-

ating permits. He plans to make an official report and issue a press release tomorrow morning.''

Keith stared at her. "Shit. Phil Evans."

She nodded. "Their general counsel. Exactly. And Dennis MacNichols, their CFO. Gulf Stream is going down, Keith."

"You can't believe that Pendleton was in on it."

"No. I don't. He's already fired both of them, and I believe he intends to play things clean. But the fact is, they violated the law in a big way. They bought environmental permits."

"You've got clout. With a good word from you they won't be treated too harshly."

She looked annoyed. "That's beside the point. Evans and MacNichols are going to stand trial for this, and Evans's uncle is the other major investor in Gulf Stream I. He'll view Pendleton as throwing his nephew to the wolves, and he won't take that without a fight. He'll make things tough for Pendleton—if he isn't already."

Keith drew a sharp breath. "That *is* bad."

"And besides, Gulf Stream stands on its reputation as an environmentally beneficial enterprise. All its customers bank on it. Even if Gulf Stream is given leniency for making a voluntary report—and of course that's going to be my recommendation to Enforcement—their customers and granting institutions are likely to abandon them. This will destroy them."

Keith said nothing. She saw the look on his face and sat back again, shaking her head in exasperation.

"You're throwing your career away, damn it," she said. "I haven't spent years grooming you as my replacement just to watch you pitch it in the trash can."

Her replacement? That touched him. He laid a hand on her shoulder. "I'll miss you something awful, Jen. You're the best boss I've ever had, and I've loved my job. But this is something I have to do."

Jen tossed her hands up. "All right, all right. But next month if you want your old job back—" Then she looked at him searchingly, and a wry smile pushed away the angry, disappointed expression. "Aw, hell. If you want your job back, any time, you know you've got it."

He'd never take that offer. It was time to set aside old agendas—old anger, old pain. Time to stop hunting bad guys and start working for something he believed in. Gulf Stream had become his child of the mind.

But he loved her for offering. He hugged her.

Then he stood, with a grunt of effort. "I'd better go talk to Brad Pendleton. And to Emma."

Chapter 57

Emma closed the conference room door behind her and headed slowly down the corridor toward Control.

The meeting when Pendleton had brought Keith onboard. All those times, during their dinner at the Chart House and afterward, when Keith had eluded her questions, had been silent when he might have spoken. The dinner with Gabriel, which she'd so enjoyed. And then, when Gabe had shown up for a tour, how delighted she had been. The memories rolled past, over and over, burning her inside till she could almost smell the odor of searing flesh.

It was bad enough, the way Gabriel had betrayed her. If there was an afterlife, she hoped he was burning

in hell. If not, she hoped he'd suffered horribly before
he died.

But her supposed friends had used her just as badly.
If she had guessed right about the source of that note
regarding Keith, then Phil *had* tried, however
obliquely, to warn her . . . but that probably had been
because Keith was EPA and Phil had been afraid of
what he'd uncover during his investigation.

Used. Deceived. Keith, Brad Pendleton, Phil—and
God only knew who else—knew Gabriel and his companions were going to attack Gulf Stream. And they
knew about Emma's old relationship with him. The
only person kept ignorant was the one person who
most needed to know: the one person who could have
stopped Gabriel dead in his tracks before he could
have set a toe on Gulf Stream's decks, before Gulf
Stream or its people had been put in danger. Before
Gloria's life had been threatened and maybe lost.

By then Emma had reached Control. She shoved the
door open with a bang, causing the engineers and technicians in the room to jump. Lee was there, as well as
Oleg Tashkovich and two of her young engineering
interns, Hannah and Bill. Steve Padwick was in the
switch room, working to repair the damage done by
Gabriel to their communications circuits. He gave her
a wave and a smile.

"Great news, chief. I should have at least some external phone function restored in the next hour or so."

She nodded but couldn't bring herself to reply. Lee
held the phone out to Emma, a sour expression on his
face. "Dr. Reynolds wants to speak to you."

Oh, yes. Perfect timing. She snatched the phone
from Lee's hand. Without even waiting for Reynolds
to speak, she said, "Thomas, the evacuations will take
place as scheduled. Period."

"You can't—"

She spoke over him. "That's final." Then she hung

up. "Let it ring," she told Lee, as the phone started to ring again.

"But what if it's somebody else?"

"We're getting all our structural and buoyancy reports by radio. Nothing else is a priority right now."

"But—"

"But nothing. Leave it."

Lee and the others exchanged looks. Emma lowered herself painfully into a chair at the console. Yeah, yeah, I'm being a bitch, she thought. Sue me.

Over the next twenty minutes, status reports rolled in. Results of the divers' preliminary inspections were reassuring; the most important structural feature—the line between the main anchor buoy and Residential, the anchor line between Residential and Engineering, and their beanpole connectors—appeared undamaged. Evidence of moderate to substantial strain was reported at all the catwalks and seventy-foot beams' junctions at Science and Mariculture, but nothing that posed an immediate threat, and the welding crews were already at repairs.

They also received word that all leaks at Residential were completely sealed off now, so its buoyancy was stable. With the main anchor buoy no longer at risk, *La Pescadora* could return to dock and get evacuations started.

In fact, her original expectation, that the Residential beanpole was a complete loss, seemed to be unfounded. Though they'd lost the top sixty feet of it, it seemed to be remarkably intact below that. Perhaps it could be towed back to Melbourne and repaired.

Despite sightings of major fish kills in the vicinity of Residential and the hydrogen barges, the reef itself seemed to be intact—though they'd have to do a detailed species census to see what the underwater explosions had done to the sea life. It'd be a few days before they knew if Louie had made it.

As these reports came in, her spirits lifted a bit above rock bottom. A bit.

But there was no news about Gloria and there wouldn't be for a while—the York helicopter wouldn't reach Melbourne for another fifteen minutes. She paced and answered questions in monosyllables, and hoped that Freddy was redlining the turbines to get Gloria to the hospital.

A sudden, irrational loathing for Gulf Stream welled up inside Emma, so intense it made her tremble.

It must have been more than an hour after she'd left the meeting when Lee reported Freddy was on his way back to pick up the rest of the medevac roster, but there was still no word on Gloria. At that moment the inner door to Control opened; Keith said her name. Emma felt her face muscles form a mask. She turned.

"Can we talk?" he asked.

"Actually, I'm busy. And your chopper is about to land." She turned back to the console. "Perhaps some other time."

"It's really important," he said.

"So is what I'm doing right now."

She felt him behind her, and felt the others' attention on both of them. Then, after a painfully long pause, she heard the door shut. The tension in the room eased. She put her fists together and pressed thumbs against her lips. She was devoid of feeling, as if someone had shot her up with a massive dose of Novocain.

Emma reached a decision and stood, with difficulty. The muscles in her legs were starting to stiffen up. "Where's Pendleton?"

It was Oleg who answered. "We set him up in Gloria's office."

"Thank you."

Feeling as if she were moonwalking, Emma left Control and went there.

Entering the room was like putting a knife into her own heart: the gonzo decor, the tapestries and photos and piles of geodes, crystals, and rocks, the silly sayings and buttons, the weird screen-savers on all the computer monitors.

Pendleton was on the phone. He hung up when he saw her.

You bastard, she thought. She picked up Gloria's egg-shaped quartz rock, the geode with the pink crystals, a smoky quartz crystal spear, a garnet, and a polished malachite nugget the size of her fist, and slid them into the pockets of her shorts.

"I was just about to call you for an update," he said.

"Preliminary indications are that the structures are sound."

He appeared relieved. "Good. Thank you." He paused. "I wonder whether, since that's the case, Dr. Reynolds's desire to keep a skeleton staff on-board over the next couple of days could be accommodated . . ."

So Reynolds had been calling him up and complaining. Part of her wanted to be a jerk and say, *Fine, whatever; I don't care. You decide.* Another part of her wanted to make Reynolds suffer. She knew Pendleton wouldn't nay-say her, if she told him the risks were too great.

But that would be petty.

"I suppose so," she said, with a heavy sigh, rubbing her sore neck. "I didn't think we'd get off so lucky. Under the circumstances a more limited evacuation is appropriate than I'd originally anticipated. I'll call him. Flo, too."

"Very good. When do you expect external communications to be restored?"

"We'll have limited function in another hour, perhaps." He started to say something else, but she said,

"The chopper is almost here to take the last of the noncritical injuries to Melbourne. I want to go along."

He studied her face, clearly surprised.

"I have to be with Gloria," she said.

"Who will be in charge?"

"Lee Attewell will be monitoring the situation and I'll stay in touch by cellular phone."

He didn't look too happy about it, but she didn't care how he felt. Finally he nodded. "Very well."

She turned to leave. He said, "Before you go, there are a couple of important matters I want to discuss with you. Will you close the door and sit down?"

She pulled the door to and rolled a chair over from the main server.

"To set your mind at ease," Pendleton said, "there'll be no further talk of culpability due to your admitting the terrorists aboard." How very generous of you, she thought. "Everyone's story corroborated yours, and Barnes has agreed that any further suspicion of you is unfounded."

"Oh."

"Persistent post-trauma symptoms are a commonplace for people who have been in a hostage situation. The FBI will arrange for the former hostages to be given counseling by people who specialize in that sort of thing. That includes you. There'll be an eight-day, expenses-paid vacation in the Bahamas for those of you who agree to participate. We'll be making counselors available to the rest of the staff on request, and have some group debriefings and discussions."

Emma's eyebrows went up. "That's very generous, Mr. Pendleton."

"And I've just been talking to Keith Hellman. He has resigned his EPA job. He wants to join Gulf Stream."

The news made her skin tingle with surprise. So *that* was what he'd wanted to discuss with her.

"He says the firm's environmental program is poorly managed and desperately needs attention, and proposed that I create a new corporate office: chief environmental affairs officer, reporting to me."

Emma thought about the difficulties Keith had spotted and corrected during the Phase II storm preparations.

"He also pointed out to me," Pendleton continued, "that we wouldn't be in the hot water we're in now over the DEP scandal if we'd had a reliable person, a corporate officer responsible solely for environmental issues, overseeing the permitting process."

She nodded, watching him.

"And my own thinking is this," he said slowly. "If Gulf Stream has a ghost of a chance of surviving this scandal, creating a position such as he proposes, and filling it with someone with his background—well, the amount of credibility it would buy us is simply enormous. It's possible . . . if anything could salvage the CalEPA deal, that could.

"Well?" he said, rocking back in his chair. "What do you think?"

You're asking too much of me, she thought. I don't want to give a fuck about Gulf Stream right now.

She shook her head, sharply, and stood, a spring-loaded mechanism. "Mr. Pendleton, right now I'm too—I can't—" She stopped herself. "I'll get back to you on that. All right?"

He gave her a quizzical, penetrating look. "Very well. But—I know the pressures you're under right now, but—please don't wait too long to give me your feedback. Things are getting pretty damn hairy, and I'll have to act quickly."

She sighed. She didn't want to have to deal with this later, either; she might as well get it out of the way now. "Do what you think is best for Gulf Stream,

Mr. Pendleton. I think Hellman makes some excellent points, and I'll support your decision.''

"Thank you."

She started to open the door.

"Oh, and Emma—''

She turned back, hand on the door jamb.

"The company owes you a great debt. I'm deeply grateful for all you've done.''

Emma stared at him, tongue adhering to the roof of her mouth. The praise couldn't have felt emptier of meaning. She mumbled something noncommittal and left.

Ben, Nikki, Mac, and Rob were waiting for Freddy's chopper in the Mariculture conference room, along with Keith, as Emma had expected. Flo and Veronica were there with Ben, Jess with Nikki, and Charles Lawson with Mac. A few other close friends and well-wishers were also present.

Emma ignored Keith's presence. She gave each of her fellow former hostages a long hug, and then sat down with them. "Are you guys all right? No injuries?''

"We were damn lucky,'' Ben said. They all looked at each other—all lucky except for Gloria, of course. No one said it. But Nikki covered her face with a groan.

"I feel terrible. We didn't even know anything was wrong with her, coming back on the cutter. She was a little out of it, but . . .'' She shook her head, unable to finish the sentence. Flo took her hand.

Keith sat apart from the others, on the couch. He stood up with some difficulty and started toward Emma; she had an adolescent urge to bolt. But she sat rooted.

The look on his face was raw anguish.

"Can we talk?''

Be mature, Tooke. She stood and glanced at Flo,

who was watching her and Keith with an intent expression. "May I borrow your office?"

Flo waved a hand. "Help yourself."

Emma led the way, and after Keith entered Flo's office, closed the door and leaned on it. He looked beat up and forlorn, with that ridiculous splint on his arm and the old bruises on his face; he looked weary and sad. But she held on to her anger, sealing it in with arms folded tightly across her chest.

Keith walked over to the window and looked out. "I've been dreading this moment," he said.

At that, it all came up. Emma slammed a fist into the door. "God*damn* you! Why didn't you tell me what was going on?"

He didn't say anything.

She went on, "If you'd just trusted me—if you'd told me what was going on—I would *never* have let Gabriel come aboard! Your deceit may have cost Gloria her *life*!"

He lifted his hands in a remorseful shrug. "You're right. I should have. I wanted to— I even said as much to the FBI. But that doesn't help now, I know."

Emma stared at him, then backed up against the door and hugged herself. Keith came toward her, reaching out. She put her hands up. "Don't."

So he stood there, arms hanging useless at his sides. "Emma, can you ever forgive me?"

Emma clenched her fists—not in anger, but to hold back the anguish his words evoked—took a rasping breath, and shook her head. "Just go, okay?"

His shoulders slumped and his face closed down. "Okay," he said. He opened the door and left. With precise, deliberate steps, she walked over and sat down at Flo's desk, staring blindly out at the darkness. I'm so tired, she thought. I hurt. I can't go on like this.

In a few minutes, chopper blades beat the air, and

aircraft lights played through the window. Emma stood. The York Aviation chopper. It was time to go.

The admissions clerk in Holmes Regional Medical Center's emergency room directed Emma to the operating waiting room. It was near a bank of elevators, off a hallway. A short distance down that hall were the automatic double doors that opened into the operating room.

The waiting room had an atmosphere much like a doctor's office. It sported comfortable chairs, a magazine rack, and a coffeepot. It also had a TV set mounted on the wall, tuned to the local news. A small group of people who all looked a lot alike were watching TV. Sitting at a desk was a big, older woman in a pink lab coat, with a strong Southern accent. Emma asked her about Gloria. The woman took the name down, said she'd check, and left. Emma headed for the coffeepot.

A few minutes later the woman came back in.

"They're just wrapping up," she said. "They'll be wheeling her into Recovery any time now. Dr. Milhouse will be out in a few moments to give you a full report."

"How is she?"

"I'm not sure—but it won't be long now; the doctor can fill you in."

Emma paced. Finally another doctor wearing surgical scrubs and booties came through the doors. He was quite short, in his late thirties or early forties, perhaps, and had a bounce in his step and a cheerful expression.

"You're a friend of Gloria Tergain's?"

"Yes. Emma Tooke." She shook his hand.

"I'm Dr. Edmund Milhouse."

"How is she?"

He rubbed at his mouth and chin. "She survived the

surgery—and the long delay in getting to surgery—and that is a miracle in itself. One tough lady.''

A smile touched her face. "That she is.''

"She suffered a severe blow to the gut that lacerated her liver, and nearly bled to death on the way here. I've seen plenty of people with a similar type of injury die, with that kind of time interval. But the damage to the liver has been repaired and she has a fairly good chance at recovery. There is still risk of postsurgical complications, though, so we're going to keep her in our surgical ICU for a while and monitor her condition.''

A "fairly good" chance? "What kind of complications?"

"By the time we got her into surgery she'd lost between a quart and a half and two quarts of blood into her abdomen. Pulmonary distress due to prolonged anoxia is still a very real danger. Or the reduced blood flow might have damaged her kidneys. She'll have to be watched closely for a few days. She's not out of the woods yet.''

"When can I see her?''

He hesitated. "Only immediate family is allowed in ICU.''

Emma eyed him. What the heck. "I'm her sister.''

"Okay, that's fine, then. She'll be in Recovery for at least an hour.'' He glanced at his watch. "It's eleven-thirty now. She'll be in ICU by one A.M. Check at the nurse's station in surgical ICU about then.''

Emma gulped. "Right. Thanks, Doctor.''

Then she went back to ER to check on the other Streamers. Most of those who had been on the same chopper as Gloria had been treated and sent home; one was being kept for observation overnight. The medevaced man, one of Flo's people, was scheduled for eye surgery at 7:00 A.M. Ben and the others from the last chopper run were in being checked and nobody else was in the waiting room. Emma wandered over to the cafeteria to get a cinnamon roll and another cup of coffee—which she took one sip of, grimaced, and left on her tray with the half-eaten roll. She tried to read a newspaper someone had left on a chair. At about ten till one she went up to the surgical ICU.

The nurses' station was at the center of the ward, with glass-walled rooms surrounding it, satellitelike. Lights were dimmed; blue and green glows fanned out from the video and cardiac monitors behind the desk. Emma approached, and a woman in a nurse's uniform asked, "May I help you?"

"I'm here to see Gloria Tergain. I'm, um, her sister."

The lie came harder to Emma this time than the other—perhaps she'd had too much time to worry about what she'd do if they asked her to prove it—but the woman either didn't notice her hesitation or didn't mind the lie; she gave Emma a warm smile and said, "Right this way."

Emma followed the nurse to one of the glass-walled rooms. There she turned on the light at the head of Gloria's bed and then exited, closing the door behind her. Emma approached the bed.

They had her on oxygen, with an IV in her arm and a catheter snaking up under the cover. Her headboard wall unit had a call button and a heart monitor, on which a line twitched across the screen. The heartbeat looked and sounded like any other Emma had seen: an upbeat and a little downbeat, a pause, an upbeat and a downbeat . . . *beep-beep, beep-beep, beep-beep.* Next to the bed was a computer. A window by the bed looked out over a dark, empty field. Even through the closed window, she could hear the faint sound of insects singing.

By this time Emma had worked up the nerve to give Gloria herself a close look. Gloria was shrunken and pale, her eyes slitted open, the sockets sunken in their orbits. Green tubes rested in her nostrils and wires ran out from beneath the hospital gown. She breathed noisily, mouth open. Her tangled hair was splayed across her pillow and fell over the edges of the bed. Both arms were outside the cover. They looked limp and lifeless.

Fresh pain squeezed Emma's heart. She emptied her pockets of Gloria's rocks and crystals. She set the quartz egg, the geode, the smoky quartz, and the malachite on the bedside table, then pulled a chair up beside the bed, opposite the paraphernalia, and took Gloria's hand. "Hi, Gloria. It's me, Emma. Just here to keep you company for a little while."

She fingered the garnet as she spoke. Gloria had told her once that red was the color of life force; a red crystal imbued a person with strength and was useful for healing injuries.

It was all superstitious hokum, of course. But at the very least the talisman would bring Gloria comfort, and it might even provide a focus to help her find her own strength, within. Emma pressed the garnet into Gloria's hand and closed her fingers around it.

"Here's your garnet." She swallowed, and held up the quartz egg. "The magic crystal says you're going to get better." Tears started pouring down her face. "You know I need you, Gloria. And I love you. I want you to heal. Find the strength."

Gloria lay unresponding. Emma cried hard and long until she ran out of tears, and then just sat holding Gloria's hand, staring blindly out the window.

It was a long, dreary night. Every two hours a nurse came in to check Gloria's vital signs and input them to the computer at the bedside. It was the same nurse each time, the one who had showed Emma in. The two would chat about inconsequentials, whose details

Emma would promptly forget. In the stretches between, sometimes Emma talked to Gloria, sometimes she stared out the window, sometimes she dozed. Mostly, she thought.

In the early morning, at 4:00 A.M., she walked out into the waiting room and used her cellular phone to check in with Gulf Stream Control. Progress was maintained—the structure was doing finc and the critical repairs had all been completed.

"I just heard about Reynolds," Lee told her, yawning.

"What are you talking about?" Emma asked, confused and tired. "What did the asshole do now?"

"You didn't know? He resigned. He's jumping ship. Going off to some policy position in D.C. Someone heard him say he wasn't waiting for Gulf Stream to fail before looking for a new job."

"What a jerk. Good riddance. I can't wait to tell Glori—" And then grief hit her, midword, like a brick in the face—she started crying, sudden jerking sobs that shc hid from Lee by holding the cellular phone away from her.

She couldn't tell Gloria anything.

When she had her breathing under control she put the phone back to her ear. Lee was saying, "—ma? Emma? You there?"

"Sorry, Lee. Had to talk to a doctor. Look, get some sleep. I'll check in with you tomorrow. And damn good work, by the way." She hung up before he could say anything else. Before *she* had to say anything else.

Chapter 58

The phone ringing woke Keith up. He grabbed it and mumbled into it.

It was Pendleton. "My apologies for waking you."

Keith sat up, fully awake. "Quite all right."

"Let me get right to the point. I'm calling to offer you a position as Gulf Stream's chief environmental affairs officer, effective as soon as you are prepared to take it, at the salary you proposed last night."

Keith took the phone away from his ear and grinned at it. Then he put it back. "Great. Let me think. I could start as early as a week from this coming Monday."

"I'd like to add you to the payroll today, if possible. We can accommodate you with some time to wrap up your affairs in Houston thereafter." Pendleton cleared his throat. "I'll be frank. I have a press conference scheduled for eleven-thirty, and I'd like to be able to say that you are an employee effective today, if possible."

"Well, technically, I'm already on the payroll."

"True."

"But . . . I work for the government and there's a lot of paperwork that has to be filled out. I wonder if we could make the 'official date' two weeks from next Monday."

"All right. That should do. And, if I could get a copy of your résumé—your real résumé—"

"That'll take a day or two."

"Fine. And let me be the first to welcome you aboard Gulf Stream I."

"Thanks."

Keith hung up the phone, feeling a bit stunned. He grimaced, remembering Emma. Things were going to be difficult. He cradled the phone against his ear, dialed the Ramada with his good hand, and asked for Jen's room. She picked up right away.

"Hi," he said. "It's me."

"Keith! I'm glad you called. I'm on the next flight out and I wanted to give you an update, but I didn't want to wake you."

"First I have news for you. It looks like the Gulf Stream job is a done deal. I start in two weeks. I know that's short notice—"

"We'll deal with it. I . . . won't beat a dead horse; I'll just wish you luck."

"Thanks, Jen. And what's your news?"

"The Coast Guard is wrapping up their search. They didn't find any bodies, so we don't know if one of the terrorists survived the blast or not. I doubt it, myself—one of them might have survived the initial blast, but without scuba gear or someone there to pick him up right away, he—or she—would have drowned anyhow."

"Perhaps. I guess we'll never know."

"Guess not. Anyhow, Barnes has closed the book on it, so I don't suppose we'll ever know who was behind the bombing, either."

"I have my own theory," Keith said.

"What's your theory?"

"I think Boadica-slash–Joan of Arc was a mercenary, and behind her was someone—or someones—with a lot of money invested in current energy technology. Someone who doesn't mind playing dirty, as long as the dirt doesn't reach him."

"Head of an oil company? Utility company?"

"No—my guess is, the person who actually orchestrated this is some sort of renegade who believes in operating outside the law and has some sort of money or power of his own, maybe military or paramilitary. An Oliver North sort, with credibility among certain oil or utility company power brokers, who paid him and looked the other way. Or maybe an investor or cartel of investors with money in the fossil fuel industry is involved."

Jen grunted, noncommittal. "I never figured you for a conspiracy nut."

"It makes sense, Jen. It makes more sense than anything else I can think of. You know the old saying: just because you're paranoid doesn't mean they're not out to get you."

"Whatever you say." Then she yelped. "Look at the time. I have to catch my plane. Good luck, Keith."

"I'll call you tomorrow when I get back to Houston," he said, hung up the phone, and flopped back down onto the bed with a groan, pulling the covers over his head. "Make that next week sometime."

Chapter 59

EMMA: Thursday, 8 October, 7:54 A.M. EDT
Holmes Regional Medical Center, Melbourne

Someone shook her awake. She had fallen asleep slumped over the bed. Dr. Milhouse stood beside her. "Good morning."

Emma sat up and yawned. A sharp pain lanced her shoulder and neck; she rubbed at it.

"It's morning?" She glanced at her watch. It was five till eight.

In the early morning sunlight that streamed in the window, Gloria looked and sounded a little better: she was still wan, but less wizened. Less grey. Her breathing was quiet and more even. But perhaps all that was illusion.

Emma watched worriedly as the doctor examined Gloria. He spent a lot of time listening to her lungs. Then, on the computer, he called up a graphic of a human body, which had Gloria's vital signs displayed next to the relevant portions of the body.

She looked over his shoulder. The blood pressure, heart rate, and breathing she got, but the rest was gibberish, graphic or no graphic. "How is she? Any improvement?"

"I'd say so. Yes. Her lung function and blood gases seem normal. We'll know more about the kidneys once her next round of blood work is done, but right now I'm cautiously optimistic that she'll experience a complete recovery." He shrugged. "The next few hours should tell. As soon as she comes out of the coma we'll know she's going to be all right."

Emma released a long, slow breath. Her eyes burned with fatigue. "I'd like to get some sleep. She's not going to die on me if I go home for a few hours, is she? Would the hospital call me if her condition worsened suddenly?"

"Of course we'd call," he said. "Leave your name and number with the nurse on duty and then go home and rest."

Emma stood and picked up the garnet, which had rolled off onto the floor during the doctor's exam, and put it on the table. Then she kissed Gloria on the forehead and took her hand.

"I'm going to go home and get a few hours' sleep but I'll be back later. Your garnet's right beside you on the table, here. Keep healing, woman. We have a date with some rockers in an old folk's home.''

Gloria exhaled softly, turning her head in Emma's direction. Her eyes opened slightly, and she made a soft sound. It sounded like Emma's name.

Emma straightened. Her heart rate picked up. ''Gloria?''

Emma thought she detected a smile and a nod, and she *knew* she felt a gentle squeeze on her hand. Surprise and delight bloomed in her—she turned to tell the doctor, but he was already gone.

''You were injured,'' Emma said, leaning over Gloria, ''but you're going to be all right.'' Gloria's eyes closed again and she sighed. Her voice was barely audible. ''So tired . . .''

''I'll bet,'' Emma said, grinning, wiping away tears. ''I'm going to go let them know you're awake, and then I'm going to head home and get a couple hours' sleep.'' She picked up the garnet again and pressed it into Gloria's palm. This time Gloria's fingers closed around it. ''Rest and get better. I'll be back.''

She had to pass right by Keith's apartment on her way home, and some part of her mind had a mind of its own; she made the turn onto his street without thinking, blinking as she realized where she was.

He might not even be there. The hospital might have decided to keep him overnight. And if he *was* there, what was she going to say? This was really a dumb thing to do. And so on, and so forth, while she parked, locked up, set the car alarm, and went up the outer stairs to his suite.

She knocked on his door, heart pounding fiendishly. What am I going to say? she thought. What will I say? I should leave. Her stubborn feet held her there till the door opened. A sleepy, tousled Keith opened the door. His right wrist was in a blue plastic splint.

His eyes widened. "Hi."

Emma walked into his arms without saying a word. He buried his face in her hair. And the words came.

"It was the terrorists who nearly killed Gloria. Not me, and not you. It just—" Her voice broke. "It hurt like hell, not to be trusted. When it would have made such a difference."

"I know," he said. "I know. I'm so sorry."

She called the hospital to give the ICU nurses the different number and stayed. They didn't make love, not at first; exhausted, they fell asleep in his bed, nestled in each other's arms, immersed in each other's scents.

At some point she woke to his touch—he was propped on an elbow, looking down at her with a wonder-filled expression while the fingertips of his free hand roamed from her chin, down her neck to her collarbone. His fingers swirled from the outer edge of her right breast inward, to its slowly hardening nipple, then down to her solar plexus and up to cup her other breast.

"God, you're beautiful," he said, and did it all again with his mouth.

With a moan she pulled him to her. Large, crinkly bandages covered patches of his chest, abdomen, and back; she lifted his head, queried him with a touch on the dressings and a look, but he shook his head, smiling.

"Just abrasions."

"I'll be careful," she said.

It had been a very long time for her and she was nervous, making her movements hesitant, tentative. But sensation gradually overwhelmed hesitation, worry, and even thought. Bandages, scrapes, mutual bruises, all the distractions went away as they moved together—skin rubbing skin, hands wandering, stroking, pulling, probing—slowly and softly, then faster, harder, until in groans and gasps they were caught up together and swept away in their own great, sweet wave.

He rolled over, removed the condom, and they curled up again and fell asleep, entangled in each other's limbs once again, like puppies.

When she awoke again, in the afternoon, she was alone in bed. Kitchen sounds floated through the door, left slightly ajar: porcelain, glass, and metal clinked and rang against each other; cabinet and appliance doors thumped. An off-key, reedy whistle butchered "Froggy Went A-Courtin'." She smelled biscuits and bacon.

Emma pulled one of his shirts out of the closet, pulled it on, and went into the front room. The table was set. She sat down, picked up a piece of bacon, and munched on it while he carried two cups of coffee out. They ate breakfast in companionable silence, and, sipping her coffee, she gazed at him as he buttered his biscuit and thought, This is good. This is right.

After breakfast they went for a walk in the bright sunshine, amid the lush growth of trees and flowering bushes, to the estuary with its hidden life. They stood at the rail and gazed together out at the water, listening to the birds and frogs.

"I'm a Streamer now," he said.

"So Pendleton decided to make you an offer?" He nodded. "I spoke to him about it last night." She smiled and entwined her fingers in his. "Welcome aboard, colleague."

"Thanks."

"Calloo-callay. We lose Reynolds and get you, all in one go. Life is sweet."

He laughed. Emma glanced over at his profile.

Yeah, she might lose him someday. He might leave her, or die.

Grief was love's price; it harbored the seeds of grief within it, as life harbored the seeds of death. Love was worth the price of loss, just as life was worth the price of knowing someday you'd die.

And there was more to it than just that. A life of the mind—clever utility, technology, devices of complex function—delighted her, excited her. But a world without other kinds of beauty—without room for artistic creation, for instance; for a natural world, with its own complexities and life cycles; for a search for the life of the spirit—a world that didn't allow for beauty of these other kinds was a sick and dying world.

So, crazy as he'd been, she couldn't quite bring herself to forgive him, but she could—*almost*—understand why Gabriel had done what he'd done.

With a snort of disbelief at herself, she leaned into Keith. He wrapped his arm around her, gave her an inquisitive glance. "What?"

Emma shook her head, smiling. "I'll tell you later."

Available by mail from

TOR
FORGE

CHICAGO BLUES • Hugh Holton
Police Commander Larry Cole returns in his most dangerous case to date when he investigates the murders of two assassins that bear the same M.O. as long-ago, savage, vigilante cases.

KILLER.APP • Barbara D'Amato
"Dazzling in its complexity and chilling in its exposure of how little privacy anyone has…totally mesmerizing."—*Cleveland Plain Dealer*

CAT IN A DIAMOND DAZZLE • Carole Nelson Douglas
The fifth title in Carole Nelson Douglas's Midnight Louie series—"All ailurphiles addicted to Lilian Jackson Braun's "The Cat Who…" mysteries…can latch onto a new *purr*ivate eye: Midnight Louie—slinking and sleuthing on his own, a la Mike Hammer."—*Fort Worth Star Telegram*

STRONG AS DEATH • Sharan Newman
The fourth title in Sharan Newman's critically acclaimed Catherine LeVendeur mystery series pits Catherine and her husband in a bizarre game of chance—which may end in Catherine's death.

PLAY IT AGAIN • Stephen Humphrey Bogart
In the classic style of a Bogart and Bacall movie, Stephen Humphrey Bogart delivers a gripping, fast-paced mystery."—*Baltimore Sun*

BLACKENING SONG • Aimée and David Thurlo
The first novel in the Ella Clah series involving ex-FBI agent, Ella Clah, investigating murders on a Navajo Reservation.